CARPENTER MEMORIAL LIBRARY
CLE ELUM, WA 98922

Praise for Kristine Kathryn Rusch's novels

The Disappeared: A Retrieval Artist Novel

"Rusch's handling of human-alien interactions puts a new and very sobering face on extraterrestrial contacts that few authors have thoroughly explored. . . . I am hopelessly hooked. . . . Rusch's characters . . . keep you reading long after everyone in the house has fallen asleep. . . . *The Disappeared*, like all the best science fiction, achieves a higher purpose: to make us look at the world around us with a new understanding and question the status quo." —Lisa Dumond, SF Site

"An interesting and fairly original solar civilization . . . a balanced blend of police procedural and action adventure." —*Science Fiction Chronicle*

"As well known for her fantasy and horror as she is for her science fiction, [Kristine Kathryn Rusch] especially excels in tales of the collision between human and alien cultures. *The Disappeared* is a fine example of her skills." —Science Fiction Weekly

"Rusch is a talented storyteller who creates a make-believe future g   owser

"A well-conceived, well-executed novel." —*The New York Times Book Review*

continued . . .

Praise for Kristine Kathryn Rusch

"A masterful writer is at work." —Orson Scott Card

"Whether [Rusch] writes high fantasy, horror, SF, or contemporary fantasy, I've always been fascinated by her ability to tell a story with that enviable gift of invisible prose. She's one of those very few writers whose style takes me right into the story; the words and pages disappear as the characters and their story swallow me whole." —Charles de Lint

"Accomplished . . . exceptional." —Edward Bryant

"Kristine Kathryn Rusch never stray[s] from the path of good storytelling as she dissects her characters and their situations for the reader's benefit. She integrates the fantastic elements so rigorously into her story that it is often hard to remember she is not merely recording the here and now."—Science Fiction Weekly

"[Rusch's] writing style is simple but elegant, and her characterizations excellent." —Beyond

"Kristin Kathryn Rusch's . . . stories are exceptional, both in plot and in style." —Ed Gorman, Mystery Scene

"[Rusch] is already far better than should be allowed." —Nexus

EXTREMES

A RETRIEVAL ARTIST NOVEL

.

Kristine Kathryn Rusch

A ROC BOOK

ROC
Published by New American Library, a division of
Penguin Group (USA) Inc., 375 Hudson Street,
New York, New York 10014, U.S.A.
Penguin Books Ltd, 80 Strand,
London WC2R 0RL, England
Penguin Books Australia Ltd, 250 Camberwell Road,
Camberwell, Victoria 3124, Australia
Penguin Books Canada Ltd, 10 Alcorn Avenue,
Toronto, Ontario, Canada M4V 3B2
Penguin Books (N.Z.) Ltd, Cnr Rosedale and Airborne Roads,
Albany, Auckland 1310, New Zealand

Penguin Books Ltd, Registered Offices:
80 Strand, London WC2R 0RL, England

First published by Roc, an imprint of New American Library,
a division of Penguin Group (USA) Inc.

First Printing, July 2003
10 9 8 7 6 5 4 3 2 1

Copyright © 2003 White Mist Mountain, Inc.
All rights reserved

Cover art by Greg Bridges

REGISTERED TRADEMARK—MARCA REGISTRADA

Printed in the United States of America

Without limiting the rights under copyright reserved above, no part of this
publication may be reproduced, stored in or introduced into a retrieval system, or transmitted, in any form, or by any means (electronic, mechanical,
photocopying, recording, or otherwise), without the prior written permission
of both the copyright owner and the above publisher of this book.

PUBLISHER'S NOTE
This is a work of fiction. Names, characters, places, and incidents either are
the product of the author's imagination or are used fictitiously, and any resem-
blance to actual persons, living or dead, business establishments, events, or
locales is entirely coincidental.

BOOKS ARE AVAILABLE AT QUANTITY DISCOUNTS WHEN USED TO PROMOTE
PRODUCTS OR SERVICES. FOR INFORMATION PLEASE WRITE TO PREMIUM MAR-
KETING DIVISION, PENGUIN GROUP (USA) INC., 375 HUDSON STREET, NEW YORK,
NEW YORK 10014.

If you purchased this book without a cover you should be aware that this
book is stolen property. It was reported as "unsold and destroyed" to the
publisher and neither the author nor the publisher has received any payment
for this "stripped book."

The scanning, uploading and distribution of this book via the Internet or via
any other means without the permission of the publisher is illegal and punish-
able by law. Please purchase only authorized electronic editions, and do not
participate in or encourage electronic piracy of copyrighted materials. Your
support of the author's rights is appreciated.

For Jack Williamson
with love

ACKNOWLEDGMENTS

I owe a great deal of gratitude to a lot of people on this project, who helped in a variety of ways. Thanks go to Geoffrey A. Landis for help with some of the science—and so quickly, too; to the 2002 Short Story Workshop for the great, thoughtful, and timely discussions on sf; to my husband, Dean Wesley Smith, for all the support, the willingness to have strange discussions about even stranger topics at the drop of a hat, and all of his wonderful advice about the manuscript. Great advice, however, is only as good as the person who receives it, so I must stress that any errors are my own.

Thanks, all. I couldn't have done this without any of you.

Prologue

The Earth glowed in front of him, green and blue and white: impossibly beautiful against the blackness of space.

Coburn used the Earth as his marker, his goal, even though it wasn't. The horizon was so close, and the Earth so large, that he almost felt like he could catch it, then hang it, like a souvenir, on the wall of his apartment.

He followed the designated path on the Moon's surface, his feet landing in footprints left from previous Moon Marathons. The regolith was packed solid here, the trail as old as time.

He had forgotten what it was like to be alone with himself in a familiar place, the sweat from his body pooling at his feet before his suit recycled it. Earth marathons were not solitary events. Bodies bumped each other, and the narrow quarters always made him claustrophobic.

Here he was on his own, with nothing to break the gray landscape except boulders, craters, and the packed trail.

So he focused on the Earth, and tried not to listen to his own breathing. The sound screwed up the rhythm of his legs. It had been ten years since he had run a marathon in anything less than 1G. He was used to having the pounding of his feet match the force of his breath.

In.

Out.

In.

But here, on the flat, endless vista outside of Armstrong Dome, he ran with a different rhythm: step, half step, push—or launch, as his coach used to say. Only when Coburn thought of launching off the ground, he wasted energy going up, instead of moving forward.

He had to concentrate on distance and speed, not height. And while that sounded easy in gravity one-sixth of Earth's, it was not. There were too many things that could literally trip a man up.

The monitor, built into the lower half of his helmet's tinted visor, told him he had run for six miles, although it felt like much longer. The simulated programs he'd run hadn't been good enough, and the city of Armstrong did not allow any training runs on the cross-country track.

In theory, no one was supposed to be able to train on the Moon's surface—suited, in the proper gravity. In practice, a handful of extreme athletes and rebels managed it every year. If they got caught, they faced jail time and disqualification from any off-Earth marathon for life.

Normally Coburn would have taken that risk, but he hadn't had time. He'd been planning an extreme event on Freexen, and hadn't even planned to run in this thing until Jane called him back to Armstrong. Their business, Extreme Enterprises, was running into some legal troubles, and she needed his cool head to help her with the fine points.

He signed up for the Moon Marathon when he learned he'd be in Armstrong during the event. And this marathon was turning out to be a lot harder than he had expected.

The first mile had been easy. The area outside Armstrong, like the areas outside any established dome, was almost as tame as the interior of the dome itself. Several established vehicle tracks led to the dome's exterior services, from the physical plant for each dome section to exterior maintenance and repair.

A lot of private industry also had buildings outside the dome. Some of those buildings housed exterior equipment. Others had their own tiny environments for workers who had to stay outside for weeks at a time.

These businesses and buildings were the real reason no one was allowed to train outside a dome. The potential for sabotage was too great. The only way for a domed environment to survive was for the residents to carefully monitor everyone who had access to the exterior.

Coburn had understood that intellectually. He'd modified his own VR program to compensate for the changes in terrain, so he had trained in the proper conditions.

But he hadn't been prepared for the subtle things: the way the blackish-gray dirt moved beneath his feet, forcing him to sink to the harder crust beneath; the impact craters too small to show up on any map—some of them no wider than his fist, just wide enough to trip a runner and send him sprawling; the intensity of the sunlight etching everything around him in clean, rigid lines.

Yet this was one of the safest places near any inhabited part of the Moon. The area around Armstrong was mostly flat by Moon standards, but it still contained dips and hillocks and hazards too small to place on any official map. And then there were the tiny alterations in the landscape that occurred because the Moon had no atmosphere to block space debris.

Coburn had read about one runner who had stepped on the sharpened edge of an exploded shuttle, pieces of which had rained on the Sea of Tranquillity the month before. The runner severed his foot. His suit, which had been severed along with the foot, depressurized. He didn't even have time to die from the blood loss. The change in pressure and the loss of oxygen killed him first.

But cases like that were rare. The more common injuries occurred when a runner misjudged a distance—taking the wrong step before a leap up a four-meter rise, for example. Once launched, a runner was committed—there was no atmosphere to beat against, no air or water to slow him down, nothing to create friction or to use to change the trajectory.

Coburn had already seen victims of that miscalculation—good runners, excellent athletes, many of them extremists, who had fallen alongside the track, because they'd landed in an impact crater and broken an ankle or fallen against a tiny rise and ripped open one half of their environmental suit.

Most suits couldn't repair damage that great. Coburn's could, but his had been designed for conditions much more hazardous than this one—races where there were no panic buttons, and no well-worn track covered with generations of boot prints to keep the participants from getting lost.

He was grateful for the suit now. The visor reported the distance to any object up ahead, and it also warned him of potential problems below. Unless he made a careless error, he would make it to the end of the 26.2 miles just fine.

Coburn ran—if this skip-hopping movement he was making could be called running—toward a boulder. As he approached it, he realized it was taller than he was, and six times as wide. Someone had filled in the sides of its impact crater, and the path around it had been smoothed by the footprints of thousands of runners over the life of the marathon.

The path along the right side of the boulder was

thinner, not as well traveled as the path along the left. This boulder had been here for at least a hundred years, and it held no surprises. Even the tiny craters on the right side had been mapped.

He approached the boulder faster than he expected, and narrowly missed kicking its outer edge. He veered away from it, focusing on the details of running, the placement of his feet, the way he launched—almost like long jumpers on Earth, only with another jump shortly after the first.

The boulder cast a shadow that darkened part of the trail. He tried not to land there, trying instead to go past it. When he landed, he could finally see beyond the boulder.

He saw something white in his path.

Another fallen runner. Only this one hadn't crawled off the path like he was supposed to. He was curled, fetal position, as if his injury was somewhere other than his legs and feet.

New footprints on the dirt to the left of the fallen runner suggested that at least ten runners had already gone around him. None of them had stopped to see if the runner was okay. But that was normal. Coburn hadn't stopped for the other fallen runners either.

However, those fallen runners had been moving. Rocking back and forth as they held broken shinbones, pounding the ground in frustration at the lost dream. A few had been trying to get up as he passed, and a few others were stumbling along the pathside, trying to continue despite the injury.

No one just laid there.

This injury was clearly more serious than the others had been.

He wasn't going to stop—he would lose precious time—but once he reached the runner, and the visor gave him the location readout, Coburn would contact the Med Alert Team and let them know there was an unconscious runner on the path.

Then the suit came into focus.

It wasn't white. It was a pale pink with gold strips that glittered in the sunlight. The bottoms of the boots had a familiar lightning pattern, a pattern that matched the one on the bottoms of his boots.

Jane.

She had been about fifth when she left him behind. Having her pass him in a marathon was a normal occurrence. Jane excelled in the run, and her suit, like his, didn't allow her to lie unconscious for a long period of time. It should have contacted the Med Alert Team directly, rather than leave her here, where at least ten runners had passed her by.

The only way her suit wouldn't revive her was if it had failed.

Coburn found his breath coming in small gasps. He slowed his loping gait and altered his trajectory so that he stopped on her right side.

Then he crouched beside her.

Her face was turned toward the regolith, the helmet's white shell blocking his view of her visor. He had no idea how she had fallen like this—both legs together, arms gathered against her chest.

Jane ran beautifully, even in conditions like these. She should have sprawled, like anyone else, unless she had gathered herself into this fetal position to compensate for some kind of pain.

But her suit should have compensated for her by boosting her endorphins, or, if her injuries were severe, medicating her until help arrived.

Medicating her and keeping her conscious.

With one gloved hand, he touched her shoulder. The layers of fabric between them made her seem inhuman. He pushed her shoulder away from him, rocking her back so that he could see her face. One of her hands flopped into the dirt.

Coburn's mouth was dry. The monitor on the right side of his visor was blinking, cajoling him to breathe regularly and to take a drink before he dehydrated himself.

He ignored it.

Instead he was staring at Jane's visor. The sunlight filter was on low, allowing him to see inside. What had been Jane's face was black and contorted, her beautiful brown eyes bugging out of their sockets.

Coburn's stomach turned over, and he had to swallow to keep the bile down.

Somehow he managed to find his own panic button, and he pressed it two, three, maybe four times.

There was no reason for the Med Alert Team to hurry, but he wanted them here, now, just in case he hadn't understood what he was seeing.

Just in case he was wrong.

1

Fifteen days without a case, and Miles Flint was beginning to think he had made a mistake. He wasn't cut out to be a Retrieval Artist. The solitude was driving him crazy.

Paloma had warned him about this aspect of the business. A good Retrieval Artist—she said—picked cases with caution. Too many of them were fraught with dangers that weren't immediately obvious.

In fact, the systems she had designed, systems he had bought from her when he bought her business, were set up to give him ways out of a case once he had agreed to it. The worst thing a Retrieval Artist could do was find himself in the middle of a case that would destroy lives.

Flint had thought he was up to the light caseload. His caseload as a detective had been overwhelming, and the idea of being able to pick and choose his jobs appealed to him. He hadn't thought about the weeks spent sitting alone in his office, waiting for someone or something to come through the door.

The office was no prize, either. It was small, with only his desk at one end, and the door at another. He had a single chair—his own—so that his clients remained uncomfortable when he talked with them. The single chair also meant that he couldn't find another place to sit when he was at work.

There was a back room, which was well hidden, but it wasn't as comfortable as the front area. There were two other exits, also well hidden, and storage space in a secret compartment that Paloma had built herself.

The building was made of original colonial permaplastic, and the walls had yellowed over time. The floors tilted and the door appeared to be off-kilter, although it was not.

Even though the building was old, the security system was so advanced that Paloma had had to tutor Flint in its use—and he had once designed hackerproof programs for a living. Flint thought he could hack into any security system, until he had encountered Paloma's. She had modified it in ways that he had never seen done before.

Now the system was his, and he had to keep it as state-of-the-art as possible. It was more difficult than he would have initially imagined.

A large part of his job involved remaining current—on security systems, on the news, on changes in the culture. He believed that if he was abreast of things, he would have less to investigate when he did get a case.

Paloma hadn't told him this trick—he had figured it out on his own, based on his years with the Armstrong Police. In those days, he had always wanted the extra time to keep up on all the various areas that would help him with his day job. Now that he had the time, he was stir-crazy.

Even his routine didn't help. He went to a downtown gym in the morning before coming into the office, exercised for an hour, and then walked to work. Most of his human interactions were shallow: ordering from waitstaff at various restaurants, conversing with acquaintances from the gym, and nodding at his neighbors as he walked to and from the office every day.

Flint lived alone and hadn't had more than a casual

relationship since his daughter died more than ten years before. He had thought that he liked being solitary—his ex-wife had even accused him of liking his own company better than hers (an accusation that, after his daughter's death, turned out to be true)—but he was discovering that until the last year, he hadn't been solitary at all.

He'd had friends at his job, people he saw every day and had real interactions with. He'd also struggled with criminals, and people who had accidentally broken the law. When he had worked for the Armstrong Police, he hadn't been alone at all, not until he went to his apartment for his four hours of sleep every night.

Now he slept eight hours and no one noticed. He went days without having a conversation about anything deeper than the kind of food he wanted for breakfast. And even though he was doing a lot of studying, he lacked stimulation of the kind that had always fascinated him: finding out what made other people—and aliens, for that matter—act the way that they did.

No wonder other Retrieval Artists took too many cases, or the wrong kinds of cases. The sameness of each and every day was beginning to drive Flint nuts.

Day sixteen looked like it would be no different from the preceding ones. The morning had bled into the afternoon, and Flint still sat behind his desk, reading the day's news.

The hand-held reports contained color graphics that swirled, but he didn't touch the screen to open them. He found lately that he preferred reading text only; audio, flat vids, holographic reporting, all added a level of noise that distracted him, made him wonder just how much was news and how much was made up.

Perhaps it was the silence. Flats and holographic news all had the audio track, which felt out of place in this office. Paloma had always kept the tiny room quiet. Not even the computer system hummed. Flint could hear the sound of his shoes sliding along the old permaplastic flooring.

A screen opened on his desktop, and he glanced at it. The screen opened only when someone had triggered his perimeter alarm. The perimeter alarm was located half a block away from the office itself. About a dozen times per day the alarm went off, usually showing local residents or tourists.

Old Armstrong attracted a handful of tourists each week, all of whom wanted to see what remained of the initial colony. Most of the initial colony had been rebuilt in Armstrong's Museum of Moon History, which was part of the City Center downtown. About four blocks of the old buildings survived, however, and tourists came for those.

At this moment, the screen showed a woman striding purposefully toward his office.

Her hair was pulled back, her pointed chin jutted out, her gaze directly on his door. Her clothing was inappropriate for this part of Armstrong; her long coat covered a tight skirt with a slit up the side, and her bare legs were already coated with dust. Her shoes were as flimsy as her clothing—the heels high in a fashion sported only by the extremely rich of both sexes—and she wobbled as she walked.

Flint studied the screen, then pressed its right upper corner to zoom in on the woman. She didn't look familiar, so she wasn't a resident of this section of Armstrong, but she had walked some distance or she wouldn't have had dust along her legs.

If she had an aircar, she had parked it a few blocks away, probably where the streets narrowed to the early colonial width.

Flint hit the small button on the front of his desk that slid the keyboard from its pocket. Paloma hadn't believed in voice recognition or in touch screens. She thought they were too easily compromised by even the most average of hackers. She preferred a silent keyboard, so that no one could use audio of the clicking to break into her system.

Eventually she convinced Flint that her method was the best. He still missed the convenience of a touch screen, but the keyboard made him feel as if he had the secrets of the universe at his fingertips—a feeling he never had before, not even when he had designed computer systems.

Flint tapped a special key three times, and more images appeared on the screen. He got a 360-degree view of the block around his office. More ancient, yellowing permaplastic buildings, dusty streets, and some slapped together, postcolonial rock homes filled the block.

The only local merchant, owner of a discount grocery selling dry items past their use-by date, stood outside his store, arms crossed. He spent a lot of his time standing like that, looking at the street, as if he were waiting for someone to take him away from his life.

He and the strange woman were the only people visible in Flint's security perimeter. Still, Flint didn't like it.

Flint tapped the keyboard again, moving her real-time image into the corner of the screen so that he could watch her current movements. Then he called up all the images of her that he had, from the moment she had arrived in the perimeter until now.

One of the images caught the woman's face. She wore expensive jeweled frames around her eyes. The jewels seemed bright against her golden skin. Her hair was dark, her chin narrow, and her thin mouth had no lines around it at all, indicating either youth, enhancements, or both.

She had crossed into Flint's security perimeter and headed straight for the office. Flint backed the images up even further, caught a glimpse of an aircar, hovering in one of the pay parking spaces near a newer section of dome.

Flint fast-forwarded again, caught the image of the woman's face, and sent it through the extensive database Paloma had left him. The database contained all the information that Paloma had gathered through her long career—or at least the stuff that she did not consider confidential. It included histories of people she had never encountered as well as histories of people she had; it included as much information about the various known worlds; in short, it included everything Paloma felt relevent to a Retrieval Artist, whether the information was or not.

When Flint put in an image of a human face, what usually came up on the screen was a primary identity—the kind found in news reports and official biographies. Only he wasn't getting anything on this woman.

And that bothered him. It meant the system would have to delve into government identification records and private company databases to discover who she was. The search would take longer, and probably wouldn't be completed by the time she knocked.

Another screen went up, and a silent alarm buzzed against Flint's hip. He had added that alarm so he would know if someone came close to his building. He shut off the hip alarm, powered down all the screens but one, and waited.

The woman paused outside the door. Most people did. Flint liked it that way. The more he could do to discourage a client from hiring him, the better he felt.

Retrieval Artists specialized in finding the Disappeared, people who went missing on purpose, usually to avoid prosecution or death by any one of fifty different alien cultures. The Disappeared were usually guilty of the crimes they'd been accused of, but by human standards, most of those crimes were harmless. The problem was that the Earth Alliance, in making treaties that allowed trade with various alien cultures, also allowed instances in which humans could be prosecuted for crimes committed against those cultures. Those prosecutions were often brought before one of thirty Multicultural Tribunals. If the human was found guilty, she would be remanded to the offended aliens for punishment.

In many cases, punishment for the simplest crime was death.

Over the years, humans found a way around the tribunals' verdicts: the humans disappeared—vanishing under a new identity into the known worlds. Gradually, companies that disappeared people for a fee sprang up, and some of these companies were sponsored by the very corporations that needed trade with the alien cultures.

Helping established criminals disappear was illegal; finding them was a matter for commendation.

Except for Retrieval Artists.

Theoretically, Retrieval Artists did not work for the law. They worked for the Disappeared's family or for an insurance company who needed the Disappeared to settle a claim or for a variety of other business reasons. Retrieval Artists did not reveal the Disappeared's location without permission nor did they ever retrieve a Disappeared for a legal proceeding.

If a Retrieval Artist screwed up, more often than not, the Disappeared died.

So discouraging a client was always good. Casual clients did not belong in Flint's office.

He watched the woman hesitate. She pulled down the frames she wore as decoration around her eyes, and examined the plaque on the wall, which mentioned that the building was a historical landmark. Beneath it was the tiny sign—barely as wide as a standard-issue wrist computer—advertising that a Retrieval Artist worked in the office.

Her eyes had tiny tucks in the lower corners, and

her nose was wide in the center, almost blending with her cheekbones. The decorative frames had added structure to her face, accenting the narrow jawline and hiding the flatness of her central features.

This was a woman who knew what made her look good.

Flint glanced at the other section of the remaining screen. No history on her, no identification, not even preliminary.

She raised her hand to knock. He shut down the entry protocols, deciding to listen to what she had to say, but he turned on an added security feature. If she touched anything inside or outside of the office, he would collect a small DNA sample. If he needed to, he would use it to identify her.

Using DNA for ID without the person's permission was illegal, but he didn't care. So much of his work since he'd become a Retrieval Artist had been illegal, and he found that bending laws he didn't like suited him better than enforcing laws he hated.

Her knock was as confident as her walk had been.

"Come in!" Flint called.

She grabbed the door and pushed in, blinking at the interior darkness. A bit of dust swirled in after her—apparently the material of her skirt attracted it, almost like a magnet.

She seemed startled as she walked across the threshold, not just because the eight-by-eight office was so small, but because Flint had just shut down all of her personal links.

Her links had to be subtle. Most people wore them like decorations on the skin, but she didn't. The links hooked her up to someone or something on the outside, although Flint couldn't tell who or what.

"If you want to come in here," Flint said, using the script that Paloma had given him, "you come in alone. No recording, no viewing, and no off-site monitoring."

The woman blinked at him, almost like someone

coming out of a deep sleep. So she was someone who preferred to be linked, who used her links for downloads to keep part of her brain constantly entertained.

People like that bolted when their links were severed. Flint waited for her to leave.

Instead she shut the door, and the lights went up ever so slowly. Flint wanted to see her better.

"You're Miles Flint?" she asked, still clutching her frames in one hand.

"Yes," he said, seeing no reason to deny it.

"You've taken over Paloma's service?"

"This used to be her office." He leaned back, pretending at a relaxation he didn't feel. He was excited about having a potential client, and he knew that emotion was bad. He would have to proceed with caution. He couldn't let his enthusiasm get in the way of his judgment.

"But you are a Retrieval Artist too, right?" For the first time, she sounded uncertain.

"Yes," Flint said.

His computer finally found her identification. From the city courthouse's database, one used to confirm the ID of lawyers to be admitted into one of the courtrooms.

Astrid Krouch, granted her degree ten years before from Glenn Station University, passing the difficult Armstrong bar on her first try, hired directly out of law school by the large and well-heeled law firm Wagner, Stuart, and Xendor, Ltd. She hadn't yet appeared in a courtroom, although she'd been to the court many times to do filings for other attorneys.

So she was still at the beginning of her career, a lawyer with a good salary whose entire life was at someone else's beck and call.

No wonder Flint had trouble finding her. She wasn't anyone important yet—and that alone put him even more on alert.

"I have a case for you." She made it sound like a gift.

"Well, that's good," Flint said. "I wouldn't want to think you stumbled in here by mistake."

She blinked once, as if she were reassessing him, and then smiled. The smile was as artificial as the silk in her suit.

"I work for Wagner, Stuart, and Xendor, Limited. We have a client—"

"Excuse me." Flint stood up. He decided to play her differently than he played most of his clients. "You look uncomfortable in those shoes. Have my chair."

He lifted it around his desk and set it in the center of the small room. She looked confused, glancing at the chair, and then glancing at him.

"I really don't have time, Mr. Flint. I was just going to tell you about our client—"

"Have a seat, Ms. Krouch."

Her mouth opened, then closed, before opening again. "I didn't tell you who I was."

"It's my business to know everyone who comes through my door," Flint said, crossing his arms and leaning against the front of his desk.

"You scanned me without my permission? I'm not in any public databases." She shook the frames at him. "If you figured out who I am, then you went through illegal sources."

"Really?" he asked calmly. "You don't think your office could have notified me of your pending visit?"

Two spots of color rose on her cheeks. "You're toying with me, aren't you, Mr. Flint?"

Yes, he wanted to say, *and it was remarkably easy.* But he didn't. Instead he shifted slightly against the desk. "Has your office ever used a Retrieval Artist before?"

"Of course," she said. "In case you didn't catch my credentials, I work for—"

"I heard you. Am I supposed to be impressed?"

"We have offices all over the known worlds."

"If you're that important a law firm," he said, "then you probably already have a Retrieval Artist or two on retainer, along with your Trackers."

"We don't use Trackers, Mr. Flint. We're a corporation-friendly organization."

The assumption being that corporations, more than any other business, needed to disappear their employees. Corporations didn't want the employees caught any more than the employees wanted to get caught, and so the corporations wouldn't work with Trackers.

Flint had known that assumption was wrong back when he worked as a detective. A lot of times corporations hired their own Trackers to go after one of their former employees so that person could take the fall for something someone else did.

"But you do have other Retrieval Artists on retainer," he said.

She shook her head. "Not that I know of."

Because she was a new attorney, and this was her first visit to a Retrieval Artist. Someone had planned this visit well.

"We have done business with Paloma in the past," she said.

Flint nodded, waiting.

"I'm sure my superiors thought she was still around," she said.

He doubted that. He was certain they knew exactly when Paloma quit. He was also certain that they knew exactly how new he was.

Paloma had warned him that he'd get a lot of lawyers, insurance agents, and other people who fronted for Trackers in his first few years of business. These people would have assumed that any new Retrieval Artist was too green to figure out that a Tracker could piggyback on their research and then find a Disappeared.

Eventually the requests from lawyers, insurance agents, and others would become the foundation of his business—the honest group who didn't hire Trackers. But up front, Paloma had warned, Flint would have a hard time telling the legitimate cases from the manipulative ones.

"Well, she's not," Flint said. "Let them know that. Tell them to go to their second choice. I've already got enough work."

Krouch frowned at him, as if she had never heard anyone say they had enough work. "I think you might want to take this case, Mr. Flint. It's easy and it's quick, and if you're just starting up, it'll be good money for you."

Now she was moving into the financial argument, one he was also insulated from. A year ago he had stumbled into a case that had paid him so much money he would never have to work again.

"Thanks but no thanks," he said, reaching for the chair she was obviously not going to use. He lifted it over his desk and placed the chair in its usual spot. "I'm not interested."

"Not interested? But it's easy."

"You already said that." He walked around the desk and sank into the chair. "Believe me, that's not a selling point."

"Fast money isn't a selling point for you?" Apparently she hadn't run across anyone like that either.

He shook his head. "Easy cases that offer me fast money are precisely the types of cases I avoid."

"But—"

"Good day, Ms. Krouch," he said.

She didn't move. "But—"

"You can leave the office now," he said.

"I'm—"

"Or," he said, raising his chin, "I'll show you out myself."

She did that odd little open-close thing with her

mouth again, only this time she apparently decided to
keep her mouth closed. She spun on one of those
uncomfortably high heels, and let herself out of his
office, shutting the door so hard that the permaplastic shook.

Flint keyed on his security screen. Krouch stood
outside, her back to his door, as if she were trying to
decide whether or not to come back in. He smiled.
She had thought this assignment would be easy. He
wondered if it was the first assignment she'd failed for
her powerful bosses.

After a moment she stalked away, leaving the perimeter as quickly as she had entered it. He watched
her struggle with her skirts for a moment before she
turned a corner and disappeared from view of his primary security systems.

Flint leaned back in his chair. Something about this
meeting disturbed him. He should have gone back to
his reading—after all, he had just rejected the case—
but he was too intrigued.

Why had WSX come to him? And why had they
sent someone like Krouch, someone whose identity
didn't show up on the traditional image-ID search?

Were they trying to get him to investigate them?
Why would they do that?

The only reason he could think of was that they
wanted to use his search as a back door into his security systems. But there could be a hundred other reasons, and discovering which of them was the truth
would take some research.

Flint double-checked his system. So far, no
breaches. He set everything on highest alert, so that
he would know if anyone tried to access his files.

Then he stood up. He would go to a public-access
portal to do his research on Astrid Krouch and WSX.
And maybe, just maybe, he would find out what they
were up to.

2

Noelle DeRicci reached the edge of the marathon spectators' area and tugged on the wrist of her environmental suit. The suit, not yet activated and with its hood down, felt hot.

DeRicci's latest partner, Leif van der Ketting, had parked the aircar in front of the *No Parking During Special Event* sign, and was struggling to get his environmental suit out of the backseat. Like all of DeRicci's most recent partners, van der Ketting was a newly minted detective. This would mark his first official case outside of the dome.

Lucky him. He would see this as an adventure, bouncing in the light gravity, wandering around rocks that most Moon residents were forbidden to touch. But the novelty would wear off quickly enough—especially if the marathon organizers were as uncooperative this time as they had been in the past.

It would take van der Ketting another five minutes to get ready to leave the dome. DeRicci turned away from him and studied the crowd instead.

Several thousand people sat on the bleachers especially set up for the marathon. No spectators were allowed Outside. They had to see most of the race on live feed, just like everyone else. But the bleachers gave them the perfect view of the finishing line, and

they'd be able to see their favorites stumble across—
or leap across, as was usually the case.

Thousands more spectators watched the feeds from
hotel rooms and bars scattered around Armstrong.
Those folks hadn't been able to afford bleacher seats,
but they still wanted to be part of the excitement.
Armstrong was stuffed with strangers—every hotel
room filled, every possible rental jammed—and all of
them wanted some connection, no matter how small,
with the marathon.

DeRicci had never understood why anyone would
watch this sport. She appreciated the folks who
watched the Armstrong Marathon, held every fall inside the dome—it was a novelty to see a pack of dedi-
cated human runners jog through your home
neighborhood—but to sit on hard plastic bleachers for
hours, waiting for a runner to break a white paper
streamer, seemed like a complete waste of time to her,
especially when that runner's entire body was hidden
by an expensive environmental suit.

DeRicci tugged at the pants legs of her cheap environmental suit. She'd put on weight since the last time
she'd needed this thing. She hoped the suit would
hold.

The suit alone would have made this case a pain in
the butt, although DeRicci hated going Outside for
any reason. Now she would have to negotiate her way
through one of Armstrong's greatest tourist draws of
the year just to investigate a death.

DeRicci had investigated deaths at the Moon Marathon before, back when she was a brand-new detective
and the job seemed endlessly fascinating. She'd found
an end to the fascination at least ten years ago, and
she hadn't been brand-new in more than twenty years.

She'd been promoted during that time. She was lead
detective on most of her cases now. But those promo-
tions were only technical. The kinds of cases she re-

ceived were the crappy ones, the ones the real
detectives with real power managed to avoid.

DeRicci was too mouthy, too independent, and too
difficult to work well within the system. It also would
have helped if she believed that what she was doing
was just: Most of the time, she felt worse than the
criminals she pursued.

The crowd was subdued, watching their own personal feeds, waiting for the lead runners to come into
view. Obviously no one had been told about the
death—but then, that was standard procedure.

Deaths at the Moon Marathon had become less
common—one every five years or so—but they still
happened. And they rarely got reported. Usually they
were listed in the statistics part of the annual account
as a footnote, and almost always, according to that
footnote, the death was caused by the runner's error,
certainly not by anything the marathon organizers
had done.

Van der Ketting finally joined her. He was a short,
slim man, barely coming up to her shoulder. When
DeRicci had first seen him, she asked the chief of
the First Detective Unit, Andrea Gumiela, how he'd
managed to pass the physical exams.

Gumiela had grinned at DeRicci. *He's a lot stronger
than he looks.*

DeRicci had hoped so. She hadn't seen any evidence of it. And it still disconcerted her that van der
Ketting was shorter than she was. She was one of the
shortest women on the force.

"How the hell do we get Outside without calling
attention to ourselves?" van der Ketting asked, parroting the words Gumiela used when she had given
them the assignment.

"Trust me," DeRicci said. "The organizers aren't
going to allow the crowd to figure out what we're
doing."

She checked his suit as if she were his mother making certain he was dressed properly for the first day of school. His suit was newer than hers, but no better. The material was thin and not nearly as sturdy as it should have been. She checked the hood and the faceplate, looking for rips and finding none.

"Do I pass?" van der Ketting asked.

"You joke," she said, "but one mistake and you die out there. That's probably what we're investigating."

"My death?" He always seemed to have a quip, especially when he was nervous.

"No," DeRicci said. "Someone's mistake."

She grabbed the evidence kit that she had set on the ground and carried it toward the bleachers. The air smelled of fried pork, slow-cooking sugar candy, and instant chips. Not the healthiest of foods for people who seemed to have an interest in watching healthy athletes test their own limits.

Van der Ketting let her take the lead, as he always did. Just once, DeRicci would like a partner who had more experience than she had, who knew exactly what he was doing and why.

She had a hunch she would never get that. Not without a lot of work cleaning up her reputation.

She headed down the makeshift aisle, weaving underneath the stands. They wobbled a little, unsteady even though the crowd wasn't doing a lot of moving. She was glad that the stands weren't set up for more boisterous events—then she might be investigating an even worse disaster.

Of course, if something horrible happened, such as the stands caving in, other detectives would investigate, detectives with less seniority, but a lot more clout.

Van der Ketting followed closely behind her. She could hear him breathing through his mouth. He did that when he was nervous, and anything out of the ordinary seemed to make him nervous. His nervousness didn't affect his performance, just his metabolism.

The bleachers narrowed as they got lower, and the aisle seemed even more cramped. The spectators' area smelled strongly of spilled beer and cheap wine. This part of the bleachers had been set up on a sidewalk, and the surface was sticky. Her boots made small sucking sounds as she walked.

"They're so quiet," van der Ketting whispered.

DeRicci nodded. She'd always hated that too. The crowd should have been louder, conversing among themselves about trivial things while they were killing time, or cheering runners even though the runners couldn't hear the cries. But year after year, the crowd watched in silence. The cheers never started until the first runner appeared on the horizon.

She reached the other end of the bleachers. The front row was only two meters from the dome. This section had been cleaned and some of the panels replaced, so that the view Outside was clear and crisp.

DeRicci stared through it for a moment. The finish line was painted across the surface built for near-dome vehicles. The paper ribbon stretched between two temporary posts. One year the winner came through the posts so hard that he knocked them over, sending them bouncing into the dome itself. The dome hadn't shattered—it was built to withstand greater forces than that—but the event scared a lot of spectators, causing quite a scandal.

The deaths and injuries never caused scandals, unless they happened inside the dome.

DeRicci sighed. She wished she could see more of the surface than this small section through the cleaned dome; she loved the Moon's bleakness, its clean lines and vast expanse of dark.

Two elderly men whose long and lean bodies marked them as former competitors in the Moon Mar-

athon flanked her. Like many athletes, they had es-
chewed enhancements rather than alter their bodies.
As a result, their faces were wrinkled, their hair—
what was left of it—the steely gray of moon rocks.

"Officer?" one of them said softly.

"Detective." DeRicci always corrected people who
called her by the wrong rank. She had worked hard
to become a detective, and even though the brass gave
her the worst assignments, she still ranked higher than
a simple beat officer.

"Come with us," the man said, ignoring her correction.

She looked for van der Ketting. He walked just behind her, taking in the spectators instead of the view.

The spectators were mostly human. Track-and-field
sports didn't appeal to most of the alien races. The
Disty liked tennis, which seemed to match their passion for Ping-Pong, and the Rev liked hockey, boxing,
and wrestling, probably because the sports were so
violent. But endurance sports seemed to appeal only
to the race involved. Humans thought the Pochae's
eating contests as ridiculous as the Pochae found
marathoning.

"This way," the man was saying, hurrying DeRicci
and van der Ketting along.

DeRicci had to hurry to keep up with the man in
front of her. Finally they reached the far side of the
bleachers. A small white bungalow, temporary and
movable, had been set up as a gathering place for
participants.

The man ushered DeRicci and van der Ketting inside. The other man closed the door behind them.
They walked through a small anteroom into the main
part of the bungalow.

The live images of the race covered all the walls.
On two of them the image tracked a single runner.
On the other two walls, tiny images of all the runners
aired simultaneously.

Three women and a man, all of them as elderly and

gaunt as the two who had found DeRicci, sat in white plastic chairs, watching the race. They seemed oblivious to the newcomers in the room.

"Sorry to hurry you out of there," the man said to DeRicci. "We didn't want any of our people asking questions."

It took her a moment to realize that "our people" meant the spectators, many of whom had paid small fortunes for seats.

He held out a hand. It was bony and bent, looking as used as the rest of him. "I'm Alfred Chaiken, the chair of this year's race."

DeRicci took his hand gingerly. "Noelle DeRicci, and my partner, Leif van der Ketting."

"Thank you for coming so quickly," Chaiken said. "We were hoping you'd arrive before the first runners crossed the finish line."

DeRicci glanced at one of the wall-sized images. A runner, wearing an environmental suit with a real helmet, half ran, half jumped past a small group of pointed rocks. She had no idea where he was on the trail, and she had no idea how the people watching their tiny screens knew either.

"How long do we have before the winner arrives?" van der Ketting asked.

DeRicci frowned. With that question, van der Ketting put the investigation on the race's timetable, not theirs. She would change that later.

"About thirty minutes." Chaiken glanced at the same wall DeRicci was looking at. The runner looked like all the other runners, face hidden by the helmet's reflective visor. The runners wore numbers on their fronts, but that and the design of the various suits seemed to be the only differences.

"You can stay out there as long as you need to," Chaiken was saying to van der Ketting, "but we'd like to get out through the dome as quickly as possible."

So that the attention wasn't on the police when the first runner arrived.

"All right," van der Ketting said. "What do—"

"First," DeRicci said, stepping in front of him as if he weren't there, "tell us what you found."

Chaiken glanced from her to van der Ketting, then bobbed his head, as if suddenly realizing who was in charge. "We didn't find anything. This is the management team. We stay inside the dome. We have staff outside the dome, including a medical response team."

"All right," DeRicci said, pressing a tiny chip inside her suit's glove. She was going to record this interview after all. "Who found the body?"

"One of our runners, a Mr. Brady Coburn. He has since left the course, even though we offered the opportunity for him to finish the race."

How kind of them to let him finish. DeRicci wondered if he got a time break for finding one of the more unfortunate contestants.

"There've been deaths at this marathon before," she said.

"It's one of the risks of participation, although not something that happens as much as it used to," Chaiken said, and it was clear he had launched into remarks he made often. "We still have a number of injuries every year, but we've modified the system so that those injuries rarely result in death."

"Our runners do sign a release," said the other man. He was still standing by the door, almost as if he were guarding it, so that DeRicci and van der Ketting couldn't escape and alert the spectators of the crisis outside the dome.

DeRicci gave the man a sideways look. "You are?"

"Jonathon Lakferd. I'm the assistant chair."

"You have them release you of all responsibility in their deaths?" DeRicci asked.

"Or for injury," Lakferd said. "We're very clear about the risks. We don't want anyone to be surprised."

"We also don't want the negative publicity," Chaiken said. "We'd prefer it if you don't speak of this—"

"How we handle this is the department's call," De-Ricci said. "If it's anything like the last few deaths I've investigated in the marathon, caused simply by the race itself, you can bet the department won't say a word."

She had to struggle to keep the sarcasm from her voice. She hated being asked to do a job, only to have the department ignore her work for political reasons. And the marathon was definitely political.

Chaiken smiled at her, as if his greatest concern was not the dead body out on his track, but the negative publicity that body would generate.

"Where is this Mr. Coburn now?" DeRicci asked.

"He's in one of our buildings nearby," Lakferd said. "Would you like to see him?"

"Not yet," DeRicci said. "How did he notify you?"

"With his panic button," Chaiken said. "Every runner—"

"I'm familiar with the system." DeRicci frowned, staring up at the walls. "The runner who died didn't contact you?"

"No," Lakferd said.

"Isn't that unusual?" DeRicci asked. "Wouldn't someone with a serious problem push the button?"

"If she could," Chaiken said. "Sometimes things happen quickly and a situation might not allow it."

"She?" DeRicci asked. "You know who the victim is?"

Chaiken nodded. "One of our more experienced participants, and a former winner. Her name is Jane Zweig. She runs Extreme Enterprises. You've probably heard of them. 'Extreme sports for the adventurous traveler.' That's their tag line."

DeRicci had heard of them. She had seen their ads—happy, thin people with too much time on their hands, swimming in pale red liquid, and climbing gray spirelike mountains in obviously alien places.

She said, "I find it odd that someone who specializes in extreme sports would die on your course. I thought the Moon Marathon went mainstream more than a century ago. The extremes don't even bother with it."

Van der Ketting watched the whole proceeding with interest. He caught her hint that he had been out of line and he hadn't tried to participate since.

"This is still a difficult event." Lakferd's thin body seemed to close in on itself. "We have a number of extremes each year. Jane Zweig participated every time she could."

"Why?" DeRicci asked. "I would think that extremes wouldn't find this marathon to be a challenge."

"But it is," Lakferd said. "As you can see by today's event."

He seemed almost buoyed up by it, as if the death had proven the race's legitimacy yet again. DeRicci gave him a hard look. His face was as grooved as the Moon's surface. She had taken him for being a natural—someone who never had enhancements. But he might have enhanced at least once. If so, he was old enough to have been part of the race when it was an extreme event. Perhaps that meant something to him.

She filed the theory away, just like she filed all other random thoughts away. At this early part of an investigation, she wasn't going to throw anything out.

Besides, if she could stop the deaths at the Moon Marathon, she'd feel better about it. She'd love it if the city prosecuted the marathon for reckless conduct, but as long as the marathon brought in this many tourists and this much money, she knew that wouldn't happen.

"My point is," DeRicci said, "that an extreme athlete should have prepared for all the dangers. I always thought it was the first-timers who died here, not the most experienced people."

Lakferd shrugged. "She was probably overconfident. That's usually what happens with these people. They forget to take the normal precautions. A first-timer would risk losing the race—or not concentrate on a personal best—just to make sure that everything was fine. Someone as experienced as Jane . . . well, you know."

DeRicci didn't know, but she was sure she would find out.

"You knew her?" van der Ketting asked Lakferd.

"Of course," Lakferd said. "Everyone did."

"And liked her?"

Lakferd frowned. "What does it matter? Her death was accidental. How I felt about her should be irrelevant."

"We haven't seen the body yet," DeRicci said. "We have no idea if her death was accidental."

Two of the women looked up, as if they had just noticed the conversation. Lakferd bowed his head, revealing a thin spot in the hair over his crown.

"Well, then," Chaiken said. "Let's get you to the investigation site."

DeRicci didn't move. "How long ago did Mr. Coburn discover the body?"

"Whenever you folks received the call," Chaiken said.

"How long ago?" DeRicci asked.

"An hour, maybe less. Mr. Coburn was up near the front of the pack. He was the first to call in."

"You let the race continue?" van der Ketting asked.

DeRicci suppressed a smile. She couldn't have put that level of shock into her voice even if she wanted to.

"We have no choice, young man," Chaiken said. No "Detective," no sign of respect. Just a sharp tone and an even sharper phrase.

DeRicci could feel van der Ketting stir beside her. He was angry, just as she would have been in his place, just as Chaiken wanted him to be.

She put a hand on van der Ketting's arm. "You didn't divert?" she asked. "You made the runners go past the body?"

"It's not as heartless as you make it sound," Chaiken said. "We don't dare divert. We don't have alternate routes. If people went around the body, even more runners would get hurt."

"How many injuries have you had in the race so far?" DeRicci asked.

Chaiken shrugged. "The usual number."

"Which is?"

"About fifteen up front, nothing really serious," Lakferd said. "Just serious enough to put the runner out of the race. We expect more as the race continues. Usually around the twenty-mile mark or so, where the average first-timer 'hits the wall,' as they used to say. Tired runners are careless runners."

"How many medical teams do you have?" De-Ricci asked.

"Ten," Lakferd said. "more than enough for a race of this size."

His sudden defensiveness surprised her. Apparently he didn't think ten were enough. And if they didn't have a large enough medical staff, then a few deaths might be due to negligence.

She wondered if that was what he believed had happened to Jane Zweig, if someone hadn't responded quickly enough. DeRicci would have to get someone on that part of the investigation quickly. She had a hunch the organizers could hide information if they thought it necessary.

Chaiken looked at the clock running near the ceiling of the wall across from the door. His movement was ostentatious, his meaning clear.

This time, DeRicci would let him hustle her out of the building. The short interview she had done with them had raised a lot of questions.

The body would provide the answers.

3

Miriam Oliviari leaned against the emergency medical scooter. She stood just outside the dome, watching the spectators inside. Her borrowed environmental suit was a good one, bought by the marathon committee especially for the medical team. She had a better environmental suit on her ship, but she didn't dare use it. The only thing she liked about this suit was the gloves—they were so thin that they felt more like she was wearing lotion instead of material.

Still, this suit did a good job of protecting her from the boiling heat of a Moon day. The sunlight, unfiltered and brilliant, fell on the surface road, gray as the dust it was made of, revealing all the pocks and flaws in the design. The road covered most of the first mile, and small side trails went off in all directions, leading to maintenance buildings, and storage units for surface equipment.

Armstrong had all of its Outside buildings tightly locked. A few were guarded. At one of the early marathons, a spectator had sneaked into one of the buildings and sabotaged all of the city-owned vehicles. Three vehicles failed while in use, causing city workers to die, and resulting in two decades of lawsuits.

The marathon had somehow managed to survive that tragedy, but only by making a lot of concessions—including keeping spectators and unauthorized personnel inside the dome. The rules had gotten so tight that it had taken Oliviari six months to figure out how to get Outside herself. The organizers were an in-group of people who had known each other since they all raced six or more decades ago. The only opening Oliviari had found had been within the medical teams, and it had stretched all of her resources to obtain it.

Around her, other members of the medical team waited. Teams One, Two, and Three had already been called out on emergencies. She was in Team Five. The teams were not linked via a comm system, which she wished she had known about from the beginning. She would have insisted on a group link, claiming it would make for a safer race.

She would have been lying, of course. She really didn't care about a safe race. What she wanted was the opportunity to collect DNA from all the female runners.

Her own private links were off. She didn't want them to trigger the marathon's high-tech security system. She had allowed the organizers to link her to the emergency personnel, as well as to the race's security system. Theoretically, she was supposed to return those links when the race was over—and she would. But the clones she had made of them would remain in her system so that she could investigate at her leisure if her DNA plan didn't work.

It was beginning to look like the plan wouldn't. The organizers had changed policy this year. They had hired a medical team leader who, in turn, hired the medical teams. During the race, he managed the medical teams' crisis responses.

In the past there had been one large medical team, which coordinated its own efforts. Apparently there had been a lot of miscommunication at the last two marathons, and one of those miscommunications had been serious. A runner had nearly died because no one had responded to his panic button for more than half an hour. The team who should have responded claimed they hadn't received the initial alarm.

The other teams ignored the alarm, thinking it was not their problem.

It took three different runners, going past, to query via their links about the runner down at milepost fifteen before a med unit went out to investigate. Oliviari never did find out what the runner had nearly died of; it had taken her a lot of oblique conversations and delicate probings to find out this much of the story.

The race's organizers maintained a lot of secrecy around the deaths and injuries. Oliviari had a hunch not all of the deaths were reported on the field. That way, the numbers remained within the "acceptable" range for a tourist event of this nature, and Armstrong wasn't put into the difficult position of investigating one of its most popular sporting events.

It made her job even more difficult, however. She had been tracking Frieda Tey for years now, always edging close, and somehow getting thwarted.

Oliviari was one of the best Trackers in the business, and she had been fooled several times by false information planted by Tey. The tangle behind Tey's disappearance was even more muddled than most; the false information had a lot more solidity than information created about most Disappeareds.

And that was the other problem: Oliviari had never been able to identify Tey's disappearance service. It appeared, from all the evidence Oliviari had gathered so far, that Tey had Disappeared on her own.

Oliviari didn't believe it, though. No one was that good. It took entire teams of people, along with very sophisticated systems, to properly hide a Disappeared.

Most Disappeareds did not vanish as well as they thought they did; it was just that the roadblocks set up to finding them were solid enough to discourage the casual searcher. A real Tracker, like Oliviari, was expensive, and most governments did not have enough resources to hire a Tracker for every Disappeared.

Generally, the governments hired Trackers for only the most grievous cases. In all others, the governments did a cursory search themselves—a search that usually failed.

Oliviari hadn't failed yet. The Tey case, however, was testing her limits.

The whistle of a panic button echoed through the earpieces in her soft-sided helmet. At the bottom of her visor, the location of the injured appeared, along with a bio readout.

She studied it closely, hoping that Team Four wouldn't get an assignment she wanted. Finally the information that she was interested in crossed her screen.

The injured party was a male runner. Already there'd been two calls involving women, and Oliviari hadn't been involved. Her best opportunities for DNA sampling had already been taken.

Still, she finished looking at the readout. Male runner, mid-forties, first time in the race. Insufficient oxygen. Probably a problem with his environmental suit. A lot of the suits sold to athletes for this event were untried. During training, the medical recruits had all been warned that they would primarily be dealing with various forms of suit failure, mostly with the breathing systems.

Oliviari had been glad about that. She had a dozen years of off-and-on-again medical training, augmented by field experience, but there were gaps in her knowledge wide enough to drive a shuttle through. One thing she did know, though, was how to deal with oxygen problems—bad suit flow, high carbon dioxide, too much pure oxygen.

The information feed started again, this time with an image of the runner. Oliviari watched it, feeling no

sense of urgency. This emergency was Team Four's
problem. The next injury that came up would be hers,
and she would have to respond to that.

The members of Team Four split into their two
smaller units—two on the swift-moving emergency
scooter, carrying their med kits, followed by the other
two members in the field ambulance.

The ambulances were parked behind one of the
maintenance buildings, hidden from the crowd. The
scooters were parked near the organizer's table, but
anytime a warning resounded, the drivers had been
instructed to launch behind the buildings. The crowd
needed to know that there were medical facilities, but
they didn't need to know when the facilities would
be used.

As Team Four headed off, the feed at the bottom
of Oliviari's visor shut off. All med team members got
the initial information—it was one way of preventing
the disasters of the last few years—but the moment
a team launched, the information no longer had to
be shared.

Oliviari sighed. Her plan wasn't perfect. She had
hoped she would be on a quicker response team, like
Team One, so that she would get into the medical tent
sooner. At the end of the race, all of the runners had
to come through there—even the runners who did not
finish—so that they could be processed.

It irritated her that she hadn't gotten inside so far.
She wanted to see these runners without their helmets on.

Long ago, Oliviari had memorized Tey's features,
as well as her movements and the sound of her voice.
All of that could be changed through enhancements,
but generally the Disappeared didn't use enhancements. The money always went toward the disappearance itself instead of the reinvention.

Trackers also had another advantage: People didn't
change their fundamental natures. They were in-

structed to modify their interests, to avoid things they
had done before, but usually they found ways to get
involved in similar occupations.

Frieda Tey had always been a fitness nut. Even
when she had been stationed in isolated labs in the
most remote places, she had kept herself in immacu-
late physical condition. Toward the end, she had
started to focus on the human body's physical limitations, with and without enhancements.

Oliviari figured that Tey was probably not doing
official science any longer. No more experiments, no
more high-profile projects. But Tey's interest in the
edges of human existence probably hadn't changed.

That was what Oliviari gambled on. She followed
hints in Tey's record that could have led Tey here.

Oliviari looked back at the crowd. The spectators
noticed nothing. They couldn't hear the panic whistles,
and the feeds they watched cut to a different section
of the course whenever a problem developed.

A movement in the aisle between the bleachers
caught Oliviari's eye. Two people, a man and a
woman, strode toward the dome, wearing environmental suits. The suits had hoods instead of helmets, and
the hoods were down.

The woman appeared to be in her mid-forties,
though appearances were often deceiving because of
enhancements. She had short black hair with gray
highlights that caught the dome's artificial light. Her
angular face had stress lines; the mouth seemed permanently downturned in anger or disappointment. She
was surveying everything, her expression wary.

The man behind her was younger—maybe twenty-
five—and shorter than the woman. He still had a
young man's thinness, although something in his
movements suggested a wiry strength. He too tried to
take in everything, but he seemed easily distracted, his
head turning this way and that.

As the woman and the young man became visible

between the bleachers, two of the race's organizers hurried to their side. The organizers hustled the pair toward the organizers' in-dome booth, closing the door tightly behind them.

Most of the spectators hadn't even noticed. Those who had didn't seem to think anything of it. The medical teams were staring at the empty path that led to the finish line or examining their vehicles, obviously hoping for a run.

The woman and the young man had been police. Probably a detective and a recruit. Armstrong didn't dare send high-profile officers to the marathon; someone was bound to notice. But a low-ranking detective and a patrolman to back her up would be able to take charge of any accidental death scene, even one that occurred outside the dome.

Oliviari frowned. She hadn't heard anything about a death, and she should have. She placed her hand on the scooter's climate-controlled seat, unable to feel anything but the seat's hardness through her glove. She flicked on her visor monitors, adjusting the information until she got only the medical reports.

The scooter part of Team Four had arrived at the male runner's side. Insufficient oxygen due to a clogged interior line; he was light-headed and sick, barely alert enough to push the panic alarm at all.

Team Three's injured woman had a broken ankle. She was being moved off course now. Team One's injured woman had a broken wrist and a poorly sealed suit—she had tripped in one of the craters, fallen, broken her wrist, and scraped the suit open. It had sealed, but not well enough to allow her to continue. They were all still debating in field about whether or not she should go on.

Team Two had responded to a male panic alarm about six miles in. His bio readout had been fine, but sometimes bio readouts malfunctioned just like everything else. Team Two had not come back with a follow-up report, like the teams were supposed to, and they'd been with the man for more than an hour.

Oliviari frowned. She hadn't paid a lot of attention to Team Two's call—she wanted to keep track of the injured women, not the injured men—but it seemed suspicious. Especially with the arrival of the police and the lack of follow-up.

She wondered if she should bring this to the medical leader's attention. Maybe if she offered to follow up, she would be allowed to find out what was going on.

The gamble was that the man had accidentally hit his button and the team hadn't thought the follow-up worth anyone's time. If Oliviari involved herself in someone else's case, she might hurt her chance to attend at least one woman on the field. The more chances she had to work in the field, the less she had to do when the race ended.

The other problem with approaching the team leader was that Oliviari would call attention to herself. The key to her success as a Tracker had always been in maintaining a low profile. She never even checked in with local governments the way Trackers were supposed to.

She had found, over the years, that the locals sometimes had moles that fed information to the Disappeared. Sometimes, the Disappeared had gotten government jobs just to have the chance to monitor Tracker arrivals.

Oliviari never allowed anyone to get ahead of her— which was why Tey annoyed her. It felt like Tey had had the better of her from the very beginning.

Oliviari shoved the thought away. She wanted to find out about that mysterious call Team Two had gone on. Tey was the kind of woman who would find a race like this a challenge, and Oliviari was afraid that if she ignored any detail, she might miss Tey altogether.

Oliviari summoned all the vid images of the race,

and let them stream across her visor, with the real
lunar landscape in the background. She had the suit
add the coordinates and mile markers. Logically those
would all be consecutive. Since she was part of the
med team, her feeds should have remained unblocked
and she should have seen the emergency care under
way.

The two first-response members of Team Four were
huddled next to the male runner. He was sitting down,
his feet shaking as if they wanted to continue on the
race alone. Team Three was loading their victim into
the field ambulance, and a member of Team One was
spraying something on the arm of the injured woman,
probably an additional sealant for the suit.

Like so many of these athletes, the woman probably
felt she needed to finish this race to prove something.
As if competing in an artificial environment like a
marathon proved anything. A person never knew what
she was made of until she faced a life-or-death situation that surprised her, not one she had spent the last
five years training for.

There was a gap between miles five and six. Proximity cameras focused on a large rock, almost as if they
had been broken and pointed in the wrong direction.
When Oliviari tried to compensate, her visor went
black.

The images were gone, leaving only the moonscape—the man-made road, the runner's path leading
off into the distance, the dark horizon that still seemed
too close.

She tried to call the images back, to get the feeds
provided to the medical teams, and they wouldn't
reboot.

Obviously her query had come to someone's attention—and that someone hadn't liked what she was
doing.

Oliviari sighed. The only thing she could do now
was go to the medical leader and ask about Team

Two, pretend ignorance and assume that there was a problem in communication, rather than an attempt to hide something.

Even though she knew what that something was. Someone had died on the course between miles five and six. That was why the police had been called; that was why there was video silence. Someone had died and the circumstances were odd. The initial readout had listed that a healthy person hit the panic alarm. Either there was something wrong with the bio readout, or a runner had stumbled on another runner's body, literally.

There were very few cases in which runners lacked the time to hit their own panic alarm. Sudden suit depressurization would be the worst. But those deaths were messy, and hard to miss. Usually people talked about that sort of thing, especially civilians like runners, who had to be passing by the body.

But no one was saying anything.

And Oliviari found that strangest of all.

4

Flint sat in a research café three blocks from Dome University's Armstrong Campus. Paloma had introduced him to this place. The café provided net linkage for poor students whose families couldn't afford standard enhancements. The café was funded with grant money, and augmented by paying customers like Flint, who had a favorite corner in an alcove just off the bathrooms.

Because of its location, the alcove was usually empty and therefore private. The screens here were smaller than the others, and voice commands did not work because of a slight echo effect that the café couldn't afford to get rid of.

The screens were touch screens or, for an extra fee, the café provided a keyboard. Flint used the touch screens here. No sense in calling attention to himself.

He did, however, wear gloves. A clear skintight pair that weren't visible to the naked eye. They even had ridged fingertips so that they seemed like real fingers, since a lot of touch screens didn't operate for people with gloved hands.

He had chosen this place to research Astrid Krouch and WSX because the café was far from his office. Eventually WSX would note the queries, but it would take a while for the WSX system to realize the queries had come from Flint.

Because the café was close to the university, the system might ignore Flint's queries altogether. A lot of university students researched law firms before sending in applications. The only thing that might trip the system to Flint's presence was the mention of Astrid Krouch.

He spent a few minutes reading about WSX, finding only their promotional materials and transcripts of court cases they'd filed. He realized quickly that this particular search would get him nowhere.

So he turned to Astrid Krouch instead.

Because he was curious, he had decided to see why Astrid Krouch had kept such a low profile for the past ten years. Usually lawyers—even baby lawyers—did everything they could to get as much publicity as possible. But Krouch hadn't.

Was she working her way into becoming one of the firm's secret weapons, one of those talented but hidden lawyers who seemed new to the competition, but turned out to be better than all of them? Weapons like that fired only a few times, but they were useful in important cases.

He found only her school records, her family history, and her résumé. Once she had gone to work for Wagner, Stuart, and Xendor, Astrid Krouch had lost her interest in courting the public eye.

A shape loomed behind him, reflecting in the touch screen. Flint hit the lower right-hand side, making the screen go dark.

A man stopped beside Flint's desk. The man was beefy, his arms barely remaining contained in his black business suit. His face had the rounded cheeks of a person who tended toward fat. He looked like he used slimness enhancers to keep his weight under control. But, like so many people who could afford the enhancers, he ate even more once he had them linked, and so the enhancers always fought to keep up.

The man folded his manicured hands, their backs

dotted with tiny security chips, and smiled. "Mr. Flint? I'm Ignatius Wagner, Astrid Krouch's boss."

One of the Wagners of Wagner, Stuart, and Xendor, Ltd. Flint kept his expression neutral even though he was surprised. Big-time attorneys like Wagner didn't come to cafés near Dome University, especially to seek out a Retrieval Artist.

"And," Wagner added, "in case you're wondering, I'm the junior Wagner, the son everyone assumes will inherit the company only if I learn what the law is truly about."

Flint deleted his files and shut down the screen he'd been working on. He pressed a small indentation on the desk in front of him, confirming that he wanted to pay for his time with the credit he had on file.

Wagner had probably traced Flint's search, using the WSX office systems to find out who had been probing into Astrid Krouch's background. But the trace had occurred much quicker than Flint had expected.

He also hadn't expected anyone to show up at the café. Flint had expected WSX to monitor his movements, not confront him.

"You must really want to hire me," Flint said without moving away from the screen. It took a while for public systems to purge information. He wasn't going to move until he was certain what he'd been looking at would vanish into the ether. "Aren't there any other brand-new Retrieval Artists in town?"

"Our firm has a history with Paloma."

Flint shrugged. "She hasn't worked for a long time. Surely you use someone else."

"We were happy when we learned that she'd trained a successor. It means that you're as ethical as she is."

Assumptions again, this time flattering ones. Flint could believe that the law firm was looking for an ethical Retrieval Artist, that they had done a minimum of research and decided that Flint would do. Or he could believe that he was being manipulated at the highest level for a reason he couldn't fathom yet.

"I turned down Ms. Krouch," Flint said. "I'm not interested in the case."

"She said you didn't even listen to her," Wagner said.

"I never do," Flint said. "I make my decision based solely on whether or not I can trust the client. Frankly, Mr. Wagner, I find your presence here simply confirms that I made the best possible decision."

A Peyti college student staggered toward the rest room, trying to adjust its breathing mask with its long, twiglike fingers. Its translucent skin picked up the white of the walls, making it seem ghostlike. It disappeared into the women's rest room.

"You need to hear me out, Mr. Flint," Wagner said. "I really don't want to take this to anyone else in Armstrong."

Flint was getting intrigued, despite his misgivings. "Because someone else, you have to figure, would already know the rules of whatever game you're playing."

Wagner sighed. "Look, Mr. Flint. I really can't go into why we want to hire you here. Let's just say there are some legal reasons that have nothing to do with your competence that make it imperative that we work with you."

Flint raised an eyebrow. "That's a new one."

Another Peyti slunk toward the rest room, obviously looking for the first Peyti. This Peyti had its breathing mask on properly, and its skin didn't pick up as much white from the walls.

It knocked on the bathroom door with the tips of its long fingers, then said something that sounded like a cross between a sigh and a groan. Peytin was hard to understand in the Peyti's natural environment. Through a breathing mask of the kind all Peyti had to wear in Armstrong, their native tongue was nearly impossible to understand.

"This clearly isn't private," Wagner said. "Should we go outside?"

Flint shook his head. "I've paid for an hour's worth of time here and I plan to use it. Make an appointment with me, Mr. Wagner, and I'll listen to your legal reasons. But stop trying to flatter me with the ethical crap. You have no idea who I am or what my relationship with Paloma really is. One thing you can be assured of is that I won't take any case if I feel manipulated."

"The ethics are part of the legal reason," Wagner said.

The Peyti knocked on the rest room door again, then pushed it open. A series of chirrups resounded from inside as the door closed.

Wagner was trying to talk over the noise. "But I will make an appointment with you. Shall we do that verbally or do you have an appointment manager that I can link with?"

Flint didn't let anyone close to his links. "We'll do it now."

"All right." Wagner looked pleased with himself. "I'm free later this evening at six. If you could come to the office—"

"I don't come to you, Mr. Wagner. If you want me to work for you, you come to my office in Old Armstrong and we talk there. Or we can end this association right now."

Wagner looked surprised. Then he nodded. "All right. Six?"

Flint nodded.

"I'll see you then." Wagner looked at the narrow desk area, than at the nearby bathroom—from which more chirrups resounded.

Flint had a hunch the Peyti were a couple and they were having a fight.

"I don't see how you can get any work done here," Wagner said. "I, at least, would move to a screen closer to a window, where it's quiet."

"I'll see you at six, Mr. Wagner," Flint said, and powered the screen back up. He punched in his code, determined to use the rest of his credits. He wouldn't be coming back here, not when his identity had been so easily breached.

Wagner sighed, then left. The chirruping continued in the rest room, but Flint ignored it. He was more interested in tracing the café's access.

He wanted to know how the hacks in Wagner's law firm had found him so quickly, and he wasn't going to leave this tiny desk until he found out.

5

DeRicci and van der Ketting stepped inside the air lock between the interior and exterior of the dome. The airlock was small, little more than two doors and a corridor.

DeRicci's heart always started to beat a little harder in an airlock, from both nervousness and excitement. She loved going Outside, something she rarely admitted, even to herself.

When the airlock door closed, DeRicci lost sight of the dome's interior. Lakferd had hustled her and van der Ketting inside the airlock—apparently to keep them out of view of the spectators—but DeRicci didn't know where he was now.

She was just glad that Lakferd hadn't accompanied them. DeRicci really didn't want to deal with a race organizer during the Outside portion of this investigation.

She sealed her environmental suit, and had the suit's smart chip check for leaks. Air puffed around her. A small green light appeared on the cheap see-through fabric of her hood. No helmets for low-grade detectives who had to investigate outside the dome. Just sealable hoods and a short-term air supply.

Just once she'd like to know what it was like to venture Outside in proper gear, like the kind the runners had. Stuff made to last days should the wearer get into trouble, with its own water recycling as well as the recyclable air. All bodily fluids cleansed and reused. Efficiency instead of economy.

DeRicci glanced at van der Ketting. He stood behind her as close to the dome entrance as he could get. His lank brown hair puffed up around his forehead, once, then twice.

He was double- and triple-checking. She wondered if he'd ever been Outside before.

"You're not just wasting time," she said through their link, "you're wasting oxygen."

That wasn't technically true, but if he was as green as he seemed, he wouldn't know that. She had taken a lot of new partners Outside for the first time, and most of them did what van der Ketting had been doing. She learned that lying to them about their oxygen made them stop a lot quicker than ordering them to quit.

The problem new detectives had wasn't the environmental suit or even leaving the safety of the dome. Schoolchildren took excursions Outside during every year of schooling, and the police academy spent an entire semester on Outside investigations.

The problem was a lot more complex. It took DeRicci years to figure out why new partners on their first Outside case were so nervous.

The entire concept frightened them.

Not the concept of going Outside—by the time they'd risen to detective, they'd gone Outside two dozen times or more—but the investigation itself, the open-ended nature of it. There was no instructor with emergency training beside them, no structured itinerary, and no planned route. Every cadet heard the horror stories of investigating officers who wandered in the wrong direction, who got confused by the large expanse of rock and craters only to be found days later dead of dehydration or oxygen deprivation.

DeRicci, to get over her own fear, had investigated

some of these stories and found all but one to be a myth. The one that was true happened when the dome was small, the police force new, and the equipment primitive. Apparently the policeman's death had been horrible—he'd been conscious and radioing for help throughout most of it, but he hadn't known his exact location—and over the years had become an example of the dangers of Outside.

Right now, she didn't have the time to warn van der Ketting about all the myths. She needed him alert and focused, not worried about whether he would survive the investigation.

"I can do this alone if I have to," she said to him.

He gave her a startled look through his hood's plastic face panel, and then shook his head. "I'm all right."

"I'm not going to take care of you out there," she said.

Van der Ketting's shoulders straightened. She had offended him. "I don't need help Outside, Detective."

He only called her detective when he was irritated at her. DeRicci turned away so that he couldn't see her smile. She had gotten him to focus on something other than his fear of the Outside, and that was good. With a limited time on this investigation and all the hassles the marathon organizers would throw her way, she would need his observational powers as much as she needed her own.

"We're heading out then." DeRicci opened the code box beside the door. With a gloved finger, she typed in the day's police code, followed by her badge number. Then she pressed a chip in the corner and leaned forward, letting a small red beam of light examine her right eye.

For a moment nothing happened, and she wondered if the eye scan had failed to identify her. That happened a lot to people in police-issue environmental suits. The hood's plastic panel distorted the beam of light just enough to give the system a variety of misreads.

Then a warning buzzer sounded, followed by an androgynous voice. "Dome door will open in thirty seconds. If you are not wearing an environmental suit, you have fifteen seconds to vacate the airlock. Repeat. Dome door . . ."

DeRicci suppressed a sigh. Thirty seconds seemed like forever while a buzzer clanged over her head. Finally the buzzer stopped, along with the voice, and the door slid open.

DeRicci loved the contradiction of Outside. The sunlight was so much brighter than anything she'd ever experienced inside the dome, yet the ground was dark gray, and the sky black. It didn't feel like day or night out here, at least a dome day or night. Instead it was something different, something that felt, to her, like an alien planet, which she always thought odd because she had been born and raised in Armstrong.

She stepped through the door, feeling a wave of cooling air run through the suit's interior as it tried to compensate for the exceptionally hot temperatures. She'd been told that more expensive environmental suits didn't have that moment of adjustment; that when you wore one of those, stepping from inside the dome to Outside felt no different from crossing a street.

One of the organizers waited for her, standing on the entry platform, white suit glowing in the sunlight. The visor was tinted, so DeRicci couldn't see the organizer's face.

"Noelle DeRicci," she said through the link that the marathon had provided. "And my partner Leif van der Ketting."

"Gordon Frears." The responding voice, male, startled her. For some reason she had been expecting a female guide. "Come with me."

He didn't wait for her to reach his side. Instead he used an odd loping gait to take him to one of the surface cars. He was clearly a veteran of the marathon as well, just like Lakferd and Chaiken had been.

DeRicci didn't have that kind of grace in the Outside. Besides, she wanted to take the opportunity to observe. To her left, maintenance buildings, storage sheds, and a few unmarked metal shacks clustered, most of them city-owned, but a few belonging to the bigger corporations that were headquartered inside Armstrong.

The small staging area for the race stood to her right. The organizers' table, a place where they double- and triple-checked the identification of the suited participants (in the past, too many people had sneaked onto the course—something caught only when the finishers numbered more than the starters), seemed small against the curved edge of the dome.

Even farther to the right stood a variety of scooters, used by medical personnel, and some field ambulances, although not nearly as many as required by the city, which meant that several were already responding to calls.

Medical personnel waited beside the ambulances. A small knot of organizers stood around viewing stations, and two people still manned the table, as if they were waiting for more runners to join the race.

Behind the field ambulances, a small semipermanent tent had been set up as the medical facility. After the race, all runners had to be cleared to reenter the dome. Outside workers had their own facility for that, but they wouldn't rent it out for the race. They were worried about volunteers contaminating the site. DeRicci didn't blame them; she had seen what kind of damage volunteers could do.

Van der Ketting had stopped beside DeRicci. He too was looking around. She wondered if he was tak-

ing in the setting or worrying about the case. Maybe
he was doing both.

Frears waited for them at the surface vehicle. His
arms were crossed, his back straight, his body lan-
guage so clearly irritated that DeRicci wondered if he
hadn't struck the pose on purpose.

She turned away from him. No runners yet, although she suspected the first ones would be crossing
the finish line soon. Then this area would be complete chaos.

Before heading to the surface vehicle, she walked
to the medical tent.

"I thought you wanted to see the body." The voice
in her link was Frears. He sounded as impatient as
he looked.

"In a moment," DeRicci said. "I have one other
stop to make first."

"I need to be here when the first runner comes
back," Frears said, but DeRicci ignored him. If he had
to be here when the first runner crossed the finish line,
the organizers wouldn't have sent him. Still, it was a
good ploy and one a newbie like van der Ketting
would have fallen for.

Van der Ketting had trouble keeping up with her.
He was tripping along the surface, trying to remain
low. Obviously he had never really learned the Outside gait.

She wasn't going to instruct him either. Most of the
time he would be on the vehicle, and she'd give him
tasks that would keep him there. With a walk like
that, the last thing he needed was to cross an unpaved
surface, with its rocks and fist-sized craters, perfect for
catching a boot in.

The medical tent had clearly been assembled for
days. It had its own atmosphere. The tent's rear exit
was attached to one of the dome's maintenance entrances; that way, cleared runners could go inside the

dome without donning their environmental suits all over again.

DeRicci headed for the main door, which faced the finish line. A tall person in another white environmental suit extended a gloved hand, stopping her.

"Sorry. Only race participants are allowed past this point." This time, the voice in the link was tenor. DeRicci couldn't tell if she was speaking to a man or a woman. Even the face, which she could see faintly through the tinted visor, seemed androgynous.

Van der Ketting glanced over his shoulder, as if he were looking for Frears. Maybe Frears was communicating to van der Ketting directly, not that it mattered. Van der Ketting couldn't leave DeRicci's side on this investigation.

"Police," DeRicci said.

"I'm sorry. I'm not authorized to let anyone inside before the race ends."

"That's fine," DeRicci said, even though she knew she could push the point if she wanted to. "Just let me look inside."

The organizer turned, the movement almost a pirouette, and skipped toward the door. DeRicci hadn't realized how different everyone's walks were on the surface. In her investigations at previous Moon Marathons, she had either gone directly to the death site or been taken into places with atmosphere.

DeRicci followed, feeling clunky after the organizer's graceful movements. If DeRicci felt awkward, she wondered how van der Ketting felt as he stumbled along behind her.

The organizer stopped at the door and lifted a flap covering a large window. DeRicci placed one gloved hand on the window's surface as she peered inside. Police suits did have a lot of job-specific extras. The gloves had extra chips for touch analysis, and she also had ways of recording everything the suit processed, even the visuals.

Through her personal link, she sent van der Ketting a single message: *Record.* She would take care of her own backup, but she wanted his to be primary.

The glove registered the window as clear plastic, the visuals inside as the actual interior instead of a feed flowing through the surface. DeRicci would double-check that when she got back to the station, but she had a hunch the glove was accurate on this. Since no tourists or reporters were allowed in this part of the race setup, there would be no reason to mask a window with a fake visual.

She peered inside. Empty beds extended all the way to the second door. Three medical personnel sat in various parts of the room, watching wall screens of the race. Another medical person was setting up silver, finger-sized diagnostic wands on a long table in the center. Even though medical personnel could use their own chips for diagnosis, most preferred the wands. The wands made it easier to share the information with the patient.

"No patients yet?" DeRicci asked the organizer.

"We've had a couple of calls and sent out several teams, but so far no one has brought an injured runner back. We're expecting one shortly."

DeRicci had encountered this on a previous race. The med team waited—if they could—to bring injured runners here until someone had crossed the finish line. That way it wouldn't look so odd to see a runner, supported by a few "friends," being carried to the checkout tent.

A few times, however, runners were brought in early. On that investigation, DeRicci learned that a particular part of the course had been hit with a rock in the year between races, and the committee hadn't changed the path to compensate. That little mistake had caused several injuries and the death DeRicci had been investigating.

DeRicci took her hand off the window, nodded at

the organizer, and headed back toward the surface vehicle. She was aware of the spectators inside the dome watching her movements.

The police environmental suits were not obviously marked; no one from Inside could tell she was anything more than one more race volunteer, albeit one with a very cheap suit. Still, she felt conspicuous, and she had a hunch it was because the organizers had been so careful to hustle her and van der Ketting away from the spectators.

Frears was already inside the vehicle when she and van der Ketting arrived. The vehicle was a large one, built for carrying personnel and cargo. Two seats up front, two benches in the back, and a long open area with an optional roof that closed at the touch of a button.

"Ready?" Frears asked, and even though the question seemed innocuous, DeRicci heard a faint edge of sarcasm in his tone.

"Let's go," she said.

The vehicle lurched forward, bumping off the paved road onto the unpaved trail. DeRicci loathed the surface vehicle, and not just for its bumpy ride toward the victim. She loathed the way it destroyed evidence by trampling it, loathed the way it created its own trail as if nothing else mattered.

She didn't ask Frears to drive around the footprints left by the runners, however. Following trails was very important Outside. The surface could be deceptive. Sometimes craters looked smaller than they were, or weren't visible at all, causing vehicles to get caught, jackknife, or flip over.

Everything Outside was fraught with what DeRicci thought was unnecessary danger. Sometimes she thought if she were ever elected to the Board of Governors (like that was going to happen), she would vote to dome over the entire surface and be done with it.

The trip was short. DeRicci watched the rocks and

flatness go by. There were no runners on this part of
the course; even the slowest, apparently, had gone past
the five-mile marker.

Of course, this marathon, unlike the ones in the
dome, took only people who qualified by winning or
placing in other marathons. No one was going to walk
for exercise out here. This marathon was for the best
of the best, or at least the best of those who felt the
need to prove their worth.

Van der Ketting was staring at the Earth, looming
large in the darkness above them. DeRicci looked at
it too, its surface providing the only visible color. She
loved the purity of the blue, the way the white drifted
across everything, the brightness of the green. One
day she wanted to go there. She had never been to a
place where the Outside had more variety than Inside.

The vehicle went over a rise, and slowed. Before
them, a large boulder dominated the horizon. The
path split around the boulder, and each side of the
split showed signs of foot traffic.

A field ambulance was parked on the right side of
the boulder. The attendants were leaning against the
ambulance's side. One of them was pointing at the
Earth, as if identifying locations for the other
attendant.

DeRicci felt a tingle of anticipation run through her,
and she immediately tamped the feeling down. She
loved this part of her job, the moment of discovery,
of learning what this case—if indeed it would be a
case—was actually going to be about. She tried not to
look like she enjoyed it, though, because no matter
what else had happened, someone had just lost a
loved one.

The vehicle pulled up beside the field ambulance,
and Frears contacted the attendants. They turned,
clearly surprised by the vehicle's proximity. DeRicci
wondered if anyone ever got used to the silence out
here.

Everyone got out of the vehicle, and Frears introduced DeRicci and van der Ketting. The two attendants, Molly Robinson and Colin Danners, were now in charge of the police visitors. Frears made that plain even before he returned to the vehicle, turned it around, and headed back to the dome.

DeRicci watched him go, and saw how the vehicle kicked up the dirt. The dirt didn't have atmosphere to fly through, no air to slow it down. It flew behind the wheels in a fan pattern, each particle keeping its position until it landed on the ground.

"All right," she said to the attendants after Frears disappeared over the horizon. "Take us to the victim."

"She's just around the rock," Robinson said. Her voice was high and breathy, the voice of a young girl, even though the woman before DeRicci was taller than the men.

Danners nodded. "I think she probably dislodged—"

"Please," DeRicci said. "No theories yet. Let us take a look and then we can talk."

She didn't want any more preconceived notions than she already had. It was always best to approach a new scene with the freshest possible interpretation, the most open mind she could have.

Danners and Robinson started walking side by side around the boulder. This time, it was van der Ketting who stopped them. "Didn't you go in single file?"

All med techs were taught to approach a dead body down the same trail. That way evidence, if it was needed, wouldn't be compromised.

"We were told it was a medical emergency," Robinson said in that breathy voice. "We had no idea the runner was dead."

"Besides," Danners said, "the entire field of runners has gone through here. We're not destroying anything."

"You don't know that," DeRicci said, even though

she suspected Danners was right. "Just point us in the right direction and we'll go. Wait for us here."

Robinson pointed around the boulder. "She's a few meters on the far side. You can't miss her. She looks like she curled up there for a nap until you get close enough to see inside her visor."

DeRicci shuddered, glad the motion was hidden by her suit. Outside deaths were ugly things. Sometimes DeRicci preferred a rapid-depressurization death. At least then she could imagine that the death was quick and painless.

Oxygen-depletion corpses bore their suffering in every pore of their bodies.

"I'll go first," DeRicci said to van der Ketting, hoping that she would now pick the right trail. She walked around the boulder, noting that its shadow fell on the forward part of the path.

The sunlight blazed, reflecting off nearby rocks. They glittered, showing mineral components that had excited the first settlers.

Most of the footprints followed the paths that merged a few meters away, and then disappeared over the horizon. The most recent boot marks were distinctive and clear, but the earlier ones had already been destroyed by too many feet stepping on them.

DeRicci had no idea how many runners had signed up for this year's marathon, but all of them had gone past this point. What had they thought, seeing the field ambulance and the runner on the trail? Or had the attendants been pretending to help until the last runner passed?

Once DeRicci made it around the boulder, the body was clear. At first she thought the suit was a typical organizer's white, but as she got closer she realized that the suit was a pale pink. Where the sun hit it, the pink got a rosy gloss—a festive, fanciful suit as well as a functional one.

DeRicci felt her heart twist. The woman, the dead

woman, had a nontraditional streak, something that had encouraged her to buy this particular suit. The suit's unusual color made the woman seem real somehow, in a way that her body did not.

But the body's position was already bothering DeRicci. The position seemed almost fetal, legs up, arms crossed, hands cupped beneath the helmet as if in sleep. Not a natural position for someone to die in if they had lost oxygen or if their suit depressurized.

DeRicci approached slowly, recording everything with a simple movement of her hooded face—the nearby boulder, the trail, the other scattered rocks, and the tiny craters no bigger than her hand. Near the boulder, she saw vehicle trails, and she wondered if they were from surface vehicles or field ambulances. She could hear her own breathing, raspy and shallow, and she made herself take deep breaths.

The last thing she needed to do was get light-headed again, this time because she hadn't been breathing properly.

She took careful note of the footprints going around the body. Some were large, some small, and a number were deep. She couldn't tell if everyone had leaped the body or if only a few runners had.

There was also no way to tell from this distance if anyone had landed on the body itself, although she suspected one or two people might have. After all, the body lying across the trail, just a meter or so from where it met the other trail, might have been enough of a surprise that a runner might not have been able to correct in time.

DeRicci shook her head slightly and followed the trail of narrower prints, prints that seemed to have been made by the attendants, to the corpse's head. Then DeRicci crouched, bracing herself.

The visor's faceplate was nonreflective, although it had a special coating that protected the wearer's face from the sun. A scratch in the faceplate formed a jagged bolt that worked its way to the plate's bottom.

But the faceplate hadn't cracked through. It looked, at first glance, like the suit's seal remained. The woman hadn't died from rapid depressurization. The victim's face was intact, but grotesque. Her eyes bulged out of a blackened and distorted face. Her mouth was worse; it took DeRicci a moment to realize that the large purplish thing sticking out of the mouth was the woman's tongue.

She had died of oxygen deprivation.

Van der Ketting crouched beside DeRicci, and then nearly toppled forward onto the body. He caught DeRicci's arm, and used it to brace himself.

"Suit malfunction?" he asked via his personal link.

"Don't know," DeRicci said.

She rose slightly, looking at the helmet. It was covered in dust, looking grayer than the suit itself. DeRicci wasn't sure why the helmet would have more dust on it than the suit.

The victim's hands were wearing standard-issue gloves, thick and heavy, not made for fine work like DeRicci's were. She tried to remember what the other runners had worn, and couldn't. She didn't know if these fit within the regulation or not.

"Double-check the information we were given," she said. "Did this woman hit her panic button?"

"I thought Chaiken said that some guy did," van der Ketting said.

That was DeRicci's recollection as well. "Make sure."

Van der Ketting nodded. He remained crouched, looking at the body while he reviewed the early interviews.

DeRicci continued to examine the area around the body. Aside from footprints, there were no other marks in the dirt. No glove prints, no swishes showing a struggle, and, most important, no fan of dirt, like DeRicci would have expected if someone collapsed and fell without bracing herself.

"No contact from this runner," van der Ketting said. "A male runner found her, pressed the panic button, and everyone thought they were going out for him. In fact his bio read was so healthy that a few of the med staff thought this was a prank."

Van der Ketting had done more than review the interview. He'd accessed some of the other files, the ones DeRicci had planned to look at only if this case was suspicious.

Which it was.

"Get her recorded, then check her for a panic button. See if she's one of those extremes who believe that they shouldn't ask for help."

Van der Ketting nodded, then extended his arm over the body. He was going to do a surface record as well as a contemporaneous record.

DeRicci peered behind the body. Still no more scuffs in the dirt, besides the footprints, and only the imprint of a light fan of particles, so close to the suit that she probably wouldn't have seen it without looking.

The body hadn't fallen from a standing position. If anything the woman had eased herself to the ground, like a person about to go to sleep.

Then DeRicci frowned. She looked at the helmet again, and the dirt covering it. No large fan around it, and no small fan. Either the head went down so lightly that it barely made an impact into the dirt, or it had been set down gently.

DeRicci didn't like that last thought. She shouldn't have let it creep in. Deaths should have been expected on marathon day. The organizers should celebrate whenever they got through a marathon without losing a runner.

Van der Ketting was still moving his arm above the

body, probably taking microscans as well as images. Good. They would need all the information they could get.

DeRicci backtracked in the trail they'd made, careful to put her feet only where she or van der Ketting had walked before. She moved only half a meter, so that she could examine the body's lower section.

Legs lined up perfectly and bent at the knee. No obvious tears or rips in the suit anywhere, even at the top. No twists in the fabric, no bunching of the material.

DeRicci had seen some expensive environmental suits in her day, but none as precise as this one. The suit was incredibly sophisticated. She'd seen advertisments for suits like this one. They stretched when the body stretched, shrank when the body curled up. They were self-repairing and self-diagnostic. They also, if DeRicci remembered correctly, had several different emergency services programmed in. If this runner had bought the Moon Package, she could have been anywhere on the surface or anywhere within Moon space, and received help for everything, including catastrophic suit failure.

DeRicci finally leaned backward as far as she could without overbalancing herself. She gazed at the boots.

They were the same luminescent pink as the suit, but they were made of a different material, which meant they came from a different manufacturer. They were ridged, as so many Outside marathoners' boots were, the runners believing that the ridges somehow gave them more traction.

But running down the center of the boot was a jagged crack. DeRicci recognized the pattern as a lightning bolt, even though she'd never seen an actual lightning bolt in real life.

She was about to glance at the jagged scratch on the faceplate, to see if it really matched or if it was just her fervent imagination that made it seem like it would match, when she froze.

Her movement must have seemed abrupt, because van der Ketting looked up from his work. "You okay?"

"Come down here and get the boots," she said. "Stay in our trail."

He frowned, but backed toward her, his arms still extended. When he saw the boots, he whistled. "Expensive."

"The whole package is expensive. Tell me what you see."

"It sort of resembles the mark in the visor."

"And?" DeRicci asked, glad he found that bolt as strange as she did.

He peered at the boots. "No 'and.' "

"There's a big 'and,' " she said. "One Gumiela, the chief of police, and hell, probably even the mayor, aren't going to like."

He braced his hands on his knees, leaned closer to the boots, and would have fallen forward if DeRicci hadn't caught him.

"Sorry," he said.

"Be careful," she said. "You almost ruined our most significant piece of evidence."

He frowned at her again, then examined the boots without touching them. "I don't know what you're seeing."

"The dirt pattern," she said. "Look at the dirt pattern."

He shrugged. "A little spray on the toes from passing runners, but nothing unu— Oh, my. There's no dirt on the treads. They're as clean as a brand-new pair."

"Exactly," DeRicci said. "And you know what that means."

He raised his head. The sun glinted off the plastic of his hood panel. "She was dumped here."

"That's right," DeRicci said. "She was dumped here. After she had been murdered."

6

It took Oliviari nearly fifteen minutes to find the medical team leader. All of Oliviari's links to the med teams—except the links to the panic alerts and the initial readouts—had been cut off. She couldn't access any information at all.

None of her team members seemed surprised as she left her post near the scooter. No one tried to stop her from walking to the organizers' table, which had been her first stop, then continuing all the way across the main staging area.

As she reached one of the maintenance buildings, she saw one of the surface cars drive away, hurrying down the track used by the field ambulances. She had been right: The police were here to investigate a death on the course.

She was trying to keep her movements easy, her breathing calm. She didn't want her own readouts to show any agitation, even though she was feeling some. Mostly anger at her own curiosity, and at the fact that her curiosity had led her to make a blunder.

Her scans of the course had led to someone shutting down her access. Even though she'd made clones of the access information, she couldn't use them now. She would have to wait.

If Oliviari could cover, though, she might be able

to make this blunder into a tiny mistake, something no one knew about except herself.

The medical team leader, Mikhail Tokagawa, was a tall, slender man with lightning-quick reflexes. During the training sessions, Oliviari had often speculated about his background. He had almost a paranoid's re-action to surprise.

He reacted like that when Oliviari approached, turning, stepping forward as if he had been doing something wrong. He hadn't been, so far as she could tell. He had been standing near one of the mainte-nance buildings, talking to a guard, when Oliviari fi-nally located him.

Funny that he would know she was coming. Her footsteps made no sound out here, and she hadn't been in his line of sight. Perhaps the guard had warned him.

"Excuse me, Dr. Tokagawa," Oliviari said, going on the offensive as she had planned. "My med links seem to have shut down."

His visor was tinted like most of the others, but she could see his face through it. He seemed tired, almost as if the race had been too much for him. "Shut down?"

She nodded. "I get the panic alerts and the initial readout, and then nothing."

"Strange," he said in a tone that led her to believe that he didn't find it strange at all.

"I was hoping I could piggyback on someone else's link," she said. "My team's about to be called up."

He shrugged, the movement making his entire suit rise and fall. "I'm sorry. I would have no idea how to do that."

"But you could authorize it."

"I'm not even sure I could. You'll have to go inside."

She sighed. They wanted her away from the runners now. Why? Had the organizers finally checked her credentials?

"I will go inside," she said, "but there was one other thing I wanted to talk with you about."

He lifted his head slightly and looked past her. She turned. There was movement on the horizon. Something faint and small. The first runner was coming in.

"Make it quick," Tokagawa said.

"I was just wondering about Team Two. They haven't followed up, and I tried to see their response on my visuals. That was when my links crashed." A little grain of truth added a lot to credibility.

He looked at her. "Why would you check up on another team?"

"You asked us to, sir, at our first training session. You told us about all of the changes that had occurred because of the unfortunate lack of response to a panic alert a few marathons ago, and you said should any of us notice anything that seems unusual, we should come to you."

"Oh." It was clear he didn't remember that statement, but this time Oliviari wasn't lying. He had said those things; she supposed he just hadn't expected someone to take him quite so literally.

"Two unusual things happened as far as I'm concerned," she said. "First, Team Two didn't report, and then when I check to see if I'm the one who missed anything, my links fail."

He put a gloved hand on her shoulder. The touch felt oddly impersonal through the suit layers. "Thank you for bringing this to my attention. Clearly something has to be done."

Patronized and dismissed. She was beginning to think all doctors were the same everywhere, believing they were smarter than everyone else around them.

Then a panic whistle went off inside her helmet. She winced, wishing she could find a way to turn the damn sound down. A readout trailed along the bottom of her visor: *female runner, age thirty-five, ruptured suit (repairing), dislocated right kneecap, tears in multiple ligaments in the right leg. Mile 14.3.*

Oliviari was about to press her response when the readout and the whistle shut off. Someone else on the team had signaled then.

She moved to return to her scooter, but Tokagawa's hand tightened on her shoulder. She hadn't even realized he was still touching her until he held her in place.

"You can't go without the proper links," he said.

"But I'm on Team Five," she said. "We're up."

Not to mention that the victim was female within the right age bracket; this was the opportunity Oliviari had been hoping for.

"Don't worry," he said. "I'll move a member of Team Ten up. You can go when they're called, so long as your links have been repaired."

"Obviously my standard communication links are working, and since the rest of the team—"

"No," he said, letting go of her shoulder. "Go inside the dome. Get the technical difficulties resolved."

The scooter shot past. Oliviari frowned at it, seeing two suited people on it as it headed onto the trail. Her place had been on that scooter and she had jeopardized it. Chances were that her links wouldn't be repaired by the time Team Ten left either.

Oliviari sighed and left him, heading back to the organization table. Everyone there was on their feet, staring at the finish line.

She turned so that she could see.

A single runner, bent almost in half, headed toward the tape. Another runner had appeared on the horizon, taking large leaps, low to the ground.

A push to the finish, a chance for a real race this year.

Oliviari forgot both her mission and her own disappointment in herself as she watched the competition. The first runner continued at the same pace, clearly at some kind of personal limit. The second runner was gaining, the leaps surprisingly effective.

They were side by side as they headed toward the tape. Then the first runner attempted a leap—

—and the second runner broke through, arms raised.

The first runner had used too much energy going up instead of forward. The change in stride had ruined a beautifully run race.

Oliviari shook her head. That was precisely what she had just done to herself. She had run a beautiful race and then, at the last minute, had blown it by being too curious.

She watched the runners attempt to slow down, the volunteers gather around them to assist, the beginning of the last part, which would include examinations as well as trophies and media interviews.

Maybe she could salvage this after all.

Tokagawa had headed toward the finish line. He wasn't watching Oliviari at all.

She took a deep breath and headed toward the medical tent. A guard stopped her and she flashed her medical clearance. The guard let her through.

She stepped into the air lock, felt her own movements slow as the heavier gravity settled on her, and then she pushed open the door to the medical tent.

"Some race, huh?" she said as she stepped inside, flipping the controls so that her helmet would disengage.

A med tech, someone she didn't recognize, frowned at her.

"I just spoke to Tokagawa," Oliviari said. "He sent me in here rather than keep me on Team Ten, since we'll be getting a lot of people in here in the next few hours."

"You've got about five minutes before the winners arrive," the tech said. "Better take the suit off."

Oliviari smiled. Mistake repaired. Now she just had to get through the next six hours without calling attention to herself all over again.

7

Flint walked on the sidewalks under the glassed-in high-rises in Armstrong's newest, most exclusive neighborhood. Flint had never been inside one of these places before, and he was uncomfortable going there now. He'd always thought them extravagant and wasteful. He would rather have seen poorly functioning sections of the dome repaired and replaced than have the city help fund exclusive housing like this.

But he felt he had no choice. He'd spent nearly an hour tracking Wagner, Stuart, and Xendor's hacking systems, and found that they were very sophisticated. They had traced him within minutes—and could have done so even if they hadn't been expecting him to try to find more information on Astrid Krouch.

It was clear that WSX had the resources to find out anything the lawyers wanted. They didn't need an outside Retrieval Artist. Yet they seemed determined to hire Flint.

He had to know why.

Since Ignatius Wagner had mentioned WSX's previous dealings with Paloma, Flint felt that Paloma was the place to start.

Normally he would have called her to his office, but she would have asked why he sent for her. This time he wanted to catch her off guard.

Paloma's building was part of a high-rise complex on

Armstrong's outer edge. The city had approved a new section of dome to surround them. Somehow the high-rises owners got the council to change zoning regulations. One entire wall of the high-rises was actually attached to the dome, so that residents got to see the Moon's surface from the inside of their homes.

Paloma had loved that feature. She had told Flint so when she used some of the credits he had paid for her business to buy a one-bedroom on the dome side. She still said it was the best investment she'd ever made.

Paloma seemed to have no trouble with the unnecessary luxury. She liked spending her wealth. Flint had barely touched his. He still had the same apartment he had had when he was a police detective. He had upgraded his security system, but had changed little else.

His greatest expenditure so far had been his purchase of Paloma's business. Otherwise, he spent less now than he had when he worked for the city.

A set of clear steps, built against the far wall, circled their way into the building. They seemed indulgent. Part of him felt annoyed; why couldn't the place have solid steps like everywhere else?

But he mounted them, his boots whispering on the clear surface. As he walked, he got slightly dizzy. The see-through steps and the see-through walls made it seem as if he were walking on air. Only the ceiling, as solid as any other ceiling he'd ever seen, gave him a sense of perspective.

The stairs became solid once he went into the main part of the building. They opened onto a corridor that led to a steel door, making him feel as if he were walking into a fortress.

When he had bought the business, Paloma had given him a guest code for her building. He hadn't needed it until now. He had stored it inside his links, and it took a moment for the code to access.

He typed it into the keypad beside the door, an old-fashioned system that seemed odd in such a modern building. He guessed that the keyboard probably had hidden features: a fingerprint gathering system or a DNA-capture system, to be used only in cases of emergency.

He hoped so. Otherwise this building advertised under false pretenses. He could break through a keypad security system—any keypad security system—in less than fifteen seconds.

When he finished typing in the code, the door clicked and slowly swung inward. As the building's interior appeared, Flint caught his breath.

The lobby was spectacular. The floor was as black as the lunar sky. Furniture and plants were scattered along it. The air smelled faintly of lilacs, making it seem fresher than it probably was. Only a handful of people were in the lobby: two security personnel dressed as doormen, standing near the occupants' entrance; a woman working behind a black onyx desk; and three people sitting on the couches, watching tiny screens.

No one was looking at the view, but Flint couldn't take his gaze off of it. The lunar landscape, with its black dunes rising in the distance, dominated the room. For the first time Flint felt as if he were Outside without wearing the uncomfortable suit and breathing the stale air. This was Outside as he wished it could be—accessible and comfortable.

"May I help you, sir?" A woman had approached him from the side. He didn't even see where she had come from, and he was usually aware of such things.

"I'm looking for the elevator," he said.

Her smile was conspiratorial; she knew as well as he did that he had forgotten all about what he had been planning to do until she broke into his reverie.

"Over there," she said, pointing toward a door kitty-corner from the one he had just entered in. It was part of a black wall that, from here, had looked like an extension of the floor.

"Thanks," Flint said, and walked purposefully across

the floor, trying not to look at the Outside. But it was there, so much a part of this place that thinking about anything else was impossible.

He had lived on the Moon his entire life, and sometimes he went days without thinking about the lunar landscape. He could have been in any domed colony on any inhospitable world; it wouldn't have mattered at all.

Often the dome around his office was so covered with dust and dirt and general grime that he couldn't see the moonscape even if he wanted to. When a nearby section of the dome had been replaced and the moonscape was suddenly visible, Flint found himself staring at it at odd times, almost as if it were a secret that had suddenly been revealed.

Perhaps that was what made this lobby seem so decadent: the unobstructed view of a place that a person couldn't visit without permission, money, or connections.

Flint was almost disappointed when he reached the elevator. He wasn't ready to leave this view behind, wasn't ready to reenter the mundane world of other people's concerns.

Still, he pressed the call button. The elevator door slid open, and Flint felt his breath catch again. On three sides, the elevator was glassed in. As he stepped inside, he realized that the floor was mirrored, reflecting the view from the windowed sides.

He spoke the number for Paloma's floor and the doors closed silently behind him. The elevator rose. He walked to the closest window, and saw the moonscape grow smaller. It felt like he was flying without an aircar.

He had never done anything so simple that had been so exhilarating. He wondered how anyone could be depressed living in this building, or sad or even angry. The views alone should have been enough to lighten any mood.

Too soon, the doors behind him opened. He turned his back on the moonscape, sighed, and stepped into a carpeted hallway. A soft voice announced his presence.

A door opened in front of him, one he hadn't even noticed because it had seemed like part of a smooth wall. Paloma stood there, watching him, one hand on the frame, as if she weren't certain whether or not she wanted to let him in.

She looked frailer than she had in her office. The majesty of this building accented her small stature and her unnatural thinness. She hadn't used age enhancers. The skin was stretched over her delicate bone structure, giving her a birdlike appearance. Her white hair, flowing down to her shoulders, looked almost like wings.

"Miles," she said in a voice that belied all the frailty in her appearance. "I thought I wasn't going to coach you anymore."

"If I were asking for coaching," he said, "I'd invite you down to the office."

She stepped away from the door, as if those were the words she'd been waiting to hear. "This is a social call?"

The surprise in her voice made him feel guilty. He hadn't visited her socially since she had retired.

"It's not that either." He crossed the threshold and saw a white wall covered in still images. The images were black-and-white, mostly ancient collectibles of the Moon.

"You've never been here, have you?" she asked.

He shook his head.

She led him around a corner and into an open living room. The moonscape was here too, but not quite as dominant as in the lobby. In this room, the Outside almost seemed like a flat vid or an image that had been tamed.

Perhaps it was the brown carpet or the upholstered furniture. The illusion of being Outside didn't exist here, and Flint was glad for it. He didn't need any more distractions.

"Drink?" she asked. "I have sun tea."

A favorite of Armstrong's rich: tea made with water heated by the sun, tea that could be brewed only in

clear terraces near the dome. Most connoisseurs claimed
they could taste a difference between tea brewed this
way and tea brewed by boiling the water, but Flint
couldn't.

He thought it was all pretension, something he never
would have associated with Paloma. But then, he had
been surprised when she had moved here.

"Just some water, thanks," he said.

She smiled, and squeezed her hands together. Then
she sat down on an armchair with a central view of the
lunar landscape.

A tray with two glasses of ice water floated into the
living room.

"Sit down, Miles," she said.

He did, nearly colliding with the tray as it tried to
serve him his water. He caught the bottom of the tray
with his left hand, and took his water off with his right.

"I'm not used to all this fancy stuff," he said.

Her smile widened. "You'd be surprised how quickly
you become accustomed to it."

And how quickly you come to expect it? The question
reached his lips, but he didn't allow himself to speak it.
He didn't want to offend Paloma. In some ways, she
was the truest friend he had ever had.

"So," she said, taking her drink off the tray, "if it's
not coaching, what do you need that's so urgent you
had to come up here?"

He said, "I need information about your past
dealings."

"You know I can't do that," she said.

Retrieval Artists kept confidentiality so that they
would get more work. Legally, the confidentiality had
no standing. Even the clients knew that a Retrieval Artist would break confidentiality if she had to.

But Paloma had always been ethical. She had told
Flint from the start that she wouldn't betray a client,
and so far she hadn't.

"I'm not asking you to reveal client details," Flint

said. "All I need is to confirm something someone's been telling me."

"Miles, you put me in a delicate position."

He held up a hand. "Hear me out first."

She sipped her water and gazed Outside. The room was very light. The actual lunar day, not the dome day, lasted two weeks. He wondered if the room was always this light or if the window he was looking out of—which was part of this new dome—changed color the way the rest of the dome did.

Distracting. He made himself look away, focus on the water beading against the side of his glass.

"Did the law firm Wagner, Stuart, and Xendor, Limited, send you regular work?" he asked.

Paloma looked at him. Her brown eyes seemed wider than they had a moment ago. "Why?"

"They sent an associate to me, saying they'd always done business with you. She had never dealt with Retrieval Artists before, and assumed I'd be grateful for the job."

Paloma grinned. "She doesn't know you, does she?"

"I thanked her, and turned her down. Then Mr. Wagner Junior, son of the bigwig, turns up at one of my research cafés while I'm working there."

Paloma's grin faded. "You allowed yourself to be traced?"

"I expected it," Flint said. "I was curious about the associate, so I figured WSX was using her in some way. The only thing I could think of was that they expected me to research her, maybe as a way to access my files. So I went to the research café."

Paloma nodded. She obviously approved of his reasoning.

"And they confronted you? In person?" she asked.

"Wagner Junior did," Flint said, "which clued me to how sophisticated their tracking system is. He found me quickly and easily. After he left, I neutralized all links to me, but I'm going to be a lot more cautious with WSX from now on."

"I would hope so," Paloma said.

Flint recognized the tone. She had used it during their teaching sessions, when she thought he had made a rookie mistake. He didn't try to defend himself, but he knew that Paloma, for all her skill, wouldn't have seen the traces either.

He said, "It also made me realize just how much they want me to work for them."

"All the more reason to say no."

"I'm inclined to hear what they want," Flint said. "But first I need to know what kind of lies they're telling. Did you work for them?"

Paloma nodded. "I worked for most of the lawyers in Armstrong at one time or another. I did a lot of superficial investigative work, seeing if someone who was assumed to be Disappeared actually was, finding old clients, determining whether or not a litigant was still alive."

"So did you work with them or were you on staff?"

Her shoulders straightened. The question offended her. "I've never worked for anyone else, Miles."

"They paid you by the job?"

She nodded.

"Did you do a lot of jobs for them?"

"In the beginning," she said. "But none in the last ten years or so. Most of my work was with Wagner Senior. He's still part of the firm, but he hasn't done any real lawyering for fifteen years or more. And I didn't like the new blood."

"Because?"

"Because they use sophisticated tracing systems, and do things that are better left to the professionals," she said.

"Like us," Flint said.

Paloma nodded. "My sense is that they don't need a

Retrieval Artist. I got the impression that when I stopped working for them, they decided they would do everything in-house."

"Then why come after me? Do they want some Tracker to piggyback on my work?"

Paloma shook her head. "That makes no sense. They probably don't distinguish between Tracking and being a Retrieval Artist. Lord knows, there were times I accidentally Tracked for someone."

Flint frowned at her. She had never admitted that before. "You have?"

Paloma shrugged. "Every Retrieval Artist does at one point or another. We can't help it. We're vulnerable to it. And some Retrieval Artists realize there's a lot more money in Tracking for the aliens who caused someone to go into hiding than there is in recovering a Disappeared for some distraught family member, so a lot of people start out as Retrieval Artists and become Trackers."

"Do you think that's what happened in-house at WSX?" Flint asked. "Do you think their staff has become Trackers and they don't trust anyone in the office with this, thinking the staff will sell out the clients to whatever alien is looking for them?"

Paloma templed her fingers and leaned back in her chair. Then she frowned, waved a hand, and the window across from her opaqued. It got so dark that the view completely disappeared.

"Damn thing becomes a distraction when I'm trying to work," Paloma said. "I bought this place because I don't think about important things here, and now you're asking me to."

Flint almost apologized, but he couldn't bring himself to do so. He needed her to be as focused as she could be.

"Are you using my guidelines?" Paloma asked after a moment.

"With clients?" Flint asked.

Paloma nodded.

"To the letter," he said. "I'm still using your wording."

She smiled at him, then reached for her drink. Beside her, a light went on. This entire apartment was linked to her; she was clearly controlling it with just a thought.

"At some point you're going to have to develop your own career," she said.

"I'm still a beginner, Paloma," he said. "I don't have enough experience yet to let go of all of your systems."

She sighed and stood up, turning her back on the opaque windows. Another light went on across the room, and then some music, very faint, too faint to actually make out what it was.

"They sought you out twice," Paloma said. "First with an associate who really had no idea what we do."

Flint noted the "we," and found a bit of comfort in it. Maybe he wasn't as much of a loner as he thought he was.

"Then with the son of the senior partner." Paloma ran a finger across her lip, a nervous gesture, one Flint hadn't seen often from her. "Was this Ignatius or Justinian?"

"Ignatius," Flint said. "I didn't realize there was another son."

"Old man Wagner had four sons and two daughters, but only two sons stayed in Armstrong." Paloma walked across the room. Flint had never seen her so restless. "Ignatius, huh?"

"Does that mean something?"

"He was never the brightest Wagner," Paloma said. "But that should mean nothing. Most of the Wagners are geniuses, especially with multicultural law. Ignatius is merely brilliant."

"Merely," Flint said.

"He came to you, after setting up their internal system to track you down."

Flint nodded. "He did want me to come back to his office."

"And you refused."

"He'll be at mine at six."

"Interesting." Paloma sighed. "I would have thought he had no support from WSX, but since he invited you back there, he's not trying to hide anything."

"Can we be sure of that?" Flint asked. "I'm assuming that since I'm a new Retrieval Artist, they're going to count on my incompetence."

Paloma turned, her frown deepening the wrinkles in her face. "You think Ignatius is playing those kind of games?"

"I don't know what to think," Flint said.

"They're going to a lot of trouble to bring you in," Paloma said.

"Which is why I came to see you, to find out your relationship with the firm."

She shook her head slightly. "My relationship with the Wagners isn't relevant."

Interesting switch of terms. Flint wondered if she even knew she had done it, saying *Wagner* when she meant *law firm*. But he didn't underestimate Paloma. Perhaps she was trying to tell him something too.

Maybe she didn't think her apartment was as secure as it could be. The thought hadn't crossed his mind until now.

"Why don't you think you're relevant here?" Flint asked. "The associate seemed surprised that you were gone."

"The associate is irrelevant too," Paloma said. "She was just the first volley to send you astray. Ignatius is the one who has me curious. If they were interested in me, they wouldn't have come back when they found out that I sold my business to you. They want you, Miles. The question is, do they want you because you're a new Retrieval Artist, because you're a former cop, because of your ties with the city, because of your family, or because—"

"My family?" Flint said. "My parents are dead, Paloma, and I have no siblings. There is no family anymore."

"There's a former wife, and a—forgive me—deceased child. These people are brilliant, Miles. They might want to play on sympathies that you may not even be aware that you have."

This time Flint stood. He could never sit still when someone mentioned his daughter. Emmeline had been dead for a long time, but he still wasn't over it. He had learned that last year, during the case that had led him to quit working for the city, and to work for himself.

"Don't be offended, Miles," Paloma said. "They went to the trouble of tracking you down, and doing it in an obvious way. That's a message right there. They're letting you know they have the capability of tracking and they're willing to use it."

"What would you have done in my place?" Flint asked, shaking off the disquiet that the mention of Emmeline always brought to him.

"They wouldn't have come to me," Paloma said.

"If you were me, Paloma. What would you do?"

She gave him a mysterious little smile, and then walked back to her chair. "This is precisely the kind of advice I will not give you anymore, Miles."

"But—"

"I won't always be here. You have to figure this stuff out on your own. I've given you enough direction. Now you work it out."

"You're intrigued, Paloma."

"Yes." She sat down, picked up her water glass, and drained it. "But being intrigued was never enough reason for me to take a case. Of course, I had a different life, a different history, and my own reasons for being a Retrieval Artist, very different from yours."

"Meaning?"

She looked down. "You have enough money. You're set for the rest of your life."

"So? What has my financial situation to do with any of this?"

She took a deep breath. He could feel her exasperation, even from a distance. "You don't have to work, Miles, and yet you do. Why?"

"I'd be bored," he said.

"This is a big universe. I'm sure you'd find something to amuse you."

"I don't want to be amused," he said. "I want to be useful."

"And there it is." She looked at him, her dark gaze meeting his. "Something is happening at Wagner, Stuart, and Xendor. Something important enough to involve a rookie Retrieval Artist with connections to the police force. It might have nothing to do with anything you care about. It might affect your future in ways you can't imagine."

"You think I should take the case," Flint said.

"Miles, what I think doesn't matter. But you can't seem to move beyond me. You need to graduate. I've passed my wisdom on to you. I have nothing left to offer you, no more advice. You're a full-blown Retrieval Artist now, and Retrieval Artists work alone. What I think doesn't matter."

He felt his cheeks heat. He hadn't expected to be this dependent on her. He hadn't expected to need someone else in his life, a confidant, someone he could trust.

She had explained it to him before. Anyone he trusted could be used—against him, against a Disappeared. He was putting her in a difficult position, as well as himself.

"I'm sorry, Paloma."

"Go to your office, Miles. Let me enjoy my moonscape. I've served my time."

His cheeks were so hot that they burned. For the first time in a decade, he felt both needy and rebuffed.

He slid across the couch, then stood as well, heading toward the door, trying not to make his movements seem like the flight that they were.

"I won't consult again, Paloma," he said, careful not to let any emotion into his voice. "Next time I see you, I'll make sure to keep my conversation limited to the merits of sun tea and the way a view like that can spoil you."

She didn't look at him. "I've been alone most of my life, Miles. It's too late to change that habit."

"Yet you want me to make the same choice."

"You already made it," she said, "when you took on the title of Retrieval Artist."

He nodded, then sighed, wishing he hadn't come. He felt less confident, and even more confused, than he had when he arrived.

"Be careful with the Wagners," she said. "Make sure they know your rules."

She assumed he would take the case. She was probably right. He had probably decided to take the case the moment he spoke to Ignatius Wagner.

"Thanks," Flint said, although he wasn't sure he meant it. Then he stepped out of her apartment, feeling alone, and oddly enough, feeling free.

8

"Murder?" van der Ketting asked. "Isn't it a long way to go from a dumped body to murder?"

DeRicci glanced at him. He seemed small, his shadow stretching toward the boulder. The forked trails spread behind him, going wide to avoid the largest thing in the area. She could barely make out the attendants, pacing around the field ambulance while they waited.

"Tell me why someone would dump a body here if the death was of natural causes?" DeRicci said.

"Maybe she died just after the race started," van der Ketting said. "Maybe the organizers didn't want the spectators to see, so they brought her here, and would later say that she died while in the middle of the run."

"Brought her here, instead of hiding her in the medical tent?" DeRicci shook her head. "Taking her to the tent would have been a lot easier."

"But they're supposed to leave a body where they found it. They couldn't leave a body near the starting line while they waited for us," van der Ketting said.

"And they wouldn't," DeRicci said. "They would give us some crap about thinking she was alive, and they'd whisk her off to that tent."

"You're basing the murder theory on that?" van der Ketting asked.

DeRicci shook her head. "There's a million things."

"Like what?" he asked, and she didn't like the challenge in his voice.

Still, she responded to it, mostly because he was angering her. She was the one with experience. She was the one looking at the details—and the one who understood what she saw.

"Like the scratched faceplate," she said.

He shrugged. "It probably happened postmortem, when a runner went by, and kicked a rock into the plastic."

"Really?" she asked. "Can you be sure of that?"

"Seems logical. She didn't die from rapid depressurization."

"Of course not," DeRicci said. "The scratch didn't break through the plastic. But I would wager that someone had been trying to break the faceplate when they were interrupted."

"Why would anyone do that?"

"To hide any evidence on the body," DeRicci said. "The corpse would have depressurized quickly. We would have had a mess to deal with, not an actual body."

"If this is murder," van der Ketting said, "why not kill the person that way? Why have the suit run out of oxygen and then depressurize it? Why not do it the quick way first?"

DeRicci shrugged. She looked down at the corpse, the pristine suit, the blackened face behind the visor. "That's just one of many questions we have to answer."

"I still say the scratch was caused by a rock." Van der Ketting started to cross his arms, but stopped halfway through the movement. He put out a hand to steady himself.

DeRicci ignored his difficulties. She was still concentrating on the body. "Okay, say some runner caused the scratch. Then that means the pattern of the scratch—which almost exactly matches the lightning-bolt pattern at the bottom of the boot—is just a coincidence."

Van der Ketting glanced at the boots. "And you think it isn't?"

"That's right," DeRicci said. "I think someone made that mark deliberately, so that we would notice the relationship between the boots and the faceplate."

"Why would they do that? Isn't the coincidence more logical?" van der Ketting asked.

"One of my former partners said he never believed in coincidence," DeRicci said.

"Do you?"

She smiled at van der Ketting. "No, I don't. Not around murder."

"A scratch isn't evidence," said van der Ketting. "It certainly doesn't convince me that this is murder."

"Then let's talk about the position of the body," DeRicci said. "Have you ever seen anyone who died from oxygen deprivation?"

"Not until today." The challenge was still in van der Ketting's tone, but not as strong as it had been before.

"Do you know how long it takes to die when your oxygen goes?"

He touched his suit, another involuntary movement. She was gong to have to teach this kid to play poker or something. He gave himself away with every movement.

"I don't really want to think about it out here," he said softly.

"Well, this is precisely the place to think about it." DeRicci looked up at the dominating Earth. So strong and powerful, the place where humans had come from, and yet a place where they could go outside without fearing death.

"How long does it take, Leif?" DeRicci asked, deliberately using his first name.

"I dunno. A couple of minutes," he said.

"What do you think you'd be doing for those minutes?" DeRicci asked. "If, for example, your suit malfunctioned and you realized you were no longer getting air."

"I'd try to fix it. I'd be sending for help and trying to fix the damn thing myself."

"Right." DeRicci waited for him to make the connections, but he didn't say anything. "Did you find a panic button on this suit?"

"I haven't looked yet. I was still recording when you had me look at the boots."

"Look now," DeRicci said.

Van der Ketting leaned across DeRicci, nearly lost his balance again, and was about to put a hand in the dirt when she caught him.

"Careful," she said. "I don't want you contaminating my crime scene."

"I wouldn't—"

"Just record. Backup record. And find a way to stay balanced, all right?"

He sighed so loudly she could hear it echo inside her suit. Then he stood up, which was probably the best thing he could do.

She leaned slightly to her right, and gingerly touched the victim's hands. On the left forefinger, a marathon volunteer had drawn an O in permanent red marker. It was this year's sign that the runner had received a chip—called the panic button—so tiny that it attached to the pad of the thumb, and was not linked into any main personal systems.

DeRicci wasn't ready to pull off the gloves—she'd leave that for the coroner—but the O symbol was more than enough confirmation that the runner had at least started out with the right equipment.

"Looks like she had a panic button," DeRicci said.

"Why didn't she use it?" van der Ketting asked.

"One of many mysteries." DeRicci frowned. Rigor mortis always hit the extremities first. But this body's hands were mobile. Either the woman hadn't been dead very long—and DeRicci knew the body had been here for more than an hour, time enough to make it hard to move—or the woman had been dead more than a day.

The coroner would have to confirm, but DeRicci was pretty sure that this woman had been dead long before the race started.

"She doesn't have excess oxygen bottles," DeRicci said. "We're only at mile five, right?"

"So?" van der Ketting said.

"So, all runners carry extra oxygen, just like they carry extra liquid. There is a refueling station around mile twelve, where they trade in the bottles for fresh ones, but that's still seven miles away."

"Maybe she didn't want the excess weight," van der Ketting said.

"They're required," DeRicci said. "You can't leave the dome without your extra oxygen. It's one of the rules the organizers instated years and years ago. It's essential."

"Maybe she threw the bottles away once she took off," van der Ketting said.

"Maybe," DeRicci said. "We'll have to look for them."

But she doubted that had happened. The tiny hip rings that everyone used to hold their extra bottles still had their plastic coating. That coating came off the first time a snap connected with the ring.

DeRicci studied the suit. It looked as new as the boots. Unused, untested even. She knew a lot of runners wore new suits in the Moon Marathon, but *new* here was a relative term. It meant that they hadn't used the suit in a marathon before, but they had done practice runs in it. All of these runners were experienced; they knew better than to use a brand-new piece of equipment on race day.

The dirt covered only the parts of the suit that were

touching the ground. A bit of splatter fell elsewhere, but DeRicci could trace the pattern. It came from footfalls. Other people's footfalls.

Her frown deepened. DeRicci scanned the dirt around the body again. There were dozens of different boot prints, many of them obliterating the prints below. She doubted anyone swept the course from year to year, so she suspected some of those boot prints were decades old.

Still, she looked for prints with a lightning bolt running down the center, and she found them. At least ten of them, all in a patch around the body.

Her breath caught, and she crouched as low as she could, studying the prints. They were wider than she would have expected and longer too. They seemed to be made by a bigger foot.

These prints were all beside the body, pointing to the body. An associate, perhaps? Someone who had something in common with the victim?

The killer?

DeRicci couldn't tell. "We need records of all these prints too. Make sure you get holographic as well as flats, and I want measurements as well. And compare the lightning-bolt prints to the bottoms of the victim's boots."

"We already know that she didn't walk on those boots," van der Ketting said.

"Actually," DeRicci said, "we don't know that. We don't know if the boots and suit have an automatic cleaning system that is malfunctioning now. There's a lot we don't know."

Van der Ketting nodded, sighing.

"But I do want to know how she got here," DeRicci said. "If she didn't walk or run here, she was brought here, and I want to know how."

Van der Ketting peered at the prints. "There're vehicle tracks beneath some of these footprints. Lots of vehicle tracks."

That was what DeRicci was afraid of. The evidence here had been badly compromised, and whoever had dumped the body had known it would be.

DeRicci sent a message to both the coroner and the forensics team to get here as soon as possible. Then she sent another message to Gumiela, warning her that this was an unusual case, and that the body would have to remain on the course.

That would bring the big guns here. Maybe, once they saw the body, DeRicci wouldn't be blamed for disrupting the marathon.

Van der Ketting was taking excess vids, examining footprints, and being as precise as DeRicci had hoped. DeRicci followed the upper layer of vehicle tracks— or at least what she assumed was the upper layer.

They followed the path exactly. For all she could tell, the vehicles belonged to the marathon, making certain everything was fine along the track.

She crossed her arms, staring at the curving landscape and the Earth beyond. Visibility was only a mile or so. Anyone could work here without worrying about being seen.

But that begged a lot of questions. If the body had been moved here, as the evidence suggested, how had it been moved? Where did the death occur? And how did an unauthorized person get on the track?

"Crap," DeRicci whispered.

She hadn't been completely clear in her message to Gumiela. DeRicci and van der Ketting would have to disrupt the marathon even more than DeRicci had planned to.

The only people with access to the track after the marathon started were medical personnel, race personnel, and the runners themselves. The singlet and the outfit suggested that this runner had started the race, died elsewhere, and then was brought here. But the body itself contradicted that assumption. If the woman had died the day before, she wouldn't have been able to get her singlet.

But maybe the singlet was a misleading clue. Maybe the runner never made it onto the course. Maybe someone had put the singlet on later, and left the body out here to mislead.

DeRicci had a lot of things to check. The vids of the runners getting their singlets and signing in, the vids of the starting line, the information concerning each entrant and each employee.

She needed to know if this number was even one of the numbers issued by this marathon. There was a possibility that the number was fake.

But why leave a body on this course? Why not hide it deeper in the Outside, where it would take days, weeks, maybe years to find? Why make it look like part of the race?

For that matter, why do it during the race?

"Noelle?" van der Ketting asked. "What's the problem?"

"We can't let anyone leave," she said. "Every single person connected with this race is a suspect."

"Oh, God." Van der Ketting shook his head. "And they thought they were running a marathon. We're going to be here forever."

He was right. The investigation had just taken on staggering and immediate proportions.

DeRicci would have to page Gumiela again, this time sending a small oral report. Her superiors weren't going to like this. No one was going to like this, particularly the Armstrong Board of Tourism.

Gumiela had sent DeRicci out on an easy case, and she ended up with the political nightmare of the year, as well as a mystery she wasn't sure anyone would be happy to have solved.

9

Oliviari found herself in charge of the environmental suits. She got to see everyone who came in off the course, and she got to do the first diagnostic pass. It was a job she hadn't even known existed when she drafted her undercover plan.

If she had known, she would have angled for it, but she doubted she would have gotten it. Most of the people in the tent had been with the marathon for a long time.

She was stationed in a small changing area just off the main door. Her partner, a woman named Hayley, took the suits, labeled by singlet number, and hung them in a special decontamination room.

Decontamination was something that most domes required when people went from an unenclosed environment to an enclosed one. The Moon's surface had no known contaminants on it; the fear in this instance was disease or a manufactured toxin.

Oliviari liked handling the suits. She got her DNA samples, along with the singlet number, so the very problem she'd been fearing from the moment she had decided to search for Frieda Tey here had been alleviated: Oliviari was able to get her samples and label them at the same time, without anyone noticing.

The runners were coming into the medical tent regularly now. Oliviari took their suits before doing the diagnostic pass, handing the suits to Hayley. As Oliviari took the suits, she used a small fingertip-sized DNA net to swipe globes of sweat and sloughed skin, moving each sample to a collection bag on her hip. Then she had the net tag the samples with the singlet numbers. If she got caught, she could always say that someone had told her to do this, and she would give over her evidence.

The preliminary information, taken off the DNA net, would be enough to run a cursory investigation. Of course, it would be best to hang onto the entire sample, but she was prepared in case that wasn't possible.

The runners seemed dazed and tired, unable to immediately adjust to their change in environments. As the runners stepped out of their suits, it seemed like they were stepping out of their skins.

Most runners didn't even wear anything underneath, except special lotion designed to keep the material from chafing. They seemed embarrassed by their nudity, as if they hadn't thought this last part through. And generally, Oliviari noticed, the runners who weren't wearing undergarments were first-timers, people who were just proud to finish anywhere in the first hundred runners.

She looked up, studying a wall screen for a moment. Runners were still approaching the finish line in clumps. And there would be even more clumps as the afternoon went on. The bulk would finish in between four and six hours, with a few stragglers taking anywhere from eight to ten.

So far she hadn't had a DNA match. Her links would have sent her a signal, so that she would be able to follow the person who might be Tey. Oliviari thought it odd that Tey hadn't come in yet.

If Tey had been participating in the marathon, then she should have finished in the top one hundred, maybe even the top ten.

But that was Oliviari's expectation. She had no real basis for that in fact. So she continued to work, hoping she would find Tey somewhere in the group of runners.

A man was holding up the line. He was too thin, and he seemed to be having trouble removing his suit. Oliviari grabbed her diagnostic just as he pitched forward.

She caught him, his body unusually cold, and staggered backward. "Need some assistance here."

Hayley had taken the suits into the main room. Another medic came running, took the man out of Oliviari's arms, and then took the diagnostic.

"Fluids!" the medic shouted. Then he looked at Oliviari. "We need to get him to one of the stabilizer beds."

She glanced at the line. She would miss an entire group of runners just because she was helping this one. But she could still feel the man's chilled skin against hers. The smell of his sweat clung to her clothes. She slipped an arm around his back, and helped the medic drag him into the main part of the tent.

A handful of runners sat on bedsides while medics looked at sprained ankles, torn ligaments, pulled muscles. A few were lying on beds, while IVs poured liquids into their systems. One or two more wore breathing masks, while someone monitored the readouts bedside.

A gofer brought a cup of miracle water to the medic who was helping Oliviari. Miracle water wasn't a miracle at all, just water filled with electrolytes, proteins, a touch of salt, and a lot of sugar, guaranteed to revive the most dehydrated soul.

The medic stopped dragging the runner forward. He tipped the runner's head back.

"Hold him still," the medic said.

Oliviari braced the runner as the medic tried to

pour water into him. Half of it trailed out of the man's mouth and down his face, dripping onto Oliviari.

She tried not to grimace. The runner coughed, put up a hand to stop the flow of liquid, then shook his head. He looked more lively than he had just a few minutes ago.

"It's a start," the medic said. "Let's go. Bed three."

Bed three was about two meters away. Oliviari helped the medic drag the runner there, then eased the runner onto the bed. The man's skin was gray, his eyes sunken. He had clearly pushed too hard. Oliviari wondered if his suit had malfunctioned as well, maybe not controlling temperature as well as it should have or giving him too little oxygen.

"Thanks," the medic said, bending over the runner. Neither of them looked at Oliviari. She backed away, scanning this part of the tent.

Most of the people getting treatment were men. Oliviari saw nothing suspicious about that. It was just the luck of the draw. Besides, the marathon always drew a lot more male first-timers than female ones, so the chances of a man being in this part of the tent were greater than the chances of a woman being here.

Still, Oliviari made sure she looked carefully at the women. None of the women looked like Tey, and most were too young to be her, even if Tey had had a lot of enhancements. Oliviari went to each bed, though, and put a reassuring hand on the women's shoulders, asking each one if they needed anything extra.

To a person, they all said no.

Then Oliviari went back to her post.

Hayley looked overwhelmed. The line had bunched together, people crowding in three and four across. The diagnostic was on the table behind Hayley, obviously unused and unseen.

Suits had piled up behind her as well, since she clearly hadn't had a chance to take them to the closet.

That made Oliviari smile. Maybe helping that poor man hadn't harmed her search at all.

Oliviari picked up the diagnostic and walked over to Hayley.

"Hey," she said softly. "Leave the suits. I'll help you gather them later, okay? We're in the crunch period and we're going to have to work hard to get caught up."

Hayley flashed her an angry glance. "You're not supposed to leave your post."

"Except for an emergency," Oliviari said. "That man fainted against me. That constitutes an emergency."

Hayley pressed her lips together, but didn't say anything as yet another runner forced a suit into her arms. Oliviari pushed forward, getting Hayley out of position. Oliviari wanted to be able to touch all of those suits.

She ran her diagnostic over the runner, said, "You need some fluids, and probably something to eat. There's a juice bar just through that door. I'd suggest liquids before you clean up. Otherwise, you're fine."

The runner smiled at her, and she smiled back. She slipped his DNA sample into her bag, and continued, dispensing advice as she stole a tiny piece of each person who stopped in front of her, expecting a little help.

10

When Flint returned to his office, he immediately set his security system on highest alert. He had the system double-lock the doors and seal them, then he had his internal net lock itself down, severing any contacts it had with the outside world.

He ran a diagnostic, looking for trackers, tracers, ghosts, and bugs. He found echoes at the edges of his system, places where various people had tried to break in since Paloma had left, but no evidence that anyone succeeded.

He reprogrammed the diagnostic, taking out all of Paloma's codes and back doors. He should have done this when he bought the business from her, but, despite her warnings that he could trust no one now that he was a Retrieval Artist, he had trusted her.

He had always thought Paloma's warning that Trackers, aliens, and others could get to Retrieval Artists through their loved ones was a fairly obvious warning. Threaten a loved one and of course a Retrieval Artist would give in to any demand.

But her warning was more complex than that, the problem subtler than he had realized. No one looked as closely at the people they cared about as they did at strangers. A loved one could compromise a Retrieval Artist's business better than anyone else could.

Flint cared about Paloma and trusted her more than

he had trusted anyone in years. But even she had secrets, secrets that might hurt his work.

The fact that he hadn't taken her out of the business completely was his fault, not hers. If he had problems because of that, well, then he couldn't blame her for them either.

She had warned him right from the start.

Flint tapped a button on his keyboard, and upgraded the airflow system inside the office. He wanted to stay awake and alert; fresh, cool air would do that.

After he cooled the air, he got up and paced. Paloma's reticence on Wagner, Stuart, and Xendor, Ltd., bothered him. If she had been keeping information confidential, and struggling to tell him something without revealing secrets, he wouldn't have been upset.

But she had hinted at other things, an involvement with that office that went beyond what she had led him to believe a Retrieval Artist did.

He had gotten the same sense from Ignatius Wagner—that something in the relationship between Paloma and WSX led him to believe that Flint would be flexible in his dealings with them.

Perhaps he would be; he was never known for following the rules—at least not when he had been a detective. Since he had become a Retrieval Artist, he had followed the rules slavishly; Paloma had predicted dire consequences if he did not.

But had she been teaching him to be the Retrieval Artist she had always wanted to be and had never been? Had she bent all of those rules she claimed no one should bend? Was that how she knew what the consequences were?

He stopped pacing near the door, slipping his hands in his pockets. He knew she would never tell him if she had made those mistakes, and she had made it clear she wasn't going to tell him anything else about WSX.

He did have a way of finding out her involvement

with them, a simple and direct way, one he had avoided until now.

Paloma had made him promise that he wouldn't investigate her cases. What files she kept, she had taken with her. Most of the information she had gathered, she claimed, she never wrote down.

But that the last statement had to be a lie. Paloma believed in doing reports—expense reports for the clients, and a final report, depending on the case. Of course, she had said that the reports weren't always accurate—that they couldn't be if she were to keep some secrets—but, she added, they always had a grain of truth.

Deleted reports left ghosts in the files.

Flint had known that when Paloma had initially told him of her system, and he had wondered then if she had known that she left traces of herself throughout the internal net. Paloma hadn't been as good with computers as he was; she knew a lot, but she didn't know everything.

He went to his desk, sat down, and flexed his hand over the keyboard. Paloma's question haunted him: Why did he still work? He didn't need the money.

He had told her he wanted to be useful, but that wasn't true. He felt that everything—right, wrong, good, bad—had been turned upside down by the agreements between the known worlds. People were punished for things they hadn't even known were crimes—for things, even if they had known, that wouldn't be considered crimes under human law.

Flint had been forced to enforce those rules, sometimes sacrificing children for their parents' crimes, sometimes sending people to their deaths for carelessly walking along the wrong patch of ground.

He had gazed along the path of his future and had seen his own morals become twisted or felt the impending bitterness of a man continually forced to do things he did not believe in.

He had become a Retrieval Artist because he had watched Paloma. It seemed to him then that she had the perfect job: She could determine who she worked for and why; she never had to make tough moral choices, leaving them to other people; and she could rescue people if she felt they needed saving.

She wouldn't endanger lives, not even accidentally, and she would—more often than not—help families get together rather than use the law to force them apart.

He rested his fingers lightly on the keys, not depressing them, staring at the empty screen before him.

Paloma had warned him. *You have a romantic view of the Retrieval Artist, Miles,* she had said. *You must realize that nothing is easy or straightforward any longer.*

He had felt she was wrong when she had said that to him. The choices he made in his last days as a detective—they had seemed easy and straightforward. He had saved lives, countless lives, and he had felt good about his work.

Then he had come here to continue that work, wanting to be Sir Galahad, a hero of old.

He had always been fond of tales of heroes. He'd even read them to his daughter before she fell asleep. His wife had laughed at him, saying Emmeline was too young to understand what he was saying, let alone understand the stories themselves, but he had believed that stories planted early would become a healthy foundation for Emmeline's life as an adult.

The life she would never, ever have.

He raised his right hand from the keyboard and wiped his face. A sheen of sweat coated his skin, even though he had cooled down the room.

Emmeline. How had he gone from ethics to Paloma to Emmeline?

Perhaps ethics and morals and his daughter's short, tragic life were all tied together in his mind. Maybe the guilt he carried from her death—from failing to check the care providers' backgrounds more carefully to failing to understand how one accidental death could become the first murder when everyone realized that Emmeline's had been the second.

How awful it must have been for her in those last few minutes, being held by someone larger and more powerful, someone angry who had shaken her. . . .

He stood. His breath was coming in short gasps. He walked back toward the door, not pacing this time so much as trying to get away from his desk, where the emotion had built to a fever pitch—as if it were the desk's fault instead of his own.

Maybe he didn't want to work for ethics and morals at all. Maybe he simply wanted to defend the small, helpless, and uninformed against anyone larger, stronger, and angrier. Maybe he was just trying to right a wrong—a wrong that could never be fixed.

He made himself breathe evenly. Examining his own motives wouldn't help him here. They would only twist him further.

For the first time since he had purchased Paloma's business, her past was influencing his. She had always told him that he could not make decisions without all of the information he could find.

The biggest problem he had this afternoon, however, was that Paloma refused to share information with him, information that clearly pertained to Wagner's insistence on Flint for this job—whatever the job was.

Flint ran a hand through his hair. Sweat had beaded beneath the curls, but he wasn't hot. He was nervous.

He had felt quite an obligation to Paloma, one that had extended throughout everything he did—using her systems, her office, her well-worded client agreements. In some ways he felt like her placeholder, someone who ran her business while she took a much-needed vacation.

You need to graduate, she had said to him. *Retrieval Artists work alone.*

He sighed. He had promised Paloma that he wouldn't investigate her past cases, but it was a promise he wouldn't be able to keep.

Perhaps she had known that. Perhaps that was why she had taken the remaining files with her.

However, if she wanted to have complete privacy, she should have taken the entire office network, all the way down to the security system. He would be able to find traces of anything within that system, especially now that he knew it better than its designer.

Paloma knew how good he was with computers. She had once told him that his computer skill would make him a better Retrieval Artist than she could have ever been. Perhaps she had known about the ghosts in the system and expected him to find them.

But he had to stop worrying about what Paloma wanted. She would never know what he did, how he conducted his business, why he made the choices he had, unless he told her.

And he wasn't going to tell her. Not anymore. He had graduated. He no longer needed an instructor, and he couldn't afford to have a close friend—at least not one who knew about his business.

He returned to the computer. He would capture all of the ghost files Paloma left in the system, and he would store them in a special place, someplace that no one else would ever think to look. Then he would wipe them out of the system forever.

That was step one.

Step two was even simpler. He would read the files that pertained to WSX, but he wouldn't read any other files. He wouldn't snoop unless the situation forced him to.

He had a hunch that this wouldn't be the only time that Paloma's past would influence his present. He would use what she had left him when he had to, and only then.

He had to this afternoon.

Flint took a deep breath and sat down at his chair. The restlessness was gone. Now he had to concentrate to get all the work done before Wagner arrived for his appointment.

11

DeRicci stood inside the bungalow, her hood down, the environmental suit off. Sweat slicked her body, and her cheeks felt flushed. She longed for the opportunity to remove the suit, but knew it probably wouldn't come anytime soon.

Chaiken, Lakferd, and five other race organizers were gathered around her. She could feel their anger already, and she hadn't even spoken to them yet. Perhaps what she felt was her own anger, suppressed after her conversation with her boss.

DeRicci had contacted Gumiela just before coming into the bungalow. With an investigation this complicated—a murder at the marathon—DeRicci had asked for someone else to take over. Someone with diplomatic abilities, political skill, and a little bit of clout.

Someone, in other words, as far from DeRicci as possible.

Gumiela had turned the request down. A younger, more naïve DeRicci would have been ecstatic that she remained in charge of this investigation. The older, cynical DeRicci knew that she had gotten the job because she gave the city the ability to blame every tough position, every unpopular move, on her. They might even fire her if she did her job extremely well—especially if it turned out that the marathon was somehow at fault for the corpse that still rested on the regolith.

The live feed of the race now focused on the finish line. Runners came across in clumps, arms raised.

DeRicci thought it odd that to a person they all leaped across, no matter how tired they were. It was as if, in that final moment, they summoned the strength to fly.

The organizers were staring at her. She hadn't told them anything yet. She had asked Chaiken to gather them as she returned from the murder scene, then she had come straight here.

At least the coroner and the forensic team had arrived quickly. DeRicci had sent them a message through her link the moment she realized that the corpse was a murder victim. Forensics was guarding the scene now, preventing anyone else from getting close.

She had left the coroner with specific instructions: DeRicci needed time of death as soon as possible. She also needed cause of death. Even though the corpse's face had the look of an oxygen-deprivation victim, the position of the body had not.

DeRicci wanted all of the contradictions explained. The more information she had when she started the interviews, the better off she would be.

"Where's your partner?" Chaiken asked.

He crossed his bony arms and stared at her, as if he wanted her to get another message. She got it: He wanted this meeting to go quickly.

So did she, but she wasn't going to let him control her actions. If Gumiela wanted DeRicci in charge, then DeRicci would stay in charge.

"He's doing some follow-up for me," she said.

She had sent van der Ketting to the organizer's table to investigate the singlet number, figuring he could do that without harming any evidence, even if the low gravity made him topple over. This investigation had suddenly become too sensitive for him, only he didn't know that yet. He didn't have the skills to conduct the kinds of interviews she needed, and he didn't have the political background to handle the kind of diplomacy she now found herself faced with.

"Follow-up?" Chaiken asked. "Then the investigation is nearly done?"

She didn't like the note of superiority in his tone. In the past, the marathon organizers had controlled the length of police investigations into the deaths. That control had been possible because the deaths were clearly accidental, the fault of the type of event rather than any human agent.

They wouldn't have that kind of control this time, no matter what it cost DeRicci.

"No," she said. "The investigation has barely started."

The organizers shifted. One of the women, whose name DeRicci hadn't caught, looked at Chaiken in alarm.

"You know we have to clear the course by the end of the dome day," he said. "We have an agreement with the city—"

"The city has other priorities now," DeRicci said, "and you will too in a few minutes."

"That sounds like a threat, Detective," Lakferd said.

Were all former runners paranoid? DeRicci wanted to snap at him, but she didn't. She had to present her case as best as possible, without angering the organizers.

She needed them, for the next few hours at least.

"No, it's not a threat," she said, making sure her voice remained level. "We all have a serious problem here."

Chaiken moved in front of the wall of images. Runners moved behind him all over the course, a not-so-subtle reminder of the importance of the race.

"A serious problem?" he asked. "What's so different about this death?"

DeRicci clenched a fist, but kept it hidden at her side. His tone was so matter-of-fact, as if the end of someone's life meant nothing in comparison to the race.

She hated people like Chaiken. She had to take a deep breath, so that she wouldn't tell him what she thought of him.

"What's so different about this death?" she repeated, her voice low. "Well, it's pretty simple, actually. This death is a murder."

Lakferd gasped. The other five stared at her as if she had gone crazy. Behind them, more runners floated across the finish line, arms raised.

Chaiken didn't look at his colleagues, or at the wall screens. Instead he stared at DeRicci as if he could see through her. His posture hadn't changed, nor had his expression. She could have just as easily told him that she preferred reconstituted chicken to the real thing.

"How can you possibly know someone was murdered?" he asked.

He wasn't challenging her data. He was challenging her expertise. He wanted her away from his marathon, as if the murder were her fault.

"I found a variety of things that convinced me this was murder." DeRicci wasn't about to tell him what those things were. Right now, everyone connected to the marathon was a suspect. She didn't think the organizers were involved, but she was operating on a hunch, not fact. And frankly, she didn't like Chaiken's attitude.

Maybe her gut was wrong.

"Right now," she added, "the forensics team is out there, seeing what they can find."

"We can't deal with a murder," one of the women said. "This'll shut us down forever."

Lakferd nodded. He started to say something, but
DeRicci spoke first.

"I think shutting you down might have been the
intent."

Everyone looked at her. Even Chaiken seemed
stunned. Finally he had shown some emotion. It was
as if he couldn't bear losing the marathon, as if it were
as alive as he was.

"Why?" he asked, his voice shaking. "Why would
anyone do that?"

"We're a long way from why," DeRicci said. "But
I suspect that someone set you up. It looks like the
body was dumped here, so that it would be found
during the race."

"That's not possible," Lakferd said. "We have security measures. No one gets Outside before the race
starts."

"No one?" DeRicci asked.

"No one," Lakferd said. "Except staff, of course."

DeRicci waited for him to realize what he had said.

His cheeks grew red, and his eyes widened. The
other five organizers were shaking their heads.

"It couldn't be staff," Chaiken said. "We've all been
part of this event for decades. None of us would try
to ruin it."

"But you have volunteers, don't you? People who
must man the tables, people who help set up. And
what about the medical staff? Surely they aren't the
same year to year." DeRicci spoke softly. Right now
the organizers' shock gave her an advantage. She
planned to use it.

"We check them out," the woman said.

"I'm sure you do," DeRicci said. "Checking people
out doesn't always stop them from doing something
bad."

"If this person was dumped onto the track,"
Chaiken asked, "how did she get a singlet number?"

"That's one of the questions we have," DeRicci said.

Chaiken sank into a nearby chair. "This is a mess." He was finally beginning to understand.

"It's going to get worse," DeRicci said. "We're going to have to interview everyone connected with the marathon."

"I figured as much," Lakferd said. "We get names and addresses as a matter of course. Everyone is linked. It's a requirement of entry. Since we have all the information, you'll be able to contact them at your leisure."

DeRicci clasped her hands behind her back, like a schoolteacher facing a recalcitrant student.

"We have no leisure," she said. "We have a small window of opportunity before everyone in the race scatters. We have to take it."

"What are you talking about?" Lakferd asked.

"We're going to interview everyone today. You'll have to clear out this bungalow for us. You'll also need a place that the runners can go after they finish. I would suggest one of the utility buildings Outside. I'm sure the city will give permission for that."

"You want people to stay here? They'll be tired and hungry and they'll feel trapped. You can't do that. Imagine the publicity it'll garner us." Lakferd twisted his thin hands together.

One of the other men bowed his head as if he had already given up. Chaiken was watching a wall screen. More people crossing the finish line.

DeRicci could only imagine what he was thinking. It was quite possible that no matter what happened, no matter how careful everyone was, this would be the last Moon Marathon ever run.

It was one thing to have people die accidentally on the course. Everyone who had ever been in an environmental suit knew that accidents happened—

sometimes caused by a person's own stupidity, and sometimes not.

But a murder on the track, after the race started, would be a sensational story, picked up all over the known worlds. Reporters from all media would come in from various planets. Alien groups who thought marathoning unusual would use this as filler, or as yet one more way to prove that humans were unstable.

The Moon Marathon would get a terrible reputation. Big-name runners didn't come to marathons with bad reputations. If the bigger names weren't here, the tourists would drop off.

And since this event brought in a large portion of Armstrong's tourist revenue, any decrease in attendance would have a profound impact on that sector of Armstrong's economy.

"The publicity is why we have to do this quickly," DeRicci said. "If we allow the investigation to drag on, then the marathon is tainted forever."

The organizers were nodding. She had them on her side, finally. The next thing they would try to figure out would be how to keep the murder secret, which, in the short term, wouldn't hurt her investigation at all.

But that wasn't what she wanted the organizers to do next. She wanted them to make her job easier. She needed them to rearrange this temporary complex so that she could conduct interviews in private.

DeRicci knew she had only a few minutes to take control of this investigation before Chaiken got over his shock and started to fight with her.

"I suggest," she said in a tone that made it clear her suggestion was really an order, "that you feed these people, make sure they have enough to drink, and find some chairs for them. I also suggest that you keep them Outside if possible. Once they get inside the dome, they can scatter all over the city. It would be better for all of us if they didn't."

"You're going to arrest one of our runners?" Chaiken asked.

"I don't know," DeRicci said. "I'll need to talk to everyone connected to the marathon. If you can find a way to keep the spectators here as well, that would be helpful."

"You realize that you'll have to talk to hundreds of people." Lakferd seemed like the only person who wasn't in shock. DeRicci made a note of that, although she wasn't sure what it meant at the moment. "You and your partner can't do all of that in one day."

"I know," DeRicci said. "I've already been in contact with my boss. We're diverting a lot of police to these interviews. We want them done as quickly as possible. This is a full-blown crisis for the city. We're going to deflect as much of it as possible."

"You can't conduct all of the interviews in here," the woman said. "You're going to need other facilities."

"Yes," DeRicci said, relieved someone was going to help with this. "Places with private rooms would be best, so that we can interview without being overheard."

The woman nodded. She stood. "I know just the place. I'll get you set up."

No one else moved. Finally the woman touched Lakferd's arm.

"Come on," she said. "The detective is right. We have to move quickly, and we have to make these runners comfortable. We have the dining hall. We may as well use it. I think I can arrange for more food to be brought in."

"Dining hall?" DeRicci asked.

The woman nodded. "I know it's not what you asked for because it's inside the dome, but I think it'll work better than anything else. We were planning a dinner for the first twenty runners, along with a medal

ceremony. The area is big—we were going to feed
some city luminaries, but I'm sure you don't want
them here. So we'll have food for about two hundred
people. I'm sure we can scrounge up even more."

"It's a disaster," Chaiken muttered.

"Not if we handle it right," the woman said. "We'll
feed the runners and the volunteers, and you can put
some police on the doors so that no one leaves until
the interviews are done. Would that work?"

"It might," DeRicci said. "But I'd prefer it if people
stayed Outside."

The woman shook her head. "Logistically that just
doesn't work. They go into the med tent when they're
finished, get cleared, and come into the dome. The
runners are already following that procedure. Changing it now would make things even harder for you."

DeRicci thought about it. Saving time was her top
priority. Saving time and making certain that everyone
went through a preliminary interview.

"All right," she said. "I'll get some uniforms on the
doors. You'll make sure no one leaves. If we lose even
a single witness, I'll blame the marathon organizers."

"Threats again, Detective?" Lakferd asked.

"Threats for the first time," she said. "And this time
it's a serious one. I have to talk with everyone connected
to this event. If anyone slips through, I'll look harder at
the organizers. The last thing you folks want to do is be
in trouble for interfering with a police investigation."

"We won't interfere," the woman said. "We'll do
what we can."

Chaiken made no such promises. He continued to
stare at the wall screen.

"Right, Alfred?" the woman asked, elbowing him.

Chaiken looked up at her. "You're not in charge,
Dorthea."

Dorthea Jonston. DeRicci nodded slightly. She was
going to have take notes, because she was going to
hear a lot of names before the day ended.

"I am now," Jonston said. "No one is going to sabotage my marathon. I'm going to do everything I can to save this event."

She looked at DeRicci. DeRicci saw both anger and determination in the woman's face.

"You tell me what you need and when you need it," Jonston said. "I'll make sure you get everything."

"Thank you," DeRicci said, feeling absurdly grateful. At least she wouldn't have to fight the organizers as hard as she had thought she would.

For a while, all she would have to do was concentrate on finding a killer. And that was always the part she did best.

12

Oliviari had lost track of time and she had lost count of the runners. This had to be the crunch—six exhausted runners stretched across the narrow corridor, lines going back as far as Oliviari could see. She wondered if people were bunched in the small airlock and knew there was no way for her to tell.

The recycled air seemed thin here, perhaps because so many exhausted people were breathing it. The temperature in the arrival area had risen dramatically, and Oliviari was sweating, even though she'd stripped down to her T-shirt and pants.

Two other medics had joined Oliviari, all of them doing diagnostics, some of them taking suits and putting them away. Somehow Oliviari still managed to touch each runner, grabbing them and pulling them forward or helping them step out of a suit.

No one seemed to notice her extreme helpfulness. No one seemed to notice that she was doing anything out of the ordinary at all.

Several other runners had collapsed against her, but none as badly as that first man had. Oliviari thought she could still smell his stale sweat mingling with her own, as if they'd had a night of passion instead of a momentary touch.

She hadn't had time to check on his condition. The afternoon was at its busiest pace, and she had to concentrate just to get DNA from all the runners. She kept reciting singlet numbers to herself, so that she could keep track of the people she'd touched. She also tried to focus on their faces, doing her best to make certain no one slipped past her.

Few of the runners spoke, and those who did were ignored. Most of the runners were too tired to compare notes, and some were irritated at the end-of-the-race procedures, even though everyone had been warned about them. Except for a few murmurs, Hayley's short and repetitive instruction speech, and the occasional cough, the only sounds in the room were the rustle of fabric and the shuffling of feet.

Oliviari almost felt as if she were still wearing her environmental suit. She wasn't used to large groups of people being so silent. But then she'd never worked in a situation like this before.

Every now and then she'd stop, take a moment to look at the rows of runners, and scan for Tey. So far there had been no sign of the woman, and Oliviari was beginning to doubt the wisdom of her plan.

Oliviari smiled at a thin, unenhanced woman with exceptionally dry skin. The woman looked exhausted as she handed Oliviari a damp environmental suit. Oliviari slipped a bit of the DNA off, bagged it, and ran a scan of the woman.

"You need fluids," she said, as she so often did. "And check in with one of the medical personnel. You'll need a thorough going-over."

"No," the woman said.

Oliviari had already moved to the man beside her. It took a moment for the woman's refusal to register. "What?"

"I'm not going to see anyone. I didn't come here for treatment. I came to run. I've done that, and I'm going home."

"Ma'am," Oliviari said, wishing this weren't happening at the moment, "you're dehydrated, and your skin is slightly blue. I have a hunch that for the last few miles, your environmental suit wasn't operating at peak efficiency."

"Which is my problem, isn't it?" the woman snapped. "I can deal with it inside the dome with my own doctors instead of the quacks you people hire."

The runners in the narrow corridor looked at the woman. Whispered conversation began in the back, near the entrance. Oliviari couldn't tell if the sounds were agreement, disagreement, or just information being passed back and forth.

"Ma'am," Oliviari said, "just go into the main part of the tent. They'll work with you there."

She had almost said "deal with you there," but some measure of self-control had prevented it. One thing she did know: She would never go undercover in a job like this again. She didn't like being at other people's beck and call, working so hard for very little return, and dealing with people who had tested their own limits—and were cranky about the results.

"Hand me my suit," the woman said, holding out her hand. It trembled.

"You'll have to wait until it comes out of decon," Oliviari said.

"I'm not waiting for anyone. I want to get out of here. I heard that you're holding people against their will, and I won't stand for it. You hear me?"

The woman shoved her way toward the open door where the suits were being taken. A large man in a uniform who acted as the med tent's security wrapped his arms around her and moved her to one side.

But Oliviari had stopped working. The entire team had. They were staring at the woman being carted toward the main area of the medical tent.

"What did she mean, being held against their will?" Hayley asked, her voice so breathy she was almost whispering.

"I don't know," Oliviari said. "I hadn't heard anything."

"A few of us who've been doing this for years don't go through the tent." The man Oliviari had been about to help spoke as softly as Hayley had. "We tried this year, and we were redirected here. When we asked about it, one of our friends, a guy who's been volunteering for thirty years, said no one gets to leave until some investigation gets completed."

Oliviari remembered the police heading off on the surface vehicle. She'd been trapped in here ever since, so she hadn't seen if more police had arrived. Odd that they wouldn't come inside the medical tent.

"What kind of investigation?" she asked.

The man shrugged. "No one knows. I've asked a few times. They were adamant, though. Everyone through the medical tent. Allison thinks that we're all being checked for something."

"Allison being the woman they just carried off?" Oliviari asked.

He nodded.

"What do you think?"

"I don't know," he said, "but I saw a lot of runners down out there this year, and at least one of them wasn't moving."

The murmuring got louder as word traveled backward. Something strange was going on. Oliviari wondered how she could find out what it was without blowing her cover.

She extended her hand for the man's suit.

"Well, let's keep going through the motions, shall we?" she said. "I mean, if there were some kind of contamination, we'd be looking for it on the prelim diagnostic, and I haven't been told about it. I also haven't been told about everyone staying here. So that might just be a bad rumor, designed to make you guys follow procedure."

His gaze met hers, and he shook his head ever so slightly. But her small speech, spoken louder than the rest of the conversation, seemed to calm the murmuring. The runners shuffled, but didn't seem as nervous as they had a moment before.

Still, long after the guy left, Oliviari pondered what he had to say. An investigation put her in a difficult position. Armstrong required Trackers to register with the city, theoretically to discourage vigilantism. Mostly, though, Armstrong, as the Moon's main port city, used its own resources to help Trackers, figuring Disappeareds were bad for business.

If she got caught, she would be charged significant penalties by the city, penalties that would go on her record. Earth Alliance would immediately review her license, and she might find herself restricted to certain worlds, or have to requalify for her job all over again.

Sweat rolled down Oliviari's face. She was very hot. So were Hayley and the others. Someone had to complain about the environmental system. Someone had to find out what was really going on.

Oliviari couldn't do it. She'd already attracted too much attention, and she didn't want to attract any more. Particularly if the police were investigating the marathon's volunteers as well as the participants.

Maybe this was all a blessing in disguise. If Tey had joined the marathon, then she would be trapped here too. If Tey wasn't here, Oliviari wasn't sure where to look anymore.

Sometimes Oliviari felt as though Tey were a figment of her own imagination.

Oliviari smiled at the next runner in line, even though she didn't feel like smiling at anyone. She held out her hand, and the runner handed her the damp suit. Oliviari pulled the DNA sample, and tucked it away.

She would continue to work here until someone made her stop. No matter what setbacks she had today, Oliviari would catch Tey. And all of this would come to an end, for Oliviari, for Tey's victims' families.

For everyone.

13

The system had more ghosts than Flint expected.

He spent the remaining hours of the afternoon capturing and retrieving the ghosts, putting them in a separate system where no one else could steal them. He felt a mixture of anger and worry as he worked, primarily because Paloma hadn't been as cautious as she had led him to believe she was.

Anyone with a hacker's knowledge of systems could have broken into her files and stolen whatever they needed.

Flint wondered if that had happened. He wondered if she had had any inexplicable failures in her career, or if a Tracker had worked off her systems, finding people Paloma thought were safely hidden.

Maybe that was why Wagner had come to him, because they knew this in-house network was so very vulnerable.

There was no way Flint could find and download all the information, read the necessary files, and be finished in time for his meeting with Wagner. Flint would have to finish after Wagner left, provided he had time to do so, provided he didn't take the case Wagner was so hot for him to have.

As Flint worked, he also grew angry at himself for not double-checking everything Paloma had left him. A sense of disillusionment was growing in him, and

he found that ironic. He had thought all the illusion
had left his life ten years before.

An hour before his scheduled meeting with Wagner,
Flint set up a program within the system to net all the
ghost files imprinted on the system's memory. He
would deal with those later.

While the system worked, he made the files he had
found solid, then searched them for mentions of the
Wagners. To his surprise, hundreds upon hundreds of
files scrolled down his screen, all of them with at least
one mention of the WSX or one of the Wagners.

The files dated back fifty years or more.

That surprised Flint too. Paloma had updated her
system several times in her career, but apparently she
had simply expanded the existing system, letting information flow between the old and new parts, rather
than moving information to the newer system and destroying the older one.

Not that information could ever completely be destroyed. Perhaps that was why she operated the way
she had. Perhaps she felt that she had to keep her old
systems here, hidden within any upgrades, so that no
one could scan her discarded systems for deleted
information.

It didn't help him, though, and there was so much
about the Wagners in her files, he didn't know where
to start. He wouldn't be able to go through everything
in a week, let alone an hour.

Flint scanned some of the early files and saw that
Paloma had not lied to him about her position with
WSX. She wasn't on payroll, but she seemed to have
handled any job they had for a Retrieval Artist. Her
early reports were crisp and to the point: She wrote
about the status of a Disappeared, even to the point
of advising WSX as to whether or not to pursue a case.

It seemed that most of the early cases revolved
around estate work: a Disappeared would inherit significant funds, and Paloma would evaluate the case.

She would determine the cost of finding the Disappeared. If the cost exceeded the amount of the inheritance, she recommended that WSX put the inheritance into some kind of escrow, and had them flag the file for review every three years.

It looked, at first glance, as if she had a cushy relationship with the law firm. They would give her more than enough work to keep her busy for years at a time, and they seemed to pay her a handsome amount as well.

Paloma had been rigorous about billing WSX, and the payments were tracked on the bills, as well as in an accounts receivable file. She seemed so concerned about money that Flint wondered if she had financial problems. Had that been why she had taken the work WSX had sent her?

A Retrieval Artist who was constantly short of money, she had told him time and time again, risked compromising everything he believed in.

Had she told him this, not as a caution, but out of experience? Had she risked everything? Had she paid a huge price for her lack of financing—or had someone else?

A shiver ran down his back. He glanced at the timer he had set up along the screen's edge. It was set for 5:30, so that he could open up the office net before Wagner arrived.

Flint had thirty minutes until he had to open the system, not long enough to get any answers at all. He found that this search had given him a lot more questions, and he didn't want that.

He skipped ahead and saw that Paloma's later dealings with WSX weren't as detailed. Her later reports simply expressed whether or not she felt a case was worth following, and the attached bills had not itemized her expenses.

Had she stopped trusting people in the office or had they worked out a shorthand?

Flint stood, frustration making him restless. She should have told him what had been going on. He wanted to know, rather than having to dig like this. Had she been ashamed of whatever happened with WSX, or had she felt that the past had no bearing on the present?

He stretched, reaching toward the ceiling. The muscles in his back ached—he had been sitting in one position too long—and his spine made small cracking noises.

Maybe everything was exactly as Wagner said it was; maybe they had come to Flint for his connection to Paloma, his newness, and his ties to the police department.

Flint sat back down. He tried one last thing: he searched for files that mentioned Ignatius Wagner. It took the system a moment to find everything, which Flint found odd.

He glanced at the clock. Only fifteen minutes before he had to unlock his net and open it so that Wagner could come inside the office.

Flint cursed silently and wished for more time.

Then the system stopped searching. It had found thousands of files listing Ignatius Wagner.

Flint stared at the results. He couldn't believe those either. Why would Paloma have so much information on Wagner? Was that why she had warned him?

He opened a few of the files at random, double-checking the system. Every file mentioned Wagner, and as Flint opened more and more of them, he grew cold.

Paloma had gathered information on Wagner's life as if Wagner were a client or a Disappeared. She had the time and date he left for school on his very first day, the date of his first kiss, the location of his first job.

Paloma probably knew more about Ignatius Wagner than his parents did.

Flint scanned some of the later files, just for informational purposes. Wagner was Claudius Wagner's youngest son, and hadn't made partner in the law firm when Paloma wrote her last entry. He had always been contrary, having trouble following WSX policy. As a punishment, his father hadn't sped Ignatius's partnership through. Unlike his brother, Ignatius would have to earn his place in the law firm.

Apparently he had earned his place, because the information Flint had gathered on Ignatius listed him as a partner. But Paloma's records showed that Ignatius wasn't happy with the direction WSX was going. There had been some kind of power struggle going on at WSX, and both brothers were involved with it.

The alarm on Flint's computer beeped. Five-thirty. Time for him to open the systems.

He frowned. He was further behind in his research than he had expected to be. But he had no real choice. Now that he had spoken to Paloma, found all these records, and seen some of the gathered information, he wanted to meet with Wagner again.

Flint moved the files to a private area of his system, knowing he was going to have to find an even better hiding place for all of this information, but that he didn't have time this afternoon. He would do it after Wagner left.

Flint sealed the private area, then reopened the system, reestablishing all of the links with the outside. He had a lot of work to do. He might even overhaul everything, put in a completely new system that was strictly his own.

Fortunately he hadn't had many cases yet, and he had been careful about the kinds of reports he had written, so there weren't many of his ghosts in the system.

He had decided to read just a bit more about Wagner when Flint's perimeter alarm went off. The security screen rose, revealing an airlimo floating about two meters off the ground, going very slowly, as if it were looking for something.

Flint glanced at the clock. Five-thirty-five. People like Wagner were seldom early for appointments. Still, Flint let his security system run the airlimo's identifying numbers, and clear the tinted windows.

The last thing he wanted to do was assume he knew who was coming to the office when, in fact, he didn't.

The airlimo continued to move slowly, searching for an address. It took Flint's system only an instant to break through the tint and reveal the two people inside the limo.

Ignatius Wagner and his driver.

Flint felt his stomach twist.

The case was about to begin.

14

The moment the organizers left DeRicci alone in the bungalow, she shut off the wall screens. She hated being surrounded by the finish line of the race. Not only did she think the participants foolish, but she also saw the finish line as just a bit too ironic for her tastes.

Her personal marathon was just beginning, the finish line so far in the future that she wasn't even sure she knew when or where it was.

She did keep the race on a small screen on the wall behind her, knowing she could increase the image if she had to. She wanted to keep track of the race's progress. She also wanted to have a live feed in case something else went wrong.

DeRicci moved the table to the center of the room, placed chairs on each side as if she were holding a party, and closed the door to the entry.

Then she established two uniformed officers to act as guards for each entrance. Another uni would shuffle in runners for their interviews. DeRicci was taking the primary interviews, the ones that had the greatest chance of panning out. She would interview the organizers and the maintenance team—anyone with access to the course before and after the race started. She would speak to the runners who went around the body, and she would also interview the person who discovered the body.

The remaining interviews went to the rest of the force. They would talk to the runners who hit mile five after the body had been discovered. If the interviewer heard anything even slightly suspicious, that interview would then become DeRicci's responsibility.

Van der Ketting would probably get some interviews as well, but at the moment he was watching the vids of the early part of the race. Since the organizers monitored each patch of ground on the 26.2 mile course, there had to be vids of the area where the body had been found.

What DeRicci hoped was that the killer didn't know about the monitoring system. She hoped the entire crime had been recorded.

Some of the investigation she had assigned to the organizers. She had sent Chaiken and Lakferd to count the participants in this race and see if the number that started was one more than the number that finished.

If DeRicci was lucky, someone else would be missing.

The third uniformed officer, the one she had bringing the interviewees back and forth, also set up a secure recording system, so that DeRicci's personal links had a backup. The last thing she wanted was important information to disappear because she hadn't kept up her link maintenance.

Someone had brought her coffee, and one of those real pork burgers the organizers had been selling outside the stands. She had eaten about half of it when the uni brought in her first witness.

The first was the most important, because he was the best suspect they had. Brady Coburn was Jane Zweig's business partner, and from the information that DeRicci had managed to gather hastily, the business had faced various difficulties over the years.

The unis opened the door. Coburn stood just inside it.

He was a slender man, almost gaunt, with weather-roughened skin and short, dark hair. His eyes were red-rimmed, his mouth downturned. He seemed to have none of the confidence that DeRicci would have expected from someone who ran a business called Extreme Enterprises.

"Come in," she said, as if she were inviting him to tea.

He glanced at the uni who had brought him, as if asking the man for permission. DeRicci felt a flicker of irritation—she was in charge, after all—but then she realized that Coburn probably didn't know that.

Coburn took two hesitant steps inside, and the uni closed the door behind him. Coburn whirled as though the sound surprised him, and DeRicci saw the athletic grace in his sudden movement. He wore a light T-shirt and a pair of formfitting pants obviously designed to go beneath an environmental suit. The clothing wasn't even sweat-stained; either he hadn't tried very hard in the first five miles of the marathon or he was so in shape that he hadn't worked up a sweat yet.

Or he might not have run that first five miles at all.

"Sit down, please," DeRicci said.

Coburn turned away from the door. His muscles were ropy, unlike the bulky muscles that men who worked out in a dome usually got. He gave her a small smile and walked to the chairs, slipping into one as if his feet couldn't hold him much longer.

"I'm Detective DeRicci," she said. "I'm in charge of this investigation. Your interview will be recorded. At any point, you have the right to ask for counsel. You do understand these facts as I've given them to you?"

"Am I being charged with anything?" His voice was deeper than she would have expected, given his slight frame.

"Not at the moment," DeRicci said, "although that could change."

He studied her. "You don't think Jane's death was an accident."

"Do you, Mr. Coburn?" DeRicci asked.

He pursed his lips and shook his head slightly, the movement almost involuntary.

"I'm going to have to ask you again," DeRicci said, "do you understand the proceeding inside this room as I have explained it to you?"

He nodded.

"Aloud, Mr. Coburn."

"I thought you were recording everything." His words were snide, but his tone was not. He seemed to be unusually distant, the way people were in the first stages of grief.

DeRicci found that interesting. "We are, but it's always best to have an aural and visual record."

He grunted, crossed his arms, and slumped.

"Mr. Coburn?"

"Yes," he said. "I understand, and no, I don't want an attorney at the moment, but I'm going to reserve my right to hire one if you start badgering me."

His moods were mercurial, exactly the way someone who had just started grieving would be. However, grief did not absolve him from being a suspect in Jane Zweig's death. DeRicci had seen a number of killers become grief-stricken as they realized that what they had done was irreversible.

She sat down, deciding to play this one gently. "I understand you found the body."

He nodded, then seemed to catch himself. "Yes."

"Tell me about it."

He shrugged. "There's not much to tell. Jane was ahead of me, but that wasn't a surprise. She's good at simple events, like marathons, and she's worked out in low gravity forever. So she does well in the Moon Marathon."

He hadn't caught himself using the present tense yet, and DeRicci wasn't going to point it out to him.

But she made a note of it. He had spent time with the body, and Jane Zweig's death still wasn't real to him.

"I was having a good run until I found her." He shook his head, eyes downcast. "I probably wouldn't have stopped at all, but I recognized her suit. . . ."

His lips thinned again, and a small wash of color brushed his temples, as if he were trying to hold back tears. DeRicci hoped the recordings she was making caught things this delicate. They might be important later on.

He kept his head down. After a moment, DeRicci realized he wasn't going to continue.

"Then what, Mr. Coburn?"

"Hmm?" He looked up. His eyes were redder than they had been a moment before.

"You recognized her suit, and then what?"

"I stopped." He spoke as if that were the most obvious thing in the world. "I bent down to see if she was okay, and I saw her face."

Anyone looking at that face would have known she was dead, but DeRicci pressed on, not just trying to get Coburn to state the obvious, but also to find out how much knowledge he had and how much he lacked.

"What about her face, Mr. Coburn?"

"Didn't you see it?" His voice rose. "I thought you were in charge of this investigation. Didn't they let you see her?"

"I just want you to tell me what you saw." DeRicci kept her tone even. She made no quick moves, did nothing to unsettle him further.

"Oxygen deprivation." He spat the words. "She died from oxygen deprivation, and that's just not possible."

DeRicci kept herself very still. "We lose runners every few years to oxygen deprivation, Mr. Coburn. It's one of the risks we all face when we go outside the dome."

"You don't know Jane," he said. "She's cautious. She knows the limits of everything. It's one of her hobbies. She knows how far you can stretch things, how much punishment something will take."

"We all make mistakes, Mr. Coburn."

He shook his head. "Jane couldn't make that mistake, not with this suit. Don't you see? We have the top of the line in everything. She was using the best environmental suit made. Me too. Its systems have redundancies upon redundancies built in. The oxygen can't fail."

"No suit is perfect," DeRicci said.

"No, this one has its flaws. Extreme cold, wet. The suit gets brittle after too much use. But her suit was new, and we knew we'd be running in the lunar day when heat was the issue, not cold."

"She didn't die from the extreme temperatures," DeRicci said. "She died from lack of oxygen."

"And that's what I'm telling you." He slapped his hand on the table and stood up, spinning away with that effortless grace DeRicci had noticed before. "She couldn't have."

"Why not?" DeRicci didn't move from her chair. Let him pace this time, let him burn off the restlessness. She was going to be his rock, his strength, his confessor. She would get more out of him this way.

"Because I always test the oxygen systems of any suit we buy. I've seen too many people die like that, or nearly die—"

DeRicci wondered about the correction. It was interesting.

"—and I vowed it would never happen again to anyone I knew. Some suits, they have fragile oxygen systems. Step wrong, you can cut off flow. Have too much fluid so that it backs up, and it slops into the oxygen storage. Bad CO_2 filters, you name it, I've seen it. And these suits, they're the best in two areas— oxygen flow and fluid manipulation. And that's all you need in the Moon Marathon. That and temperature regulation, which the suits do reasonably well, particularly in heat."

"You tested the suit she wore?" DeRicci asked.

He shook his head. The movement was dismissive, as if he were growing impatient with this line of questioning. "We ordered from the same batch. The suits came in while I was gone, but mine was fine. I'm sure hers was too."

"But you never checked it."

"I didn't have to." He turned toward DeRicci. His body was agile, his movements so poetic they caught her every time. DeRicci didn't find him attractive, but she did find him unusual. She had never seen anyone who moved with such ease.

"Why not?" she asked.

"Have you ever see the oxygen system in these suits?" he snapped. "It's almost impossible to manipulate. I poked holes in the test suit and they healed. I poisoned the oxygen reserve, and the suit immediately switched to the backup oxygen—no delay. The entire system changed over immediately so that the wearer wouldn't breathe in the bad air."

His cheeks were flushed, his breath coming unevenly. His anger was too strong. He had been going over these questions in his own mind, worrying about them, wondering if he had missed something important.

"So," DeRicci said, "this backup system. Is it why she didn't have any reserve oxygen bottles, as required by the rules?"

He froze, almost as if he had been following one script and suddenly found himself in the middle of another. It seemed to take him a moment to process the question.

"Jane had reserve bottles," he said. "I saw them at the table this morning."

"The table?" DeRicci asked.

"The sign-in table. I waved to her, she waved back, and that was that."

"No conversation?" DeRicci asked.

"Jane and I don't talk much." Again with the present tense.

DeRicci raised her eyebrows. "You're business partners. I would assume that means you talk a lot."

He pulled his chair back and sat down. The movements weren't as graceful now. It was almost as if he had learned how to behave in a small setting so that he didn't call attention to himself.

"Jane handles the business side of Extreme Enterprises. I handle the trips." His breath caught, and awareness flickered across his face. He blinked twice, hard, as if he had just heard what he had said, and understood what it meant. "Jesus. The business. What the hell are we going to do about the business?"

"We?" DeRicci asked, deciding to let this train of thought follow its own course. "You have other partners?"

"No," he said, and the word almost sounded like a moan. "There's just me and Jane. But I can't run things while I'm leading excursions, and I'm heading out on Monday."

"You'll probably have to cancel that trip."

"The fees alone'll eat us alive. God." He put his face in his hands. "I hope she kept up the escrow account."

He hadn't followed the business side at all—either that, or he was putting on a very good act.

"Escrow account?" DeRicci asked.

"Everyone who goes on a trip gives us a down payment when they make their reservation. We're supposed to keep a percentage of it in escrow, so that we can refund if the trip gets canceled." His voice was muffled against his hands. "Jane was always lax about this part. We even—"

He stopped himself. His hands clenched into fists, and he wiped his eyes.

"You even what?" DeRicci asked softly.

"I guess you'll find out soon enough." He raised his head. His eyes were red from being rubbed, the pupils small. "We were sued for breach of contract a few times, and our business manager raided the escrow account to pay for the court settlements. Jane found out about it, and fired the business manager, swearing she'd reinstate the escrow accounts. I thought she had until a few years ago, when I went to refund a large deposit for a well-known client. There wasn't any money in the accounts. Jane fixed it. She always could. But I'd been planning to see if she was still stiffing the escrows. I just hadn't gotten around to it."

"Court settlements," DeRicci said. "It sounds like you had some bad years."

He rose again, as if he found staying still completely impossible. "Jane liked edges. She thought everyone else did. She cut some of the wrong corners and we got sued. I made her stop. That's when I started inspecting equipment, investigating travel destinations myself, doing the adventures with a handful of highly trained guides before we took any amateurs. Jane always said I was too cautious, that the name Extreme Enterprises should tip off anyone who wanted to come with us that they had to face some risks."

He walked around the room as he spoke, almost as if it caged him in.

"She hired some lawyers, got this really airtight release, and had our new clients sign it. But even that wouldn't be completely suit-proof. When someone died on one of our trips, we had to handle it. I finally convinced her to set up a death-benefits account, especially for trips too dangerous for our insurer to cover, but she didn't like it. I had to force her every time we used it."

His tone was bitter, and he wasn't making eye contact. DeRicci felt stunned by his revelations. Either he truly didn't realize that Jane had been murdered—and that each word he uttered could have been used against him—or he didn't care.

"You've lost clients?" DeRicci tried to keep the incredulousness out of her voice.

"Of course we have. It's the nature of extreme sports. In that, Jane was right." He was using the past tense now. Was it because of the argument he and Jane had had or because his mind was finally accepting her death?

"How many have you lost?" DeRicci asked.

"I've lost ten, mostly in the early years," he said. "I don't know about the company. For a while, Jane had set up some excursions on her own, using guides she chose. I ended that too. She was getting into my end of the business and she knew nothing about it."

"How many did those other guides lose?"

He shrugged. "I don't have those numbers right off the top of my head. But there was the accident. . . ."

He winced as if he immediately regretted mentioning it.

"Accident?"

He sighed. "We lost an entire group, ship and all, because no one went through the proper decontamination procedures. Those new guides were awful. Clients died because no one had checked their suits, because no one had scouted locations, because the treks were too difficult for anyone human, even me."

Even me. He spoke those words without pride, just acceptance. Either he was arrogant by nature, or he believed himself to be very talented. Maybe he was both.

"I'm amazed you managed to stay in business," DeRicci said.

"We're not a heavily regulated industry," he said, "and we had enough money to fight off any judgment. Besides, most of these things happened after Jane developed the ironclad release. A lot of judges just threw these cases out."

"It sounds like quite a headache for you," De-Ricci said.

"It was a headache for her." He stopped beside the small screen still showing the race, but didn't look at it. "It was her mess. I made her clean it up."

This time, he met DeRicci's gaze, and she thought she saw a challenge in his eyes.

"You're very angry with her," DeRicci said softly, making sure she was using present tense too.

"So I killed her? Stupidly? On some marathon track that I had no control of?" He crossed his arms.

DeRicci didn't answer any of his questions. Instead she said, "I had thought, when you first came in, that you'd been crying, that you felt something for her. But now I realize that all you feel is anger."

"That's not all. Jane and I . . ." His voice rose and then broke. "Jane and I . . ."

He turned away, clearly unable to finish the sentence.

"Were a couple?" DeRicci asked.

He nodded, head still down.

"Even though you spent no time together?"

"Before," he whispered.

"Before what?"

He wiped at his face again, then glanced at the screen. DeRicci could see shadowy figures moving along its path, but not how many or what they were doing.

"Mr. Coburn?" DeRicci made his name sound like a command.

He turned toward her.

"You were telling me about your relationship with Jane Zweig."

"Business." He cleared his throat. "These days, it's just business."

"But before?" DeRicci asked, using his word.

"Before, we were lovers. We started out as lovers." His right hand ran through his hair again; a nervous gesture, almost as much of a tic as his relentless pacing.

"And then what happened?"

"What happened?" He shook his head. "Jane happened. She—I don't know. She decided it was over, I guess."

DeRicci let the last two words resonate, but Coburn didn't elaborate. She would get him to eventually. "When?"

"Just after we started the business. But we stayed friends." He paused. "Sort of friends."

"What does that mean?"

He gave DeRicci a small smile, then came back to his chair. "It means she stayed friends with me. I was ready to cut all ties. I kind of did. I'm rarely here in Armstrong, and when I am, I don't see her unless I have to."

"But you're here now," DeRicci said.

He nodded, but didn't elaborate.

"For the race?"

"No." He sat down. "Jane said there was trouble, so I came back."

"What kind of trouble?"

"She didn't tell me the details."

"But you don't know?"

"I only got back a few days ago. We were going to meet after the marathon."

"Why not before?" DeRicci asked.

"Because we both wanted to train. I'd qualified before, but never run the marathon, and Jane loved it. She wanted to finish better this year than last. I think she was on pace, too, at least in the beginning."

His voice quavered. So many emotions about one woman. DeRicci had learned long ago that volatile emotions were often the most dangerous—and the most likely to lead to murder.

"You watched her run?" DeRicci asked.

"She always starts quicker than me. She's a runner. I told you that."

"And you are?"

"A nut." He laughed weakly. "At least, that was what she called me."

"I thought you excelled in a number of sports."

He looked up at her, his expression suddenly blank, as if he had just remembered who she was and why she had brought him to the bungalow. DeRicci cursed herself silently. She hadn't planned to reveal any of the cursory research she had done while waiting for him.

"It's easy to excel," he said, "if you know where to participate."

"Where to participate?" DeRicci didn't understand him.

"Know your skills, know the races." He waved a hand dismissively. "I don't like running in low gravity, but I'm good in one-G. I like climbing and swimming, and I do both well, so if a sport combines them, then I participate. I always did that, and then I started designing trips for myself at first, bringing some friends. It was Jane who convinced me to open the excursions to the public. She said a lot of people wanted to test themselves, and she was right. She was right about a lot of things."

"Like what?" DeRicci asked.

He shook his head. "Little things."

He wasn't going to answer that yet. DeRicci felt as though she were circling him, trying to find an opening, a way to pry open the door leading to Coburn's secrets.

"You said you just got back," she said. "From where?"

"Freexen," he said. "Jane wanted an event there."

DeRicci thought his wording was interesting. He didn't want an event there. Jane did.

"What kind of event?" she asked.

"Whatever I could design." He spoke too quickly. He had already planned that answer when he mentioned Freexen.

"Freexen's a long journey from here," DeRicci said. "Jane must have contacted you a while ago to get you back."

"Yeah," he said, not elaborating further.

He no longer paced, and no longer spoke as freely. DeRicci wondered if that was because of the topic or because of her blunder a moment earlier.

Time to change the interview's nature and focus.

"What did you do when you found Jane's body?" DeRicci asked.

"Hit the panic button," Coburn said, frowning. He obviously hadn't expected to change the topic.

"Hers or yours?" DeRicci asked, even though she knew the answer.

"Mine."

"Why not hers?"

His mouth opened, then closed, as if he thought the better of what he had been about to say. "I don't know."

"You don't know?" DeRicci let doubt creep into her voice for the first time. "You could have pushed her panic button, then kept going. No one would have blamed you. You would have been able to finish the race."

He let out a small snort, as if her words had shocked him. "Jane's dead, Detective. Why would I want to finish some stupid race?"

The right answer said with the right amount of indignation. In spite of herself, DeRicci was convinced.

She didn't want to be. Coburn had a traditional motive for murder, and enough volatile emotions within him to carry it out. Although she wasn't sure how, not if Jane Zweig had been alive when the race started.

He seemed to understand the direction DeRicci's

thoughts had turned, because he said, "I'm not the only person who had troubles with Jane."

"Really?" DeRicci wished he had stayed silent. One of her old partners, back in the days when the police department thought she would amount to something, said that anyone who volunteered information in a murder inquiry, particularly about other suspects, was usually guilty.

"Really," Coburn said. "Jane's a difficult person."

DeRicci already had the sense of that.

"I had to vouch for her," he said.

"For what?"

"The marathon." He stared at DeRicci as if he couldn't believe she didn't know this information.

"The marathon organizers?"

Coburn nodded. "She tried to take over the event last year, make it one of ours. They didn't like that."

DeRicci felt a chill run down her back. "How could you vouch for her?"

"I had to promise them she wouldn't disrupt the proceedings, that I'd take full responsibility if she did." He sighed. "But I guess I was wrong, wasn't I? She disrupted things after all."

"Somehow," DeRicci said, "I don't think it was intentional."

"Me, either," Coburn said. "I suspect no one was more surprised than Jane. She always thought she'd find a way to live forever."

DeRicci let that thought filter through her consciousness for a moment, not quite sure what to make of it.

"You know what the funny thing is, though?" he said.

"What?" DeRicci asked.

"I always thought that if Jane came face-to-face with death, she would win." He stood, the restlessness obviously back. "I guess I believed her. Jane was such a force. I never thought that she could lose."

15

Oliviari had lost count of how many runners had removed their environmental suits and handed them to her. The runners' faces had blurred together; she had even stopped searching for Frieda Tey's features in the crowd.

Oliviari's back ached, her finger—with its little DNA swipe—hurt, and her head throbbed. Sweat drenched her. The space she was working in—with all the tired runners, Hayley, and two security guards—seemed even smaller than it had before.

The runners weren't happy any longer. They were just as tired as the others who had come through, but that glow of accomplishment didn't fill this group. They knew they wouldn't be allowed out of the race area, and they were angry. They wanted to take out that anger on someone, and Oliviari was the closest target.

She wiped the sweat off her forehead, ignored the questions being shouted around her, and concentrated on swiping bits of DNA as she moved the suits to Hayley.

Hayley was being quiet too, keeping her head down as she worked. Perhaps she felt that if she didn't make eye contact, no one could yell at her.

"Ms. Ramos?" The male voice carried over the din of exhausted conversation.

Oliviari took the next suit, its material damp, its neckline sweat-stained. The young woman who handed it to her had high cheekbones and almond-shaped eyes. Her hair was a light shade of green, but Oliviari couldn't tell if the green was an enhancement, a genetic alteration, or an affectation.

"Ms. Ramos?" Louder this time.

Oliviari turned, remembering only a half second too late that Ramos was the false name she was using for this job.

The medic who had helped her with the exhausted man stood at the door to the main part of the tent. The medic looked exhausted now. Exhausted and worried.

His gaze met hers. "Can you come with me?"

She shook her head, sweeping her hand toward the group filling the entry. "I've got to stay here."

"Someone'll cover for you. I need you in the main part of the tent." He clearly wasn't making a request.

Oliviari cursed softly. There was no way her luck would hold twice. She wouldn't be able to find out which runners she had missed.

She slipped the DNA swiper into the pocket of her pants.

"I'm sorry," she said to Hayley.

Hayley looked up, as if she had just realized that something was wrong. "Now what?"

Oliviari pointed with her head toward the medic at the door. "They need me."

"They need a pair of arms. Have them get someone else. We need you here." Hayley spoke loud enough for the medic to hear.

"Ms. Ramos." This time, his tone held a warning.

"I'm sorry," Oliviari said again to Hayley. "I have to."

She handed the diagnostic wand to one of the security guards as she passed him, then stopped at the medic's side.

"What's so important?" she asked.

"Not here." He held the door into the main part of the tent open for her. She stepped inside.

The air here was cooler and smelled fresher, probably because there weren't so many bodies packed into the place. A lot of people sprawled on beds, though, and even more stood near the refreshment stand, downing glasses of liquid as if they were having a contest to see who could drink the most.

The medic put his hand on her back and propelled her toward yet another door. She'd never been through this one. It led into a windowless office with a makeshift desk stacked high with equipment boxes. The only chair was covered with boxes as well.

"You feeling all right?" The medic was tall, muscular; he had circles under his eyes, and sweat streaks on his brown skin. A name tag on his shirt identified him as G. Klein.

"Tired," she said. "But that's to be expected. Why?"

"Because." He leaned against the wall and ran a hand over his face. "The man we helped—the one who finished the run? He just died."

Oliviari felt her breath catch. "Of what?"

"That's just it," Klein said. "I'm not sure."

"You're not sure." Oliviari shook her head. She hadn't expected this. "What do you mean, you're not sure? If someone died after a race like this, cause of death should be pretty straightforward. Either the strain triggered something already wrong, or he had some kind of suit malfunction, or——"

"I checked all of that. I've been with this race a long time. I thought we'd seen everything."

She was getting chilled. The cool air, which had felt so good a moment before, seemed frigid.

"So I have to ask you again," he said. "Are you all right?"

"You think this is something contagious." She

wasn't asking a question. It was clear from his behavior that he did.

"Please." He sounded tired. "Just answer me."

She shrugged. "I've been working hard. Sweaty, tired, exhausted. I have no idea how I am."

"He fell against you," Klein said.

Her skin crawled with the memory. The man's sweat had long since mingled with her own.

"Yes," she said. "So you figure if anyone would get infected, it would be me?"

Klein didn't answer her.

Oliviari ran her hands over her arms. They were covered in gooseflesh. "You took readings. I know you did. What did they show?"

"Nothing that should have killed him," Klein said.

"What did they show?" Oliviari deliberately raised her voice. It was an old technique but a good one. People generally responded to a command tone.

"He had a mild viral infection," Klein said. "Nothing much."

"A viral infection?" Oliviari's chill deepened. Domed communities tried to prevent all kinds of viral infections. They were virtually unheard of out here, thanks to vaccines and health boosters. "What did your diagnostic wand say about it?"

"Nothing much. The problem was that he died so fast—his lungs filled, and he drowned before we could do anything about it. I've been talking to everyone who came into contact with him. I'm worried that this thing might spread."

Oliviari's chill grew. She finally had her evidence. Frieda Tey had been here after all.

"If it's what I think it is," Oliviari said, "it'll spread. It'll spread fast."

"You know what this could be?" He sounded surprised.

"I have my suspicions," Oliviari said. "Let's just hope that I'm wrong."

16

Flint braced himself. The air in his office seemed cold, and he raised the temperature slightly. He was too nervous about this meeting.

His curiosity was roused, and he knew that could be a problem. Paloma had warned him from the start not to take a case because he was curious about it. The case itself had to fit several criteria, the most important being that it had no suspicious elements— no way for Trackers or others to trace the same Disappeared that Flint was looking for.

This case had been suspicious from the beginning.

Still, Flint wanted to hear what Wagner had to say.

Wagner's airlimo had been parked across the street for more than five minutes now. Perhaps he hadn't liked the seedy look of the building's exterior, or maybe he hadn't realized he would be coming to this part of Old Armstrong. The driver appeared to be arguing with him, and Wagner was shaking his head forcefully.

Finally Wagner got out. The driver leaned out the passenger window and shouted at him. Flint did not turn up the audio, so he couldn't get the words, but the gist was pretty clear: The driver didn't want Wagner to come into the building alone.

After a moment, Wagner ran across the street as if something were chasing him. He reached Flint's building, scanned the doors as if he couldn't quite believe he was coming in here, and focused on the Retrieval Artist sign.

Wagner raised his hand to knock, seemed to think the better of it, and turned the knob. He looked surprised when the door opened, and then even more surprised when he stepped inside and all of his links cut out.

"Mr. Wagner," Flint said dryly.

Wagner frowned at him.

"Your links will work outside, but in here you'll be as alone as a person gets. If you don't like that, don't hire me." There. The challenge had been issued. Wagner would know from the beginning that Flint wasn't as easy to manipulate as the average first-time Retrieval Artist.

Flint's security system traced two more sophisticated links, and shut them down. He tapped a key on the board, making certain the security system looked for every possible worm and mole, then templed his fingers and smiled at Wagner.

"Change your mind about hiring me now?"

"How did you do that?" Wagner's hand was still on the door, holding it open. "How did you shut me down like that? No one's ever done that before."

At least not noticeably. Flint always made certain that when his security system severed someone's links, they noticed. That way they knew exactly what they were getting into.

"Stay or leave," Flint said. "I don't care which you choose so long as you close the door."

"Reinstate my links, and I'll come inside," Wagner said.

Flint shook his head. "You're on my turf now. You follow my rules or you get out."

Wagner studied him for a moment, then pushed the door open even wider. "I need to be in touch with my people."

"Then you have your answer," Flint said. "Find a new Retrieval Artist."

Wagner came inside, still looking disconcerted at the silence Flint had engineered in his head. "Look, I don't want anyone else—"

"Fine." Flint tapped another key on the board and the door slammed shut.

Wagner jumped in surprise. His eyes widened. "But," he managed to say in the same tone of voice, "I can't work with you in this manner. I must stay in touch."

"I trade in information, Mr. Wagner," Flint said. "I can't allow information to flow freely into and out of this place. If I do, it puts a lot of people in jeopardy. Many of those people paid a lot of money to escape the kind of troubles you and your links would bring to them."

"I can assure you that nothing confidential would slip through my links."

"You're right," Flint said, "because I won't let your links be on anywhere near me. This is nonnegotiable. Most of my terms are."

Wagner sighed. Flint had a hunch this stalemate would continue as long as Wagner focused on the links. So Flint moved the meeting forward.

"Let me tell you the rest of my terms so that you understand them. Then you can decide what you want to do."

Wagner watched him warily. Clearly this had all surprised him, which was well and good for Flint. It kept Flint in control of the meeting, which was where he wanted to be.

He then launched into the prepared speech he gave all of his clients. So far, all of the terms—indeed, all of the words—were Paloma's, but after this week, Flint would even reevaluate that.

"I charge a minimum of two million credits, Moon issue, not Earth issue," Flint said, "and I can charge as much as ten million or more. There is no upper limit on my costs, nor is there one on my charges. I charge by the day, with expenses added in."

This was one of Paloma's rules that she hadn't had to convince Flint of, not because he needed the money but because he understood the principle. Make the service so expensive that no one could pay the asking price casually, and yet again, an entire group of potential clients went away.

He went on. "Some investigations take a week. Some take five years. I cannot predict up front how long an investigation will take."

Wagner was staring at him, as if he were trying to memorize everything. The man seemed almost naked without his links. Flint wondered how long Wagner had used them to supplement his own memory.

"I have a contract," Flint said. "It holds up beautifully in court. You cannot nullify it."

Of course, he had never tested the contract, but Paloma had, many times. The contract was beautiful. No client could argue that he wasn't going to pay because the Retrieval Artist refused to turn the Disappeared in. It didn't state that the agreement was between a Retrieval Artist and a potential client, since some courts would want to know what the Retrieval Artist would do once he found the Disappeared. The rest of the contract was straightforward. In the end, the courts always had forced the clients to pay, no matter how the cases had turned out.

"I do not take charity cases," Flint said, "and I do not allow anyone to defer payment. The minute the money stops, so do I. If you don't like these terms, leave now. I won't change them for anyone. I do not negotiate."

"You can terminate but I can't?" Wagner asked, the lawyer in him obviously intrigued in spite of himself.

"That's right," Flint said.

"All the control in this relationship is with you, then."

Flint nodded. "Once you've hired me, you've put the situation—whatever it is—into my hands. I make all the relevant choices. That's part of what you hire me for."

"Because I'm not smart enough to deal with the ethics of Disappeareds?" Wagner asked, an edge in his voice.

"You're the one seeking me out, Mr. Wagner," Flint said. "I didn't come for you. I'm not giving you any rules I don't give other clients. However, I am telling you the rules sooner because you seem so alarmed at my severing of your security links—something, I'm sure, your office does routinely without informing its clients."

Wagner started, then covered the movement with a shake of the head. "We wouldn't do that. We don't violate privacy like that."

"Stop," Flint said. "We both know that private companies can determine what nets operate within their offices. So long as people have immediate access to emergency services, severing links in these circumstances does not violate the law."

Wagner's shoulders slumped, as if they and they alone were conceding defeat. "People said that if Paloma trained you, you'd be the best. Obviously they were right."

"My knowledge of the law has nothing to do with my abilities as a Retrieval Artist," Flint said. "Don't try to flatter or manipulate me, Mr. Wagner. I already trust you less than I trust the average person who walks through that door."

"And you don't trust them at all."

Flint smiled. "That's right."

Wagner nodded. He seemed to have forgotten his desire to leave. "Okay. If I accept your terms, then what?"

"Then you can tell me about the case."

Wagner nodded. "All right. It seemed straightforward enough—"

"Mr. Wagner," Flint said. "You haven't told me what you think about the terms yet."

Wagner's cheeks flushed slightly. It was clear he had tried to avoid committing to them.

Lawyers. Flint didn't have to be warned about them. He'd dealt with them enough as a detective. Lawyers hated to commit to anything.

"All right," Wagner said, his voice reluctant. "I accept your terms. What do I have to do? Sign something?"

"A verbal agreement works in this case," Flint said, "as I'm sure you already know."

"So long as there's a record of it." Wagner held out his hands. Their backs were dotted with flesh-colored links. "I haven't made one."

Flint smiled. "I've made two."

Actually he'd made four, using different systems to keep track, but Wagner didn't need to know that.

"I'll make certain you have a copy," Flint said.

Wagner crossed his arms. "Is there anyplace to sit?"

"No," Flint said. "Sorry."

He liked this old ploy of Paloma's, and planned to keep it. The lack of a chair made powerful people even more uncomfortable than they already were when they asked Flint for help. It also took away any feeling of superiority they had in towering over him.

"Okay," Wagner said. "If I don't have to sign anything, we can move forward, right?"

"Right," Flint said. "Then I'll take a few days to see if I'm interested, and I'll get back to you. You'll pay me a nonrefundable retainer up front for those days. Chances are, I will not take your case."

"How do you know that?" Wagner asked.

"Because people lie," Flint said. "They usually can't help themselves. But if one of the lies is detrimental to me or the Disappeared, then I'm going to refuse your case."

"You've already checked up on me," Wagner said. "You know I'm not going to lie to you."

"Everyone lies to me, Mr. Wagner," Flint said, not denying that he had checked up. "You will be no different. You have secrets you don't want me to know. Those will be lies of omission. You have things you consider unimportant, but embarrassing. Those will be little white lies, harmless ones, you'll think, and with luck, you'll be right. And then there are the big lies, ones you promised someone else you'd never reveal or things you lie about automatically, or lies you tell me deliberately to manipulate me."

"We're going to have full trust in this relationship," Wagner said.

Flint smiled. "You and I? Full trust? I don't think so. Especially with all your attempts at manipulation in the beginning. You don't really trust me, Mr. Wagner, and I don't trust you. We share that. But we have a difference that's pretty fundamental."

Wagner shifted from foot to foot, looking very uncomfortable. "What's that?"

"You've sought me out three times," Flint said. "It seems that you need me for one reason or another. I don't need you. If you walk out that door right now, my life will be no worse. It might actually be better, given your firm's recent history."

"I'm not here for the firm," Wagner said. "I'm here for myself."

"Really?" Flint asked. "Then why did you want to meet in your office? Why did you send your assistant?"

"Astrid's a good judge of character. I wanted her opinion. And as for my office, it gives me a measure of control." Wagner looked around Flint's as if it were the most ornate office on the Moon. "I'm sure you understand that."

"I do," Flint said. "So what you want to discuss with me has nothing to do with the firm?"

"I didn't say that," Wagner said.

"But the firm won't mind if you take its business outside its walls."

Wagner frowned. "What're you getting at?"

"Wagner, Stuart, and Xendor have three Retrieval Artists on staff, and a relationship with at least two others in Armstrong, not to mention Retrieval Artists scattered throughout the known worlds. You certainly don't need me."

Wagner crossed his arms. "You've done your homework."

Not enough of it, Flint wanted to say, but didn't. Let Wagner think Flint knew more than he did.

"It's probably better that we're meeting here," Wagner said. "I'm so used to using my office systems, and they're protected, but probably not protected enough. I could get disbarred for what I'm about to do."

Flint felt a shiver run down his back. That was quite an admission for a lawyer to make.

"Sometimes, though, you have to follow your gut. That's one of the reasons I came to you. You're a friend of Paloma's, and she always followed her gut."

"I'm not Paloma," Flint said.

"No, but you're her handpicked successor." Wagner walked toward the wall and leaned on it. It creaked under his weight. He looked at the wall as if it had betrayed him, and stood upright.

Flint didn't mention that the wall was reinforced, more than strong enough to hold a dozen Wagners. One of the nice things about this building was that it looked seedier than it was.

"Paloma once told my father that she wouldn't sell her business to anyone. When he found out that she had, she had laughed at him, and said that you were the most trustworthy person she had ever met."

Flint started. She had never said that to him. He had trouble believing that she had talked about him with anyone.

"Paloma doesn't use the word 'trustworthy,'" Wagner was saying. "I had always thought she was too cynical to believe there were trustworthy people left in the world."

Wagner's familiarity with Paloma disturbed Flint. He had gotten no sense from her that she had known these people well, yet she had worked for the firm for a long time, and obviously had maintained a relationship with the elder Wagner.

Then there were the files that Flint had found this afternoon. Such detail implied some kind of relationship, but not necessarily a healthy one.

"Let's forget Paloma," Flint said. "Tell me about your case."

Wagner sighed and gave the wall one last look. Flint almost felt sorry for him. He was beginning to realize the man hardly exercised, let alone spent this much time on his feet.

"You didn't mention it," Wagner said, "but I'm assuming you know that we had four Retrieval Artists on staff until a week ago."

Flint hadn't known that, but he nodded just the same. He wished he had had time to gather more information.

"Dambe—Dambe Rabinowitz—started at the same time we contracted with Paloma, only he stayed with us." Wagner looked down at his hands, at the useless links. "I knew him all my life."

That last sentence had a mournful quality. Flint leaned back in his chair, watching Wagner closely.

"He died last week. No one seems to have thought much of it. I mean, he was a Retrieval Artist, so he didn't have family or close friends. Just his colleagues."

Flint winced. Fortunately, Wagner wasn't looking at him, so he missed Flint's expression.

"They seemed relieved that he's gone. He was old-school." Wagner's voice held contempt, but Flint couldn't tell if it was for the other Retrieval Artists or for Rabinowitz. "But if you look at what he was working on and then you look at how he died, things don't entirely add up."

"Are you saying he was murdered?" Flint asked.

Wagner nodded once, then looked up. "At least I think so."

"I don't investigate crimes anymore, Mr. Wagner. Perhaps you should take this to the police."

"Give me a minute," Wagner said. "Listen to the whole thing. Give me that courtesy at least."

Finally the big-time lawyer showed through. Flint had pushed him around as much as he possibly could.

"What I'm going to tell you is privileged information, Mr. Flint. I expect you to keep it confidential." Wagner stared at him.

"I don't make those kinds of promises," Flint said.

Wagner continued to stare at him. Flint recognized the power of the look—he was certain it got clients to change their minds all the time, maybe juries as well—but it didn't influence him.

Finally Wagner sighed. "You're going to let me hang."

"I'm going to let you choose," Flint said. "There's no obligation on either side at this point. You can walk out right now and keep all your secrets."

Wagner broke eye contact, looked at the wall as if its blankness gave him guidance, and then shook his head once. "You ever hear of Frieda Tey?"

The name sounded vaguely familiar, but Flint couldn't place it. "No."

"I thought everybody had." Wagner sighed. "About ten years ago, she supposedly killed about two hundred people in a lab experiment. Some kind of government thing. It was big news here because her experiments involved domed colonies."

Ten years ago, Flint had been mourning his only child. He hadn't paid attention to anything else. "I don't recall anything about the case."

"Then this is going to take longer than I thought." Wagner crossed his arms. "Frieda Tey was a really well known scientist. She was doing medical research, trying to find out how quickly diseases spread and mutated in enclosed environments. She had a lab on Io, and she managed to get permission from the governments of the Earth Alliance to set up a small domed colony there, as an experiment."

Flint was beginning to remember some of this, but he let Wagner continue.

"She had done enclosed-environment studies before, mostly working with the common cold virus. She had worked in large ships before, but they had had short runs. This experiment was supposed to be of a working colony, so she set that up with human volunteers, and then she introduced the virus."

Flint let out a small breath. "She was the one who didn't let her subjects out when they got sick."

"Yeah," Wagner said. "That's the case. You do remember it."

"Vaguely," Flint said.

Wagner nodded, then clearly decided to continue rather than rely on Flint's memory. "The colonists got sick, then they got better, then they got sick again. The virus she'd put in there had been tampered with. It mutated quicker than any cold virus scientists had seen before. Earth Alliance charged her with deliberately infecting these people with a dangerous disease, not the common cold."

"She's disappeared, then, I take it."

"She stuck around for a while, trying to defend herself and her research assistants. But they didn't stand by her, saying she prevented them from releasing the dome doors, cut off the decontamination units, and wouldn't allow medical supplies inside when it became clear the mutated virus was lethal." His voice rose. This topic obviously bothered him. "She claimed that the virus's mutation was spontaneous, and that the decontamination units wouldn't fix it. The last thing she wanted to do was release that virus into the known worlds."

"So she let hundreds of people die?"

"She claimed there was no choice. The virus mutated quickly. By the time she got word out, asking for help, everyone was dead. She actually had some sympathy for a while."

"And then what?" Flint asked.

"Then her assistants spoke out, making the charges I mentioned and saying there had been time to save the colonists."

Flint shuddered.

"That," Wagner said, "was when she disappeared."

"Ten years ago," Flint said.

Wagner nodded.

"And your firm would like to what? Prosecute her?" Not that Flint blamed them, but that wasn't why he had become a Retrieval Artist. "If you want to find her for that, you need a Tracker, not a Retrieval Artist."

"I understand the difference between the two jobs," Wagner said. "I know that it's a subtle difference, but an important one to you guys."

Flint wasn't sure if he meant to Retrieval Artists, to Trackers, or to both, but he didn't ask for clarification.

"Frieda Tey's father relocated to Armstrong about fifteen years ago. My father handled all of his business, and then when my father retired, Tey became my brother's client."

Flint shifted slightly in his chair. This, apparently, was the unethical part.

"When Tey died two years ago, he left his entire estate to his only child."

"Frieda," Flint said. He was beginning to understand where this was going now. It was quite common for attorneys to hire Retrieval Artists to find beneficiaries of a will.

"There's a lot of money involved," Wagner said. "More than enough to justify the expense of a long search, and still have money left over. In fact, my brother argued that even without the will's other provisions, setting up a trust for Frieda Tey would be unethical."

"What other provisions?" Flint asked.

"Frieda Tey's father thought she was innocent. He wanted part of his estate to go to proving that she had simply suffered bad fortune. He wanted us to clear her name."

"He couldn't do this while he was alive?" Flint asked.

"He was trying. He had gathered a lot of rather contradictory information. When my brother presented it at the partners' meeting, it even convinced me that the entire sad thing might have been an accident of fate."

"What do you mean, even convinced you?" Flint asked.

Wagner walked around the room, then clasped his arms behind his back, like a lecturer in front of a difficult class.

"I followed the case when it first broke," Wagner said. "I've always been mildly phobic about living inside a dome. I went to school on Earth, thinking I'd like the open air better, and I found that it scared me even worse. So I figured I'd spend the rest of my life in a dome, and that meant I was subject to things—fires, bad air, fast-spreading disease. What happened to those people was—hell, is—my worst nightmare, so I kept track of that case."

He tugged at his chin, the chips on the back of his hand glinting in the light.

"And you know, I gotta think that human compassion would force you to open those dome doors. Maybe find a way to get those people to one of a ship's decontamination units or find a way to get one of those units to them." His gaze met Flint's. "You don't let them die like that, choking in their own fluids, and you sure as hell don't let them do it in front of you."

"I thought you said the fact that she watched was an exaggeration."

"She was a scientist," Wagner said. "She didn't just watch. She kept notes. That's what got her indicted in the first place, and then convicted in absentia."

"She wasn't convicted when she disappeared?" Flint asked.

"She wasn't even indicted yet," Wagner said. "It just looked like she was going to be."

"But her father thought she was innocent."

Wagner nodded. "And the evidence he had showed that whatever scientific curiosity she had was irrelevant. Getting help was impossible, predicting the deadly mutation was unlikely, and all the circumstances—including the setting—combined to create a situation in which everyone died."

"Everyone." Flint rested his elbows on his desk and templed his fingers. "You'd think someone would survive."

"That's what I said. Say, actually." Wagner glanced at Flint's chair. A contest of wills.

Flint pretended not to notice.

"But," Wagner said, "the scientists Tey's father hired had reasons for that too. They said that cold viruses will affect anywhere from one-quarter to three-quarters of the people they come into contact with, depending on the type of virus."

"The type?" Flint asked.

Wagner shrugged. "I don't remember the terms. Just that what Earth calls a cold is really five different virus families, and they all infect at different rates and all cause similar symptoms."

Flint's security screen flicked on. He hadn't lowered it when Wagner entered—he hadn't had time—but with the audio off, Wagner had no idea that anything had changed.

"Tey's original virus had a pretty standard infection rate," Wagner was saying. "About fifty percent."

Flint nodded, and maintained eye contact with Wagner, but all the while monitored the screen. Wagner's driver had gotten out of the limo and was standing in the middle of the street, staring at Flint's office.

"But each mutation—and I guess there were several—had a higher infection rate. What the scientists said was that the sample was too small."

The driver put her hands on her hips, glanced at the limo, then looked at the door again. She was going to come in here, and it was going to annoy Flint.

"Chances were," Wagner continued, "that by the end, one person in five hundred or one person in a thousand would have survived the virus. But there were only two hundred people in that colony, not nearly enough—"

"Sorry," Flint said. "Your driver is getting worried about you. You want to calm her down?"

Wagner didn't even look surprised that Flint knew what was going on outside his office. "Has it been thirty minutes?"

"Yes."

"She's just following instructions. I'm not supposed to be out of touch that long." Wagner went to the door and pulled open just as the driver reached it. Flint watched the interaction before him, and on the screen. He could barely see the driver over Wagner's shoulder, but through the security system Flint saw her take an involuntary step backward.

"Not done yet," Wagner said, his voice carrying back to Flint. "Give it thirty more."

"You know that I'm not supposed to do that. I'm supposed to notify the firm if you've been out of contact for thirty minutes—"

"And I just contacted you," Wagner said. "So start the clock from right now."

Then he slammed the door. The entire building vibrated. Flint hit a key on his security system so that it would recheck Wagner for any links that reactivated.

The driver stood outside, staring at the closed door. She rubbed the back of one of her hands, and Flint wondered if she had contacted someone after all.

Not that it mattered to him. It would just be inconvenient to have more people swoop down on his office, demand entry, and be refused. The only person it might matter to was Wagner, and he seemed more intent on continuing the conversation.

He gave Flint a crooked grin. It seemed familiar, although Flint knew that he had never seen Wagner before today.

"Think I deserve a chair now?" Wagner asked. "I've been a good boy so far."

"You could have one if I owned another," Flint lied. He wasn't about to go into the back and pull out the extra chair.

"With all the money you earn, you should be able to afford an army of chairs." Wagner started to pace again. "Where was I?"

"Almost convinced that Frieda Tey was innocent."

"Oh, yeah." Wagner sighed. "We decided to pursue the case on two fronts—we'd assign a Retrieval Artist to finding Frieda Tey, and while that search went on, we'd see if we could get enough evidence to provide her with an airtight defense in court. Because if she came back, she would have to go to court. There was no doubt about that."

"You think anyone accused of a crime like that would want to face that sort of trial?"

"For this kind of money, maybe," Wagner said.

"Most estates that go to Disappeareds go to them whether or not they return."

"This one was tied to proving her innocent. Otherwise she would get a smaller lump sum."

"Her father was going to bribe her to return to her old life?" Flint asked. "That made no sense, not if he was dead."

"I think the old man cared more about the Tey name than he did about her. Not that it mattered. You know how it is. The client's wishes are our wishes."

"Actually." Flint smiled. "I don't know that."

Wagner did not smile in return. "We assigned the search in-house. Rabinowitz was the best man for the job. He was an old-fashioned Retrieval Artist. Cautious, meticulous. No Tracker had ever piggybacked on him."

"Not even ones you assigned to do so?" Flint asked.

Wagner's cheeks reddened. "I never worked with Trackers."

"But your firm has."

Wagner nodded. "Trackers are one of the points of contention in the firm. My brother likes them. I don't. Unfortunately, my brother has more clout than I do."

So the hints that Flint had seen of an internal power struggle were true.

Flint frowned. "I'm still not understanding why you need me. Why not reassign this to one of your other Retrieval Artists?"

"I'm going behind Justinian's back to hire you."

"I gathered that," Flint said. "But you have the resources. You don't need me."

"Actually, I do need you. You have police contacts. You know how to investigate a murder."

"If it was a murder," Flint said, "the police'll handle it. The Armstrong detective units are overworked, but they eventually get the job done."

"I'm the only one who thinks Rabinowitz was murdered," Wagner said.

Flint crossed his arms and rocked his chair back. "The police don't think so?"

"They haven't even been called in. I argued with Justinian. I said that they should be called, but he says I'm being paranoid."

"Paranoid about what?" Flint asked.

"Rabinowitz," Wagner said. "He died of complications from a virulent cold."

17

The coffee the marathon organizers had brought De-Ricci was the real stuff. Real beans with real caffeine, strong and potent and extremely delicious.

Unfortunately, she was already feeling the effects. Her hands jittered and she had too much energy. Her stomach churned too; the brew was much too strong. She had switched to water about half an hour ago, but that didn't help much. She had to pace herself, keep her blood sugar level and her reactions under control. There were a lot of people left to interview, and not a great deal of time.

But she was taking a break from the interviews for the moment. Van der Ketting had the results of his investigation, and he wanted to see her personally. Part of the reason was so that he could ask for some interview time all his own, but there seemed to be something else he didn't entirely trust to links.

Van der Ketting sat next to her at the table in the main room of the bungalow. Together, they stared at the tiny screen on van der Ketting's hand-held.

On the wall in front of them, the marathon played in real time. The crush of runners had slowed to a trickle, and they no longer flew across the finish line. They still jumped when they got there—but it was a weak jump, with height and distance gained only because of the low gravity.

These runners were exhausted and showed it. A few of them had even collapsed when their feet touched the pavement on the other side.

A small screen on the corner of the wall reran the press conference from earlier that afternoon. Against DeRicci's wishes, her boss, Andrea Gumiela, had notified the media about Jane Zweig's death. Gumiela's reasons—or so she told DeRicci when DeRicci paged her across the links—were simple: someone might have information about Zweig's murder, someone who wasn't anywhere near the marathon.

And, DeRicci had said to Gumiela, *you just gave that someone a good reason to leave Armstrong.*

Gumiela had missed the point, as usual. She wasn't really an investigator, never had been. Or, as one of DeRicci's old partners, Miles Flint, had once said, Gumiela had always seen investigation as one step closer to promotion.

The Gumiela announcement had also put more pressure on DeRicci. Now there were press inside the dome, waiting around the cordon the police had established. Usually the press couldn't get into the marathon. They had to rely on the feeds provided by the organizers, who had been controlling information ever since the marathon's first accidental death.

The organizers couldn't have been happy about this announcement, and DeRicci wondered if the mayor was. Perhaps Gumiela had finally screwed up for good.

DeRicci hoped so, because that announcement had made her job a lot harder. A few enterprising reporters might have actually sneaked in—or even had seats in the bleachers, against marathon organizers' best plans, of course.

DeRicci supposed those reporters were already interviewing people, ruining any advantage the police might have in this case.

"Okay," van der Ketting was saying, "are you going to pay attention to me or are you going to stare at the reruns of Gumiela ruining our investigation?"

DeRicci made herself look away from the small screen. She hadn't even realized she'd been watching it again. The sound was down, but she almost had Gumiela's words memorized.

There will be inconvenience, of course, Gumiela had said in that unctuous tone she seemed to think was soothing, *especially for the participants and their friends and families. However, the sooner we resolve what actually happened on the Moon Marathon course today, the sooner we can put this entire case to rest.*

At least, DeRicci thought, she hadn't said that they could go back to celebrating the riches the marathon brought into Armstrong, although that subtext was there. A few reporters had even asked Gumiela about it.

The woman hadn't been too dense. She'd managed to deflect those questions.

"Noelle." Van der Ketting was sounding annoyed.

"Sorry," she said, forcing herself to look from that small screen to the even smaller screen he held in his hand. "What've you got?"

"Some strange stuff." He extended his arm so that the screen was between them. "Look at this."

He pressed the side of his hand-held, and an image started to play. Runners thronged around the organizational table and the starting area, picking up singlets, standing with heads together, or pacing to and from the starting line. Every runner in the race had to be in that grouping, but on the tiny screen they looked like little stick figures, players in a drama she knew only the ending to.

"Let's feed this into their wall system." She didn't ask his permission; she just took the hand-held from him, and checked the links built into the wall. It took only a moment to figure out how to synchronize the systems.

She hadn't quite finished when van der Ketting said, "They'll know what we were looking at."

DeRicci shrugged. "You got all this information from the organizers, didn't you?"

"Yes," he said.

"Then they'll know anyway. And what they know today may not matter tomorrow. Despite what Gumiela says, we have a lot of work ahead of us to figure out what's really going on here."

Van der Ketting slumped in his chair like a schoolboy who had been rebuked. DeRicci still wasn't sure how she felt about him. Sometimes she liked his combination of paranoia and enthusiasm, and sometimes she thought it interfered severely with his job.

She finally got the link hooked up. She turned on yet another wall screen, so that she could still get the marathon feed.

"You sure it's not going out into their system?" he asked.

"You want to check for me?"

She had meant the question as an aggressive, rhetorical one, but he stood up and came over, touching the links, examining the portals, and touching parts of the synch in his hand-held.

"I guess we're fine," he said, as if he had just accomplished something spectacular.

She studied him, wondering if it was worth telling him she had already done all of that, plus a few more things.

Then the screen across from her lit up. The images she had seen on the hand-held a moment before were suddenly life-size, the angles constantly moving.

"What kind of system did they use?" she asked.

"It's a blend of several," he said. "I adjusted it for the correct angles, but I managed to get all of the

information. We can change it as much as we want,
look at everyone as closely as possible, and then some.
I just figured this would be the quickest for right
now."

DeRicci shoved her thumbs in the waistband of her
pants and watched. The runners milled about, mostly
with the dome as their backdrop. It actually took De-
Ricci a few minutes to realize that she saw twice as
many runners as she had initially thought. Everything
was being reflected in the dome, which was still dark
with Dome Night.

"How early did this thing start?" DeRicci asked.

"Runners started showing up at six," he said. "Start
time was eight-thirty. This is from about seven. It's
the first time I located Zweig."

He pointed to an image on the wall. A woman, not
too much taller than DeRicci, stood in front of the
organizers' table. The woman wore a light pink environmental suit similar to the one that the corpse had
worn.

The suit was as attractive as these things got. It was
formfitting, which was how DeRicci knew for certain
she was looking at a woman, and it glowed in the light
of a Moon Day.

"Let's enlarge that," DeRicci said.

Van der Ketting did without complaint; apparently
he liked manipulating the technology. Good thing to
know. She would make certain he did a lot of it. Normally she found technology more of a hassle than a
help.

The woman's image grew until it filled the wall. The
helmet had its sun tint on, so the woman's face wasn't
visible. But DeRicci wasn't looking for the woman's
face.

DeRicci was interested in the suit.

It had dirt in the creases, like suits that got used a
lot often did. The dirt was gray, like most of Outside,
and it was thick. It coated the pink, dulling it. Even

though light reflected off this suit, it didn't do so as brightly as on the suit DeRicci had seen on the corpse.

Her breath caught. "You're positive this is Zweig?"

"She's holding the singlet," van der Ketting said. "She had to present identification to get it."

The image swirled in front of DeRicci until the singlet came into view. The numbers matched.

"Identification Outside, not Inside," DeRicci said. "Why is that?"

"Oh, they do ID inside as well. Then they double-check the suits to make sure they meet regulation. But to get the singlets, the runners have to go to the organizing table Outside. That way, they can't pass off the singlet to someone else."

DeRicci nodded. The organizers seemed to think of everything. "This is an hour before the race?"

"An hour and a half."

"Does she just wander around?"

"I lost her for about forty-five minutes," he said.

DeRicci nodded, not liking this at all. "Show me when she reappears."

Van der Ketting skipped forward, the images appearing fleetingly across the white walls. Portraits of the day already mostly gone: people standing, peering into the distance, trying to put on their singlets. DeRicci got that in single images, almost too short to truly register on her brain.

Then the images slowed. Zweig emerged from one of the maintenance sheds.

"How'd she get in there?" DeRicci asked.

"I already asked," van der Ketting said. "It's a secondary dome door. Normally no one can use it, but the marathon has limited permission. They use it for one half hour before the race, when the crush at the regular door is too severe to get everyone through the airlocks on time. No matter how early the runners get told to arrive, a large group of them always comes late."

That last sounded like he was parroting one of the organizers. DeRicci was still frowning at the maintenance shed.

"What's in there?" she asked.

"Nothing, so far as I could tell," van der Ketting said. "They're supposed to clear it out before the race. That whole tampering thing, you know."

DeRicci didn't respond. Instead she continued watching. The singlet flapped on Zweig's chest. She walked up to a man in a reddish gold environmental suit of the same make, and nodded at him. DeRicci wished she could hear the conversations, but they had occurred across private links. The organizers had only emergency links and an announcement link that the runners shared.

Apparently an announcement came across the main link, because runners started lining up according to their qualifying times.

"Blow up her image again," DeRicci said.

Van der Ketting froze the frame on Zweig as she crossed the pavement. She was very much alone. Somehow, despite the swarm of environmentally suited bodies, Zweig managed to keep herself isolated.

DeRicci was grateful for it: Zweig's isolation gave them a clear view. "Can we make this into a hologram?"

"Not here," van der Ketting said. "At the station."

DeRicci nodded so that he couldn't see her disappointment. She got as close to the wall as she could and looked at the boots. In the white light of the sun, they looked gray.

"Zoom in on the boots," she said.

He did.

"Okay, now rotate the image one hundred and eighty degrees."

He did that as well.

Zweig was walking in the image van der Ketting had zoomed in on. She had lifted one foot so that the sole of that boot was completely visible. The boot's lightning-bolt zigzag was barely visible. Moon dust had gathered in the boot's ridges and along the edges.

Van der Ketting came up beside her. "Wow," he said. "I have no idea what to make of that."

DeRicci studied the sides of the other boot. The dust had collected on the boot in a uniform pattern. A few lines of dust weren't uniform, and she blamed that on the 1G inside the dome.

"These aren't the same boots," van der Ketting said, showing that he did know what to make of this after all.

"This isn't the same suit either," DeRicci said. "This one's been Outside a number of times."

She frowned. Coburn had told her that the suits were new. He had also said that they often ordered suits for the tourists who went on their excursions—and that the suits were usually tested by the staff first.

DeRicci cursed silently. She hadn't wanted to do follow-up interviews if she could at all avoid it, and she wouldn't be able to avoid it in this case. She hadn't asked Coburn how many suits he'd ordered or when they had arrived.

She had been under the impression, though, that they were new. Which meant that Zweig had worn hers Outside a lot recently.

"You need to check dome logs," DeRicci said. "You need to look for Zweig's name on them."

"How far back?"

DeRicci shrugged. That was one of the pieces of information she didn't have. "A year to start. Maybe more."

"You think that the fact that she was Outside a lot had something to do with her death?"

Who taught these new detectives anyway? All of her young partners had asked a variation on this question at one time or another, and she was getting to the point where she wanted to slap them.

"I'm not thinking anything in particular right now," she said, and that was true. Too many preconceived notions, and the case would dissolve before her. She'd see only what she wanted to see and would miss the important stuff.

Van der Ketting was studying the boot too. He ran his finger along the image, as if he could feel the lightning bolt pattern through the wall.

"How many other people had these suits?" DeRicci asked. She really didn't want to go through the two hours of the recording by herself, double-checking van der Ketting's work. She would if she had to, but this would also slow down the investigation, because she couldn't do much research until she'd finished the interviews.

"I only saw one," van der Ketting said, "and that suit was slightly different."

"Different how?"

"It was kind of a goldish red," van der Ketting said. "I thought it belonged to the guy who found her."

So that was who Zweig had been talking to. DeRicci had suspected as much.

She said, "Get Coburn's environmental suit. Bag it for evidence. Make sure you get everything, including the boots."

Van der Ketting studied her. "I thought I was going to help conduct interviews now."

DeRicci shook her head. "There's too much to do right now. You and I have to split the duties. I'm afraid you're going to have to spend a lot of time staring at images from the race."

Van der Ketting didn't move for a long moment; then he said, "You done with this one?"

"Yes." DeRicci moved away from the wall. On the opposite wall, a runner walked across the finish line. The runner's arms were down, body hunched. Each movement spoke of extreme exhaustion.

And the sad part was, none of the medical staff or

the organizers moved to help the runner. The runner had—his? her?—moment of triumph all alone and in what appeared to be great pain.

DeRicci made herself turn away from the race. The wall was white and bare now.

"What about miles five and six?" she asked. "Did you get the footage from there?"

"Yeah," van der Ketting said. "It's not real helpful, though. Apparently the system is tied into sensors that turn on when a runner approaches."

"I guess we'll have to make do. Show me the segments when Zweig approaches."

Van der Ketting used his hand-held as a guide and set the program already in the wall unit. Then the barren landscape appeared: the boulder, looking ominous, its closest side hidden in shadow; the trails forking around it; and the edge of the horizon in the distance.

It took DeRicci a moment to get her bearings. For some reason she had expected the image to face toward the finish line, with the Earth in full view in the dark sky.

But the system looked toward the starting line, which, of course, wasn't visible because of the short horizon. After what seemed like a long pause, but which couldn't have been more than thirty seconds, Zweig glided toward the boulder.

DeRicci could see only the pink helmet bobbing above the boulder at first. Then Zweig took one of the side paths. She loped past wherever the cameras were, and disappeared.

Then the image cut off. Apparently no one had been following her closely.

"What about other angles?" DeRicci asked.

"That's the only one we got," van der Ketting said.

DeRicci bit back her irritation. "Get the rest. I thought you were going to be thorough."

"I was thorough," he said. "They only have one angle out there. Costs again."

174 *Kristine Kathryn Rusch*

"This marathon doesn't need to save costs," De-Ricci said. "They could afford cameras on every centimeter and from all angles. Who told you this hogwash?"

"Several people, actually," van der Ketting said. "They all had the same story. They didn't need much, especially early on. All they wanted was a full face view of the runner's approach and nothing more."

Full-face view. DeRicci frowned. She hadn't seen Zweig's face. "Run that again."

Van der Ketting did. As Zweig rounded the boulder, DeRicci had him freeze the image.

The Earth reflected in Zweig's visor. Her helmet's tint was on full. It was impossible to see her face.

"You'd think if they wanted faces," van der Ketting said, "they'd tell the runners to turn off the tint."

"They don't dare." DeRicci felt cold. "The sunlight is unfiltered. Without the tint, the runner would be subject to all sorts of nastiness."

Van der Ketting grew up on the Moon; he should have known that. But he probably wasn't thinking about it. He seemed to miss a lot of things because he hadn't thought them through.

"Then what's the problem?" van der Ketting said.

"There's a couple of problems," DeRicci said. "She doesn't look like a woman who's having breathing troubles."

Van der Ketting looked at the frozen image, and his mouth gaped open. "You're right," he said. "How could I have missed that?"

"I don't know," DeRicci said, "but it's a pretty big miss."

He turned toward her, the shock that had been on his face a moment before even worse. "Is that why you don't want me doing interviews?"

She sighed. It didn't pay to point out this man's flaws. "I already told you. We have too much ground to cover to do it together. But if you keep missing things, I'm going to have to review what you've done."

"So the filter doesn't bother you." His tone edged on belligerent.

"The filter bothers me," DeRicci said, "although not because I can't see her face. I would be stunned if I could see her face."

"But we saw her face when she was dead. We—" He stopped, looked at DeRicci, and shook his head. "That's what bothered you, isn't it? That we could see her face then. Someone wanted us to know who she was and how she died."

"You're not thinking about this as if it's an Outside case," DeRicci said, unable to control her impatience any longer. "The scratch in the visor, the open filter. What does that tell you, Leif?"

She would lead him by the nose if she had to. She would force him to the realization, with all the strength that she had.

"Someone got interrupted."

"Yes." DeRicci extended the word, exaggerating her usual patient tones. "I already told you that."

His lips thinned. He looked at the image still large on the wall.

"Obviously you can shut off the filter without opening the helmet," he said, and that caught DeRicci by surprise. She'd never heard of that feature on an environmental suit, but he was right. The killer had shut off the filter from the outside—the pressure had remained even.

Van der Ketting was looking at her. "But that's not what you wanted me to see, was it?"

DeRicci shook her head. "It's good, though. It's exactly the kind of thing you should be thinking. Look for the logic flaws, look for the holes."

He was still staring at Zweig's image. "Why would you shut off a filter?"

"Why would you scratch the visor?" DeRicci said.

"He wasn't trying to scratch the visor," van der Ketting said. "He was trying to crack it."

DeRicci waited.

Van der Ketting ran his palm over his open mouth. "My god," he said slowly. "The corpse got found too soon. They didn't care if we saw her face or not."

DeRicci didn't nod, even though van der Ketting was right. She continued to wait for him to complete the realization.

"They wanted to make her completely unrecognizable." His hand still gripped his chin, thumb and forefinger pressing against his jawbone as if he had forgotten to let go. "Why? Why would anyone want that?"

"In the middle of the marathon," DeRicci said.

"Do you think he cleaned her suit?" van der Ketting asked.

Another thing DeRicci hadn't thought of. She felt her shoulders relax slightly. Maybe he would be a real partner after all.

"Depends on how much time he had," she said, noticing that they were both using the male pronoun. She would have to put a stop to that soon, but not yet. Not when van der Ketting was finally learning how to think properly.

"I'm going to have to look that up, aren't I?" he said, the excitement back in his voice. "See who came next?"

DeRicci nodded.

"You're going to want to interview them, right?"

"Those are the people who are most important to me, yes," she said.

"And the more information you have the better." This last wasn't a question. It was muttered, almost as if van der Ketting were making a memo to himself. "I'll get right on it."

He started to walk away.

"Wait," DeRicci said. "What about the discovery of the body? Did they have that recorded?"

"Yeah, and it's just what we expected." He paused at the door, then shook his head, as if he couldn't believe it himself. "It's just what *I* expected. Want to look at it?"

"Yes," DeRicci said.

Van der Ketting came back and moved the recording ahead again. DeRicci stared at the white wall, waiting for the images to return. She could see faint reflections of the other screen, light and shadow playing across the whiteness here, signifying nothing.

But she didn't turn, didn't look at the other runners coming in. Nor did she watch Gumiela while she waited. It was time to stop thinking about her career and to start thinking about this case.

This case required her full concentration.

"Here," he said, and suddenly the images returned.

The perspective seemed slightly different. The boulder loomed larger, but didn't seem as dark. In fact, DeRicci could see the streaks of gold in its stone, glinting in the sun.

She also couldn't see the body. She thought for certain the section of the track where the body had fallen had been visible in the previous scene.

"Is this a different angle?" she asked.

Van der Ketting shook his head. "They only have one, remember?"

"It looks different."

He studied the image too. "I'm sure they only had one camera out there. But it does look like it was moved. Do you think the killer knew where it was?"

Score another point for van der Ketting. DeRicci almost smiled at him.

"If the killer did know," she said, "then we have to find out who has access to these cameras, and who knew where they were placed."

"And whether they're moved from year to year."

"I would assume that they'd have to be," DeRicci said. "No one would leave valuable equipment out there."

"It's not going to get stolen," van der Ketting said.

DeRicci suppressed a sigh. He had come so far, only to forget about the Outside again.

"Of course not," she said. "But it might get hit with space debris. Lots of stuff comes down every year. I'd assume that any equipment left out there would have to be really hardy or really cheap. And this doesn't look cheap."

"I'll check on it." Van der Ketting's tone seemed muted, but the excitement lingered.

DeRicci would still have to supervise him, but perhaps not as much as she had worried about. "Let's watch this."

He started the images, letting them move forward.

Once Coburn started to appear in the frame, the images looked very similar to Zweig's. The helmet bobbing up and down, then Coburn appearing beside the boulder large as life.

Van der Ketting had been right: Coburn's suit was a reddish gold. It sparkled like the light pink suit did—obviously the same design and make—but Coburn's seemed sturdier somehow. Or maybe DeRicci thought that only because Coburn hadn't ended up dead.

Unlike Zweig, Coburn's steps slowed as he passed the boulder. The Earth had been reflected in his visor, but that reflection faded as he looked down.

Zweig's form, huddled in a fetal position, covered the golden filter. What Coburn saw was very clear. He had studied the body as he pulled up close to it.

By the time he passed the camera, he had almost slowed to a stop. DeRicci started to turn away, but the image shifted, and suddenly she was seeing Coburn from a different angle—one farther away.

Coburn stopped near the body, then walked over to it. After a moment he crouched down, put a gloved hand near the visor—and pulled away as if touching it would hurt him.

He thrashed, apparently searching for his own panic button. He did seem panicked—just like he had said he had been.

DeRicci wondered if he was a good actor or if this reaction had been real.

"Where are we looking at this from?" DeRicci asked.

Van der Ketting was staring at the images as if he hadn't seen them before. Maybe he hadn't. "I don't know."

"I don't recognize this camera angle from the earlier footage," DeRicci said.

"It's definitely different." Van der Ketting sounded almost angry. "I searched for more angles, too. I even went to mile six, to see if that camera had picked up something from mile five, but I couldn't see the body from there. And there was certainly nothing from this camera."

DeRicci frowned. "Anything from it on the runners between Zweig and Coburn?"

"I don't know," van der Ketting said. "I only scanned them, waiting until I found Coburn. You said you wanted this in a hurry."

She had said that. "Interesting that all of this is missing from the Zweig footage."

"Maybe the sensors didn't pick it up, so they didn't turn the camera on," van der Ketting said.

"Didn't pick up a woman dying of oxygen deprivation? Are you kidding? All of the sensors should have been on at that point."

"But we already determined that she didn't move," van der Ketting said.

"And that determination might be wrong," DeRicci said. "Whoever killed her had time with the corpse. He might have cleaned off the suit, like you said, and then he might have tried to bust the faceplate."

"Why wouldn't he do that first?"

"I don't know," DeRicci said.

"Do you think he was part of the race?"

"In one capacity or another," DeRicci said, "which wouldn't surprise either of us, I think."

Van der Ketting shook his head. "I did check the singlet numbers. There weren't any extras so far as I could tell."

DeRicci nodded.

"And, according to the organizers, the right number of people have crossed the finish line or are still being tracked on the course."

"I didn't say that the person involved was a runner," DeRicci said. In fact, her doubts about that had grown. "There's too many pieces that don't fit."

Van der Ketting watched her as if he were waiting for her to list them. But she'd already told him enough.

"Watch the rest of this," she said. "Watch for the smallest detail. And look for stuff from miles four, five, and six from before the race. If the cameras were set up early and the sensors activated, they might have picked up movement from earlier. It would be nice to know what that area looked like before the runners showed up. We might even be able to isolate the newer footprints from the old."

"All right." Van der Ketting was no longer complaining about this part of his job. "You think everything'll be on these vids?"

"I think a lot of the answers are here, yes," DeRicci said. "I'm just not sure yet what they are."

"You want to keep this stuff?" Van der Ketting swept a hand toward the image on the wall.

"No," DeRicci said. "It'll be a distraction. And let's not leave it for the organizers either."

Van der Ketting gave her a small smile. Apparently that had been what he was thinking of. He went to the unit and destroyed his initial download.

"Do you want me to send anyone in particular for the next interview?" he asked. It almost sounded like he had someone in mind.

DeRicci shook her head. "I'm going to contact the coroner first. I want to let her know about the face-plate filter. I also want her to check the suit. Maybe that suit has a download as well. It would be worth seeing."

"I'll get it," van der Ketting said.

"No," DeRicci said. "I need you here."

She glanced at Gumiela, whose image still talked on the small screen. DeRicci was really glad that the sound was off.

"You think there'll be problems at the station?" van der Ketting asked.

"Yeah." DeRicci reached inside the wall unit and shut off the small screen. Gumiela disappeared as if she had never been. "I'm sure of it."

18

Oliviari's skin was covered with goose bumps. She was freezing now, where fifteen minutes ago she had been so hot she was sweating.

She tried not to worry about it. Worrying about it would get her nowhere. First she had to see if her concern about Frieda Tey was forcing her to make things up.

"Let me see what you've got so far," she said to Klein.

His eyes seemed too large for his face. She had scared him. Or maybe she had just reinforced his fear. After all, he had dealt with the dead man.

"You want to see the body?"

Oliviari suppressed a shudder. "Not yet. I want to see the virus."

She was glad she masqueraded as a medic. If she had masqueraded as some other kind of volunteer, she wouldn't have had access. And she was probably the only person here who could identify the Tey virus—except Frieda Tey herself.

Klein handed Oliviari his hand-held: An image of the virus floated on it, a thousand times too large. It looked like the map of a misshapen crater or a puddle of spilled coffee.

"I'm going to need net access," she said.

"The hand-held can do it. Go ahead."

"Standard access?" she asked, not even waiting for his answer as she touched the surface. The virus disappeared for a moment; then she fingerprinted one of her codes into a locked file, and downloaded the virus information.

She didn't want to rely on her memory of this one. She had all of Tey's research—even the stuff that hadn't gone public—scattered throughout her holdings on the web. Oliviari just had to get the right file.

Klein watched her face instead of his hand-held, and somehow that made her nervous. The little room had grown cold again, the boxes and the furniture making it seem even smaller than it was.

As Oliviari worked, she wondered if Tey had slipped by her, if she hadn't been running after all, but working the marathon just like Oliviari had.

What would have been the point of infecting people out here, though? They could be forbidden access to the dome if the virus was caught in time. And since the virus was so fast-acting, getting caught early was a possibility.

Unless something happened to prevent that. Perhaps another emergency, something that might actually make people go into the dome instead of remain outside of it.

Another chill ran through Oliviari, and she suspected it had nothing to do with the cold room. "Why aren't we allowed back into the dome? It's not because of this disease, is it?"

Klein studied her. His look changed with her question, became more measuring somehow. "Didn't you get the message?"

She shook her head.

"There was a murder out on the track."

"A murder," she said under her breath. So the missing response team had found itself on the scene of a murder. That was why the police had come. "What kind of murder?"

She was thinking of Tey and the virus, the way that it killed without the killer being anywhere nearby. If Oliviari was right, there had been more than one murder at this marathon today.

"I don't know. The med team said it was oxygen deprivation, but for some reason the cops think it's murder."

"You don't think it could be the virus, do you?" Oliviari asked. He had seen the poor man die of this virus. He knew what the corpse looked like, at least inside the proper atmosphere.

Klein shook his head. "I don't think a person who died like our runner, even in an environmental suit, would look like someone who died of oxygen deprivation."

Neither did Oliviari, but she had to check. She frowned. A murder was just too much of a coincidence.

"You're sure it wasn't an accidental death?"

"Yes," Klein said.

Oliviari finally found her file. She downloaded the images of the virus that she had, the ones the scientists had managed to isolate from various mutations of the disease.

She compared them to the images Klein had and found exactly what she'd hoped not to: The virus the runner had died of was the final mutated version of Tey's cold virus.

Oliviari read the specs she had on the virus: It took four to six hours from exposure to the appearance of symptoms; from the onset of symptoms to death took another four to twelve hours; and the rate of infection, so far as anyone could tell with the limited evidence that they had, was one hundred percent.

She put a hand over her face. Her skin was clammy. She leaned against the desk and made herself remain calm.

"It's bad, isn't it?" Klein asked.

Oliviari nodded. "But not unsolvable."

That much they had learned. Because Frieda Tey had escaped, and because so many believed that she had escaped with some of the virus, the decontamination company who had initially underwritten her experiments modified its decon units to destroy the virus in its early stages.

"Have you ever heard of the Tey virus?" Oliviari was beginning to get a headache, and her throat felt raw. But sometimes her throat felt like that from too much dry air, and she often got headaches when her blood sugar was low.

She had been infected, but only a few hours ago. She couldn't have symptoms yet.

"The Tey virus?" He frowned. "It sounds like something I should know, but I specialize in sports medicine. I'm not a virologist."

Very few people were anymore, at least in this solar system. The virologists had moved farther out, where viruses were still common and deadly.

"I'll tell you about it when we have time," Oliviari said. "For the moment, though, I need to see the specs on your decon unit."

"Why? What is this?" He sounded panicked, and why wouldn't he? He had just seen a man, ruled healthy enough to run in a difficult marathon, die of a virus that probably hadn't even shown up on the morning tests.

"One of the ugliest diseases I've ever seen," Oliviari said. "It destroyed a domed colony about ten years ago."

Klein stared at her, as if he couldn't believe what she had just told him. "I suppose we should isolate the body."

Oliviari shook her head. "It's too late for that."

He took a deep breath. He clearly understood that. He also understood its implications—for all of them.

"All right," he said. "We need the specs for the decon unit. What else?"

"Modify your diagnostic wands to recognize the Tey virus." She handed him the hand-held, with her entire file still on it. "We need to know who was infected and when."

So that they could triage. Those most likely to survive would get treated first.

If they could treat anyone. That was what she wasn't going to tell him, at least not yet. Because if the marathon didn't have an up-to-date decon unit, and there weren't any mobile ones in Armstrong that could handle the Tey virus, Oliviari wasn't sure anyone would survive.

The problem was that this virus killed quickly. The virus was so rare that most domed colonies didn't have vaccines available. Decontamination units were supposed to stay up-to-date, but not all of them were. In fact, a decon unit in a city as old as Armstrong could have been made from five to fifty years ago. If the unit's owner had failed to keep the updates current, there was a good chance the unit couldn't handle the Tey virus.

The medical unit had only a few hours to work with. Once those hours were past, no one who had been infected would live through this.

No one at all.

19

"My God," Flint said. "This is a dome. What the hell are you thinking? If your suspicions are right—"

"Then we'll all die, I know." Wagner walked to the office door and back, as if he couldn't remain still, not for this part of the conversation. "I've been trying to talk to my brother about this."

"Talk?" Flint said. "You should have gone to the police."

Wagner stopped walking. "And say what, exactly? That I believe we're all in danger because a Retrieval Artist who didn't believe in enhancements died from complications of the common cold which, I grant you, is not so common here on Armstrong, but does occur. You think I didn't look that up too? People do get infected, though God knows how. The decon units are supposed to take care of any diseases that come in through the Port."

Flint sighed. Everyone trusted the Port, but it wasn't the perfect gateway. People slipped past the decon lines all the time. The Port security was too busy with major breaches to do much about it.

"I can't even prove he had contact with Frieda Tey, and until I can prove that, I can't even mention her name in connection with him, not legally or ethically." Wagner put his hands on his hips, as if he were angry that Flint had queried him. "See why I came to you?"

"You want me to go to the police?"

"I want you to back trace what Rabinowitz did, see if he was close to Tey, and if he even saw her. If he did, I want you to go to the police. They'll believe you."

They probably would, not because he had more information than Rabinowitz had, but because Flint had been a cop. He had a lot of credibility because of his past.

It was a neat plan. So Paloma had been right in part: Wagner had come to Flint because of who Flint was, not just because of his connection to Paloma.

"How much time do we have?" Flint asked.

"What do you mean?"

"If this is thing is as contagious as you made it sound, then I want to know when someone else is going to get sick and die from it. Do I have hours? Days? Weeks?"

Wagner shrugged. "That's part of the problem. If everything I read about the most virulent strain of the virus is right, we should be dead already."

Flint started. Whatever answer he had expected, it hadn't been that one.

"Tey's file said that the most virulent strain killed within a day. But Rabinowitz has been dead for two days, and as far as I can tell, no one else has gotten sick."

"So you're just being alarmist," Flint said.

"Cautious," Wagner said. "If you look at the earlier trials, some of the strains of the virus took weeks to incubate. And Rabinowitz had been calling in sick for a few days."

"How long exactly?"

Wagner took a deep breath. "Four days. I have all his stuff. He didn't do anything for the last four days of his life except stay home and rest. I'm not even sure he saw a doctor."

"But you're positive about time of death."

"Oh, yeah," Wagner said. "I had my assistant check in on him every day."

"Ms. Krouch?"

"No." Wagner smiled. "My real assistant. Ms. Krouch is an attorney, just like she told you. She usually handles her own stuff."

"Only this time, she handled me."

Wagner took a deep breath. "Look, I know this all sounds kind of crazy. I know that I'm probably worrying about nothing. But I can't rest unless I know that Rabinowitz died of natural causes."

That sounded sincere. Flint's gaze met Wagner's. The man wasn't trying to hide the fear that guided him. In fact, he seemed to want Flint to share it.

"Before I make a preliminary decision on whether or not to take this case," Flint said, "I have one more question. Let's say you're right. Let's say that Rabinowitz found Tey, and that somehow contact with her made him ill. What do you want me to do?"

"I already said. You should tell the police." Wagner sounded annoyed. "God knows how many people Rabinowitz infected."

Including the entire staff at WSX, most likely. And now Flint. But he wasn't going to let a hypothetical illness get in his way.

"I will tell the police." Flint lowered his voice, even though he knew no one else was listening. "But that wasn't what I was asking you. If Tey is alive, and Rabinowitz found her, then I will find her as well. Had you thought of that?"

Wagner looked down at the floor. Flint missed the moment of eye contact. He wanted to see Wagner's true reaction.

"Technically," Wagner said, "she's my brother's responsibility."

"Your brother will pay her the inheritance, let her help in her own defense, and maybe help her disappear again."

Flint stood for the first time since Wagner had come into the office. The movement seemed to startled Wagner.

"But think this through," Flint said.

Wagner's shoulders were hunched forward, as if he didn't want to hear this.

Flint stepped around the desk. Wagner looked up, swallowing hard.

"If I find Tey, and I can prove that it's Tey, and she's the one who made Rabinowitz sick, even with a lesser version of her virus than the one that killed all those people in that dome, this means that she's guilty of the crimes she's charged with."

"No," Wagner said, a little too quickly. So he had thought of it. "It doesn't mean that. It means that she's guilty of this crime. One case of manslaughter if she didn't know the virus would kill him."

"Homicide if she did," Flint said. "And she would have done it to save herself. People usually don't use elegant diseases to kill other people. Elegant diseases generally rule out a crime of passion. If what you're telling me is true, Rabinowitz died slowly. Tey would have had a chance to back out once her passion cooled. To warn him, to warn others. She didn't."

Wagner was watching him, his expression completely neutral. Flint couldn't tell if Wagner was really letting the information in or not.

"A person who kills in cold blood, for intellectual reasons, is precisely the kind of person who would allow a domeful of people to die to get the results of an experiment." Flint leaned against the desk. "So I ask you again. What do you want from me if this scenario plays out?"

"Are you telling me you could kill her?" Wagner asked.

Flint started. He hadn't been saying that at all, although he could understand how Wagner had misunderstood him.

"No. I'm saying that if we give her to your brother, and if she disappears again, she will continue to kill."

"I thought you're not a Tracker," Wagner said. "I thought you don't care what a Disappeared has done, and I thought you'd never turn one in."

"I'm not a Tracker," Flint said. "It's not my job to turn anyone in. But I do care what a Disappeared has done. And if this woman is guilty, she's very dangerous."

"Then you stay away from her," Wagner said. "Don't let her get you like she got Rabinowitz."

Flint felt a flash of annoyance. Wagner wasn't answering him, not in the way he wanted, and Flint knew what that meant. It meant that if Flint found Tey, Flint would have to choose what to do with her. Wagner didn't want any part of that.

Flint was not willing to accept this case on those terms.

"Tell you what," he said. "If I find Tey, I won't let her know I'm on to her. I'll let you know who she is and where she is. She becomes your responsibility then."

Wagner took a step backward, as if even having this part of the conversation was toxic for him. "I'd have to turn her over to my brother. And you know what would happen then."

"You'd have to?" Flint asked.

"I'm ethically bound to. You know that."

"Actually, I don't," Flint said. "You're ethically bound to keep the confidentiality of your law firm's cases as well, and you decided finding out what happened to Rabinowitz was more important. It's not that much of a leap, then, to doing the right thing with Tey."

"I'll do what I have to," Wagner said.

Flint suppressed a sigh. What had seemed straightforward not half an hour ago no longer seemed that way. Perhaps Wagner did have a hidden agenda, one that Flint couldn't see. Maybe it had something to do with the power struggle in the law firm, or maybe it had something to do with Tey herself.

Flint would investigate all of that. He would have to, before he even considered looking for Frieda Tey.

20

DeRicci couldn't get through to the coroner. Instead she left a message for him. She explained that the filter had been down when Zweig last appeared on camera, and it was up after she had died.

DeRicci also mentioned the lack of rigor, and her concerns about time of death. She figured a few messages on this issue wouldn't hurt, and it might actually get the coroner to contact her with some speed.

The race still showed on the wall. She tried not to stare at it. It seemed so unimportant now.

After she finished with the coroner, she'd contacted van der Ketting for the names of the runners who had passed the body before Coburn had arrived. Van der Ketting had gotten the information by scanning through the images between Zweig and Coburn and writing down the singlet numbers.

Not surprisingly, all of the people who passed Zweig—with the exception of one—had finished in the top twenty of the race. The one exception had broken her foot at mile thirteen. DeRicci would either have to go to the medical tent to interview her or send someone else there.

What was surprising was that van der Ketting reported that all the other runners showed up in the second camera, the one that Coburn had shown up on when he was looking at Zweig's body. That camera, however, didn't seem to be working when Zweig came by.

"I think the killer might have shut it off," said van der Ketting. "Maybe he was waiting for her right by it."

DeRicci had been noncommittal. The theory had a nice logic, but it didn't make all the details mesh.

She had given the singlet numbers to the uniform outside the room, and had him track down the people she needed to talk to. The first one was the woman who had won the race, Shira Swann.

Swann was a large, powerfully built woman. Her tight, curly hair was cut so short that for a moment DeRicci actually thought Swann might have been bald.

Swann strode into the room, not looking the least bit tired from the day's ordeal.

"What is this about us being kept here?" she asked DeRicci before DeRicci could speak. "We should be free to go."

"A woman was murdered. We're interviewing everyone." DeRicci indicated one of the chairs.

Swann ignored the gesture. "Do I need a lawyer then?"

"I don't know," DeRicci said. "Do you?"

They stared at each other for a moment. It was clear that Swann wasn't going to make this easy.

Finally DeRicci had to make the concession. "This is just a preliminary interview, mostly for informational purposes, so that we can put a timetable together. Everyone is a suspect, but that's mostly a formality. You can get a lawyer if you want, but that'll only prolong the experience, especially since we're only going to have to talk to you once."

Swann was staring at the screen behind DeRicci, and for a moment DeRicci wasn't even sure the woman had heard her.

"You know," Swann said in her deep voice. "It has always been my dream to win this marathon. The

Earth marathons were important, but this one—it is the one I grew up watching. It is the one I value. And the day I win it, I am also a suspect for murder."

Swann was excellent at manipulation. If DeRicci had been a bit more tired, had a bit less experience, or hadn't been paying attention, she might have reassured Swann that she wasn't a suspect, making the entire interview invalid.

"At least you have the victory," DeRicci said. "Jane Zweig never finished the race."

"Is that her name, then? Jane Zweig?"

"Yes," DeRicci said. "Did you know her?"

"I knew of her." Swann pulled back the chair as if sitting down had been her idea all along. "Dangerous woman, that."

Interesting. Only the second interview, and both people had referred to Zweig in unfavorable terms. "Why?"

"You don't know about her company, the one that lets people try anything so long as they sign their rights away?"

"Extreme Enterprises?"

"That'd be the one." Swann turned her chair so that she could see the race still playing on the wall.

DeRicci walked behind Swann and turned the controls so that the race showed up on a different wall. DeRicci made certain the screen was so small that she would have to look carefully to see what was going on.

"Did you have experience with Extreme Enterprises?" DeRicci asked as she walked back into Swann's line of sight.

"Now what would I want with jumping off cliffs into fiery seas on planets so far from here that I'd spend half my life getting there?" Swann shook her head. "I'm a runner. I don't need to try risky things to prove my strength to myself."

"Seems to me that running this marathon is risky."

Swann raised a single eyebrow at DeRicci. "I suppose. And I suppose what you do is risky, dealing with criminals from day to day. But they're acceptable risks, if you know what I mean. People have made them for years."

DeRicci sat down, not taking her gaze from Swann.

"It seems to me," Swann said, "this other thing is people taking unacceptable risks for no real gain. Doing extreme things to themselves or their bodies because they're rich and bored or too cowardly to take risks that'll mean something."

"Like running a race Outside? That means something?" DeRicci couldn't resist the question, even though she felt slightly offtrack.

"To me it does, but to you, no, I don't suppose it means much. This was an indulgence, and nothing more. The fulfillment of a dream. But then I go back to London where I'm living now, and I design races for charities, something that's gone on for generations now. People collect money for each mile they run, and give that money to needy folk. It takes care of the rich and bored by giving them something to do while they put their money in the hands of those who need it."

Swann leaned back in her chair, and as she did, DeRicci could see the muscles in her stomach and chest move beneath her shirt. DeRicci didn't know anyone who was as in shape as Swann, not even the new recruits on the police force. It made DeRicci, with her diet of anything-whenever-she-could-grab-it, and fake caffeine whenever she couldn't find real caffeine, feel like a slob.

"I had another reason for being here." Apparently Swann had taken DeRicci's silence for disapproval. "I wanted to work with the Moon Marathon committee to see if they would be willing to let us sponsor another marathon on their course, for charity. But you people here don't have the same attitude toward the poor that we do."

That statement surprised DeRicci. She had never been to Earth, so she wasn't certain what could be different. "We don't?"

"No. You seem to think that if they can't fend for themselves, then they've got some sort of character flaw. I get the sense that if you could ship people out of the poor areas in your fair city, you would do so."

Even though DeRicci knew that Swann's use of the word *you* wasn't personal, she still took it that way. People who lived on Earth, with its open land and unlimited resources, didn't understand dome life. Inside a dome, if you didn't contribute, you were wasting precious resources and interfering with other people's survival.

But DeRicci didn't say that. She had to focus on the investigation, not some philosophical argument with a woman who was too wrapped up in her own agenda to understand that the universe was a diverse place.

"So the committee wouldn't work with you?"

"No. Once they found out what I was about, they wouldn't even meet with me. They thought I was going to interfere with their major tourist event."

"Wouldn't another marathon do that?"

"Of course not." Swann sounded so sure of herself. "The Moon Marathon is the one with cachet, and that wouldn't change. We'd just be pretending to be a practice run for it, and raising some funds for the needy at the same time."

"You were trying to expand your company." DeRicci finally understood now.

"Yes."

"So of course they're protective."

"We're a nonprofit. We were not going to interfere."

DeRicci wondered about that. She'd come across a lot of nonprofits over the years who had interfered with other businesses.

Would they have killed Jane Zweig to make their

point, to shut down the Moon Marathon so that they could revive it and establish their own?

It sounded unlikely, but DeRicci had seen too many unlikely things to rule it out entirely.

"But they might have seen it that way," DeRicci said. "Right? That you were going to interfere?"

"No 'might' involved. They did see it that way. And they weren't so very happy when I won today. They saw that as a threat as well."

"Or perhaps they were preoccupied with the murder victim who still lay on their course." DeRicci's tone was sharper than she intended.

"Perhaps," Swann said, but it sounded as though she doubted it. DeRicci's pointed reminder—that there was a bigger picture here, and it involved a woman's death—seemed to have passed Swann by.

DeRicci decided she was going to stop handling this woman as if she were someone important. "You passed Jane Zweig's body, didn't you?"

Swann shrugged. "I passed a number of people down on the course."

"So much for charity," DeRicci said.

Swann's cheeks flushed. "We're told not to stop, that everyone has panic buttons, that it'll be taken care of by the volunteers and the medics. You learn, Detective, that people get injured when they run, here and on Earth. It's part of the sport. You can't help them all, and you don't succeed if you do."

DeRicci let Swann's last sentence echo in the room. Swann's flush grew deeper.

"I think there's a difference between someone who is injured and someone who is unconscious," DeRicci said. "There's no way anyone would have taken Zweig's body for a simple injury."

Swann's fingers tightened on the arm of the chair. DeRicci wouldn't have noticed if Swann wasn't in such spectacular shape. The muscles in her arms moved as the fingers increased their grip.

"I'm not on the medical staff," Swann said. "I don't know how to evaluate these things."

Defensive again. DeRicci found that she liked that.

"Huddled in a fetal position, not moving, right smack in the middle of the course. You didn't think that was worth maybe a notice along the link, a warning to the other runners, a request to the volunteers to move her? You could have sent for a medic without stopping."

"I thought perhaps someone else already had," Swann said.

"Who would that have been?" DeRicci asked. "At this point in the race, there weren't many people ahead of you."

Swann shrugged. "I do not keep track of who is ahead of me."

That, DeRicci knew, was a lie. "Not even at the end? You're telling me that little burst of energy you had at the very end was just spontaneous. It had nothing to do with the fact that you knew you could win this thing?"

"I pay attention in the last few miles," Swann said. "But in the first few, it's not worth my time."

DeRicci wasn't going to get Swann to talk openly this way. She needed to take better control of this interview.

"Look." DeRicci deliberately softened her tone. "I'm mostly talking with you as a witness, and all I want to know is what you saw when you came up to mile five."

Swann shrugged. "Nothing unusual."

Not the body on the course? Was that nothing? But DeRicci bit back those words. She was trying the conciliatory tack this time. It was difficult to play both good cop and bad cop, but she was trying.

"Well," DeRicci said, choosing her words with care. "Maybe you don't realize that you did see something."

Swann's eyes narrowed.

"For instance," DeRicci said, "there were cameras located throughout the course, which were activated by sensors. When Jane Zweig came up to mile five—and she was ahead of you, right?"

Swann nodded. "She usually was at this point in the Moon Marathon, but every year I've beaten her."

DeRicci was surprised. For some reason, she thought this was Swann's first time in the race. "But this is the first time you've won."

"I came in third twice," Swann said, "and have been in the top ten all the other times. Most of the time, I was a few places ahead of Zweig."

"So you did know her."

"I knew of her," Swann said again. "I don't think we spoke more than fifty words in all the years we've competed."

"Because you didn't like each other?"

"Because there was no point." Swann crossed her arms. Her biceps muscles bulged. "Besides, this was the only race I saw her at. Have you tried to talk to someone when you're wearing those suits? It's pretty near impossible."

Unless you were linked. But again DeRicci didn't say what she was thinking. Still, this brought up a few other questions. "Why didn't you go to Zweig with your idea for a charity marathon Outside? She would seem like a logical candidate to help you."

"We're on opposite sides, detective," Swann said. "Zweig's business is for profit. Mine is not. She would want a take, and I wouldn't want to give it to her."

So Swann had thought of it. DeRicci made a mental note of that, deciding that either she or van der Ketting would check to see if Swann had had an appointment with Zweig in the last few weeks.

"Just curious," DeRicci said in that lighter tone. "As you can see, I'm not a specialist in this area. I've only been to the marathon when someone dies."

"There have been other murders?" Swann sounded startled this time.

DeRicci shook her head. "All accidental deaths, which is what I expected this one to be. Obviously, it was not."

"How was it obvious?" Swann asked, trying to take control of the interview again.

DeRicci smiled. "There are some things I'm not allowed to talk about at this stage of the investigation."

Swann nodded.

"As I was saying," DeRicci said, "when Zweig came up to mile five, her arrival was caught on the nearby camera. But when she passed the camera, that was it, we couldn't see her anymore. However, when you came up, all the cameras in that area seemed to be working."

"I am not a technical person," Swann said. "You can ask my staff back home. I can barely operate my links."

"I'm not accusing you." DeRicci wasn't sure how this interview had gotten so out of hand. "I was wondering if you saw anyone, maybe even a marathon volunteer, working in the area."

Swann turned her head upward, as if the answer were on the ceiling. She blinked a few times, closed her eyes, and frowned. DeRicci's heart pounded. Swann was actually trying to remember. Maybe the interview wasn't so wrong after all.

Then Swann opened her eyes. "You believe that the killer was still there when I went by?"

"That's one theory," DeRicci said.

"How long between Zweig's appearance and mine?"

DeRicci hadn't asked for that information from van der Ketting, and of course, he hadn't volunteered it.

"Not long," she said, wondering if that was a lie.

"Then I should have seen something." Swann

frowned. "I don't remember much, though. You get into a zone."

DeRicci nodded, even though she doubted she'd been in a zone ever in her entire life.

"There was a boulder, and the path split. In the past, I went to the left, and this time, I decided to go right, to see if it would shave some microseconds off my time. Sometimes that's what this race is about. Not miles, but microseconds."

Swann leaned forward, as if finally getting enthusiastic about the conversation. DeRicci nodded, pretending interest, although she really could care less about the intricacies of marathon running.

"The Earth was just there, you know. Quite visible. In all the years I've run, it's never been that clear before. It's always been someplace else in the cycle. This was also the first full daylight run. I'd never done that before. Even though we have the suits on, it puts a different stress on them."

DeRicci wondered if she should be paying attention to this. Maybe it did have a bearing on Zweig's death—or at least the physical condition of her corpse.

"So I came around the boulder and nearly tripped. I was moving awkwardly when I came up to the body. Only I didn't know it was a body then. I just thought it was someone who was injured." Swann grimaced and shook her head. "I cursed her. Not out loud, but quietly. I didn't know it was Zweig, although I had a hunch. I thought it was typical of her not to move off the course when she was hurt."

DeRicci almost commented on that, but decided to wait. Sometimes letting the narrative flow uninterrupted was better.

"I had to do a vertical leap to avoid her, and that adds seconds to your time. You wouldn't think that if you're used to one-G, but in one-sixth-G, it feels like you're hanging there forever. And I hung there, and cursed her, and flailed my arms like I was swimming and trying to tread water, which was stupid because there's no atmosphere to push against. All I was doing was tiring myself, and I figured that was what she wanted."

Swann seemed to know Zweig pretty well for a woman she'd hardly spoken to.

"It took me a good mile or two to regain my gait. I have a hunch everyone'll tell you that, if you can get them to talk about it. Having her there was disturbing, because it really throws your rhythm off, and even more than regular marathons, the Moon Marathon is all about rhythm."

DeRicci made a sympathetic noise, so that Swann would continue.

"I guess it didn't matter, though," Swann said, "because we all had to deal with her just lying there—or at least, those of us up front did."

DeRicci wondered if this woman realized she was talking about another human being.

"It makes sense that someone way behind me stopped. He didn't have a chance anyway, so a few seconds off his time wouldn't matter."

DeRicci wondered if Swann knew who really stopped or if she was guessing that the person was "way behind" her.

"How did you know who stopped?" DeRicci asked, making certain none of her people had let information slip.

Swann shrugged. "I don't know who stopped. I just figured it was one of the dilettantes."

"You said that you tripped near the boulder." DeRicci was careful not to comment on any of the conclusions that Swann had just made. "What did you trip on?"

Swann was watching DeRicci as if she could read DeRicci's reaction. DeRicci hoped she couldn't; DeRicci found that after this part of the conversation, she disliked Swann even more than she had earlier.

"Who knows," Swann said. "Perhaps a small crater, or a deep footprint. You can never tell. So much pockmarks this course."

"Try to remember anyway," DeRicci said.

Swann took a deep breath. "I don't know," she said again. "I wasn't looking down."

"This could be important," DeRicci said. "You might have tripped on something the killer left."

Swann looked at her with alarm. "I would have noticed that."

"You said you weren't looking down."

"Anything unusual on the course, you see that as you're approaching. That's why I noticed Zweig. You don't see the pockmarks so much because they're the same color as the dirt itself, but you see man-made things. Especially in that sunlight. Although—"

She stopped herself and shook her head.

"Although what?" DeRicci asked.

Swann kept shaking her head. "It's not important."

"I'll judge that," DeRicci said.

"I came around that boulder, and thought I saw a movement. I think that's why I tripped. I shied, you know, like you would if you thought someone was sneaking up on you."

"Was someone sneaking up on you?" DeRicci asked.

"No. It was the boulder's shadow. It was pretty deep there."

DeRicci remembered that from the vids she'd watched with van der Ketting.

"The shadow must have fallen across the path. I'm sure that's what spooked me." But Swann didn't sound sure. In fact, now she sounded uneasy. "The killer couldn't still have been there, right? Watching me go by?"

DeRicci didn't answer. She didn't want to state the obvious.

"So it could've been me as easily as Jane?" Swann hadn't called Zweig by her first name before this.

"I doubt it," DeRicci said, although she didn't. She wouldn't know anything until she found out why Zweig had been killed.

"What would they have been watching for?" Swann said. "There would've been no reason to hang around."

Except to finish smashing that faceplate. But it would stand to reason that if Swann set off the camera sensors, the killer would have too.

Unless the killer knew how to turn those sensors on and off.

"How close behind you was your nearest competitor?" DeRicci asked.

"Not too close," Swann said, belying what she had said earlier.

"What does that mean?"

Swann shrugged, her all-purpose gesture for this part of the interview. "A few minutes, perhaps."

The time frame wasn't working out.

"Was Jane Zweig moving when you passed her?"

"Not that I noticed." Swann looked down. DeRicci had no way to know if she was telling the truth this time.

"What did she look like?"

"I barely saw her."

"You nearly tripped over her."

"And I was looking forward. That's the only way you can run out here. You have to plan ahead, and if you don't, you're done. Why do you think so many people get hurt?"

DeRicci didn't answer that. She just waited.

Swann sighed. "She was on her side, her knees up near her chest, almost like she was sleeping. I noticed because I had room to get around her. If she'd been sprawled lengthwise, I would have fallen on her for sure."

So Zweig was already in the position she'd been in when they found her.

"Are you sure you were right behind her?" De-Ricci asked.

"I told you, I don't pay attention to those things."

"But you knew about the person behind you."

Swann sighed. "I knew they were far enough back that I couldn't see them. I couldn't see Jane either. She was too far ahead of me. But whether that was thirty seconds or five minutes, I have no idea."

"What is the most she could have been ahead of you at that point?" DeRicci said.

"I have no idea."

"Yes, you do," DeRicci said.

"Wasn't your camera time-coding stuff?"

DeRicci felt a chill down her back. The time-coding had been missing. Wiped off? Or never set? No wonder they had missed the timing. The normal clues weren't there.

More things to talk with van der Ketting about.

"It wasn't my camera," DeRicci said, "and no, there were no time-codings."

Swann seem to relax with that. "I could tell you on a one-G marathon, but this one, I have no idea. It was only mile five, but Jane liked to go lights-out in the beginning, which was stupid, because then you had nothing left for the end. I always beat her in the last four miles or so."

"So give me a guess," DeRicci said.

"She could have been as much as ten minutes ahead of me, if she went really fast and knew what she was doing."

Ten minutes was enough time, barely, for the murderer to kill her then. Two minutes for capture, another minute or so of struggle, then the time it took to disconnect the suit's oxygen—DeRicci still didn't know whether or not that had happened—and four minutes or so for the actual death. Unconsciousness would come first, and the body could get posed.

But even then, Swann should have seen something more than a movement near the boulder.

"You don't believe me, do you?" Swann asked.

DeRicci looked up at her. Swann's arrogance was gone. For just a moment, she seemed like an insecure girl.

"I do believe you," DeRicci said. "And that's where the real problem lies."

21

.

"I thought I told you to go inside the dome."

Without his environmental suit, Medical Team Leader Mikhail Tokagawa had a formidable presence. His slenderness accented the wide bones of his face, giving him a regal look. His black hair somehow lightened his blue eyes, so that they seemed almost colorless.

Oliviari leaned against the wall, arms crossed. Several other runners had come down with cold symptoms, and Klein had left to tend to them. Oliviari was still feeling chilled, but she attributed that to Tokagawa's attitude. He had come storming into the medical tent when he found out that Klein had tried to requisition decon units from other parts of Armstrong.

Tokagawa had cleared the boxes off the desk with a swipe of his arm. He now sat on top of it, staring at her.

"Well?" he said. "I thought I told you to leave."

"You told me to fix my links," Oliviari said, amazed that he cared about that conversation. "Look, we're wasting valuable time here—"

"No," he said, "we're not. You've been acting strangely all day. You're one of the few people I've never worked with before on the medical team, and now you claim that one of our runners has died from an obscure variation on a cold virus that hasn't been

seen outside some disappeared scientist's lab. Sorry,
Ms. Ramos, but I see no reason to believe you."

"I don't suppose you do," Oliviari said. "But—"

"No buts." He slid forward on the desk and dangled
his legs off the edge. "You're part of the plan,
aren't you?"

"Plan?"

"To ruin the marathon. First there's the body, then
the enforced isolation, and now this, a fake quaran-
tine. Who was supposed to have planted this virus?
Tey herself?"

"Look," Oliviari said. "I don't know about any of
this other stuff, but I do know this virus. If we don't
act quickly, a lot of people could die."

"I read about it too," Tokagawa said. "It's rare, it's
essentially man-made, and it hasn't been seen in this
part of galaxy. Not ever. So unless you give me one
good reason to believe you, I'm going to treat this
infection the way I treat all viral infections. I'm going
to put people in our decon unit just as a precaution,
and then we're going to zap the things away, like
we've been doing for more than a century."

"Zap them, and they'll get worse."

"If they've got Tey," Tokagawa said. "But they
can't have Tey, can they?"

Oliviari took a deep breath. She had known when
she told Klein about this that she had little hope of
remaining undercover.

"There's a really good chance that's exactly what
they have," she said. "I—"

"Really good? What's that? Point one percent?"

"Let me finish." She kept her voice as calm as she
could. She was getting angry at all the time he was
wasting. "You're right. I have been acting strangely.
I'm a Tracker. I've been assigned the Frieda Tey case,
and I have good reason to believe she's been participating in this marathon for years."

"Frieda Tey? The woman who butchered hundreds

of people for science? She would run in the Moon Marathon?" He shook his head.

Oliviari wasn't going to fight his skepticism point by point. There wasn't time. "I have been on this case for years. I've been following a lot of leads, and they all brought me here. There are three women who could be Frieda Tey. I ruled out two this afternoon, while I was in the medical tent."

"How?" he asked.

She made herself remain calm. The last thing she wanted to do was admit to her illegal DNA scans. "Look and voice mostly."

"That's not enough, and you know it. You need fingerprints, retinal scans, maybe even permission for DNA scans. You can't be sure—"

"No, I can't be sure. But I felt like I had enough to rule them out," Oliviari said. "That leaves only one woman and she was my prime suspect anyway. I'd been trying to get appointments with her for months, but she kept canceling. The marathon was my back-up."

"You wanted an appointment?" He frowned. "I thought you were a Tracker. Couldn't you spy or something?"

"There's only so much you can do from a distance," she said, hoping he wouldn't push her any harder.

"You think Frieda Tey is here," he said.

"I think the virus confirms it." A shiver ran through Oliviari. This one had nothing to do with the conversation. It had come from inside her. She wondered if the illness was finally manifesting itself.

"Of course, and I suppose you saw her, and were about to arrest her when this whole problem came up."

Oliviari didn't like the sarcasm in his voice. "I wish it had been that easy. She's the one woman I didn't see. Maybe releasing the virus had been her plan all along. Maybe she was scoping this place out in the previous runs, trying to see whether it would work for her."

"You think she's experimenting with us?"

"I don't know," Oliviari said. "The virus's presence actually makes no sense at all."

Something in her voice seemed to have caught him. He frowned. "You actually believe this."

"Yes," she said.

"Okay," he said. "I'll bite. If Frieda Tey has been around the marathon for a few years, I'd know her. Who would I know her as?"

"One of your top runners," Oliviari said. "Jane Zweig."

22

Rabinowitz had been a good Retrieval Artist. His research seemed to be quite thorough, but his notes were sketchy. He didn't write down anything that anyone else could trace.

At least, that was Flint's first impression as he went through the files Wagner had given him on the handheld. Flint hadn't merged the hand-held's files with any of his systems, and he wouldn't until he was certain that no bugs or traps were buried inside.

But the hand-held itself posed no dangers; Flint started looking through it the moment Wagner left his office.

Before Wagner left, he downloaded funds to one of Flint's many accounts. Flint gave Wagner a paper business card with the account number embedded in it and an identification number written across it.

The ID number was mostly for show; each account was tied to a different client. Flint moved money through more than a dozen of them before he put the money in his main account. With the way things were changing, he was beginning to wonder if a dozen accounts were enough. So many bugs and spies in the systems, he suspected someone could track everything he did, if they wanted to.

He didn't want people to track the names of his

clients nor did he want his clients to be able to use his accounts to track his own monies. The last thing he needed was for a Tracker to pretend to be a client, then trace all of Flint's movements through his finances.

Flint sat at his desk, propped his feet on one side, and leaned back, reading the hand-held. His first scanning of Rabinowitz's notes made for interesting reading. Rabinowitz completely ignored the issue of Tey's guilt or innocence. Like any good Retrieval Artist, he focused on finding the Disappeared first, probably feeling that evidence about her crime would appear at the same time.

He spent weeks—Flint couldn't tell how many from the notes—looking at her initial disappearance, and concluded that she planned it herself, without going through a disappearance company.

But she left a lot of false trails, including two co-workers who disappeared with her, both of whom met her physical description, and both of whom used disappearance companies to help them escape.

Rabinowitz, with typical reticence, didn't comment on the other women's disappearance, but those extra cases made Flint uneasy. Either they thought they had something to hide as well, or they owed Tey.

The security screen slid into his desk, as it was programmed to do when it wasn't monitoring anything. Still, the movement of the screen startled him.

He hit the lock on the doors, realizing that he hadn't been paying enough attention to his surroundings as he read.

But this was the first time he had ever read another Retrieval Artist's notes. He'd seen a few of Paloma's reports—she left ones that breached no confidences, mostly insurance records from Disappeareds who had died while missing—but he'd never before had a chance to look at actual notes.

They were terse and fascinating. He was able to follow them only because Paloma had trained him well.

Rabinowitz had looked at a lot of the false clues Tey had left, and ignored most of them. A few he had followed to their logical limit, such as the ones with the similar Disappeareds. Those women had both been found by a Tracker named Oliviari, whose reports on those cases were also in Rabinowitz's files.

Oliviari had turned those Disappeareds over to Earth Alliance, and the women had been prosecuted as coconspirators in the case of the dome deaths. They had received consecutive terms of life in prison for each death.

There were hints in the records that Tey wouldn't be considered for life; that she would be tried in the nearest jurisdiction with a death penalty. Apparently, the thinking was that she was too dangerous to let live—even if she were in prison.

Flint frowned and pulled his feet off the desk. He stretched and realized he hadn't had dinner. He and Wagner had been talking too long.

But Flint wasn't really hungry yet. He wanted to finish scanning Rabinowitz's files before getting himself a meal.

He also had to figure out what to do with the handheld. He needed to store it, because he didn't want to risk carrying it with him.

He continued to scroll through Rabinowitz's notes. Rabinowitz had taken a step back from the case. He'd obviously followed enough leads to learn that anomalies told him more than common events.

Rabinowitz thought that Frieda Tey's father was the key. The man had changed his will a few years before he died. Up until that point, the will had put Tey's money in trust until she reappeared or until her heirs had been located. No one was to start a search for her for one hundred years after her father's death,

probably to give her time to live out her life in relative safety.

Then her father had abruptly changed the will. Tey
would get his fortune once her name was cleared. That
had happened two years before the father's death, and
Rabinowitz could see no obvious reason for the
change.

The only thing, he postulated, was that somehow
Tey had gotten hold of her father, and the old man
had promised to help her. They had been close once,
and the old man had believed in her innocence from
the very beginning.

Flint opened the attached documents. The attach-
ments contained copies of the both wills, the notes
and documents surrounding those papers, mostly
drafted by Justinian Wagner, and a certification,
sought by WSX, that the father had been in sound
mind when he had completed the new will.

Apparently the Wagners had thought the new will
odd as well.

Flint flicked back to the main file. As he did, his
perimeter alarm went off.

He cursed. He didn't want the distraction now. He
finally had something to keep himself occupied. Even
if he didn't go far with this case, he was learning a lot
about methods, about choices, and about ways to track
a Disappeared.

The screen came up from his desk, revealing the
perimeter around the office. An airlimo—looking sus-
piciously like Wagner's—drove down the same street
that the previous limo had driven away on. Had the
driver come back to check up on Flint? Or had WSX
sent someone else, perhaps to tell him to ignore anything that Ignatius Wagner had said?

Finally the license came into view and Flint ran it.
It was the same limo. He had the security system pull
down the window's tints as well. Inside the limo,
Wagner was arguing heatedly with his driver.

Interesting. Flint took the hand-held into the back room and set it inside one of the locking file cabinets. He wasn't willing to give the hand-held back, even if Wagner had changed his mind about the case. Flint wanted to study more of Rabinowitz's methodology.

Flint returned to the front. Wagner was already out of the airlimo and heading toward the building at a full run.

Flint frowned. Wagner looked concerned, almost upset. He hadn't been gone very long. Flint had no idea what could have changed.

He quietly unlocked the system, and as Wagner stopped outside the door, raising his hand to knock, Flint had the system ease the door open.

Wagner peered inside. "Flint?"

"Sitting right where you left me." He put his feet on the desk for effect.

Wagner stepped inside, and looked startled once again. Apparently he still wasn't used to having his links cut off.

"I don't suppose you hurried back because you missed me," Flint said.

Wagner shook his head, his expression serious, as though Flint's joke was inappropriate.

"I don't suppose you heard today's news?" Wagner asked.

"Everything up until six o'clock." Flint pressed the key that controlled the door. It swung shut. "What's happened now?"

"A woman died at the Moon Marathon."

Flint shrugged. That happened almost every year. He'd even had the misfortune to tag along on one of those cases during his second year in the academy. The death had been easily solved—the runner had fallen, punctured her suit, and died before anyone could reach her.

"How does that concern me?" he asked.

Wagner took a step deeper into the office. "I'm

assuming you're linked somehow. You just shut off my access to the news."

"I know," Flint said, referring to Wagner's second statement and ignoring his first.

"The woman who died—they think she was murdered." Wagner had reached the desk. He extended his hands, as if they could speak for him. "She—Rabinowitz visited four women before he died. They were his last interviews. She was one of them."

Flint put his feet down. "You think she's connected somehow?"

"I'm wondering if she died of the same thing he did." Wagner rubbed his hands together. "They're not releasing what killed her, but if she had cold symptoms before she started to run—"

"The marathon's system should have caught that, and kept her off the course."

"Unless she had a way around it," Wagner said.

"Around the system?"

Wagner nodded. "She was influential in the athletic community here in Armstrong, and she was one of their main runners. They might have bent the rules for her."

"If that's the case, then the marathon committee will have a lot to answer for."

"Don't you see, though?" Wagner leaned on the desk, making the security screen wobble. "If she died of the same disease, we're all in trouble."

"But she couldn't have contracted it when he did," Flint said. "She'd be dead already."

"What if she got it from him?" Wagner said.

Flint felt cold. If this was a slower-moving version of the virus that killed everyone in Tey's research colony, then Flint didn't like the odds.

"I'll make a few calls," he said, "and see what I can find out."

The police might not talk to him, but if he could prove that he had a connected case, they might. Or at least a few officers in the precinct might. He didn't really want to go through official channels.

"What was her name, so that I'm not cross-checking all this stuff myself?" Flint asked.

"Zweig," Wagner said, as if Flint had known the woman. "Jane Zweig."

Flint nodded. "I'll do what I can, but I'm not going to make any promises. Sometimes cases like this take time."

"That's what I'm afraid of," Wagner said. "I'm not sure how much time we have left."

23

After Swann left, DeRicci put the image of the race back on the main wall. No one was crossing the finish line, but volunteers remained Outside, staring at the horizon. Obviously more runners were out there. DeRicci just didn't know how to use this system to find out how many runners were left.

The caffeine high was wearing off, leaving her lethargic. She'd asked the unis to bring her more coffee and something to eat when they brought the next runner in here. She actually hoped the food would arrive first. She needed to be as alert as possible when she spoke to the rest of the team.

Before they came back, she contacted van der Ketting. She wanted him to figure out the time lapse between Zweig's disappearance behind that camera and Swann's appearance on it.

DeRicci also wanted him to examine the Swann footage to see if he could find any suspicious movements around that rock.

She had just finished giving instructions to van der Ketting when the door opened. One of the unis came in, carrying a pot of coffee and a tray covered with pastries.

"Sorry," he said as he set everything on the table. "They ran out of sandwiches already. It's going to be a mess pretty soon."

DeRicci eyed the pastries. They looked like they were made with real flour and sugar. Some had a glaze, and others had real fruit centers.

"Oh, I don't mind not having a sandwich," she said. A plateful of pastries would take her through the night comfortably. She grabbed one of the glazed. It was still warm.

Heaven.

"Where's the mess?" she asked.

"In that banquet hall. They had to take out the round tables that were scattered around the floor, put in banquet tables, pushing them against the wall and placing the food on them. There aren't enough chairs, so a lot of people are sitting on the floor to eat. I haven't heard that much complaining in my entire life. I thought these people were healthy."

"Physically healthy," DeRicci said. "Not mentally healthy."

The uni grinned at her. "Or at least we'd like to think that to justify all our pastries."

She grinned back. She would have to learn his name. The problem was that she'd been talking to him all afternoon, and hadn't let on that she didn't know. Now she'd have to do the socially awkward thing and admit that she had no idea who he was.

"I have the next interview outside," he said. "He's a bit testy. He's eaten and everything, but I guess he was looking forward to something else this evening— maybe some kind of press recognition or a big party or something. He's not real cooperative."

"I'll take care of him," DeRicci said.

The uni grinned. "Yeah, I bet you will."

He grabbed a pastry with too much frosting, and carried it toward the door. As he did, DeRicci's private link pinged.

She held up a hand.

"Hold on," she said. "Don't go yet."

She might need him, especially if this message was coming from Gumiela.

The link pinged again, and then a message scrolled across her eye, something that startled her. She thought she had that function shut off.

Noelle:

Contact me immediately.

Ethan Broduer
Coroner, Armstrong City Division

DeRicci looked at the uni. He was frowning at her.

"Keep the next interview out there for a few minutes," she said. "Offer him a doughnut."

The uni came back to the table and grabbed a napkin. "Mind if I take a few for the guys working the front?"

"Go ahead." The message scrolled across her eye again, only this time the words were flashing red.

Ethan, that irritating son of a bitch. Why did her case get assigned to him, anyway?

The uni took five pastries and carried them before him as if they were made of glass. He had trouble opening the door, but he managed.

DeRicci took a bite of her pastry, knowing she probably wouldn't get to the rest of it until much later. Then she poured herself a cup of coffee.

The message scrolled past a third time, every other letter flashing neon. This thing was designed to give her a headache. When this case was over, she was going to the police links department and ask how to shut the eyescroll off permanently.

She got up and went to the wall screen. She shoved her right fist into it, letting the chip in her middle knuckle establish a police band link. The police band link immediately disabled the other system, knocking out any attempts to listen in—at least if the other system were not as sophisticated as the police system, which didn't always happen.

At this moment, she didn't really care for the niceties. She just wanted the eyescroll to stop, and she knew from past experience that it wouldn't until she got in direct verbal contact with the message sender.

The message scrolled again. All of the letters flashed neon this time. And Ethan's name bounced up and down, as if it were doing a special little dance.

"Stop," DeRicci muttered, and linked directly to the coroner's office.

A visual popped up on the wall. Some flunky, hand on chin, reading something he wasn't supposed to. He looked startled when DeRicci's face appeared on his screen.

"Get Broduer," she snapped.

The man looked at her.

"Now!"

He got up so fast that she heard a clang. His chair had toppled over. He scrambled away from the camera, leaving the empty room for her to look at.

Not that there was much to see. A few light posters on the back wall, changing according to the concerts they were advertising. A sink, with all sorts of bottles around it. Some old-fashioned labels, and neatly wrapped see-through bundles of what looked like clothing.

Then the scene wavered, and Broduer's face covered the wall. Magnified two hundred times, he looked scary. If she wanted to, she could see inside his pores.

"Noelle." His baritone fondled her name, and she felt a slight shudder go through her. Most of the women on the force found him attractive. She had no idea why she didn't.

The message scrolled again. This time all of the letters bounced, and she swore she saw some glitter mingled in the red neon.

"Shut off your damn message."

"Message . . . ? Oh! You came through the public links." He squinched his features together—frowns should not have been that big either—and the scrolling stopped.

Her eye hurt. She rubbed it, sure that a headache would come now, whether she wanted it to or not.

"Yes, I came through the public links," she said, letting all her bad temper emerge in her voice. "I'm in the field, remember?"

It was difficult to respond visually on private links. DeRicci actually couldn't. She couldn't afford the upgrade, and the First Detective Unit provided audio and text links only.

"Sorry. I've had a busy day. Haven't been able to keep up with your schedule." He spoke lightly, as if they were having a dinner party conversation.

"Yeah, well, I have a couple of hundred people to interview, so you want to make this quick?"

The humor left his face. "You're going to want to hear this, Noelle."

"I figured as much." She powered down the screen, making his head life-size. There was only so much Broduer that she could take. "You got a time of death for me?"

"I have a number of things," he said, "all of them important, but none more important than the last."

Great. Cryptic talk. That was just what she needed.

"I want you to take notes."

"You have the notes," she said. "Why do I have to take them?"

"Because you won't remember everything."

"Sure I will." She tried not to bristle more than she already had. As if she wouldn't be able to keep track. She had been a cop longer than he had. She always kept track of things.

"Trust me on this one. Just record or something."

She sighed, tapped yet another record chip, and pulled over a chair. "Okay. I'm ready to go, sir."

"And none of the 'sir,' crap, Noelle. This is serious."

She picked up her coffee as well. It saved her from answering him directly. "I don't have a lot of time here, Broduer."

He nodded. "All right. First, cause of death: oxygen deprivation, just like you thought."

"No surprise there," DeRicci said.

"Well, there is, but I'm not going to get to that yet."

She hated it when he was being mysterious. Sometimes she thought he did it only to anger her, but she'd heard from her colleagues that he did it to them as well. He also did it in court, which made him a good witness, so there were trade-offs.

"Second," he said. "Time of death: Can't pinpoint it to the moment, but I would say thirty-six to forty-eight hours ago."

"What?" DeRicci asked. "I've got a vid of her on the course, not half an hour before the body was found."

He held up a hand to silence her. The movement wasn't that effective on the smaller screen, but she shut up anyway. If he didn't think that part was shocking, then she wasn't sure what he thought would be.

"Third," he said, "she was murdered. I can tell you that for certain."

"Even with oxygen deprivation?" DeRicci had thought that would make murder harder to prove, no matter what else they found. Everyone knew that suits failed. She thought it would be harder to show that someone could make a suit fail on purpose.

"Even with oxygen deprivation," he said. "She wasn't wearing that environmental suit when she died."

DeRicci felt the pastry she'd eaten turn in her stomach. "Excuse me?"

"The suit," he said as if he were speaking to a child. "It had been put on after death."

"The suit didn't kill her?"

"Not unless someone held it over her nose and mouth for five minutes. And even then, I doubt it, since we didn't find any fibers in her throat and lungs."

He sounded annoyed that she had questioned him.

"What did you find?" she asked.

"I'm telling you that," he said.

"In her throat and lungs," DeRicci said, wishing she could just grab his notes from him.

"Nothing," he said. "Exactly what you'd expect if she were in an airlock or spaceship and someone shut off the oxygen. No fibers, no little pieces of suit. She thrashed and struggled and bit her tongue, but she didn't do any of that in a suit. In fact, she had the bruises to prove she wasn't wearing a suit."

DeRicci cursed to herself. She had already thought that part of this death had been staged. In order for the body to have rigor, someone else in the same suit had to pick up the singlet—probably the murderer. But she hadn't realized that Zweig hadn't even been wearing a suit when she died.

"So," Broduer said, "this was staged and planned to the last detail. If whoever did it had a few more minutes, they would have been able to burst that visor and the body would have destroyed most of the evidence. We probably wouldn't have even caught the staging."

DeRicci thought of the clean boots, the lack of dirt-fall pattern. "We might have," she said.

He shook his head, but he clearly didn't want to argue with her. "The staged part of this was important, but not the most important reason for busting that visor."

"What do you mean?"

"If the body had depressurized, it would have swollen to three times its normal size and then leaked fluids. Most trace evidence would have been ruined.

And that's if we found her after the swelling had gone down and the body had mummified."

"Yeah," DeRicci said. She'd seen more of those than he had.

"We would never have done an ID."

"Why ID her?" DeRicci asked. "We know who she was."

"We know who someone wanted us to think she was," Broduer said. "I actually got an expedited warrant. I had the goods for it. First time ever, in fifteen years."

DeRicci gripped her coffee mug so hard the plastic groaned in protest. She set the mug down on the floor. "What do you mean, an expedited warrant?"

"For a DNA ID. The fingerprints and retinal scan did not match Jane Zweig's. I thought maybe we had bad information, but the death was so suspicious and so high-profile, I knew I could get a judge to hurry a DNA. And I was right."

He sounded pleased with that. She might have been too, if she weren't reeling from the thought that the body didn't belong to Jane Zweig.

"What did the DNA show?" DeRicci asked.

"Well, a couple of interesting things. First, we learned that we had no DNA for Jane Zweig. It wasn't on file anywhere. There wasn't even anything with any of the medical units in the city, and that's just plain weird. I've never encountered that before."

DeRicci had, but only with people who later turned out to be Disappeareds. She didn't say that, though, wanting to hear his analysis.

"But that was only a minor setback," he said, "because we know now that the body didn't belong to Zweig."

"For certain?" DeRicci asked.

"For certain," he said.

That changed everything. Time of death had already

screwed DeRicci around, but changing the victim changed motivation and everything else.

She hoped that Broduer had the dead woman's name. If he didn't, DeRicci's investigation had just gotten more difficult.

"Who is she, then?" DeRicci asked.

"Eve Mayoux," he said. "Longtime resident of Armstrong. Reported missing by her employer just this morning."

"Eve Mayoux?" DeRicci asked. "Should I know that name?"

He shook his head. "Lived alone. Hardly any friends. Never missed a day of work until today."

"What did she do?"

"She worked in the Growing Pits," he said.

The Growing Pits were what the residents of Armstrong called the greenhouses that clustered on the east side of the dome.

"She worked Outside?" DeRicci asked.

"Every day," he said. "She was a master gardener. She knew more about oxygen deprivation and one-sixth gravity than most people learn in their lifetime."

"So she would never have died that way," DeRicci said. "Not by accident."

"That's right, sweetheart," he said, and she didn't even get irritated at him for the endearment. "Eve Mayoux may just be the secret to your entire investigation."

24

Tokagawa laughed. "Jane Zweig? Of Extreme Enterprises? The woman who likes to court the media? You think she's a Disappeared?"

Oliviari's legs ached. It was getting harder to lean against this wall. She pushed herself against it, making certain that she kept her balance.

"Yes," she said. "I believe Jane Zweig is Frieda Tey. She has the right build and similar features. Her voice sounds right."

"That's not enough." His smile faded. He levered himself off the desk. "You're wasting my time."

"No, I'm not," Oliviari said. "I had five different appointments with Zweig. She canceled all of them."

"She probably didn't want a Tracker coming to her office," Tokagawa said.

"I didn't use my real name. I had valid reasons for seeing her. None of them worked out. The marathon was my backup."

"Backup for what?" He crossed his arms. He hadn't moved away from the desk.

"There are a few things I need to prove that she's Frieda Tey. Exactly what you mentioned. Fingerprints. Retinal scans. DNA, with her permission. I figured I'd be able to get at least one of those if I saw her face-to-face."

He frowned. "You think this woman was a Disappeared, and you were just going to ask her for some DNA? No Disappeared would do that."

Oliviari felt the tension in her shoulders grow. Why was he using past tense? It seemed odd.

"Of course not," Oliviari said. "But fingerprints aren't hard to get. And a refusal on any one of those things would take me one step closer to proving she's a Disappeared."

"Anyone might refuse you. People who know the law would refuse you. *I* would refuse you."

Oliviari smiled at him. She made sure the smile was a cold one. "Maybe you're a Disappeared, Dr. Tokagawa."

He did not smile in return. "Is that how you people do your jobs? You accuse innocent people?"

She shook her head. "I've spent years on Frieda Tey's trail, and it has led to this marathon. The virus is a confirmation, as I said. If you look at it and compare it to the Tey virus that's in the medical files, you'll see that I'm right."

"How would you have confirmed Tey's identity here? You expected to get fingerprints?"

Time to be honest. It was the only way he would believe her. "I hoped to be on the medical teams. I'd have access to all the medical records from the participants, and it would give me a legal way to compare the DNA."

"But I took that away from you." His eyebrows rose, as if her comment suddenly explained her behavior.

"So I came in here and started working with the runners who'd left the field."

"Taking their suits and their diagnostics." He tilted his head, looking at her sideways. "Would you have taken illegal DNA then, Ms. Oliviari?"

She wasn't going to admit that she already had.

"When I encountered Zweig, I planned to take her suit to the closet myself. Whatever the suit revealed would help me."

It wasn't quite an admission, but it was close enough.

"But you didn't encounter Zweig, did you?"

Oliviari shook her head. "I don't know why, either. I thought she always finished in the top ten percent."

"She used to." He paused, studying her. No one had ever examined her this closely before. She wondered if this was how the people she tracked felt when she found them.

"But?" Oliviari asked.

"But," he said slowly, "she didn't finish the race today."

Another chill ran through Oliviari. She rubbed her hands over her bare arms. The skin was covered in gooseflesh.

"Why not?" she asked, although she knew why. It was obvious now. It was the reason he used past tense, the reason that Team Two's transmissions were cut off.

"Jane Zweig died between miles five and six today," he said. "She couldn't have planted any virus here."

Oliviari stopped rubbing her arms. "Jane Zweig is your murder victim?"

He straightened his shoulders. "Not my victim," he said. "But maybe yours?"

Oliviari stared at him. Why would he suspect her? And then her sluggish mind kicked into gear. Of course, she had known Zweig. She believed Zweig was Tey.

Tokagawa stood up. "I believe I'll let the police know that we have a Tracker here, and the Tracker thought the dead woman was a mass murderer. Trackers occasionally kill their prey, don't they? Especially when they believe that the prey might not get the right punishment?"

A shudder ran through Oliviari. "It's not legal for us to do that."

"You're already operating illegally," he said. "You're not registered with the city, and you're here under false pretenses. Seems like the perfect setup for murder."

"I was on the staging area the entire time. I never got near her, and I certainly didn't go near miles five and six." Oliviari shuddered again. "Check the information if you have to."

"I won't," he said, "but I'm sure the police will."

He started for the door. She stepped in front of him.

"Move," he said.

"No," she said. "You're going to look at the virus first."

"I asked you to give me a good reason to believe you," he said. "You haven't. Instead, you gave me a good reason why one of my friends died out there today. You killed her."

"You were friends with Frieda Tey?"

"I was friends with Jane Zweig. I've known her for years. We used to make trial runs together on this very course."

"And you talked about what? Medicine?"

"My practice." He looked pointedly at the door.

"And the wonderful power of the human body? How it can and cannot compete against all those aliens out there?"

His eyes narrowed. "Sometimes."

"She used to say that it would take a lot of work to find out the limits of human potential, but now was the time to discover it. We had to learn it before they did, so that we could defend ourselves against them. We're so vulnerable in space, partly because we're outgoing. We colonize and that scares some of the aliens. That puts them at risk, and she felt it was only a matter of time before they put us at risk."

"You did talk to Jane," he said.

Oliviari shook her head. "I've read all of Frieda Tey's writings, and I saw all the recorded versions of her speeches. I've also spoken to her friends, relatives, and colleagues. They said she wanted to know what it was that made us human, how extreme situations changed us, and whether or not we could adapt to dangerous environments."

He bit his lower lip, as if he were trying not to speak. She tried not to feel time passing, how each minute, each second might cost a life. If she didn't convince him, she might lose more than a few minutes. She might lose hours to police and interviews and possible arrest.

"Frieda Tey couched all of these things in scientific terms. She believed that scientific methods would tell her more about people than people could. She used biology and psychology as well as the hard sciences to test people's limits. She felt that if scientific rigor were applied to alien-human relations, maybe, just maybe, humans would stand a better chance in this universe."

He swallowed so hard that Oliviari saw his Adam's apple bob. "I don't understand," he said. "If she cared about all of that, why would she kill so many people?"

"Her research assistants claimed it was accidental, and that's always been her defense." Another shudder ran through Oliviari. "But I believe that the experiment was purposeful. Tey knew that people would die. She expected that. She just didn't expect all of them to."

He shook his head. "That makes no sense."

"There was a decon unit in the dome," Oliviari said. "Supposedly it was there for entering and exiting. The decon unit malfunctioned early—its makers say it was tampered with, since it had been designed to cope with a variety of viruses and should have been able to handle the mutating Tey. The colonists tried to use it to get rid of the virus, but it didn't work."

"So?" he asked.

"So," she said, "I think Tey wanted to see how ingenious they all were. The tools needed to fix the decon unit were inside the dome, but the colonists lacked the expertise. Tey figured they would rise to the occasion, but they never did. Once they figured out that the units didn't work, and people were getting sicker, the colonists begged her to let them out of the dome. She didn't."

"Why would anyone do that?" he asked.

"I think she believed that if she hadn't been there, they would have found the solution." Oliviari had read her papers. "She thought that they relied on her as a crutch instead of doing the work themselves."

He nodded, just once, and then seemed to catch himself. He was beginning to understand. Oliviari hoped she could hold him. She needed him to understand.

"Was she right?" he asked.

"No," Oliviari said. "People have different skills. We think differently. And just because we're in a bad situation, we don't all respond smartly or heroically. It's a mistake to believe that we will. Frieda Tey never really studied human interaction. She read a lot of psychological theory, but that's not the same as observing people."

"You observe people." His comment was dry.

"It's my job." Oliviari tried not to sound panicked. The chills were gone now, and she was getting hot.

"Which means you know more than scientists."

"In this one area," she said. "I know that in desperate situations, you need a leader, someone who is willing to take risks, someone who is willing to try."

"You don't believe one will rise up?"

"Sure," she said. "But that doesn't mean the one who rises up will be capable. Tey was right about one thing: Her sample size was too small."

He shook his head. "She wouldn't. Jane wasn't that way. She valued human life."

"I'm not saying she didn't," Oliviari said. "Frieda Tey did too."

"She couldn't," he said. "Not and kill people like that."

"You've done triage, haven't you, Dr. Tokagawa?"

He swallowed again. The sound echoed in the tiny room.

"It's the same principle," Oliviari said. "You can't save everyone, so you sacrifice the ones who have no real chance, to do what you can for the ones who have a chance."

"It's not at all the same," he said. "Triage is for the injured. You're talking about healthy people dying of a disease someone gave them, and then watched them die."

"She gave them the disease," Oliviari said, "and she gave them the tools to save themselves."

His mouth opened slightly. If she didn't push too hard, she might convince him. The key was finding the right words, which would be hard, because her mind was becoming sluggish.

She said, "I'm pretty sure Frieda Tey thought that she would be able to use what she had learned to prove that humans could react well under stress, that we could save ourselves no matter what the problem."

"It's not the same," he said again.

"You and I don't think so," Oliviari said. "But you should have read some of her work published before she disappeared. She believed that sacrifices and failures were necessary for learning. She had good, logical arguments. She even used the laws we have with some of the aliens. We sacrifice each other all the time for the right to trade and to keep the peace."

"But to do this." He shook his head again. "No one sane could do this."

A trickle of sweat ran down Oliviari's temple. "We'd like to believe that."

He frowned at her.

"But Frieda Tey always seemed sane. Everyone said so. You say the same thing about Jane Zweig, even though you've had some of these same conversations."

He moved his head slightly from side to side, a head shake, even though he probably didn't realize he was doing it.

Oliviari winced. She was losing strength, and she didn't dare. She had to be able to keep arguing to get him on her side.

Then he closed his mouth. "Let me compare the viruses."

"I have them on a hand-held."

He shook his head. "I have to do it myself."

She wanted to argue, but she understood why he wanted to. She would have done the same. "All right."

"And I have to tell the police about you," he said.

"I know." Another bead of sweat ran down her face. "But do it after you check on the viruses. Because I'm probably the only one here who has studied this virus extensively, and I think I know how to stop it."

"We can learn."

Oliviari nodded. "Of course you can. But here's the other mistake that Frieda Tey made. This virus moves quickly, and it's already infected this tent. Your time is limited."

"You're saying they didn't have time to figure out how to save themselves?"

"Yes," she said. "And if we're not careful, we might not have time either."

"I don't scare easily, Ms. Oliviari."

She gave him a small smile. "Neither do I," she said. "And right now, I'm about as scared as I can get."

25

The moment Wagner left, Flint pulled up another screen. He scanned for news reports about the Moon Marathon. Most told him who the winner was (as if he cared) and the time in which she completed the course. Only one link led him to the death story, and it wasn't very big.

Flint followed it to find a vid of Andrea Gumiela giving a prolonged news conference about the death. He frowned when he saw her standing at the podium, her red hair easing out of its bun. She looked frazzled, even though he wasn't certain she had been.

Gumiela had given him a lot of trouble when she had been his boss: Her orders had been contradictory, and her ambition had always been at the expense of others. But she had known how to manipulate the media. That had been one of her greatest strengths.

Gumiela made a careful statement. She said that a woman named Jane Zweig, head of Extreme Enterprises, had been killed at the Moon Marathon, and implied that Zweig's death was her own fault.

But Flint had listened to Gumiela for years. He knew she would never have given a press conference if the situation weren't a difficult one. She would never have used the word *killed* if she weren't worried that the media would catch her later for saying simply that Jane Zweig had died.

Fortunately for Gumiela, the press wasn't on its toes. Flint suspected the best reporters were elsewhere, perhaps even at the marathon site, covering the event Outside.

Because if the reporters had known what they were doing, they would have asked Gumiela why she was giving a press conference when the police department hadn't done so for past marathon deaths. They would also have asked her about the cause of death—*killed* wasn't quite *murdered,* but it was still a loaded word. And finally, they would have asked why the head of the First Detective Unit, the place that usually handled homicides, had taken over what should have been a routine investigation.

Gumiela had gotten off easily, and at the end of the vid, it was obvious she knew it. She walked away from the podium, her shoulders actually sagging with relief.

Flint wondered why Rabinowitz had been in touch with Zweig, what a place like Extreme Enterprises had to do with Frieda Tey. Had Rabinowitz thought that Tey used the organization to leave the Moon?

Flint left the screen up, but set it on clear so that the edges and the material weren't visible. He could see the door through it. Nothing registered on the screen at the moment, but it would launch into life if the police held another press conference or if the words *Moon Marathon* or *Jane Zweig* were mentioned in any netcast.

He grabbed the hand-held and went through Rabinowitz's files. There was no easy way to search them— Rabinowitz hadn't indexed them—and there were a lot of odd links.

Rabinowitz had found some kind of connection between Frieda Tey and Jane Zweig; otherwise he wouldn't have tried to interview Zweig. Due to the sketchy nature of his notes, of course, he didn't make that connection clear.

Usually a Retrieval Artist didn't interview anyone

about the Disappeared. Instead, the Retrieval Artist went to various candidates who might be the Disappeared.

Zweig was an unusual choice. She seemed to be in the public eye. Most Disappeareds tried to avoid that. But most Disappeareds also didn't change their fundamental natures, and Frieda Tey had had a phenomenal ego. She might have thought she could be visible on the Moon, and no one here would have been bright enough to catch her.

Which had been the case, until Rabinowitz showed up.

If that analysis was correct, it explained why he got the virus. Zweig/Tey infected him with the slow-acting version, probably something she had planned long ago in case she got caught, and sent him on his way, so that the disease couldn't be traced to her.

But that didn't explain Zweig/Tey's death. Had she infected herself too? Had the death been accidental? Was that why Gumiela used the word *killed*?

Was she trying to cover up the possibility that a lethal virus was loose in the dome? The only reason she would do that was if the city thought they could contain it.

Flint frowned at the hand-held, looking for clues. First he went to the research articles on the virus itself. They had been written by a variety of people. Some of the articles talked about the Tey virus's scientific implications, and others discussed the social aspects of the experiment that had gone awry.

Rabinowitz had grouped the articles together into a single file, and had made a note at the top: *The same voice.*

Flint squinted at it, frowned, and then realized what Rabinowitz was saying.

He thought the articles had been written by the same person. Tey herself trying to resurrect her reputation? Possible, Flint supposed.

He scanned down the file, his eye catching words and phrases:

We have become complacent. Just because our medical technology can handle the diseases we are familiar with, we believe it able to handle the ones we have not yet encountered. . . .

. . . a reading of human history shows that whenever an isolated group encounters a new virus, the virus decimates the population. Only a select few have immune systems strong enough to survive the onslaught of a brand-new disease. What the Tey virus shows is that we are not immune from the same problems that killed our forefathers in much more hospitable environments. . . .

Flint stopped reading. He scrolled to the bottom of the articles, saw one more note from Rabinowitz—a reminder to check with the various journals and specialized publications to see how they screened their authors—and then Flint closed the file.

He went to the datebook, and saw several appointments, all with women throughout the city.

It took Flint a while to find Jane Zweig on the list. Her appointment was marked *ExEnt*. He had to click on the appointment file itself to find Zweig's name.

His notes, sketchy and incomplete, showed that he had spoken with a lower-level employee, and then with Zweig, who had been dismissive once she found out who he was and what kind of work he had done.

Rabinowitz had managed to get some kind of sample, though whether it was fingerprint, retinal, or DNA, Flint couldn't tell. Since Rabinowitz didn't say, Flint figured it was DNA, which would have been illegal without Zweig's permission.

And it didn't sound, even from these sketchy notes, like Zweig would have given permission.

A DNA sample could be something simple—a strand of hair, a skin cell, a bit of blood or saliva. Blood or saliva would also have passed along a virus.

Flint would have to contact the police. He wondered

if Gumiela would talk to him. She hadn't said a word about his resignation, nor had she acknowledged him the one time they had crossed paths on the street.

She had a low opinion of Retrieval Artists, believing them to be as guilty as the Disappeared they often helped to conceal. If she ever found out what Flint did shortly after he resigned his detective post—how many Disappeareds he had saved—she would consider him a traitor to all she believed in.

If she believed in anything.

He sighed. He couldn't contact Gumiela. She would stall him at best, dismiss him at worst.

He could go through the information office like everyone else, but that wouldn't help him. He was better off going to old friends.

Not many of them would be in a position to know what happened to Zweig, and few of them would try to find out.

But his old partner, Noelle DeRicci, would. They had stayed in touch as best as they could, and more than once she had mentioned how she envied his convictions.

She shared them, but felt that she was too old or too burned-out to try something new. She would never become a Retrieval Artist, although once he had mentioned the idea to her. She had laughed. *I'm not the courageous type, Miles,* she had said.

It had been a lie: She had more courage than he ever would. But she seemed to believe that she had no courage at all. And he wasn't going to argue with someone else's delusions.

He contacted DeRicci on her private link. She didn't answer. Not answering was unusual for most people, but not DeRicci. She thought links were intrusive. If she was driving or interviewing a suspect or sleeping, she would leave her links off.

Most people couldn't stand to be disconnected for

more than a minute. Sometimes Flint thought DeRicci couldn't stand the connection for that long.

He left a message for her, asking her to contact him as soon as her link came back on-line.

Then he contacted the Detective Division. He got Craig Booth, one of the desk sergeants. Flint put the link on holographic visual. Booth's face looked ghostly floating above Flint's desk next to the silent keyboard.

"If it ain't Miles Flint," Booth said.

Flint smiled. "Craig. How've you been?"

"Not so good as you, you dog." Booth's eyes twinkled. "I hear you got more money than God."

"Who told you that?"

"Who needs to tell anybody anything around here? We find it out sideways; you know that."

In other words, he wasn't going to give up his source. Flint had a hunch he knew. DeRicci had probably let it slip, not realizing that Flint didn't like to talk about his finances. He'd told only a few people that his financial situation had improved, mostly so that they wouldn't worry about him now that he had left the force.

"Listen," Flint said, "I've been trying to reach Noelle. Is she on a case?"

"Is she on a case? Oh, man, is she on a case." Booth shook his head. The movement made Flint slightly seasick. Next time, he'd set up the holo parameters to include a person's neck. "She's got the marathon nightmare. I swear they're going to find a way to get that girl outta here one way or another."

Flint frowned. Marathon cases usually went to junior staff, and they certainly wouldn't assign DeRicci to something politically delicate. "Did they give this to her before they knew how the runner died?"

"You ain't forgotten the way it works around here," Booth said. "Noelle rehabs herself, then says something that pisses off someone, and back she goes on the crap list, you know?"

Flint did know. He'd been on part of that ride with her in his last few months as a detective.

"She figured out it was murder, then."

"Well, who else?" Booth answered. Then his grin faded. "You ain't got a media job now, do you?"

If Flint had a media job, then Booth had just violated one of the major rules of his own employment: He'd given out information without approval from upstairs.

"No," Flint said. "I'm a Retrieval Artist now. I'm working on a case that might be related to the marathon case. I need to talk to Noelle."

"You still got a connection to her personal links?"

"Yes," Flint said, "and as usual, they're off."

Booth grinned. "That's our Noelle. I'll let her know you need to talk."

"Listen, Craig," Flint said, "maybe you can answer something for me. Did this Zweig woman die of a virus?"

"While she was running? What're you on, Miles?"

Flint deliberately misunderstood the question. "I'm tracking down some information for a friend. One of his colleagues died of a suspicious virus, and I guess the guy knew Zweig. They'd been together just before she died. So I'm checking up on it."

"A virus?" Booth frowned. "I think we'da heard. The body's back here, but I know for a fact no one in the medical examiner's office'll talk to an outsider, even if he used to be an insider, you know."

"I know," Flint said.

"So I'll see if I can flag DeRicci for you. It might be a few days. I think this case is gonna take every moment she's got."

"If I'm right about this virus," Flint said, "we don't have a few days. Can you send her a message down the emergency links?"

"That's only for in-house."

"I know." Flint made sure his voice was calm, although he was losing patience. Of course he knew that the emergency links were only for police messages. He used to have those links himself. "I'm not kidding on this one, Craig. If this virus is actually in Armstrong, we're in serious trouble."

"Thought you said some guy died of it."

"And right now, it's being seen as an isolated case. It's pretty easy to overlook in its early stages." He had no idea if that was true, but it sounded good. "If we overlook it too much, then it'll get away from us."

Booth took in a breath so sharp that the air whistled through his teeth. "You're not saying what I think you're saying?"

Flint nodded. The police had been trained in the possibilities of epidemics in the dome every year. An epidemic was one of the city's greatest fears.

"Crap. I'll see what I can dig up for you. They ain't gonna tell me much, but I know they talk to Noelle. She know how to get to you?"

"My links are the same," Flint said, just in case Booth managed to find out the information on his own.

"You got it," Booth said. "You'll hear from someone in no more than an hour or two. That work?"

"It'll have to," Flint said.

Booth nodded; then his head vanished from Flint's desk. Flint felt disconcerted, and it wasn't just from the loss of Booth's ghostly presence.

DeRicci was still getting assigned to the worst cases, and doing one of the best jobs on the force.

Flint hoped Wagner was wrong about the virus. Because if he wasn't, DeRicci had probably been exposed to it.

DeRicci and everyone in the medical examiner's office. People Flint knew. People he cared about.

People who might not know what they were up against, until it was too late.

26

Eve Mayoux might have been the secret to DeRicci's entire investigation, as Broduer had said, but at the moment, the poor dead woman had thrown the entire investigation off track. All the interviews that DeRicci and her colleagues had done would have to be redone. And all of the work that the forensics team had put together—including the work that van der Ketting had done at DeRicci's direction—would have to be reexamined with the new victim in mind.

After DeRicci ended her conversation with Broduer, she sat alone for several minutes in the bungalow, sipping her now-cold coffee. Her hands were shaking, but she doubted that was from the caffeine.

It was from stress.

She wiped a hand over her face. The room felt close. She had never completely cooled down after she had taken off her environmental suit, and her skin felt too warm now.

Maybe someday she would get enough sleep and she would know what it felt like to be healthy. She probably hadn't been in years.

DeRicci grabbed another pastry and stood up. Then she sent a message across the links, instructing everyone who was conducting an interview to take a break. She sent the message only, and then she shut down her system. Better to do that than to get the questioning responses, wondering what in the hell she was actually doing.

She wasn't sure what to do. All she knew was that she'd take flak if she didn't shut the interviews down immediately. But she couldn't let the new information out either, not until she knew what it meant.

She knew part of what it meant. It meant that she was dealing with first-degree murder, with a motive that somehow involved the marathon. It meant that the killer had access to the course, and an association with Jane Zweig.

DeRicci hadn't dealt with something like this in years—at least not something human-caused. The alien-caused murders she'd worked on with Miles Flint had been gruesome, but DeRicci had been able to dismiss the horrible nature of the crimes because they had not been committed by people.

For some reason, she felt that people should have the same values as she did, and the main value would be that of preserving human life.

After a moment, she stood and went to the door. She pulled it open to find several detectives inside, talking with the unis.

"Noelle," one of the detectives said. "You can't shut down the investigation. We haven't even gotten close to finishing the interviews. You know what Gumiela said—"

"I know," DeRicci said. "But some new information has come to light that we need to examine before we can go on."

She turned to the uni.

"Get van der Ketting for me," she said.

"Why don't you send for him? I'm pretty sure he's linked up." The uni looked tired and overwhelmed, not at all like the man who had been working with her all day.

"I'm sure he is," DeRicci said. "So you send for him. Tell him to bring all the data he's collected. He and I need to review it."

"What about the rest of us?" the other detective asked. "Shouldn't we be in on this?"

DeRicci shook her head. If she was going to get in trouble anyway, she might as well get in trouble for doing things her own way. "We'll have a meeting in an hour or so, maybe less if van der Ketting and I finish this quickly. Then you'll be briefed on everything."

Without waiting for an answer, she pulled the door closed and leaned on it.

Eve Mayoux, a woman who led a quiet little life, so quiet that no one had noticed she was missing until she had failed to show up for work, had managed to disrupt not only Armstrong's biggest tourist event, but a good percentage of Armstrong's police force.

DeRicci walked back to the table. The last pastry she had taken sat, half-eaten, on the table's plastic surface. Her coffee cup had finger stains along the side, as well as drip stains running from the side of the lip over the handle. She was such a slob, especially when she had other things to think about.

And Broduer's report gave her too much to think about.

Somehow someone had killed Mayoux by taking away her oxygen. If they killed her Outside, they had switched her environmental suits without depressurizing the body. How had that happened?

DeRicci frowned. She had no idea if that had happened or not.

She linked back up with Broduer, going through the public links once again. When the assistant saw her this time, he didn't even greet her. He just fetched Broduer.

Broduer came back, holding his hands up as if they were contaminated. They were covered with blood and bits of tissue, which dripped down the gloves that covered his arms all the way to the elbow.

"I told you everything I know," he said.

"Actually, you didn't." If he was going to be snippy, so was she. "I need to know if she was killed inside the dome or Outside."

"How am I supposed to tell you that?" He nodded toward someone DeRicci couldn't see. A towel dominated the screen; then Broduer wiped off his hands.

"You said she had the bruises to prove she wasn't wearing that particular environmental suit when she died."

"Yes?"

"Was she wearing any environmental suit at all?"

He continued wiping, cleaning off his forearms before handing the towel back to the unseen assistant.

"I mean," DeRicci said, "what is it about environmental suits that prevents bruising?"

"That's not what I meant when I said that." His thin eyebrows met above his perfect nose. She had intrigued him. "I meant that there were no stains or dents or marks in the suit that matched the bruises that she had. Environmental suits are remarkable things, but they aren't remarkable enough to prevent bruising—at least not yet."

"So if she was wearing another suit, someone removed it, then put on this pink suit before posing the corpse." She was asking a dumb question because she knew it was the only way to get Broduer to follow her line of thinking. She wanted him to be as precise as possible.

She wanted to explore all possibilities.

The door opened. Voices filled the room as van der Ketting came in.

DeRicci put a finger to her lips.

Van der Ketting pushed the door closed, and the voices vanished.

"You know." Broduer blinked a few times, as if he

were putting some details together. "There would be fiber evidence of a maneuver like that. There's no way that you can get clothing off a corpse without leaving a trace of that clothing. It's just too much work."

"Even if you cut it off?"

"That's the problem," he said. "You can't switch suits Outside. The depressurization—"

"Would change the corpse. Yes, I know," DeRicci said.

"Then why did you ask me the question?" Broduer said.

"Because there are places with atmosphere Outside," DeRicci said, getting tired of playing dumb.

"The Growing Pits," Broduer said.

That was what she wanted him to get to. But she said, "Among other places."

"If she had been killed in the Growing Pits, she would have been wearing another suit. Changing her suit there wouldn't have caused the depressurization, but she wouldn't have died of oxygen deprivation either."

"All someone had to do was shut off the oxygen in one of the greenhouses," DeRicci said.

"In order to do that," Broduer said slowly, "you'd have to shut off the oxygen, but not the rest of the environmental protocols. You'd have to check, but there's usually a failsafe in Outside buildings that provides backups. If one thing or the other goes out, then some redundant system kicks in."

"Besides," van der Ketting said, deliberately ignoring DeRicci's instructions to remain silent, "if someone shut off the oxygen in the Growing Pits long enough to kill a person, it would damage the plants as well. Wouldn't we have heard about that?"

"We might not," DeRicci said.

Broduer was looking toward van der Ketting's voice, as if he could see through the screen.

"Who's that?"

"My partner," DeRicci said.

Broduer nodded, but he seemed distracted, as if he hadn't really heard her. He was clearly thinking about the new possibilities—being killed Outside without destroying the entire body.

He said, "The killer could have removed the other, put on the pink suit, and then brought her to the marathon track."

DeRicci nodded. They would have had to travel around the dome, but that was possible. No one would have noticed a vehicle moving Outside, especially if the vehicle stayed a mile or more away.

"You have no fiber evidence, though," she said to Broduer.

"Not to support the other suit theory," he said. "Although she could have removed her suit while she worked inside the Growing Pits. She had scratches and scrapes that were consistent with the pink suit being put on her after she had died."

"No other clothing changes?"

"None," he said. "At least that we can tell at the moment. But I'm going to have to review my notes with this new twist in mind."

He moved an arm, as if he were going to shut down the link.

"One more thing," DeRicci said quickly. "Could she have been killed inside an airlock?"

"That or a ship is what I'd bet on," Broduer said. "Some contained environment where it would be pretty easy to shut off the air and leave everything else on—"

"Don't they have redundant systems too?" van der Ketting asked.

"Not all ships do," DeRicci said, "and no one expects to be in an air lock long enough to have problems. You're supposed to go in with your suit on, so the redundant systems aren't necessary. If there's a problem, you either go out or come back in. The airlock's there to protect the dome, not to protect the people."

"Dying in the airlock or a ship would explain the presence of one suit but not two," Broduer said. "It would also explain the relatively clean condition of the corpse. You'd think if a woman died in the Growing Pits, she would have knocked plants or dirt on herself. She probably fell to the floor at one point, and she would have gotten covered with dirt."

"But airlocks usually have great filtration systems," DeRicci said.

"And some of the newer ones are self-cleaning," Broduer said, "and most ships—at least human-owned vessels, coming into Moon Sector, are kept clean too, so that their own filtration systems don't clog."

"That's all helpful," DeRicci said. "I'm finally getting some kind of picture. I'm sure I'll have more questions for you."

"I hope I'll have answers for you. I've pretty much told you what I've got."

DeRicci nodded. "But you might be able to eliminate more stuff for me, like you just did. Thanks, Ethan."

And with that she signed off, then turned to van der Ketting.

He had set a pile of things down on the table, and was watching her, arms crossed. "What the hell is going on? You canceled the interviews, summon me like I'm some kind of work slave, and won't tell anyone if you found something or not. The detectives out there are planning a mutiny."

"They should be planning dinner," DeRicci said, "because they're going to be working late into the night."

"This doesn't sound good," van der Ketting said.

"It's not. Broduer discovered that our victim isn't Jane Zweig."

"Of course it is," van der Ketting said. "We have the suit, and the singlet, and the images—"

"Which is what she—or she and her friends—or some cunning killer—wanted us to think," DeRicci said. "But Broduer ran DNA, and—"

She stopped herself. DNA. There had been no DNA on record for Jane Zweig, and Broduer had called that unusual. DeRicci had agreed, although she had seen it before. In Disappeareds.

Zweig had been a Disappeared, even though she hadn't acted like one.

"And what?" Van der Ketting sounded annoyed. "Do you think Zweig's been kidnapped?"

DeRicci looked at him, feeling stunned. She hadn't thought of that option either. She had considered only two: that Zweig had killed Mayoux herself or that Zweig had been involved. But there were other options. Zweig might have been kidnapped, just like van der Ketting said, or she might have been killed as well, for being in the wrong place at the wrong time.

Or for her previous crime, whatever it had been.

"I don't know what happened," DeRicci said. "All I know is what Broduer told me, which completely turns our investigation upside down."

Van der Ketting sank into a nearby chair. "Great. All the work we've done means nothing."

"It doesn't mean nothing, but we do have to rethink things. See why I called off the interviews? You and I have to work really fast right now."

"Doing what?" van der Ketting asked. "We can't redo the interviews alone."

Maybe he simply lacked imagination. It was rare for someone who lacked imagination to get into the detective unit, but it did happen. Van der Ketting was smart, but he was smart in a once-you-tell-him-what-to-do-he-can-do-it-better-than-everyone-else kinda way.

"That's right," DeRicci said. "We can't, nor should

we. But we have to give these investigators something to go on. We need to review all the footage you have, as well as look at miles five and six from earlier in the race. We also need to see if the cameras were on before the race began, and if they picked up anything."

"Oh," van der Ketting said. "Then we'd also need confirmation that the woman who picked up the singlet this morning was Jane Zweig—the real Jane Zweig."

Which would be hard to do without DNA. DeRicci wondered if Zweig had fingerprints on file. She'd have to check the databases, and maybe even check with Coburn, to see how they secured valuables at Extreme Enterprises. Maybe Zweig's personal identifiers were on file there.

"We'll probably need some visuals of her for that. Maybe something from the airlock or the other points of entry," van der Ketting was saying. "And this puts a whole new light on the question of where she went for forty-five minutes when she was out of the staging area."

DeRicci frowned at him. "Didn't you say she came through one of the maintenance sheds?"

"Yeah," van der Ketting said.

"There were vehicles near there." DeRicci frowned. "And vehicle tracks near the body."

"You think she moved the body into one of the maintenance sheds, then carried it to a vehicle before the race started, and drove to mile five?" Van der Ketting looked at her in disbelief. "Wouldn't someone have seen that?"

"Probably not," DeRicci said. "Remember how the medical vehicles were hidden from the spectators? I don't think you could see much from the staging area either. You'll need to check that as well."

"She could have driven out there, parked the vehicle behind the boulder, and left the body in it," van der Ketting said. "No one looks behind them."

"And that would explain why there were no visuals from mile six," DeRicci said. "That camera would have caught whatever was behind the boulder."

"Do you think she was strong enough to carry the body?" van der Ketting asked.

"In one-sixth gravity? Yeah, I do," DeRicci said.

"Wow." Van der Ketting rubbed his eyes. "I'm going to have to wake up. I've been looking at so much stuff these last few hours some of it is starting to blur."

Which they didn't dare have happen. DeRicci poured a cup of coffee and handed it to him.

Van der Ketting shook his head. "This stuff never works for me."

"The fake stuff maybe. But this marathon has money. Try the real thing."

Van der Ketting took a sip, and raised his eyebrows, holding the liquid in his mouth for a moment as he tasted it. After a moment he swallowed. "Wow. Okay."

He grabbed a pastry and took a bite.

"You have to stay alert, too," DeRicci said. "We've got the most work to do."

"To double-check our theory," he said.

"More to the point," DeRicci said, "to find out what her connection is with Eve Mayoux, if there is one."

"Oh, man. You don't have anything on that?"

"Why would I?" DeRicci said. "You saw me talking to Broduer. This is all new to me too."

"Crap." Van der Ketting took another bite of his pastry and chased it down with the rest of the coffee. "This is going to take us hours."

"It can't take us hours," DeRicci said. "We have to be able to put these people back to work, with the right questions and the right attitude."

Van der Ketting shook his head. "I think we've already missed that shot. They're none too happy right now."

"They won't be happy about any of this," DeRicci said. "But they'd be even angrier if we let them continue to work with the wrong information."

Van der Ketting sighed.

"We need to find out something else as well," DeRicci said. "We have to find out who holds a grudge against the Moon Marathon. Since Mayoux has been dead for quite a while, her body could have been dumped anywhere. Someone, Zweig if we're right, chose to dump Mayoux here so that she would be found in the middle of the marathon, looking like she was a participant."

Van der Ketting's eyes widened. "So that's what Broduer was talking about."

"What?" DeRicci asked.

"If they'd succeeded in cracking her helmet, we would have had no idea that we were dealing with Eve Mayoux. We'd have no time of death. We'd have nothing, except the singlet, the environmental suit, and the position on the track."

DeRicci nodded. It always took him a while to catch up, but he eventually did. "That's right. We'd assume it was Jane Zweig without even looking for DNA."

"And the publicity would have been brutal," van der Ketting said. "Someone who runs a business specializing in extreme sports, dying on a relatively easy course from a bizarre accident. By picking a famous target—or a potentially famous target—there'd be more coverage. This could actually shut down the marathon for good."

"Which would affect all of Armstrong in one way or another." A headache built between DeRicci's eyes. She didn't want to think about all of these implications. But someone obviously had. Someone had put a lot of time into this murder, and hoped to kill a few other things in the process.

"We're not going to be able to do all of this alone," van der Ketting said. "We have to bring in more people."

DeRicci didn't want to bring in the rest of the detective staff. She didn't outrank any of them, and even though this was her case, no one would listen to her when she gave them orders. That would simply increase her irritation, make the investigation process inefficient, and lose them time instead of gaining it.

But she didn't know how to tell van der Ketting that.

"I think we can get enough information to get everyone started," DeRicci said. "You start reviewing those vids. First, I want to see the mile markers before the race began and during the first two runners. Then I want you to look at Swann's vids again. She said she saw a movement by that boulder, and I seem to remember tire tracks there. Let's figure out what was there, if we have vid of it, and who it belonged to."

"What are you going to do?" van der Ketting asked.

"I'm going to find the connection between Mayoux and Zweig," DeRicci said. She was also going to find out, if she could, who Zweig really was and why she had disappeared. "But first, I'm going to call a friend."

Van der Ketting looked at DeRicci as if she were crazy—and maybe he thought she was. Why would anyone call a friend in the middle of an investigation?

But he would think her even crazier if he knew which friend she was going to call.

She couldn't count on anyone in the department to help her and protect her reputation, such as it was.

The best person to search for a Disappeared was a Retrieval Artist. So it stood to reason that the best person to discover if an existing person was a found Disappeared would also be a Retrieval Artist.

DeRicci was willing to bet this entire investigation that her old partner, Miles Flint, could find out Jane Zweig's status a lot faster than DeRicci ever could.

Paying him would be another issue. DeRicci certainly couldn't afford a Retrieval Artist's prices, and the department wouldn't pay to have someone outside the system do the work.

But DeRicci figured payment worked a variety of ways. She would offer to barter favors—and she was willing to bet Flint would take her up on it.

She would never know unless she asked.

"You're going to have to give me a few minutes alone for my call," she said to Van der Ketting.

He grimaced. "Where'm I supposed to work?"

"Clear out the antechamber," she said. "Ignore the unis and work there."

"I have all the fun," he said, and picked up his hand-held. He left everything else on the table. Without saying another word to her, he let himself out the main door.

DeRicci waited until it latched before going back to the wall unit to call Flint. She would use public links again, in case hers were being monitored.

She hoped against hope that he was in. Because right now she really needed someone she could trust.

27

Tokagawa insisted on setting up his own comparison to see if the virus infecting people in the tent was the Tey virus. Oliviari estimated that Tokagawa's stubbornness, logical as it was, took five minutes from their precious lead time.

She followed him out of the office. A cacophony of coughs and sneezes greeted her. All of the beds in this section of the medical tent were full, some with runners lying prone, others with runners sitting on the side of the bed, holding tissue while the med techs ran diagnostic wands over them.

The man that Oliviari had helped carry to a nearby bed, the man who died—she never had learned his name, poor creature—was nowhere to be seen. Someone else lay on his narrow cot, back turned to Oliviari, covers pulled all the way up to the neck.

Oliviari was cold again. She wished she had worn longer sleeves, although she knew it would have done no good. She had the virus now; she was sure of it. Her symptoms just weren't that bad yet.

Tey had picked this race on purpose, but Oliviari wasn't sure why. Oliviari did know that Tey would have factored in several things that Oliviari could not calculate on her own.

Tey would have known how much the exertion these runners had placed on their bodies affected the rate of the disease. Some of these runners had built up their immune systems, but other runners had probably pushed harder than they had in months. That would bring their immune systems down, make them even more vulnerable to the disease.

Tey had probably counted on that, as well as the stress, exhaustion, and sheer terror that a race like this sometimes provoked in its participants.

Tokagawa was bent over a table, studying a small screen. Oliviari wanted to get behind him, look over his shoulder, and point out all the similarities in the two viruses. It should have been obvious to anyone with experience; he certainly didn't need a double- and triple-check.

But he hadn't trusted her, and with good reason. She hadn't been honest with him.

Oliviari had been afraid that Tey would eventually release the virus again. Oliviari had monitored news reports and medical journals for any strange outbreaks, and had seen none.

But Tey could have continued her experiments under new names and covered her own tracks as well. She knew how to use various aliases, and she knew how to leave false clues. Even the journal articles she wrote—brilliant pieces of analysis that became chilling when you realized who wrote them—had pen names upon pen names, little traps that would (and had) led Oliviari down the wrong path many times.

Why would Tey risk everything to release this virus here, in the heart of the Earth Alliance? Why would she call attention to her own presence on the Moon? It made no sense.

Unless someone else Tracked her, someone else found her, and someone else wanted her to pay.

But that didn't make sense either. If Tey knew she had been tracked, she would have escaped rather than risk being identified. She wouldn't have left the virus behind.

One of the med techs hurried past Oliviari, carrying three diagnostic wands. Another scurried by, holding a bag filled with a vomit-covered T-shirt, the stench making Oliviari gag.

As she stepped out of the way, she hit the small of her back on a small table. Pain shuddered through her. She used the table to brace herself, and glanced at Tokagawa.

Still comparing. Damn anal, meticulous man. She mentally urged him to hurry, sending her thoughts to him as if he could hear them. She didn't dare speak aloud. Not yet, anyway.

She glanced at the cot again. The dead man was more than a cipher. He got into the tent early, so he had to be one of the race's leaders. He might have crossed paths with Tey, and gotten infected accidentally.

Could this have been a setup? Was someone framing Tey, thinking that perhaps if she couldn't have been arrested for the crime on Io, maybe she would get charged with this one? Had her death been unplanned after all?

"Goddammit," Tokagawa said, "you're right."

He had left the table and approached Oliviari, and she hadn't even seen him. She had been concentrating so hard on the beds, on Tey, on the virus.

Tokagawa's face was gray, his lower lip trembling. Taut lines appeared around his mouth and eyes. He looked years older, and it had been only a few minutes.

"This is a disaster," he said. "It's already gone too far."

Fortunately, his voice was low. Oliviari hoped no one heard him over the rhythm of coughs and groans that were echoing in the room.

"We still have a chance," she said.

He shook his head. "That disease—"

"That virus," she said, "is defeatable, with the right

equipment. We have to check the decon unit. There's one in here. If you let me see the specs, I can see if it's the one we need."

"Decontaminate everyone? It doesn't work. You know that. If the virus has progressed to a certain point—"

"I know." Oliviari didn't want to think about that. "We'll deal with what we have. Where's the decon unit?"

He was looking at the beds. She wasn't even sure if he had heard her.

She hadn't expected him to panic. Doctors were trained in emergency situations, weren't they?

But they were trained in things like familiar diseases and trauma wounds. Not mass epidemics. Only doctors who specialized in colonial medicines and interstellar travel had to worry about things like that.

"Dr. Tokagawa!" She said his name loudly to catch his attention.

He turned to her like an old man, his movements so slow that she wondered if he even knew what was going on around him.

"It's the most lethal version of that virus," he said. "That's what I was double-checking. It's the one that killed everyone in her experiment. And fast. Like it's come on here. Why would it be here?"

"You specialize in sports medicine, don't you?" She kept her tone reasonable.

He nodded, as if they were having a conversation at a dinner party.

"You're probably not trained for things like this."

"No one is," he said, and she was relieved to hear him speak again. "No one on the team, except you. You're the only one who knows how to treat this disease, and you've got a fever. I can tell from the way your eyes glitter—"

"I'm fine," she said, and she was. At least, she was better than he was. He wouldn't take charge. That was clear now. She was going to have to do it, and she would have to do it through him. He had forgotten that she had falsified her credentials, or maybe he hadn't realized that she had falsified her medical experience as well.

"Now listen to me." She got as close to him as possible, speaking softly so that no one else could hear. "If you panic, we all die. Every single person in this race, connected with this race, or who had the misfortune to wander into areas around the race. Thousands of people. And maybe we'll miss somebody who got touched by this thing, and everyone in Armstrong will die. Do you understand me?"

"I've already thought of that," he said. "There's no hope. This thing spreads too fast."

"There is hope," she said. "There's plenty of hope, but we have to act quickly. *You* have to act quickly."

"I don't know what to do," he said.

"That's all right," she said. "I'll tell you. First things first, you have to get me to that decon unit."

He opened his mouth, as if he were going to argue, but he nodded instead. "Come on."

He grabbed her hand. His fingers were strong. Maybe she had snapped him out of the panic. She hoped so.

She wondered if this was what had happened on Io, panic once everyone in that colony realized the scientists in charge wouldn't help.

He pulled her between the beds past people coughing and crying and looking generally miserable. Oliviari couldn't see the larger mass of runners, but she wondered what they thought of this, if they even knew.

As she stumbled forward, she thought briefly of her post, how important it had been to gather all that DNA, to talk to all the runners coming in, and how unimportant it was now.

Strange to think that Jane Zweig was dead, that

possibly—probably—Frieda Tey was dead, and her virus was spreading like a giant re-creation of the experiment that had convicted her the first time.

Tokagawa pulled Oliviari past a group of runners huddled together on the floor and drinking miracle water. None of them appeared to have symptoms, but they kept touching their own foreheads as if feeling for a fever. A med tech with a diagnostic wand stood near one side of the group, as if worried about going in there.

Maybe Frieda Tey had planned this. Maybe, as she ran the marathon under the name Jane Zweig year after year, she daydreamed about doing her experiment right. Maybe she realized that with all this organization, with all this medical knowledge, she might be able to do it right this time, with a large enough sample population to see if her theories worked.

So far, they didn't seem to. If extreme crisis brought out the best in human beings—forcing them to stretch themselves beyond their own personal limits, and make important discoveries or difficult intuitive leaps—then maybe this crisis wasn't extreme enough.

Or maybe Tokagawa's reaction was a normal one. Panic. Confusion. The willingness of a brilliant man to suddenly be led by a not-as-brilliant woman simply because she was the one who had a plan.

Oliviari stepped into the curtained back area. The decon unit here was a self-contained one, of a make she'd never seen before. Tokagawa stopped in front of it.

"I don't know what you're going to do with it," he said.

She did, though. She had read all the literature. She knew that after the Tey virus became known, it became one of the recognized viruses, and the newer decon units could all destroy it. The older ones couldn't be modified to handle this, not even with a patch.

Oliviari just had to find out when this decon unit was built, and if it was programmed for the Tey virus.

Sounded simple, but it wasn't. She had to familiarize herself with the unit first.

She climbed inside, smelling the recycled air. The interior felt clammy—or maybe her body temperature had changed again. She searched for the panel, knowing that once she found it, she would get the information she needed.

Tey never respected the fact that time played such a crucial factor in her experiments. She never acknowledged it in her journal articles; she never once considered that had the colonists had more time with that last, lethal, mutated virus, they might have found a way to stop it.

If Tey had infected the marathon to start a new experiment—a so-called contained one (although that wasn't really accurate, given the space ports and the surface trains)—then she would find that the time factor was as great a problem here as it had been in her first dome.

And then the realization hit Oliviari. She finally knew what Tey was about.

Zweig *was* Tey, absolutely, positively. Oliviari didn't need the DNA scan. She didn't need anything other than logic.

Zweig and Tey had to be the same person for everything to make sense. Tey had studied the marathon, and other extreme events. She had thought about the way humans reacted and interacted. She had felt bad that there weren't enough resources in the original dome to give all of the colonists a chance, and there weren't enough colonists to make for a reasonable sample once the experiment got too big.

She had stated all of that stuff in the articles she wrote under pen names, the ones that Oliviari had traced because they so clearly matched Frieda Tey's writing and speaking styles.

Tey thought she had everything covered here, all the flaws from the previous experiment.

Which meant that Tey was also covering her own ass as well. The last time, she had been blamed for something she didn't think she should have been blamed for. Her name was at the top of that experiment. Frieda Tey had been the person in charge.

By making this seem like a random release of the virus, her name wouldn't be involved—well, the Tey name would be involved, but not the Zweig. And if anyone discovered, through new research or complete luck, that Frieda Tey and Jane Zweig were the same person, it wouldn't matter, because Jane Zweig was dead.

Truly, obviously, and completely dead. Even if everyone in Armstrong died of this hideous virus, the records would remain. And they would show that Zweig died of something else before the virus started to spread.

Before. So that she couldn't be blamed.

Or if she was blamed, it would be posthumously. No warrants, no arrests, no trials in absentia.

"Brilliant," Oliviari muttered.

"You all right?" Tokagawa asked.

No, of course she wasn't all right. She wasn't all right at all. She had been outsmarted by the woman she had been Tracking all these years.

Of course Frieda Tey would have planned everything through. That was what scientists did. They set up the new experiments so that they did not replicate the problems of the old.

One of the problems of the old was that Tey was forced to disappear. So why not disappear first?

After all, what was one life if Tey's discovery could save millions? What were a thousand lives in that context? Tey had argued that from the beginning.

Oliviari needed to speak to the police. They needed to check that body. She needed to check that body, to see if the DNA matched Tey's—or, failing that, to see if it matched Zweig's.

Because Oliviari knew with the same certainty that had brought her to this marathon in the first place that the body found on the course was not Zweig's or Tey's. It was some poor victim's, someone who had the misfortune to cross Tey's path at the wrong time.

Tey had misled everyone. She had probably planned this for years, with the help of the things she'd learned at Extreme Enterprises. She had deliberately made herself high-profile again, so that people would pay attention when she "died."

So that no one would guess that she had disappeared—again.

28

Flint had been examining the other names on Rabinowitz's meetings list when the personal link announced a call from a public node.

Flint almost denied the call, then asked who the message was from.

Someone who claims to be Noelle DeRicci, the system responded. *Claims* meant the system couldn't verify it. But it would be odd to have someone call him, claiming to be DeRicci, right as he had contacted her.

Patch her through Main, he sent, meaning that the system would guard itself against any encroaching viruses, bugs, or traps while it gave the public link visual and audio access to a single screen.

That screen rose in the center of the desk, DeRicci's face on it. Public links often didn't have the power to handle holographic messages, which was just as well. Flint wasn't sure he wanted to see DeRicci's head floating around his office.

"Noelle," he said with real pleasure. "It's been a long time."

"Yes. It's been a while." She sounded annoyed. Behind her, he caught bits of the marathon, but whether it was on a large screen or a wall, he couldn't tell.

"Thanks for calling me back so quickly," he said. "I guess Booth got the message to you."

"What?" DeRicci frowned. "Look, Miles, I don't have time for chitchat."

"I figured you wouldn't," he said. "All I need to know is what Jane Zweig died of. I have a case—"

"You need to know about Jane Zweig?" DeRicci seemed startled.

"Yes," Flint said. "Didn't Booth tell you?"

"Booth who?"

"Desk Sergeant Booth. He sent you an emergency message to contact me."

"Oh." DeRicci's cheeks colored. Flint knew what that meant. She hadn't checked her messages, even her emergency ones, in quite a while. Which was probably why she was on the public links.

He wondered who she was trying to avoid.

"I didn't get a message," she said.

"That's all right," Flint said. "You've contacted me anyway, and so we can get this out of the way. I heard about the Zweig case and I—"

"How did you hear about the Zweig case?"

"A client told me. We think it might be connected to something I'm working on. All I need to know is if Zweig died from flulike symptoms or complications from flulike symptoms or if the coroner found a viral link to her death."

"The flu?" DeRicci sounded as confused as he felt. "Why would you care about the flu?"

"Another man died of a rather bizarre virus, and just before he did, he met with Zweig. Since she died today, I wanted to make sure the virus hadn't spread."

"Virus? No. She didn't die of a virus. She died from oxygen deprivation." DeRicci sounded annoyed, as if she felt that Flint should already know that. How would he know it? Gumiela hadn't mentioned the cause of death in her press conference.

"I understand you think she was murdered," he said.

"I don't think," DeRicci said. "I know."

"Murdered by oxygen deprivation?" That had to be difficult to prove, particularly on that course. "You must have had some fairly obvious clues."

"Believe me, we do." She glanced to her right, as if she had heard something.

Flint still felt off balance. So Zweig hadn't died of the virus, which was a relief. But it wasn't much of one. He was going to have to contact the other women that Rabinowitz had met with, to see if they were ill.

"Look, Miles," DeRicci said, "I'm under a heck of a time crunch here. I need to talk to you— Wait. This is too strange. Why are you working on a case with Jane Zweig?"

"I'm not working on a case with Zweig," Flint said. "She happened to come up on another case. But you've helped me set that part aside. Why did you contact me?"

"It's about Zweig."

"How could you contact me about her if you didn't know what I'm working on?"

"Huh?" DeRicci shook her head. "Let's start this conversation over, Miles. I'm calling you because I want to barter services with you."

"Barter?" he asked.

She nodded. "I need you to investigate someone who might be a Disappeared."

He smiled. DeRicci had been right. It felt better to start the conversation all over again. "Might be?"

"Yes," she said. "It's connected to this investigation I'm doing here, at the marathon, and you have to keep this to yourself."

She looked to her right again. He strained to see what she was looking at, but couldn't see much beyond the race behind her, and a table littered with food.

"I'll keep it confidential, Noelle," he said gently.

She turned back toward the screen. Her face was lined, and there were circles under her eyes that looked like they'd been etched there permanently.

"So who is this might-be Disappeared?" he asked.

Her smile was small. "You already asked me about her. Jane Zweig."

He felt a shiver run down his spine. "Why do you think Jane Zweig might be a Disappeared?"

"She has no DNA on file," DeRicci said.

"So they can't verify the body's identity?" he asked.

"They did that," DeRicci said.

"And it's not Jane Zweig?"

Her lips thinned more. "This is a public link, Miles."

"If she's a Disappeared and it's not Jane Zweig, then your problem is solved," he said.

"And if I were that stupid, I would deserve the treatment I get at the department," she snapped. "I think I could solve that myself."

Then she looked surprised, as if she hadn't expected the words to come out of her mouth.

"Sorry," she said.

He smiled. It was nice to know she would never change.

"It's fine," he said. "I should know better than to tell you your job."

She gave him a small smile. "It's just been hell here."

"I gathered from the media reports."

"Not just here. At the unit. Everywhere. I do fine, then I say something like that to the wrong person. I should have quit when you did, Miles."

"You said you couldn't do anything else."

She sighed. "I probably couldn't."

"So," he said, knowing she couldn't go into this on public links either. "The body is identifiable, just not the identity you suspected."

"Right," she said.

"And you got a strange hit on Zweig. No DNA on record. Fingerprints? Anything else?"

"I'm going to check," DeRicci said. "But I'm really under major pressure here and I've got a year's worth of work that a team of us has to get done sometime tonight. I figured farming this out to you might be quicker and more efficient."

"And it's just between us, right?"

"Us and whoever might be listening on this link," she said.

He smiled. "No one's listening from this end."

"The whole Moon could be on this side," she said. "Can you do this for me?"

"I can," he said. "And I will check, but I have to tell you, I think I already know the information you want."

"What is it?"

"I think your Jane Zweig might be Frieda Tey."

DeRicci frowned. "Frieda Tey? Why is that name familiar?"

"The scientist who killed two hundred people in a domed colony experiment about ten years ago?"

"Her?" DeRicci's voice rose. "That's why you were asking about the flu?"

Flint nodded.

"God, you don't think that's possible, do you?"

"Someone does. I have a lot of evidence that points me in the same direction," Flint said. "Then you contact me about the same woman."

DeRicci's frown deepened. "This is too weird to be a coincidence."

"I know," he said. "I'll be talking to my client about it as soon as I can."

"There's some kind of bigger plan that I can't see yet," DeRicci said. "That much is for certain."

Flint nodded. "Let's just hope we're not following the script."

"Look," DeRicci said. "I'll contact Broduer again, and ask him if he sees any evidence of the flu in the body."

"Tell him to look for the Tey virus," Flint said.

"That's conveniently named," DeRicci said. "I'll do it. If it's there, I'll get back to you. Otherwise, you get in touch with me."

"I'm not sure how I can if your links are closed," Flint said.

She made a face. "I'm not turning them back on. It's a mess here."

He could only imagine. He wondered when they had learned that the body wasn't that of Jane Zweig. Had DeRicci already gotten into the main part of her investigation? Probably, and she was probably going to be blamed for the identity mixup.

"Tell you what," she said. "I'll check for messages from you every hour. You let me know how to find you."

Flint smiled at her. "I always leave my links on."

"You're much more sociable than I am," she said, and signed off.

Flint's smile faded. He wished that were true, that he was more sociable. But he wasn't, and he was feeling even less sociable now.

DeRicci was right. It wasn't a coincidence that he was working on a case involving Jane Zweig on the very day she died.

If Jane Zweig truly was Frieda Tey, as Rabinowitz believed, then that led to a whole new group of implications about the misidentified body. Was Zweig trying something new? Had she infected Rabinowitz herself? Or was she already gone, the unknown woman dead in her place?

Flint also needed to find out if the other women Rabinowitz had visited were ill. Flint needed to know the source of the contamination—if, indeed, Rabinowitz had Tey's virus, which was what Wagner believed.

And then there was Wagner, and whatever game he was playing. Flint would have to find that out as well.

DeRicci said she had a lot of work that had to be done quickly, and so, now, did Flint.

He pushed the button so that his screen recessed, and then he started the work a Retrieval Artist was known for—tracing a Disappeared.

29

DeRicci leaned against the wall, Flint's image long gone. She missed him. She never had to worry about him failing to think creatively. Perhaps that had been the problem with Flint the detective. He had thought creatively—too creatively—and he found ways out of problems that no one else could.

Ways that weren't always legal.

He would find out if Zweig was a Disappeared or if the lack of DNA identification was simply a fluke. He would find out, and he would find out quickly.

She shut down the wall unit, glanced at the race still playing on the other wall, and wondered if it would ever end. This group of runners seemed even more tired than the last group as they crossed the finish line. No arms raised, no final leap, no obvious sense of accomplishment.

Just like her work. She stumbled from one predesigned path to another—and occasionally, like today, found out she was on the wrong path altogether—and when she finished each race, she moved to the next without a thought of victory. Only a sense that she had put one more thing behind her.

She was burning out. She wasn't going through the motions yet—her own sense of justice wouldn't let her do that—but she always wished she were somewhere else. Although not in an environmental suit out on that course. That was the last place she would go for fun.

Then she frowned. Environmental suit. Coburn had said they got a shipment in, and that he and Zweig were testing them, but his suit was different from hers. Obviously Mayoux's suit matched the suit Zweig wore, but how many of those did Extreme Enterprises get in? If there were only two pink suits, who would know that? And who would have ordered them so that they were small enough to fit Zweig and Mayoux?

DeRicci hurried to the door. She pulled it open. The crowd had gone away—apparently van der Ketting had taken care of them, sent them off to dinner as she suggested or just got them out of the bungalow.

Van der Ketting was sitting on a plastic chair, hunched over his hand-held, his body protecting the screen so that no one else could see it. He didn't look up as she pulled the door open, but his muscles tensed.

He had seen her, but he didn't want to acknowledge her. How very childish of him.

The uni who had been helping her gave her a small grin. "Everything okay, Detective?"

She nodded, and as she did so, marveled that even a gesture could be a lie. Nothing was okay.

"Can you get Brady Coburn for me again?" she asked. "I have some follow-up questions."

Now van der Ketting looked up. "We're ready to start the interviews again?"

DeRicci shook her head. "Just that one."

And maybe not even that one if she didn't do some work first. She turned to the uni.

"Take your time getting him. I don't need him right away."

The uni dipped his head, acknowledging her. "It'll take me a little time to find him anyway. We let everyone move around a bit; they were feeling cramped in that warehouse space."

She wasn't sure what warehouse space he was referring to. "They all got food and a place to rest, right?"

"They had the option of food and a place to sit down." The uni's eyes widened. "That's what I thought you'd asked for first. They're not going to be staying the night here, are they?"

Wouldn't that be a mess? She sighed. "I hope not."

Then she nodded at van der Ketting. He continued to work over the hand-held, pretending he didn't see her.

Getting rid of the other detectives must have been difficult; he was obviously going to make her pay for it.

"Leif," she said. "let's go."

He looked up and let her see the resentment on his face before grabbing the hand-held and standing. She held the door for him, and as he walked past, he said, "Who was the friend?"

"What?" She closed the door.

Van der Ketting was standing in the middle of the room. "Who was the friend you had to call?"

"Someone who can help us out," DeRicci said, not willing to say any more. "What did you find out?"

"Not a lot." Van der Ketting's cheeks reddened. "I spent a lot of time on personnel matters."

"Thank you for that," she said, although she didn't feel grateful at the moment. "Sit down. Let's get to work."

He returned to the spot he'd carved out for himself at the head of the table. His supplies remained there, just where he had left them. DeRicci hadn't touched anything except the coffee, the pastries, and the wall unit since he'd left.

She sat down in the chair next to his and pulled her own hand-held from her pocket. It had been a long time since she'd used it; she'd done most of her work at the office or at home, and here she'd been using the public links.

"Have you investigated Extreme Enterprises at all?" she asked van der Ketting.

"I'm still working on the vids," he said.

"What have you got?"

"A few curious things." He kept his head down as he spoke, his hands busy with the small machine. "No footage of miles five and six for the early runners. The footage shows up after Zweig disappears off camera."

"So the body could have been there all along."

He nodded. "But I do have footage from the night before, as the techs tested everything. No body there and no tracks."

DeRicci felt her heart leap. Their theory had more validity now. Zweig had stashed the body in the maintenance building, and had retrieved it just before the race. Then she drove it to mile five, and left it behind the boulder.

She probably drove the vehicle back along the same trail she had gone out on. No one had noticed, or if they had, they had probably thought she was with the marathon. Her pink suit looked white from a distance, just like most marathon volunteers'.

"And," he said, "I really can't locate Zweig for those forty-five minutes. She seems to have vanished."

"What about the vehicles? Did any leave while everyone was in the staging area?"

"Not that I've found so far," van der Ketting said. "But I didn't have much time to work."

The resentment had reappeared in his tone. He felt she was taking more time from him.

She probably was.

"Let me know if you find anything," she said, and turned to her own hand-held.

She tapped into the police systems, so that she had a traceable identification. She needed to back all of this up, in case she had to take someone to trial. The judge would want to know how DeRicci came by all of her information.

First she sent for a warrant for Extreme Enterprises, citing the problems with the corpse, the suit, and Zweig's possible involvement. DeRicci also stressed a need for urgency, because she would be interviewing one of the company's owners within the hour, not to mention all of the people she was holding here while she searched for information.

If that didn't get a judge off his duff, nothing would.

Then she set that search aside, tagging her hand-held to notify her the moment the warrant came in.

While she waited, she started a background search into Mayoux and Zweig, looking for points of comparison.

Zweig had come to Armstrong from Earth by way of several extreme events all over the galaxy. Mayoux had been born in Armstrong, and had stayed there, except for her years of higher education at Glenn Station University. Her parents were dead, and she had one brother, also deceased.

DeRicci could find no evidence of friends or lovers in Mayoux's file. For all DeRicci could tell, Mayoux had lived alone since she returned from the university twenty years before. She had made two trips off of the Moon in all of those years, apparently alone, and she hadn't left at all in the last nine years.

All in all, she was about as different from Zweig as a person could get.

DeRicci sighed and rubbed her eyes. There had to be a way in which their paths crossed. How did a master gardener whose main idea of exercise seemed to be walking to work end up dead, masquerading as a woman whose entire life was about athletic feats so extreme that most people would think them crazy?

There was precious little on file for Zweig—at least in the personal categories. She was unmarried, but the media played up hints of affair after affair, even mentioning the relationship with Coburn and its rather uncomfortable aftermath.

DeRicci stopped and read the articles on that. He hadn't been completely honest, not that that surprised her. The breakup with Zweig had been a difficult one. Coburn had tried to split up the business as well, but Zweig had fought him in court.

She claimed that Extreme Enterprises needed both of them, that either it stayed in business as a partnership or it dissolved entirely. DeRicci wondered why Coburn didn't dissolve it, and start up the same business under a different name—he was obviously the talented one, the one the travelers trusted—and then she found out.

Zweig had already thought of that. One of the terms of her suit was that if the business dissolved, both she and Coburn would be enjoined against starting another extreme sports business. She wouldn't have any trouble finding work, or so Coburn claimed. He said she put in that clause simply to prevent him from gaining the business he had originally started.

Nasty, expensive, and personally bloody, that was what friends called the suit. Finally it got settled, terms not disclosed. But Extreme Enterprises stayed in business, and Coburn rarely came back to Armstrong, just as he had said.

But he was here for the Moon Marathon, for the first time ever. And while he was here, Zweig supposedly died. She certainly was missing—

"Damn," DeRicci said. She hadn't thought of everything after all. With this switch of victims midway through, she was getting confused as to what had been done before they knew the victim was Mayoux.

"What now?" Van der Ketting looked up. His eyes were bloodshot. He'd been staring at the screen for too long.

"When I had you check singlet numbers, you checked to see if someone could duplicate them, right?" DeRicci asked, praying she had asked for this, praying he had thought of it.

"Yeah," he said. "They could have if they were marathon staff, but that was pretty specific people. Each singlet is different with each marathon."

DeRicci turned her hand-held over and over in her fingers. She knew they had to look at the marathon staff; she just hadn't been ready to do so.

"So," van der Ketting was saying, "duplication would be pretty difficult."

DeRicci shook her head. If only Flint were here. He would have traced this on his own rather than have her do his thinking for him.

"Duplication sounds real easy," DeRicci said. "I'm sure they came up with the design weeks ago. Hell, I could have gotten it with a friendly 'Let me see what we're wearing this year' lead-in. I'm sure someone else could have too."

Van der Ketting's cheeks turned a dull red.

"And check for that dang pink environmental suit," DeRicci said, deciding to be as specific as possible. "If there were two out there, maybe there were three or four."

"How about if I check the airlock entrances all over the dome to see if Zweig entered or exited from one of them?" van der Ketting asked.

"Good thinking. Damn." DeRicci shook her head. "Someone has been so far ahead of us on all of this that I feel like we're not even playing the same game."

"Yeah," van der Ketting said. "Me too."

DeRicci looked at him. She had forgotten how frustrating it was to be a rookie detective. He had risen to a place of authority before, when he was a uni, and now he was a beginner again. And his investigative skills, while good for a rookie, weren't great for a detective.

"How about I bring in at least one more detective?" he asked. "We can use another pair of eyes."

"No," DeRicci said. "Get the uni outside to do it—what's his name, anyway? He's been really helpful."

"Marcus?"

DeRicci shrugged. "That the one I sent to get Coburn?"

"Yeah," van der Ketting said.

"Then Marcus. Marcus what?"

"Marcus Landres."

"Thanks." At least now she could call him by his name. She had felt embarrassed about it before. "He should have been back by now with Coburn."

"You told him to take his time."

"I did, didn't I?" DeRicci bent back over her hand-held. She still hadn't gotten that warrant. She wondered if she should wait to see Coburn before it came in, or trust him to give her the answers she was looking for.

Van der Ketting stood up. He set his hand-held on the table and walked to the door. DeRicci stifled the urge to grab the hand-held and check everything herself.

She was becoming obsessed with this investigation. That happened to her sometimes, and it never ended well for her. She always solved the case, but at some great personal cost.

She didn't know how many personal costs she could continue to take.

After a moment, she looked back at her own hand-held. She was frustrated by the lack of in-depth information about Zweig, and didn't want to go into the media accounts, searching each one for a tidbit that might be wrong.

So she did something she hadn't done before with Mayoux. She had figured that Mayoux's life was too quiet for a media search to be profitable, but she tried one now. After all, if they'd met over a lawsuit—since Zweig seemed like the litigious kind—or in a squabble about apartment rents, it might show up in both accounts.

DeRicci was going to compare both Zweig's and

Mayoux's media writeups, if she got any on Mayoux at all. But she didn't have to.

There was only one writeup on Mayoux, and it didn't mention Zweig.

It mentioned Frieda Tey.

"Oh, my," DeRicci said under her breath. She read carefully, chewing on her lower lip as she did so.

Eve Mayoux's brother, Duncan Mayoux, died in an experiment run by Frieda Tey. The domed experiment with the weird flu virus that Flint was asking about. The brother had been one of the last to go.

The only times Eve Mayoux left Armstrong had been to go to court and meet with the other families of the victims.

Had she seen Jane Zweig and realized she was Frieda Tey? The media report didn't say if they'd met, at least not directly, but they might have. Or Mayoux would have seen Tey's face all over the coverage.

If DeRicci had been Mayoux, she would have memorized Tey's face, and done everything she could to find her.

This was the link. DeRicci knew it was. As she had mentioned to Flint, there were too many coincidences here. In fact, she had to contact him. He didn't have to prove that Zweig was a Disappeared. It was obvious now that she was.

And that she had killed Eve Mayoux to keep her own cover. But why go to all the trouble to drag the corpse onto the marathon route? Why not just kill Eve Mayoux in the Growing Pits and make it look like an accident? Those things happened. It wouldn't take too much to make the police overlook an investigation out there.

The door opened, and van der Ketting came back inside, followed by Landres. Coburn was nowhere to be seen.

"Just a minute," DeRicci said. "I think I've found something."

"I don't think we have a minute," van der Ketting said.

DeRicci looked up at him. His skin was pale. The uni, Landres, didn't look any better.

DeRicci felt her own stomach twist. Not something else. She had just found the connection in this case. She didn't need another problem, a different victim, or anything else to cope with.

"What is it?" she asked, trying not to match van der Ketting's panicked tone.

"We've got three dead in the medical tent," he said.

"Murdered?" DeRicci asked, feeling cold.

"Not like you think," van der Ketting said. "They died of some famous flu."

The reason for Flint's initial contact. DeRicci hadn't initially believed him. Identifying Disappeareds was hard. Flint had a theory, but no proof.

"The Tey virus?" DeRicci asked softly.

"How did you know?" van der Ketting asked.

"Because I got warning earlier that Jane Zweig might be Frieda Tey." DeRicci shook her head, the churning in her stomach growing worse. "And now we have proof that she is."

30

Oliviari finally found the diagnostic panel for the decon unit. It was on the back side, squished against a corner. Of course it wasn't inside the unit. She wasn't sure what she had been thinking.

She was woozy and tired, and her throat was sore. Her back ached, and shivers ran through her body. While she was doing this, Tokagawa was contacting the police. He had wanted to wait until he was sure that this virus was something unusual, something that a regular decon unit couldn't handle.

The police who could go back and forth into the dome. They would spread the virus if they didn't know what was going on.

If the disease spread into the dome, no matter how many decon units were around, hundreds, maybe thousands of people would die.

Her hand was shaking. She made herself concentrate. Sweat dripped down the side of her face. She wasn't near the last stage yet. She heard a rumor—or maybe Tokagawa had told her—that two others had died.

But she wasn't that ill. Or was she? The man—why couldn't she remember his name? Had she been told his name?—he was still mobile when she saw him. Although she and Klein had had to carry him toward the back.

Maybe the man had been woozy for some time.

She really couldn't think about it. Not right now.

She touched the surface of the decon unit's diagnostic panel, and it lit up. *No Access without Authorization* scrolled across the screen.

She wasn't looking for access. She was looking for information about the machine itself.

She pressed her face close to the panel, hoping someone had given the thing voice control as well as touch control.

"All I need," she said, "are your specs. I need to know if you're recommended for Tey's virus."

The *No Access without Authorization* sign vanished, and instead a blank screen faced her. For a moment, she thought she had failed, until the machine's specs flashed across the panel.

The model was fifty years old, and had not been upgraded. She should have expected that. The decon unit was on loan to the marathon—granted, it was the biggest marathon of the year, but it was still a damn sporting event where the risk of contamination was remote. So why give the event a state-of-the-art machine? And why pay state-of-the-art costs?

The specs vanished, and in their place, another sign appeared:

The disease you named is not familiar. Perhaps you are using a slang term for the disease. Please use the name given the disease by the medical establishment of Earth Alliance.

"Crap." She turned away, staggered into the main area, and saw Tokagawa. He was talking to Klein, who was shaking his head.

"Well?" Tokagawa asked her.

"No," she said. "We need new decon units and we need them now, as many as can get here. Maybe from the space port. Usually they have stationary and mobile units, and theirs'll be up-to-date, I can guarantee it."

"I don't know how to authorize this," Tokagawa said.

"You don't," Oliviari said. "You contact the city's health department, and you get the person in charge. He'll authorize it. If he doesn't, you talk to the mayor—and impress on her the importance of all of this. We need something here within the hour, or Armstrong's biggest tourist attraction will turn into Armstrong's biggest disaster, ever."

Tokagawa stared at her, as if her words were just sinking in. Then he nodded and walked away.

Klein came over to her. His face was flushed, his eyes too bright. She wondered if hers looked that way as well.

"Let me give you something to bring down that fever." Without waiting for her permission, he jabbed something into her arm. The muscles were already so sore that she didn't really feel what he had done.

"You don't look so good yourself," she said.

He smiled. "I'll hold up. For now."

"Look," she said. "If this runs true to form, it'll hit some of us quicker than others. No one had time to study the virus, at least not while it was working in humans, but the theory is . . ."

She paused for a moment, realizing whose theory she was going to quote. She had read so many articles, most of them written by Tey under pen names, trying to justify her own reputation.

"The theory is," Klein prompted, apparently thinking Oliviari had forgotten what she had planned to say.

"The theory is that some people have certain proteins"—Proteins? Was that the right word? Her mind felt fuzzy—"or maybe it was . . . I don't know. Something on the cellular level in abundance, or at least in numbers that appeal to this virus, as opposed to other people who have less of the . . . whatever. I'm so sorry. I can't remember the details anymore."

"I'm sure we can find them," Klein said.

She shook her head. The movement made her dizzy. She put a hand on the wall to prop herself up. "Get an assistant over here, someone who isn't manifesting symptoms."

He didn't say anything, just disappeared into the throng of people. She held herself up by an arm, listening to the coughs, the complaints, the moans around her. One young man was throwing up into a bucket—the smell turned her stomach as well. An older woman sat on the edge of one of the beds, arms wrapped around her legs, rocking back and forth.

Klein came back, a young woman in tow. She was so tiny she looked no older than twelve. But she had lines beside her mouth, and her eyes, which were large and brown, had a wisdom and calmness that came only with age.

Oliviari wondered how many enhancements the woman had had—then remembered another article. Enhancements weakened the system, making the recipients even more vulnerable than everyone else.

Although it was too late to warn this woman. It was probably too late for all of them.

Still, Oliviari had to try. "One of you record this. Make sure the others know you have it."

"All right," the young woman said. She touched a chip on her hand. "I've got it."

"When the new decon units come in," Oliviari said, "make sure that everyone goes through them. There's a specs panel on all of the units. Make sure they're able to deal with Tey's virus. You've got to triage. You start with the people who have a fever, but no other serious symptoms, and work down to people who have no symptoms at all."

"What about the folks with symptoms?" the young woman asked, glancing around at the beds.

"Sickest last," Oliviari said. "Tey's virus has only turned up one place, and it was never tested in a decon unit. But all the things I've seen . . ."

A wave of dizziness swept through her. She willed herself to continue.

". . . all the things I've seen," she said, "show that it takes a while for these units to kill the virus. If the patient doesn't have a while, or there's a lot of infection, they're going to die anyway. So use the units wisely. Maybe even have someone do the math—how long it takes to go through decon times the number of people here, as compared to how quickly the virus is spreading. You know the drill."

The younger woman nodded. Klein's lips thinned.

"We're going to need a place to put people after decon, a place where they won't get reinfected. You have to find that too."

The light-headed feeling returned. Oliviari grabbed a nearby chair and sat in it, forcing herself to take deep breaths and hold them.

Just a lack of oxygen. She was getting too excited, wasn't breathing right.

At least that was what she had to tell herself.

She had to keep going.

"You all right?" the woman asked.

"I'll be fine," Oliviari lied.

Another young med tech hurried over. He looked healthy too, all fresh-faced and energetic. Oliviari envied that. She had remembered the feeling. She had had it only a few hours ago.

"The police want to talk to someone here in the tent," the tech said. "The detective in charge wants to know what makes this Tey's virus and not something else."

"I got it," Klein said.

"No." Oliviari stood. She felt as if she were made of glass. "I'll go."

"You can't go to them," Klein said. "They might not have been exposed yet."

Oliviari frowned at him. "That's what you need to find out."

He looked confused. "What?"

"How she infected your Mr.— What was his name? The first victim?"

"We don't know," Klein said. "His singlet was gone, with his environmental suit. We'll have to reconstruct."

Oliviari didn't care, not really. She waved a hand to silence him. "You have to find that out. He had to have gotten infected inside. Or before he put his suit on. Or there's contaminant in that suit. You have to find out. If he was infected inside—"

"Then it might be spreading through the dome. Oh, Jesus," the woman said. She hurried away, as if she knew what she was looking for.

"Don't let her spread panic," Oliviari said.

"I won't." Klein put a hand on her arm. His hand was cool. She felt as if she were melting. "You're really sick. Let me take that call."

"No," Oliviari said. "I have to explain in a way they'll believe. You back up Tokagawa. Make sure he gets those units coming as fast as possible."

Klein bent his head toward hers. "Are you sure there are units that can handle this? The study I saw said it was incurable."

"It was incurable in the dome situation of the study," Oliviari said. "But decon units were designed to handle it. Someone tested it on samples of the virus, and got rid of it. It's just never been tried on people."

"Great," Klein said. "This just gets better and better."

31

First Flint double-checked DeRicci's information. He hacked into every system he could think of that would contain DNA, and searched for anything under Jane Zweig's name.

He found nothing.

He then checked the groups that opposed DNA identification, to see if Zweig had supported them in the past.

Again, nothing.

He checked off-Moon records and, as best he could, examined records from various colonies and countries in Earth Alliance.

Still nothing.

Flint stood, stretched, and walked around the office. He rubbed his eyes with his thumb and his forefinger. DeRicci needed the information quickly. He might be able to get it quickly if he found the right door.

He glanced at his own, locked and encoded. It had stored Wagner's DNA along with other clients'. Not only did it have DNA, but it had fingerprints as well.

Rabinowitz worked inside WSX, so he wouldn't have had these kinds of elaborate security systems. If the law firm had them, Flint wouldn't have been able to hack them, not in the time allowed. And they wouldn't have given the information to him, since it was against the law.

But Rabinowitz might have used a hand-held system or something even smaller. He might have tried to hack into Extreme Enterprises systems on his own. Even if he didn't meet Jane Zweig, he would have been able to get a copy of her DNA from a strand of hair or from something she touched.

If he got close to her at Extreme Enterprises, he could compare her information with Tey's.

Flint didn't believe that Wagner had given him everything of Rabinowitz's. Rabinowitz probably had some files—even deleted ones—on WSX's nets. Flint wasn't going to risk investigating that from his office, and he didn't want to go to a public link.

But he would if he had to. First, however, he would see if he could find anything else in the information Wagner had provided.

Flint scanned, looking for things that bothered him. And the thing that bothered him the most was that Rabinowitz hadn't made an appointment with Jane Zweig herself.

Maybe Rabinowitz hadn't been going for DNA. Maybe all he wanted was a moment alone to slip a bug into the office systems.

Rabinowitz never claimed great hacking powers. He just might have relied on something that did the work for him, no matter how poor that work was.

Especially if all he needed was the firm's security files.

Flint felt the tiredness leave as he scurried back to his desk. He slipped into his chair, leaned forward, and found the nets that housed Extreme Enterprises. Most places had their security systems keyed to some part of their owner, usually a part that couldn't be easily obtained and replicated.

The flaw in the design was simple: There had to be an original scan, kept in the file, so that the system could compare the new scan to it.

Thieving rings had been using this system for decades. The hacker on the team would break into the system and steal the original scan, usually of a fingerprint. Then a different member of the team would make a mold of the fingerprint and gave that mold to the thief. The thief would do the actual breaking in, only he would set off no alarms because the security system would scan the thief as the owner of the fingerprint.

The detective unit where Flint last worked had the security system keyed to each detective's palm print, but the system also measured warmth and blood flow, so that it would make certain it was dealing with a living palm as opposed to one that had been manufactured—or cut off—for the purpose of entry.

Extreme Enterprises seemed to have a similar protocol, only it was retinal scans.

Flint read the instructions, something lost inside the system itself, something that Coburn and Zweig probably didn't even know existed inside their business's net. Not only was the door-locking mechanism keyed to their retinal scans, but those scans had to be done five times in the space of a minute. The eye being scanned had to move and blink, and the pupil had to dilate or shrink with the proper amount of light.

A similar scan bound their financial records, and another the company's private space yacht. Easier scans existed for the fleet of ships that the company used for tourist travel. The scan codes on those could be easily changed, and thus easily broken.

Flint didn't care about those. What he cared about was the internal retinal scan. Retinal scans made for excellent IDs. Anyone who traveled in the known worlds had had retinal scans made.

Frieda Tey's retinal scans were on file, along with her DNA and a variety of various prints.

If Zweig had been Frieda Tey—a Disappeared—then she had been careless or arrogant.

Of course, she had never gone through an agency,

so she hadn't gotten all of the verbal warnings, the kind that agencies never discussed. One of the main rules of disappearing was to never let anyone record anything that uniquely identified you—from DNA to fingerprints. A Disappeared wasn't even to do it for herself, for her own home. A Disappeared had to use some other form of security—which was often a way for Trackers and Retrieval Artists to find Disappeareds: search for the homes with security that was not keyed to personal identification.

Maybe this was just another case of Tey being smart. Maybe she figured if her actions were counterintuitive to a Disappeared's, no one would catch her. And, of course, she had been right.

It only took Flint a few minutes to find the bug that Rabinowitz had launched into Extreme Enterprise's security system. Flint followed the bug's trail into the security system. The trail led right through the firewalls the system's designers had put in place, all the way to the private information.

There, Flint found Jane Zweig's retinal scan.

Flint stored it on his system, then searched the interstellar police logs for the identifiers related to Frieda Tey.

It didn't take long to find them. The logs listed Tey as a dangerous felon, a mass murderer who might kill again. And, if Wagner was right and she had killed Rabinowitz, that was exactly what she was.

Flint pulled the retinal scan from the Tey file and compared it to Zweig's.

One hundred point match.

He leaned back in his chair and let out the breath he hadn't even realized he had been holding.

For some reason, the confirmation made him feel better. As of last week, Tey was alive and in Armstrong. He could tell DeRicci that and wash his hands of the entire case. It would belong to the police now.

Then he frowned. Something else had caught his

attention, something that hadn't really registered until now.

The retinal scan he used from Extreme Enterprises had been a recent one—one from that afternoon, in fact.

She wasn't anywhere near the Moon Marathon. She hadn't even left Armstrong. She was doing business at Extreme.

Flint logged back into their net. He saw no trace of anyone else in the system. But he double-checked just to make certain. No one was there, but someone had been there not an hour before he was.

A retinal scan logged in to open the office door. Another to open the financial records.

Flint could try hacking into those records, but it would take precious time. He had a secondary way to go. The records themselves provided direct access to the accounts, but Extreme's business net was flimsy. Flint couldn't get quick access to the accounts, but he could get quick access to the names of the banks that held the accounts. ·

He did that, then hacked into the bank records, something he had done countless times before.

He double-checked to make certain he was seeing the real information, not information that someone had planted—and he was. The information was real.

That afternoon, Zweig had liquidated all of Extreme Enterprises' accounts.

The accounts had been flush, but there wasn't enough money in them to justify this kind of scheme, at least in Flint's opinion. She probably had other credits stashed away. She had probably been planning her exit for a long time.

What she had taken, in the end, would sustain her for weeks, more than enough to get her somewhere else, wherever that somewhere might be.

Time to leave a message for DeRicci, let her know what he discovered, and that she should probably send cops to various points of exit from Armstrong. He would also have her put space cops on Extreme Enterprises' private yacht.

If only he could get to DeRicci immediately. He would have to leave the most urgent message he could.

He would have put the space cops on the yacht himself, but everyone knew he no longer had the authority. And much as the staff at the port liked him, they weren't going to do something that would anger the Armstrong Police.

Flint tried DeRicci's links, just to see if he could reach her. Of course he couldn't. Someday he would have to prove to her how dangerous it was to leave her links off.

He left a pointed message, telling her what to do, and then instructing her to call him when she had completed it.

Then he toyed with contacting Gumiela himself. But she would want to know why Flint had access to a private citizen's accounts. She'd want to know why he was messing in an obvious police case, and she wouldn't listen to his reasoning or his argument.

His best chance was with DeRicci.

Now he had to hope that she would keep her promise, and check her messages in a timely fashion.

32

"Close the door," DeRicci said to van der Ketting. She didn't care if the uni stayed in the bungalow or not. She had a few things to take care of, and she had to do it quickly.

The uni, Landres, stepped inside, apparently not wanting to be left out. He looked shaken. Van der Ketting came back to his chair and hovered there, as if he didn't know what to do.

DeRicci glanced at the wall across from her. The race—the actual race—continued. Another stupid person was crossing the finish line, and some volunteer was standing there waiting.

Didn't they know a crisis was going on here? Or were they pretending that it didn't exist?

DeRicci reached up into the wall unit and unceremoniously shut the race off. She no longer cared how many people were still out there, whether they leaped as they crossed the finish line or staggered over it like old people.

"Three dead," she said to van der Ketting. "How many ill?"

He shook his head.

"More all the time," Landres said. "It's apparently really contagious. You've got to let the others know. We can't go into the dome—or if we do, we can't get near anyone."

"It's an airborne contagion?" DeRicci asked.

If it was, they were already in trouble, because half the participants in the marathon were already inside the dome. They were having that meal she had assigned them to, and they were breathing the same recycled air as everyone else in Armstrong.

"Not from my understanding," Landres said. He was the one who should have been her partner, not van der Ketting. Landres had been efficient and informed all day. And even though he looked like someone who had just received a death threat, he continued in the same professional manner, as if death threats were a matter of course.

"I guess it's like Earth colds—you know, transmitted by fluids."

"Fluids?" DeRicci asked. If that was the case, then why was it so communicable?

"You know," Landres said, "mucus and stuff. I guess the mucus gets everywhere and—"

DeRicci held up a hand. "More than enough information. Leif, you have to get word of this to the other detectives. We're quarantined here until further notice."

"Says who?" van der Ketting asked.

"Says me, technically," DeRicci said. "But I'll get the official word shortly."

"If they know it's your order—"

"They won't pay attention, I know," she said. "So tell them it's an order from the city. That should be enough. What're we doing to stop this?"

"I don't know," Landres said. "We just got word of this."

"From someone reputable, I trust," DeRicci said.

"Yes," he said. "The medical team'll be in touch with you. They're doing what they can."

DeRicci nodded. She didn't remember much from the media reports of the Tey virus, except that the thing was highly contagious and it had killed people in that dome rather quickly. But she didn't know what "rather quickly" meant. Trying to remember a casual news report from ten years ago—granted, one of those news reports that repeated so many times you couldn't escape it if you tried—was a lot harder than she thought.

She sighed. Mucus. And everyone in environmental suits. Who knew that was possible?

She flicked her private links back on, and got bombarded with whistles and red flashing lights crossing her left eye. Emergency messages, more than she could ever deal with.

With a single command, she shut down all the emergency messages. Several didn't stop. So she sent them back, unopened, to the people who had sent them to her.

Then she linked up her private link to her handheld, and sent her own emergency message to Andrea Gumiela.

For a moment, DeRicci thought the message wouldn't go through. Then Gumiela appeared on the tiny screen.

"You have no right to go incommunicado," she said. "I've been trying to reach you for an hour. I'm getting complaints from the other detectives on-site. They say you've gone crazy—"

"I'm not crazy," DeRicci said. "We have a crisis here."

"Damn right, we have a crisis. A personnel crisis that's going to become a media circus if we're not careful. I told you to handle this with finesse—"

"I am handling it," DeRicci said, "and if you don't listen to me, I am going above your head. We have a major emergency out here, and it needs attention."

"You have no right to go above me." Gumiela's face filled the hand-held's screen, but DeRicci didn't need to see all of it to know that Gumiela was about as angry as she got. She was also cautious. DeRicci's threat to go to Gumiela's boss was an effective one.

"I'm giving you a heads-up that I'm quarantining the race and its spectators. The detectives aren't leaving here."

"Quarantining?"

"We've got three more dead," DeRicci said, "and a whole group who happen to be ill. I'm being told that it's something called the Tey virus, which is apparently really deadly. I'm going to follow up on that, but for right now, I have other evidence to suggest that there's good reason to believe that diagnosis is right."

"Tey, as in that woman who killed all those people on Io?" Gumiela had become calm. She was clearly paying attention now.

"Yes," DeRicci said. "Frieda Tey was a Disappeared, and it looks like she was here on Armstrong, calling herself Jane Zweig."

"Our noncorpse," Gumiela said.

"That's right." DeRicci glanced over her shoulder.

Van der Ketting sat down and was staring at the tabletop, but Landres was watching as if he'd never seen anything like this before.

DeRicci turned her attention back to the hand-held. "None of this is for public consumption. If the good citizens of Armstrong know there's a potential epidemic here, they'll panic."

"I got that." Gumiela didn't even sound offended that DeRicci was telling her how to do her job. "I haven't had another press conference since the first. As far as the city is concerned, they all believe that Jane Zweig is dead."

"Good," DeRicci said, "because we have one more major problem, and you'll have to deal with it out there."

Gumiela raised her chin, as if she were squaring her shoulders and bracing herself. "What?"

"I got contacted by a source earlier today, asking about the Tey virus."

"What kind of source?" Gumiela asked.

DeRicci wasn't about to give up Flint. She wasn't even going to hint at who he was. "A reliable one."

Van der Ketting made a strangling sound behind her. DeRicci looked over her shoulder. He was watching her now, but with a frown—he obviously felt that she should tell Gumiela who the source was.

"My source had seen your press conference," De-Ricci said, "and heard about Jane Zweig's death. The source wanted to know if Zweig had died of the flu, because someone else—someone who had had a meeting with Zweig within the last week—died of the flu."

Gumiela's face paled. "Are you saying this flu might be in the dome after all?"

"If it is," DeRicci said, "I think it's got to be a slower-acting version, unless all of the people who are ill here have some tie with Zweig."

That wasn't something DeRicci could rule out. But she thought it unlikely. She figured the main tie had to be the marathon itself.

"We need the name of that someone," Gumiela said.

"I'm not sure I can get it for you in a timely fashion." DeRicci had more than enough to cope with here; the last thing she needed was to get in touch with Flint again. Besides, he might not give her the name. "I think you'd better contact the hospitals, see if they have flu or viral cases, and see what's going on. Then look at death records, see if anyone in the past week or so died of complications from a virus or a cold or whatever they call it these days."

"Wouldn't the coroner have found this special virus?" Gumiela asked.

"I don't think so," DeRicci said. "I mean, if it was an isolated case, why look farther than the general type of virus? Why get really specific?"

"Oh, I don't know," Gumiela said. "To save lives?"

She was thinking from the perspective of what everyone knew now, a problem that DeRicci had always had with her. Gumiela could never look at the past as a time when information had been different. She always seemed to believe that people had the same facts she did.

DeRicci didn't have the strength or the time for the argument.

"Just assign someone to it," DeRicci said. "We've got more than enough to do here."

And then she shut down the link.

She had never done that before, just disconnected from a conversation with her boss. It felt good.

DeRicci turned to Landres and van der Ketting. "I need to talk to whoever's in charge of the medical tent. I have a lot of questions before I know what we do next."

"They already know that. They were just waiting for you," van der Ketting said.

"The person in charge," Landres said, "is Mikhail Tokagawa. He'll probably have all of your answers."

"I hope so," DeRicci said. "Someone has to have an answer or two. God knows, I'm more confused now than I was when I got here."

Even though that technically wasn't true. She wasn't confused about the big picture. If this virus was the epidemic everyone seemed certain it was, then it would spread to the dome, and there wouldn't just be a disaster.

There would be no one left.

33

The young male tech came back over. "The police just contacted us again. They have more questions."

He sounded panicked. Oliviari supposed he would be. If the police didn't know what was going on, someone might leave and spread the damn disease through the dome.

"Someone told them this is Tey, right?" She still had one hand on the wall. Sweat dripped down her face as if she were in a shower.

"Told them, warned them, told them to stay in this area." The tech bit his lower lip. Someone cried out, and he looked behind him as if he were searching for the source of the voice.

Oliviari was having trouble separating the voices and the coughs and the sneezes now. This place, so full of healthy people a few hours ago, had become a death trap.

"I guess they're quarantining the entire area," the tech said as he looked back at her. "But they still have questions. I think they should talk to Dr. Tokagawa, but you said you'd handle it."

"I'm going to do it." She had to. She had all the information and the history. Besides, she had realized something about Frieda Tey. Something important . . . if only her brain continued working. It felt like someone had packed it in cotton.

Oliviari stood upright. A wave of dizziness went through her, but she kept her back rigid so that she didn't sway.

"No offense, ma'am, but you should be lying down," the tech said.

"None taken." She made herself smile at him. She wondered how hideous that looked. "But I'm going to be useful, and this is one area where I can really help."

She looked across the beds, the sick people wrapped in blankets, some two to a cot. When did that happen? Were they all getting sick that fast?

She had. She had gotten sick that fast. She blamed it on the guy's sweat, and it probably was. She had been fine up until that point. She had been in an environmental suit.

"Let's go then," the tech said.

"Yes," she said, even though the office seemed very far away. This was not good. She had to hang on. She had to get everyone mobilized to find Jane Zweig. To get Frieda Tey.

For the families.

"You have to find the source of this virus," she said to the tech. "Figure out where it originated."

Then, without waiting for his answer, she headed toward the office. She almost put her head down and plowed her way there, like a child determined to avoid punishment. But she didn't.

Instead, she looked at the runners around her. They all had familiar faces. She had spoken to every one of them as she processed them into the medical tent. But no one had shown a virus on their diagnostic scan— not even the man who had infected them all.

What she couldn't remember was if she had spoken to them before or after she had helped him. It seemed like she had helped him right up front. Had he started near Zweig? Had he been near her when they suited up?

There was no way to know. He was dead and Zweig had disappeared.

Disappeared. That was what Oliviari had forgotten.

She whispered the word, once, as she walked. She had to tell the detective in charge that all of this was an experiment, and that someone—anyone—had to go after Tey or Zweig or whatever she called herself now, before she was gone for good.

Oliviari stumbled and the tech caught her arm, holding her up.

"Should I get Dr. Klein?" the tech asked.

"No." Oliviari made her voice sound as strong as possible. "You need the medical people out here. Go help Dr. Tokagawa. You have to get those decon units."

"He's found at least one nearby," the tech said. "It should be here soon."

"Make sure it has the right specs," Oliviari said.

"It does." The tech kept a firm grip on her arm. His fingers slid on her slick skin. Sweat. So much sweat. It was as if she had turned into a human waterfall.

They reached the door of the office. Oliviari went inside, grateful now that Tokagawa had removed the boxes from the desktop. She sat on it cross-legged, like he had.

"Would you mind getting the detective in charge for me?" she asked.

"Here?" The tech looked surprised. "But we—"

"On the link. I'm not as clear as I'd like to be. I think I need water. I'm dehydrating."

"Of course you are," he said, more to himself than to her. "Of course. I'll get you some miracle water."

"The link first," she said.

He nodded and went to the wall, establishing the link. She bowed her head, stifled a sneeze, and then ran her fingers through her hair. It was damp. She had to look a mess.

"All set," he said. "Her name is Detective DeRicci. I'll be right back with your water."

Oliviari looked up. A woman's face hovered near the wall. Holographic projection. It looked odd.

This was the woman Oliviari had seen hours ago stepping through the bleachers. She looked competent, and she was the first person that Oliviari had seen in the past hour who didn't look scared.

"I thought I was supposed to talk to a Mikhail Tokagawa," the woman said.

"You're better off talking to me." Oliviari forced herself to focus. "You're the detective in charge?"

"Noelle DeRicci. But I have no idea who you are."

The tech came through the door, handed Oliviari a large bottle of miracle water, and then left, pulling the door closed behind him. She twisted off the cap.

"You wouldn't know who I am," Oliviari said. "And that's part of the reason I'm talking to you."

"I don't have time for riddles," DeRicci snapped.

"I'm not going to give you any. I'm going slow because I'm ill. I want to get this right, because I might not get another chance."

Oliviari had to be clear about that. She needed to let Detective DeRicci know that she would be on her own shortly. If this fuzziness continued to take Oliviari's brain, it wouldn't matter whether she stayed conscious or not. She wouldn't be able to answer questions in any meaningful way.

"All right," DeRicci said. "You're the one who says this is the Tey virus, right?"

"Actually," Oliviari said. "Dr. Tokagawa agrees."

She took a swig from the miracle water. It was cool and tasted faintly of strawberries.

"My name is Miriam Oliviari. I've been Tracking Frieda Tey for years. I have followed more leads than you can imagine, and I made a serious mistake when I came to Armstrong."

DeRicci didn't move. It almost seemed like the holographic projection of her head was fake—something inserted into the room to make it seem like DeRicci was listening when she really wasn't.

"I didn't register with the police," Oliviari said. "I'm sure you'll want to investigate me and my background. Go ahead. You can check my DNA to make sure I am who I say I am. But do all this after you fight this virus."

"We've already quarantined the area," DeRicci said. "I'm not sure what else we can do."

"I am," Oliviari said. "I've already told Dr. Tokagawa and his assistants. He's taking care of it. You can make sure none of your people leave."

"I've already done that," DeRicci said.

"And that no one else comes in here." Oliviari blinked. "No one has left since they arrived, have they?"

"My assistant is checking on that." DeRicci moved her head as if she were looking at someone. Oliviari had a hunch DeRicci just used that moment to make the assignment.

"Good," Oliviari said. "Let me give you what I know as quickly as I can, because you need to be in contact with your headquarters."

DeRicci frowned. Oliviari felt like she had the detective's full attention, and she was grateful for that.

"I was hired by the families of Tey's victims," Oliviari said. "They're the reason we can even hope to save anyone here. They badgered decontamination companies to make sure their units could zap the Tey virus, even though the virus has never spontaneously appeared before today—"

"Do you think it was spontaneous?" DeRicci asked.

"No," Oliviari said, "and I'll get to that. But let me tell you this first. The families were afraid she'd strike again. They thought she was crazy—and you have to understand, there's some debate about that. Some people think Tey's a reputable scientist who became a scapegoat for an experiment that went awry. But it's not that simple—nothing is—and you have to know this."

"Know what?" DeRicci sounded impatient.

Oliviari wiped more sweat from her forehead, then made herself take a long drink from the miracle water. The dizziness was coming back.

"Frieda Tey is a spectacular scientist," Oliviari said. "All of her experiments before this, all of her work, has been to show that humans haven't reached their full potential, and that we must. In this alien-infested universe, she believes the only way we'll survive as a species is to grow, to change, to use the best of ourselves."

"I've heard this before from a whole lot of other people who haven't murdered anyone," DeRicci said.

"Exactly. It's not new," Oliviari said. "What is new—and what Tey was trying to do—is that she felt people could be forced to develop. She thought if she could isolate whatever it is that makes some people react better under severe stress, then she could teach all of us to do it."

"Do what?" DeRicci asked.

"How to step beyond our limitations." Oliviari made herself drink again. The water was nearly gone. She had no idea she'd had that much. "She had two theories on this. The first was that we learned how to become better, how to tap all of our potential. The other was that it was biological, that some people were able to do better in stress than others, and if we could isolate what caused it, we might be able to enhance the entire population, so that we'll all be super-human."

"She used that word?" DeRicci asked.

"No, it's mine." Oliviari shook her head. "It's the best shorthand I know, even with the negative connotations."

"This is background and it's not important," De-Ricci said. "I don't care why she did it. I just care that she's done it, and that now her damn virus is loose in my city."

"It is?" .

"It will be if we're not careful." DeRicci seemed to cover quickly enough, but her eyes moved sideways. She was lying. There were traces of the virus in Armstrong then, and that was very, very bad news.

"We might be too late then," Oliviari muttered.

"What?" DeRicci asked.

"If it's loose in Armstrong."

"It's only loose here," DeRicci said. "And I think we've got it contained."

"Okay," Oliviari said, even though she wasn't reassured. There was just nothing she could do about it. Not now, not in this condition.

Damn Tey, anyhow. What made her snap at this point, when Oliviari had been so close?

"You thought it was important I know this," De-Ricci said. "Why?"

"Oh." Focus. Oliviari really had to focus. "Because I think Tey's using Armstrong as her next experiment. A greater, larger site. The dome itself, with millions of people instead of hundreds."

"But she can't study us," DeRicci said. "There's no place that she could watch the experiment unfold."

"She doesn't have to watch it from here," Oliviari said. "This isn't an isolated place. We have media here, and we'll be keeping records of everything. If she's right, then a few people would survive even if we don't contain all of this. They would have been witnesses to it too."

Oliviari finished the water. She was having trouble catching her breath.

"If that's the case," DeRicci said, "and she gets what she wants, then what? What does it mean? Nothing. She will have murdered people to get the results, and everyone'll discount them."

"That's the beauty of her original plan," Oliviari said. "She wouldn't have been discounted. None of it would. No one would have known that Frieda Tey was connected to all of this—and if they figured out that she was Jane Zweig, well, then, we already have it on record from your own department that Zweig or Tey or whatever you want to call her died before the virus outbreak started. She guaranteed that there'd be media coverage by having the death—a prominent death—occur at the marathon."

Oliviari wheezed, coughed, and held up a hand. De-Ricci looked concerned. Oliviari made herself take shallow breaths. She had to finish this, had to get everything she knew to DeRicci before the virus took over.

"In other words," Oliviari said, "she wouldn't benefit from it—at least in the eyes of the public and the other scientists. She would have disappeared again, and this time no one would search for her. She would have continued writing her articles all under pen names. She probably would have established herself as a scientist under a new name, and gained respectability."

"I still don't see how," DeRicci said. "It seems like some sick person's wet dream to me."

Oliviari shook her head, and then wished she hadn't. "No, that's the ingenious part. Everyone would have looked at this as a disaster. Armstrong Dome taken out by a virus that no one expected. And science moves forward from disasters because no one wants the scenario to repeat. Human relations often move forward too. So if some unknown scientist could prove—using the Armstrong disaster—that human beings could avoid similar things, even maybe gain domination on the interstellar stage, by doing whatever it is Tey would believe she learned from the disaster, then we'd do it. We always do. We never want disasters to repeat themselves.''

DeRicci stared at her. It was an eerie effect, the clear gaze of those eyes from the disembodied head. Oliviari knew she was having this reaction, in part, because she wasn't feeling well, but she also had the sense that DeRicci was judging her in lieu of Tey. That by espousing Tey's views, Oliviari had put herself in the same category.

"So," DeRicci said after a moment, "all of this investigation, all of this mess, is a prelude to a big-scale experiment. She killed Eve Mayoux so that she'd have a body out there, so that we'd think that Zweig was dead, so that she'd disappear. Son of a bitch.''

Oliviari had to force herself to concentrate. "Eve Mayoux? Did you say Eve Mayoux? Duncan Mayoux's sister?''

"Yeah." DeRicci frowned. "You know her?''

"She's one of the people who hired me. I work for her. I work for the families of the victims. I have from the start.'' Oliviari put a hand to her forehead. She felt as if she were on fire. "Eve must have seen her, must have recognized her. That's why this year. That's why Tey was so clumsy that we caught her. I'll bet if Tey had more time to plan, we would never have known.''

"You were close to her, though," DeRicci said. "You're at the marathon.''

Oliviari nodded. But she wondered. Were those intuitive leaps she credited herself with actually hers? Or were they small clues, very tiny clues, that Tey had left for her, getting her here to get her out of the way as well?

She would never know.

"You've got to find her," Oliviari said. "If this doesn't work, she'll try again. She's obsessed with this. If you look at her records at Extreme, you'll see that she would routinely send people places they weren't qualified to go. She was trying to test on a small scale. That's one of the things that brought me here, one of the things that made me think Jane Zweig might be Frieda Tey. If she can't do it on a large scale again, she'll continue on a small scale."

"You've studied her," DeRicci said. "Where would she go?"

"She's leaving the Moon," Oliviari said. "She'll go as far away as she can, as quickly as she can. We might even have missed her. I'm sure that was part of the plan. Keep us busy so that we can't trace her if we get lucky and figure everything out."

"What a nightmare," DeRicci said.

"Oh, yeah." Oliviari took a shallow breath. She resisted the urge to cough, not wanting to alarm the detective. "And if we didn't contain this virus like we think we have, then this nightmare has just begun."

34

Flint never ordered dinner in. He always saw it as a lapse of security, one more way someone could figure out his systems and get to him. He also tried to vary his routines—which was even more difficult, given the sameness of his life when he was not working a case.

He had been tempted to break his own rule this time, and order in a sandwich, but he didn't. He ordered one through his links, and picked it up himself. He needed the chance to move around anyway. He was getting restless in his tiny office, even though he was working hard.

The evening was a pleasant one. Whoever had set Twilight in the filters had made the dome a very pleasant sienna, which, combined with the rays of the sun, made the entire area look like it had been painted with a light brown brush.

It added class to the dilapidated buildings, making them seem almost new. Flint carried the sandwich in the returnable plastic container and enjoyed the scenery, something that didn't happen much to him in this neighborhood.

He had nearly reached his building when his personal link sprang to life. DeRicci's message bounced back to him, unread, the emergency whistle blaring as if he had sent the message at a high priority to himself.

Anger flared through him. She had promised him

she would check the messages. Then he realized that
DeRicci usually kept her promises. Something had
happened to divert her attention, something that
caused her to use her links and, in typical DeRicci
fashion, clear out the messages that clogged them before she opened anything.

He tried to send the message back, but the links
were blocked again. He ran the rest of the way to his
office, double-checked as he always did to see if anyone was watching him before he opened the door, and
then, feeling secure enough, went inside.

He closed the door, reset the security, and hurried
to his desk, setting the sandwich container on a corner
as he slid into his chair. He punched up the main
screen and logged in to one of the media areas, hoping
to catch a news cycle.

Instead he got Earth's weather. He did a search for
current marathon news, and found nothing except the
rerun of Gumiela's press conference from earlier in
the day.

They weren't letting anything out. Or maybe something had happened with DeRicci.

Flint grabbed the container, opened it, and removed
the sandwich, taking a bite while he searched for news
in other venues, hoping to find something on Tey,
Zweig, or the marathon.

Nothing.

At least the sandwich was good, black beans cooked
in some kind of sauce with fresh lettuce and a real
tomato, wrapped in a tortilla that, even though it had
been made from Moon flour, didn't taste of cardboard.
He chased it down with bottled tea and continued his
search, all the while setting the message for DeRicci
on automatic—so that it would continue to send to
her until she received it.

Then his screen pinged at him. Flint looked at the
small window appearing in the upper left-hand corner.
A retinal scan was in progress at the spaceport—and

it took him a moment to realize why he was being notified.

He had left bugs in the Extreme Enterprises system in case someone tried to access the security files. Part of the bug would also show him whenever there was a personal scan, and one was going on right now.

He punched the keyboard and made the window bigger. The scan came from Extreme's personal space yacht. Apparently the yacht was tied in with Extreme's systems. Someone was trying to gain entry to the yacht itself—standing outside the door and letting the system scan her eyes.

That someone was Jane Zweig.

Flint cursed, stood, and knocked over his bottle of tea. It crashed to the floor, spilling the remaining tea on the ancient permaplastic. He didn't care.

It was too late. Zweig was going to get out of Armstrong.

Time to use his own connections. He sent a message through his links to Sheila Raye, the chief of the space cops. She was a desk cop, but she used to do field-work, and she understood procedures. He used to work for her, and she had always claimed he had made a mistake when he left.

There was a lot of goodwill between them, and he needed every bit of it.

Her holographic image appeared on his desk, her entire body standing before him, only six centimeters high. "Miles," she said with a smile. "I—"

"Sheila, I'm sorry, but I have an emergency."

She became all business. "What?"

"I've been working with Detective DeRicci, but I can't reach her. I wanted her to get some cops to a space yacht to prevent liftoff, but she has her links shut off. The yacht's being accessed right now."

"You're not with the force anymore, Miles."

"I know," he said. "I'm calling in every favor I've got."

"Whose accessing? Is it being stolen?"

"No. I'm sending you the specs now." He pressed a button and they went directly to her. "I need you to stop this woman from leaving the Moon."

Raye looked down at an unseen screen, then shook her head. "I wish I could help, Miles, but she owns the yacht, and she's not a felon. There's nothing I can do without risking my job—"

"Risk it," he said. "She's a Disappeared and she's dangerous. If we let her go, then we'll have a lot to answer for."

"Not enough, Miles," Raye said. "I wish I could help, but I can't. Besides, it looks like she's already got clearance."

Flint's system was telling him the same thing. The scan had stopped. Zweig was inside the yacht, and the yacht was powering up.

Zweig was leaving, and he couldn't stop her.

"Can't you stall? Maybe check her license, anything? Warn her of a threat, make me sound like the bad guy. Have some space cops pull her over for lift-off violations?"

"Miles—"

"Harass her for a few minutes," he said. "Give me time to get there, and at least I can tail her until I can reach DeRicci and she can give you proper authorization."

"I have no idea how you talk me into these things." Raye crossed her arms. "Consider it done."

And then her image winked out.

"Sheila, I could kiss you," he said, even though she couldn't hear him any longer. He pulled open his desk drawer and removed his laser pistol.

Getting to the port would be no problem, but what he would do when he got there would. Patrol ships had souped-up engines—they could catch anything except the latest yacht. His old cruiser couldn't get him past a thirty-year-old junker, and he had just used up a lifetime's worth of favors with Sheila Raye.

Paloma had been trying to get him to buy her yacht, and he kept saying he didn't need it. But it was state-of-the-art, and it was fast. Maybe not as fast as patrol ships, but he wasn't even sure of that anymore.

As he headed out of his office, he sent a message for her down the links, and hoped that she, at least, would respond.

35

That Tracker didn't look good. DeRicci had never seen someone whose skin was so gray she looked like she was made of Moon dust. Her eyes had sunk into her face, and at times she swayed as she spoke.

Still, she had conveyed a sense of urgency, and when they severed the connection, DeRicci knew she had to find Zweig/Tey before the woman succeeded in disappearing.

DeRicci's stomach churned. She hoped that it was the tension, the coffee, and the pastries. The last thing she wanted was this virus, and she was going to get it if they couldn't figure out a way to stop this thing.

Van der Ketting and Landres had left during her conversation with Oliviari. Perhaps they were doing what DeRicci had asked them to do—she could barely remember what that was anymore—or perhaps they, like her, could barely stand to look at the poor desperately ill woman.

How many people in that medical tent were that ill? Were the doctors surviving?

DeRicci didn't know the history of the Tey virus, not like Oliviari obviously did (and wouldn't it have been nice if the damn woman had registered with the city, so no one would have been surprised by all of this?), but DeRicci had had a lot of courses in emergency training for dome settings, and she knew that diseases, fast-spreading diseases, often took out the medical workers first.

Oliviari had said that something could be done, and they were doing it, but DeRicci was never that optimistic. She would have to get into the middle of the planning too—no matter what the risk to her own health—just to make sure everything was being done right. Not that she was better at emergency management than everyone else, but she was the person in charge of this scene, and she did know how to run staff around.

First, though, she had to contact Gumiela once again.

DeRicci pushed aside the pastries and stared at the coffee for a moment. The bungalow was too hot, and it felt cramped, even without the two men in it.

She slumped into a chair and turned on her links. Whistles, red lights flashing across her eyes, more emergency messages, half of them from Flint. Then the entire system flashed once, and winked out.

DeRicci sat up, blinking hard. She tried to reload her links, but she got nothing.

She had so many messages, they had overloaded her system.

She cursed, got up, and used the wall unit as a public link. She couldn't talk to Gumiela on it—someone might hack in—so she paged her instead, telling Gumiela that her links had crashed and that she needed to talk to her.

Gumiela—or one of her little minions—could get the links back up quickly.

Or at least DeRicci hoped she could.

Then DeRicci's hand-held, lying on the table, beeped. Gumiela's image was on the screen.

Neat trick, that. DeRicci hadn't even thought of using the built-in hand-held links. They were redundant technology, left over from the days when most people didn't have links.

"I'm in the middle of your research," Gumiela snapped—and her irritation didn't even bother De-Ricci. Everyone was on a short fuse. "I don't have time to deal with problems you caused by shutting down your links."

"That's not why I contacted you," DeRicci said, "although I do need my links back up soon. I'm waiting for an important message."

Gumiela waved a hand dismissively. "Someone's working on it."

"Good," DeRicci said, "because we have another problem. The woman who caused all of this, Jane Zweig or Frieda Tey or whatever you want to call her, is trying to disappear again. She's going to be leaving Armstrong, if she hasn't already. You've got to shut down the ports."

"Noelle," Gumiela said with no rancor whatsoever, "the last time I shut down the ports for you, the fugitive got away."

"She can't get away," DeRicci said. "She's trying to destroy an entire city. Besides, the ports should be shut down anyway. We've got a health crisis. Isn't anyone following the playbook?"

"The mayor has opted to keep it quiet so far. We don't have any proof that the virus has spread beyond the marathon site."

"And you won't get proof until someone dies," De-Ricci snapped. "By then, people will have gone all over the solar system, infecting as they go."

"No worries on that," Gumiela said. "The decon units at the port are set for the Tey virus."

"For incoming," DeRicci said. "And that's if the units work. I have good authority that they might not."

Gumiela ignored that comment. "All port decon units are set for the Tey virus and have been since they figured out how to kill it in the lab."

So she'd been reading up on it too.

"Right," DeRicci said. "That protects us from someone bringing it in."

Which, of course, begged the question of how Zweig had done it. She had probably brought it in privately. Smuggling was an easier step than murdering someone—and she'd already killed a number of people.

"But what about the rest of the solar system? We're going to be exporting this stuff."

"I don't think so," Gumiela said. "All Earth Alliance decon units are set for the virus."

"You hope," DeRicci said. "Shut down the ports, Andrea. Imagine if we start a systemwide epidemic. Imagine. Then catch Zweig. There are pictures of her everywhere in the media. She wasn't shy about that. I'm not sure how she'll be leaving—train, private vehicle, spaceport—I have no idea, but shut them all down. And check the surface-vehicle permits. She might have left in the last few hours."

"If I were unleashing a virus on an entire dome," Gumiela said, "I'd get out as fast as I could. She's probably long gone, Noelle."

"Probably, but best to cover our asses. Please, Andrea."

"You're not going to threaten to go upstairs again, are you?" Gumiela said.

"If I have to." DeRicci tucked a strand of hair behind her ear. "Do I have to?"

"No. It'll be done. Let's hope to God we catch her."

"If we don't," DeRicci said, "some other community will go through this."

And another and another. DeRicci didn't want to think about it. She shut off her hand-held without signing off again, and sent a message to Flint.

She got only audio in return.

"You promised me you'd check your damn messages." He was in an aircar. She could tell from his distracted tone. Flint sounded like that only when he was driving. "I keep getting them sent back to me."

"It's a mess here," she said. "I've got reason to believe that Tey's going to try to disappear again."

"Try?" His voice rose. "She has, Detective. That's why I've been trying to contact you. She's in Extreme Enterprises' space yacht. She got clearance and she's taken off. I got Sheila Raye to send some space cops after her, to delay her, but I don't have any authority to stop her. If I'd been able to reach you, we could have kept her in Armstrong."

DeRicci felt a flush warm her face. She was glad Flint couldn't see her. She didn't want Tey's escape on her hands.

"I just told Gumiela to shut down the ports."

"Too late," Flint said. "Tey's out and gone. Get ahold of Raye, have her authorize an arrest. That's our only hope now."

"Where're you?" DeRicci asked.

"On my way to the port," he said. "I've got a ship waiting for me. I'm heading out there to see what I can do."

"You're not using your junker, are you?" she asked. "It'll never catch up to anything."

"I've got a different idea."

"I'll get permission for you to ride with a team of cops," DeRicci said. "They'll get you into the middle of things."

"Thanks," Flint said. "It'll be my backup."

And then he signed off. Backup? Why would he use that as a backup? What was he planning?

DeRicci didn't have time to contact him in return. Instead, she used her hand-held to link with the health department herself, to see if someone—anyone—was sending the portable decon units here.

She wasn't going to worry about the fugitive right now. That was Flint and Gumiela's problem. DeRicci had something else to do.

She had a lot of lives to save—starting with her own.

36

"The first decon unit arrived," Tokagawa said.

He put his arm around Oliviari's back, holding her up. She hadn't realized she'd been leaning forward, almost collapsed, on the desktop.

"It's just inside the dome. You go through our air-lock and then into the decon unit. Come on. We're going to get you there."

She looked up at him. The office was spinning, and the lights seemed to be blacking in and out, although Tokagawa didn't seem to notice.

Oliviari wondered if that was her. It was probably her. Nothing was working right anymore.

"Is it the right specs?" she asked him, not moving.

"Yes." His arms were cradled around her. "Come on."

"Where is it? You can't have it anywhere where you'll mix the sick and the healthy. You've got to let the healthy congregate somewhere else."

"I know, Miriam." His voice was gentle. "It's just inside the dome. We've set up an area for the newly decontaminated to go. It'll work."

"Good." She leaned on him. She hadn't expected him to be strong. He'd seemed so weak before.

"Come on," he said.

"Only one unit?" she asked, her eyes closed.

"For now. It was close. One of the warehouses had upgraded just last year. The others are portables coming from various parts of Armstrong. There are built-in units, too, but the city health department and I decided not to bring anyone through Armstrong to get to them. We figure we have about six units coming our way in the next hour."

"Six units." It felt better with her eyes closed. "Seven with the one you have."

"Yes," he said.

"At what? Three minutes a person to do the full decontaminate?"

"I don't know. Miriam, let's go."

"You have to know," she said. God, she was tired. "Triage, remember? Not everyone'll get better."

"Especially if they don't get into the units. We need you well." He physically lifted her off the desk. Her legs felt rubbery. She wasn't sure she could move even if she wanted to.

"No," she said. "You forgot what I told you. People with full-blown symptoms can't get better."

"That was the earlier version of the units. They think it's fixed with the modern ones." His voice rumbled inside his chest. She could actually feel it vibrate as he spoke.

"They think." She used the last of her strength to push away from him. As good as it felt to have him hold her up, she had to show him she was still thinking clearly. And part of that was to show him that she was strong. "You're gambling too much on something untested."

"It's all untested outside the lab," he said. "You're the one who knows the most about this disease. We need you."

"Not anymore," she said. "It's out of my hands. We're in new territory now. Just do what I said. Please. Save as many lives as you can."

He peered at her. His eyes were bloodshot and his hair was damp. He wasn't much healthier than she was.

"Start with the people who've been exposed and only have a fever. Like you." She smiled at him. "You haven't sneezed yet, have you?"

"I'm fine," he snapped.

Like she was fine. "Then go to the healthy ones. The people who have no symptoms at all. Then, only then, get everyone else."

"We can't," he said. "We have so many sick—"

"Do the math." She swayed, and put a hand on the desk to steady herself. "Seven units times three minutes times how many people? Divided by how fast this thing spreads. You'll have deaths no matter what you do. More if you don't follow my advice. Please, Mikhail—" His first name was Mikhail, wasn't it? Oh, well. It didn't matter. He'd get the idea. She was trying to be as familiar with him as she could so that he would trust her. "—Please. Triage. You're going to lose a lot of people today. Make it the ones who're already doomed."

He put his arm around her and steadied her. "Come on."

"Please," she said. "Listen to me."

"I am listening to you," he said. "And I will triage, but I'm getting you through that decon unit."

"So I can contaminate the healthy people if the virus doesn't die in me? No." She dug her feet in and wrenched herself away from him. "This is all my fault anyway. If I had caught her earlier, maybe followed her more closely, could prove that it was Tey—"

"It's not your fault. She's crazy." He reached for Oliviari again, but she moved out of his way.

She opened the door and stumbled into the main part of the tent. The cots were still full, people were still coughing, sneezing, throwing up. The filtration units couldn't keep up, and the stench was growing hideous.

Oliviari leaned on the door, then let it swing her back into the office. "I'm staying here," she said. "Come and get me when the first two groups have gone through the unit."

"That'll be hours," he said.

She nodded. "I need the time. I'll be all right. You'll see. I'm only this dizzy because I've been pushing, but if I rest, I'll be fine."

He studied her for a moment. He didn't believe her; she could see it in his eyes.

"It's not your fault," he said after a moment. "You stopped it. Without you, the entire city would have been destroyed."

She smiled at him, grabbed the doorknob, and pushed him away. He stepped outside.

"Do you want me to send someone?" he asked.

"I'm a Tracker," she said. "I prefer to be alone."

Then she pulled the door closed and slumped to the floor, head buried in her arms. She had lied to Tokagawa again. She didn't prefer to be alone, but that was the life she'd chosen.

The death she'd chosen.

She closed her eyes and let herself drift into the sleep that had been beckoning—knowing there was a good chance she would never wake up.

37

Flint hadn't been in Terminal 25 in almost five years, and never to fly a ship out of the Port, only to arrest someone or to investigate a problem. Terminal 25 had gleaming walls and pristine floors. The odors of damp plastic and too many sweaty bodies that made the Port so familiar were missing from this place.

Terminal 25 was the place where the rich kept their state-of-the-art space yachts. It was home to more illegal contraband than any other two terminals combined, and yet much of the contraband slipped right past the space cops' noses here—probably because someone gave them credits, which made the space cops close their eyes.

No one had ever assigned Flint to Terminal 25, knowing he would probably anger too many people. He didn't believe in closing his eyes now; he certainly hadn't then either.

All the ships were down, grounded, so Sheila Raye said. She was in her office, handling the flak. The order had come from the mayor. All the ports were closed. But Flint had gotten special dispensation to leave—after he had gone through decontamination, losing even more precious minutes to make certain he wasn't taking Tey's virus off the Moon with him.

Frieda Tey had managed to leave before the ships were grounded. The space cops had delayed her as much as they could by asking for registrations and identifications, and by making her run through all sorts of tests and conditions. She fulfilled all of them. Her ship's registration was legal, her ID looked up-to-date, and she had kept her ship in top condition.

Then the order had come down to shut down the port, and the police identified Frieda Tey as a fugitive. Raye had been prepared for that. She had sent two traffic ships after Tey, to catch her and bring her back to the Moon.

Traffic could do that, even if the cops were out of their jurisdiction, so long as the crime was Moon-based and serious enough to justify to Earth Alliance. Tey met both conditions. Her crimes on Armstrong were serious enough that the space cops could chase her all over the galaxy and no one would complain.

Once they caught her, they would bring her back here.

If they caught her.

Flint scurried down the loading ramp, showing the special dispensation Raye gave him each time he passed a traffic cop. They all nodded to him, even if they'd never worked with him, knowing who he was. Once he'd been their hero—getting a promotion to detective, moving out of one of the most dangerous jobs in the police department to one of the most glamorous—and then he had given it all up for something most cops considered one step above criminal.

Flint was certain the cops here wondered why Raye was helping him at all.

He reached the edge of the dock and skidded to a stop. He'd never seen Paloma's yacht—the *Dove*—up close before. It was brand-new, which startled him. He thought she'd owned it for a number of years.

It was also sleek and pointed, built for speed, not luxury. He would have thought that Paloma would have gone for luxury, like she had done with her apartment.

She hadn't asked any questions when he had contacted her. She hadn't seemed surprised either. She reminded him that she had given him the codes for her yacht when he'd bought the business, figuring that he'd have to take the vehicle from time to time.

I'm charging rent, remember? she'd said, and left it at that. She hadn't even asked what he was working on.

He had a feeling she didn't have to, and that feeling bothered him.

Still, he stopped in front of the main door, feeling as though he were breaking into someone else's ship. His fingers shook as he keyed in the code—Paloma had a series of locks, each more sophisticated the deeper into the ship he went—and the main door slid upward without a sound.

Nice.

The air lock was small and efficient. Flint waited until the main door eased down before speaking the day's code into the audio pad. That opened the first door into the ship. He took a step farther, and pressed his finger on the plate above the knob on the second door. It rose as his fingerprint registered.

Then he stepped inside.

Lights came on as he moved, and he felt the rush of air as the environmental systems turned on high. He was in a corridor that led to the pilot's area directly in front of him. To his right were passenger quarters and the recreation area, such as it was in a ship this small.

He hurried down the hall into the cockpit. The yacht was set up for a one-, two-, or three-person team. He placed his palm on the main screen, and the yacht powered on around him.

He strapped in, and linked up with space traffic control.

"This is the *Dove*," he said. "I have special permission from Sheila Raye to depart the Port of Armstrong. I need emergency clearance. Please open the dome hatch above me as soon as possible."

"Acknowledged." The response was automated, which didn't reassure him, but the ship informed him that the hatch was opening over their dock.

He glanced at the controls, saw that they were standard, and looked for any special features. With the flick of a finger, he turned on audio information, and instructed the ship to tell him its specs, including any changes from regulation.

As the computerized voice droned on, he concentrated on piloting the ship upward, clearing the dock, and heading into Moon space.

Once he'd been one of the best pilots in Traffic. He kept his skills up weekly, just like he exercised, never knowing when he would need to use them.

He would need them now.

Sheila Raye had given him the coordinates for Extreme Enterprises' yacht. Flint plugged them into the navigation system, and hoped he would at least have a chance of catching up to Frieda Tey.

Although he doubted it. She had too much of a head start.

But he had to try.

38

DeRicci let herself out of the bungalow. There were no unis guarding the door. The anteroom, which had been so crowded not an hour before, was completely empty.

She stepped out to find herself in a new world. People were scurrying back and forth. Volunteers were taking down the bleachers, and other people—not wearing the bright T-shirts of the marathon—were putting up plastic barriers that the public events often used to corral crowds down a particular walkway.

An old dome wall had been lowered between the apartment buildings across the street and the main thoroughfare four blocks away. She hadn't seen an old dome wall come down in years, but it made sense.

Whenever Armstrong made its dome bigger—which seemed like it happened once a decade—the city kept the old walls. After the expansion was finished, the dome engineers replaced the old walls with retractable ones, so that the dome could be sectioned off in times of emergency.

Like now.

DeRicci stared at the old wall, and shook her head. She had asked the Tracker Oliviari if the virus had been airborne, and Oliviari had said no.

But DeRicci had forgotten to ask an equally important question—whether or not the virus had an air-

borne *stage*. If the virus did have an airborne stage—
and had hit it—then Armstrong was in serious trouble.
No lowered plastic wall would help.

This part of the dome was on its own now, and it
made DeRicci nervous. The city would do anything to
protect the rest of the dome. The reason the city isolated this section was simple: If the virus was here
and incurable, the city would solve the problem in a
ruthless way.

They'd use the air.

The city could pump anything through the air-
filtration system. This portion of the dome had been
separated out of Armstrong's air-circulation system
when that wall came down, just as the people had. If
the city wanted to, they could put in a toxic gas or
remove the air altogether. Or the dome engineers
could open one of the dome panels to Outside.

Even the most sophisticated environmental suit—at
least of human design—could protect a person for
only so long. Eventually it would fail. People in this
little sliver of dome would die a lingering death.

DeRicci shuddered and watched the volunteers
scurry around her. On the other side of the wall, air
trucks were pulling up with equipment on their flat-
beds. Pieces of the decon units.

She swore softly. She'd had no idea that the units
would have to be assembled. But it made sense. How
else would they travel through some of Armstrong's
narrow streets?

Time, time, and more time. From the look of that
Tracker, some of the people in the medical tent didn't
have time.

DeRicci turned her back on the wall and walked
toward the center of the activity. Of course Chaiken
was there, directing people as if he had expected his
day to be about surviving an epidemic instead of running a race.

"Your people are over there," he said, waving a hand toward a small dressing area that some of the runners had used to put on their environmental suits.

DeRicci glanced over, saw Landres talking to a handful of people. Van der Ketting stood near him, clutching a hand-held.

"You haven't told everyone what's going on yet, have you?" she asked.

"Well, a lot of them have figured it out." Chaiken pointed to one of the volunteers. "You! We need help on that panel. Move, and quickly. We have to get these set up before we can use the units."

DeRicci hadn't had any respect for him before, but she did now. She had worried that she would have to do this, but Chaiken already had it under control.

And she was relieved. He clearly had a lot more experience with organizing volunteers than she ever would.

"Figured it out how?" she asked.

"I guess it's a war zone in the medical tent." He stopped, put his hands on his hips, and shook his head. "We do this to celebrate life, Detective. The marathon started as a challenge, kind of a way to spit in the face of the gods, you know. Like we're human and we can conquer anything, any damn thing you put in front of us. Each person who runs this race, they come out of it saying that it's life-changing, that they realize if they can run in an environmental suit, their oxygen regulated, only a thin wall of reinforced fabric between them and death, then they can do anything."

His voice was shaking, but his eyes were dry. De-Ricci watched him. He looked away from her, snapped his fingers at two other volunteers, and directed them toward another sheet of plastic. It took DeRicci a moment to realize the plastic now being set up as walls had once formed the bleachers.

"Jane . . ." His voice broke. He cleared his throat,

took a deep breath, and started again. "Jane Zweig seemed to understand that. I'd have conversations with her about the importance of showing people what they could do, how essential strength was to living. I thought she agreed with me, and instead she used me. Why would she do that?"

DeRicci bit her lower lip, then shook her head. She knew some of the answers—the publicity that Zweig wanted so that people believed she was dead—and a few other things, but DeRicci hadn't thought about the personal side, the extreme side.

She remembered what Oliviari had told her, about the theories that Tey had regarding human potential.

Tey had chosen the marathon not just because it was the largest tourist event in Armstrong, but also because of the nature of its participants. She must have figured that if anyone would rise above the impossible problem she had set up for Armstrong Dome, it would be the people involved with the Moon Marathon.

And here they were, setting up paths in an orderly fashion, not rioting, not panicking, not trying to break into Armstrong proper, even though they had guessed, as Chaiken said.

They were working together to solve this the best they could.

DeRicci didn't know how to tell him that. She didn't know how to say that in some twisted way, Tey's choice of the Moon Marathon was a show of faith in the event Chaiken promoted.

So DeRicci patted his arm and shook her head. "She wasn't who anyone believed she was. Everything she did was a lie."

He waved a hand at a volunteer who nearly toppled her section of the wall. Chaiken ran over to help.

DeRicci remained where she was. She wondered how Chaiken would feel when he learned that Jane

Zweig was still alive. DeRicci wasn't going to tell him now, since that would simply distract him.

He had to concentrate on survival.

They all did.

It was the only way to defeat Frieda Tey.

39

Flint was well outside of Moon space heading toward Mars when he saw the first pieces of debris. Bits of metal too small to be considered chunks, whirling toward him at a speed that suggested they were part of a recent explosion.

The yacht had a reinforced hull, so small items, no matter how fast they were coming, couldn't penetrate. He would have to watch for bigger pieces, though, and he set the sensors on extra-wide scan, so that he could steer around any danger.

He tried not to think about what the tiny pieces of metal could mean.

The yacht itself had been a pleasant surprise. In addition to the reinforced hull, it had unprecedented speed. Even the traffic ships he'd used when he was a space cop hadn't had engines this refined.

He had made excellent distance in a record amount of time. And he stayed on the updated coordinates that Raye had sent him every fifteen minutes. She hadn't sent him anything for quite a while, which, he tried to reassure himself, didn't mean anything.

If the space cops were involved in an arrest, they weren't going to update their position. Even if they were involved in some kind of pursuit and thought they were undetected, they wouldn't risk sending the coordinates back to the Moon so that Raye could relay them to Flint. The last thing anyone wanted would be for Tey to scope them out.

Flint wasn't actually sure what he would be doing when he caught up to the space cops and Tey. Maybe acting as some kind of backup. The one thing Paloma's yacht lacked were external weapons, and he couldn't get the system to confess to any, either.

He knew some had to be hidden somewhere. Paloma was a cautious woman. With the amount of money she'd spent to reinforce the hull and to build up the engines, she would have thrown in some more credits to put in some weapons systems.

But because of that caution, and because Retrieval Artists worked alone, she probably didn't want someone to be able to access the weapons easily. Even though Flint had been tinkering with the ship's computers since he left the Moon, he couldn't find anything.

He was running a systems diagnostic, searching for unusual power diversions or parts of the ship that seemed to have no function. But he was having no luck.

The yacht also lacked some defensive items built into the traffic ships. There were no external lasers, designed to cut through grapplers or tunnels sent from other ships trying to illegally board. There were no double airlocks, and no small, enclosed space that could be used as a brig. He even doubted that handcuffing someone to a seat would be easy in this yacht.

His sensors picked up more debris, clouds of it coming his way. He steered around it and turned on the viewscreen so that he could see what he was facing.

Magnified at 1,000 percent the image merely looked like a smudge against the blackness of space. A lot of debris by human terms, but in space, it didn't count as much more than a speck.

Still, he had the ship analyze the debris heading

toward him. It was all man-made. Bits of reinforced plastic, more metal, and—alarmingly—bone.

He suspected that if he let the analysis continue, there'd be more than bone in the mix. Probably blood and water and flesh.

He shuddered. Something had happened out here, and had happened recently, but he had no idea what. He didn't even know if it was related to his search.

But Flint didn't like the coincidence.

If this debris was related to his case, he hoped he was looking at the remains of the Extreme Enterprises yacht. That would make everything easier for all of them.

But he would have to do something if it wasn't. That meant Frieda Tey saw the space cops, and destroyed their ships.

He couldn't go into the area like a conquering hero if he had no weapons at all except his laser pistol. He would need to let Armstrong Dome know what he'd found, and he'd have to stall Tey somehow.

He hadn't realized that in taking Paloma's ship, he would come out here essentially blind and toothless. He would have gone with a traffic ship if he'd known.

But then, of course, he wouldn't have been here yet—wouldn't have seen the debris, wouldn't be doing all this speculation. And he would be hampered by space cops who lacked the experience he had, who would question his every move because they had the right to, because they would have been the ones in charge.

The debris field had grown. It was big enough to be a good-sized ship, and the parts—what parts he could see on his screen—were black, not silver like traffic ships.

Maybe this was unrelated. Maybe he was thinking all this through for nothing. Maybe he really had lost their trail, and he was just out here on his own.

If that was the case, then he hoped the traffic cops stayed with her. The last thing he wanted was for Tey to escape.

The yacht eased around the debris field, and the perimeter scanner let him know that there were ships ahead. Flint let out a small breath. He put the images on-screen, but didn't get more than two blips, drifting apart. They were both silver—that much he could tell—and they were tiny.

He had the screen increase magnitude by a hundred percent. He still couldn't see much. Then he increased magnitude again.

The ships definitely were drifting, and he recognized their configuration. Their long, pointed shapes would have made them Moon Traffic issue even if the police logos on the side hadn't identified them that way.

One of the ships had scorch marks along its entire hull. The other had a hole blasted through the center of it. No one could have survived that, not with the design of the ship and the obvious destructive power of whatever had made that shot.

He had his yacht continue to scan for other ships. The powerful sensors Paloma had upgraded to found nothing in the immediate vicinity.

The two ships that had followed Tey were disabled or destroyed, and there was enough debris for a third ship. Apparently the Extreme Enterprises yacht had been destroyed.

Or that would have been what he thought if he were still a space cop, unfamiliar with this case. But Tey was cunning. She might have had a partner, someone who would pick up her escape pod after this fight. Or maybe someone who had been waiting out here, attacking the police ships that were following her, and then destroying the Extreme Enterprises yacht so that everyone would think—yet again—that Frieda Tey had died.

Was she that smart? Had she made that many contingency plans? Had she really believed that the police would have followed her this far, while dealing with an epidemic and a crisis inside of Armstrong?

Flint set up his scan to search for an escape pod hiding in the debris field, and found nothing. He wasn't just searching for Tey. He was searching for survivors. Then he widened the search, looking for a pod drifting away from these vessels, and still found nothing.

Flint sent his coordinates back to Armstrong, letting them know one ship had been destroyed and another disabled, and asking for backup out here. He sent the images, scrambled, so that Armstrong would realize he was not bluffing, that his word could be trusted, even though he was no longer on the force.

Raye would help him. Raye would help them.

Flint scanned the intact ship. He couldn't tell much. Police vessels were set up so that whatever was going on inside them remained hidden from criminals. The technology that made Paloma's yacht state-of-the-art also protected the traffic ships from the prying eyes of others.

The city of Armstrong insisted on that, and did upgrades every year. Apparently the upgrades had been effective.

What he learned was small: the engines had been disabled, and the rest of the ship's systems were intact. He could be certain about the engines because he knew the design of the ship, and he saw the damage where the engines had been. And he had gotten a glimpse of the cockpit as the ship slowly revolved, and noted that the main interior lights were on. If the ship's atmosphere had been compromised or its environmental systems had failed, the lighting would have changed from bright white to a pinkish red.

The system had been designed so that other space cops could know when their companions were in trouble, even if they couldn't scan inside the hull.

But the other extras on Paloma's yacht—the ability to scan for life signs—couldn't penetrate the reinforcements on the hull. If anyone was alive in there, Flint couldn't tell it from here.

He contacted the ship, sending a standard police emergency message and asking for a reply. He was being extremely cautious, he knew, but the times demanded that kind of caution. If some other ship were listening in from any distance, they would think that more of the space traffic fleet had arrived. They would think twice about returning here.

Anyone close by, of course, would see the *Dove*, and know that there was no fleet. But they would assume that there were traffic cops aboard this ship as well, making it tough to tangle with.

He only hoped they didn't scan for weapons.

He sent his message several times and got no response. That bothered him. He was no longer a space traffic cop, but he knew the procedures. If his partners were down or disabled, and help was on the way, he was to secure the scene as best he could.

He was doing that. He had scanned the area, found no suspicious vessels, and saw no evidence of other ships nearby.

The next step, then, would be to see if anyone survived, and to offer assistance that might be able to help any injured parties survive until the rescue vehicles arrived.

As a civilian, he didn't have to do any of that. He could sit here and wait—or he could fly off, trying to find Tey. But he had no idea what direction to go in: the only energy signatures in the area had come from the two ships in front of him, his own ship, and the ship that had been destroyed.

The trail ended here, whether he liked it or not.

He couldn't in good conscience stay on board the *Dove*. He checked the area near the airlock of the yacht and found some standard-issue environmental suits—he had been in such a hurry, he hadn't brought his—and he studied them for a moment.

They were in rough shape. Obviously Paloma hadn't used them much. She probably kept them on hand for emergencies among any passengers she might have.

He found one that had been police-issue when he started on the force. He ran the diagnostic, saw that the parts worked, then put the suit on, leaving the hood down.

Then he went into the cockpit to start the difficult task of boarding the revolving traffic ship.

Fortunately, the ship was turning slowly. He could get the yacht close to it and hook them up before the ship moved out of his way too far. It would be a difficult maneuver, but he'd done similar ones before.

The only difference was that he had had other traffic cops as backup, people who waited in the un-damaged ship to handle any problems that might arise.

Flint sighed and sent another message back to Arm-strong. He got a message in return: More traffic ships were on their way. Stabilize the situation; they would arrive soon.

Soon probably wasn't soon enough, especially if there were survivors. Pods could have drifted quite a distance already. If the pods hadn't been launched, then he might find badly injured people on board.

He slipped into the pilot seat. He programmed the computer to help him with the more difficult maneuvers—sending grapplers from his yacht to the ship to hold it stationary before he sent down the automatic tunnel that would link his yacht to the traf-fic ship's main entrance.

The maneuver took him nearly fifteen minutes, less time than he would have expected, considering the fact that he was doing it alone.

He set the ship on automatic, so that it would compensate for any problems that arose while he was gone.

Then he put his hood up, ran the environmental suit's diagnostic again, and headed to the disabled ship.

40

Thumps and bangs came from outside the wall. The airtrucks were lowering the parts of the various decontamination units. DeRicci had already spoken to the man in charge outside, and asked him to assemble a complete unit before starting on the next.

"We have a lot of sick people in here," she said, hoping he wouldn't pin her to a number, since she didn't have one. "The quicker we have a second working unit, the better."

He had agreed, and as she watched, several of the maintenance workers gathered around one of the units, talking and gesturing and arguing.

She hoped that was part of their work method. Each moment that clicked away could mean the loss of another life.

The volunteers had set up the plastic barriers, with doors to the various decontamination units. Only one of the barriers was operational now, and someone—she thought maybe it was Tokagawa—was funneling people through from the medical tent.

DeRicci couldn't see them come out the other side, although she knew from her discussions with the city that they'd still be isolated until upgraded diagnostic wands—and a precautionary blood test—gave them the all-clear.

She stood near the wall for a few moments, watching the workers set up the second decontamination unit. For the first time in years, she felt useless. She couldn't do much except wait.

She supposed she could continue the investigation, but they pretty much knew what was going on. Tey had killed Mayoux, probably in the airlock near the maintenance bay, put the pink suit on the body, then stashed it in the bay until the morning of the race. Once Tey had registered and gotten her singlet and her finger circled for the panic button, she had gone, removed the body, and driven it to mile five, leaving it behind the boulder.

She had deactivated the cameras—or set them up to be activated by a remote that she controlled—and then took the vehicle back to the race site, careful to stay out of sight.

When she returned to the staging area, she made a show of greeting friends and prancing for the cameras. She took off quickly and kept a good distance between herself and everyone else. When she reached mile five, she shut down the camera momentarily (mile six's was still off), carried the body to its final resting place, put her singlet on it, and circled the finger.

Then she turned the cameras back on and left.

How she got back to the dome was, at the moment, a matter for speculation. She might have run back, careful to stay parallel to the course, or she might have stashed another vehicle.

DeRicci figured Tey ran back, judging by how much time it took her to finish her escape.

DeRicci would have to do a lot of the work later to build a case for trial, but she had that investigation mapped out. It would be relatively easy once she was out of here.

If she got out of here.

She shivered once and walked toward the dressing area. It looked small and cramped. Landres was talking to van der Ketting.

"What's so interesting about this place?" DeRicci asked as she approached.

"Landres thinks this is the source of the virus," van der Ketting said. His tone held some resentment. Poor guy. He obviously didn't like to be outthought by someone who wasn't a detective.

"What did you find?" DeRicci asked.

"We haven't gone inside," Landres said. "I figure we save that for HazMat once they start working on this area. They'll be here, right?"

"As soon as we're out and cleared by the health guys," DeRicci said.

Landres nodded. "What we have is pretty simple. Actually, Leif found it."

"And I think it's just conjecture." Van der Ketting extended his hand-held. "I've got security footage of Zweig taking her environmental suit in there, getting changed, and leaving. The next person inside was the first guy who died from the virus. It seems tenuous."

"Except when we spoke to one of the medical guys," Landres said, "he thought it was odd that the guy got so very sick so fast when no one else did. He said maybe he got exposed to a more lethal dose."

"It's a virus," DeRicci said. "There's no such thing as a more lethal dose. Have you kept watching the security vid?"

"Not yet." Van der Ketting looked through the wall. "I've been a bit preoccupied."

DeRicci gave him a sympathetic smile. For all her irritation at him, she didn't blame him for being distracted right now. "We all are. But here's what I figure. I suspect everyone who got ill first went through this dressing area after Zweig got out. Did anyone collapse on the track from this?"

"I don't know." Van der Ketting looked back at her. She could actually feel his struggle to concentrate on the case and not the slow progress of the decon units.

"That's something else we'll have to find out," De-Ricci said. "When we get out of here, we're going to have a lot of backtracking to do. The more stuff we gather now, the better off we'll be. Who knows when HazMat'll let anyone in here again."

"Good point," Landres said.

DeRicci smiled at him. "And I'd like you to stay on this case, even after we've gotten out of here. You've been a big help."

He gave her a surprised look. So did van der Ketting.

"Thank you," Landres said, and it was clear that she had given him one of his dreams. Good. Let him focus on the future. She wished she could.

DeRicci glanced through the new wall again. The clump of workers seemed to have grown, but the air-truck was gone. Did that mean all the parts had been lowered?

She hoped so. She was beginning to feel restless, and she knew what that meant. It meant she needed to get out of here.

And if she was feeling that way when she understood everything that was going on, she wondered how all the others felt, the people who had no real idea about the devastating illness around them, the way they'd all been targeted, the fact that they were in jeopardy just because they had chosen to live their lives in an unusual way.

Time to take her own advice. Gather as much evidence as she could while she was still here. After all, she needed something to keep her busy. Something to keep her attention away from a tragedy she'd already done everything in her power to avert.

41

Flint climbed inside the tunnel between the two ships. His hood was on and the environmental suit's air tasted stale. It wasn't. He'd run the diagnostic so many times that he felt like he knew every inch of this suit, but he was being extremely cautious about everything.

He'd never been in space alone. Not even after his training. Space cops always had partners, and often worked in groups of four or six. Then there were always ships as backups.

And although he'd seen a lot of action, he'd never wound up in a situation like this one—one ship destroyed, the other disabled.

He had the suit's outside monitors on so that he could hear his own movement and any others. He was also hooked up to the *Dove*'s communications system. He had done that partly so that he wouldn't feel alone. But he also needed to cover his own back, and using all his senses was the only way he could figure out how to do it.

His boots hit the outside of the traffic ship. The side was scored by weapons fire, and the fire had gone deep. He wondered how much damage he'd find inside. The ship that had hit this one had a lot more firepower than any ship he'd ever come across.

He turned his body ninety degrees, and tucked his boots inside one of rungs on the tunnel. Then he crouched, using the emergency override to open the traffic ship's outside door.

The airlock was dark, just like it was supposed to be, but the warning light was not flashing. That meant that the environmental systems were still working.

He unhooked himself from the rung and floated inside, pulling the door closed. This was the first-stage airlock. There was a smaller, second stage that a lot of traffic cops used as a dressing room to remove their environmental suits.

On a whim, he typed his old override code into the keypad beside the door, and wasn't surprised when the door opened. No one changed all the codes on all the ships. It was simply too much work. The changes got inputted during a full overhaul, when the entire computer system changed.

It was a bad way to work, but so far the Port hadn't had the money to change it.

At the moment, he was grateful. He didn't want to have to disable the access panel and try to pry the door open by hand.

He slipped inside the airlock. The door closed behind him.

His movements echoed in the small space. There was gravity in here. His feet found the floor. The gravity anchored him, making him feel safe.

He had his suit run its external diagnostic. Not just gravity, but atmosphere. The lack of warning lights had been correct. The ship's internal environmental systems were still working.

Using his old code a second time, he opened the internal door. It slid sideways, and he stepped inside the ship.

There weren't any frills in traffic ships. No cushy seats, no comfortable carpets. Only plastic chairs bolted to the floor, with belts wrapped in them so that passengers wouldn't get thrown around the cabin.

The back of the ship had a large cargo hold for any items confiscated on long trips, and a small brig in case criminals were apprehended. Usually criminals were placed in these plastic chairs and handcuffed in, but every once in a while Traffic picked up people so violent that they needed to go into the brig.

Flint glanced around. The main lighting was up, and everything seemed normal. Nothing had spilled along the floor; there were no audio messages warning him of hull breaches or containment problems.

He reached to the side panel and double-checked the information his suit had given him. Yes, indeed, the environmental systems were working. The ship had sustained disastrous shots to the engines and to the weapons systems, but life support worked just fine.

What bothered him was that no one greeted him. By rights, at least two cops should have been on this ship. Were they wounded? Or were they so preoccupied with trying to effect repairs that they hadn't realized he'd come aboard?

Flint brought his hood down so that he could see and hear better. The ship was chillier than regulation allowed for, but he'd worked with partners who liked a cooler environment, so that didn't really disturb him.

What disturbed him was the faint odor of copper in the air. Someone in this ship was injured, dying, or dead.

He walked toward the cockpit. The hatch to the engines was shut and locked, the lights that indicated the lock was on revolving just like they were supposed to.

The door to the small galley was closed, which was unusual, but the cockpit door was open.

A hand stuck out of it, splayed and motionless. Flint grabbed his laser pistol and peered around the corner.

One cop, dead, his face mashed into the floor, his arms above his head. Flint didn't see any obvious blood, but he did see a big scorch wound in the man's back.

That wound didn't come from an accident with the ship. He'd been shot, and at fairly close range.

Flint brought his own pistol up, keeping it in front of him as he moved. He breathed shallowly, so that he could hear any door open or any boot thud against the plastic flooring.

Another body huddled next to the pilot's chair—a woman's, also in a traffic cop uniform. The smell came from in here. Blood still dripped off the console. A lot of blood.

Flint glanced at her as he moved closer to the controls. Her throat had been slit, and she'd bled out, unable to stop it.

Flint swallowed hard. His heart was pounding. He wasn't alone in here; that was becoming clear. Whoever was in here had killed either to survive or to take over the ship, apparently not realizing that the engines had been ruined in the firefight.

Time for him to leave, let the professionals handle this. As curious as he was, he was alone. And if he was facing Frieda Tey, as he expected, he needed support.

That much was clear.

He scanned the room, making certain she wasn't in here. He didn't want to turn his back to leave, only to give her an easy shot at him.

No one hid behind the console, and no one sat in the nearby seats.

The *Dove* was on the viewscreen, its perfect form outlined against the stars.

She'd been watching him. She'd probably heard him, too.

She had known what he would find.

And, if she was smart, she would realize that she had an advantage. He had delivered to her the perfect escape vehicle: one with working engines and more speed than any ship in the Moon's fleet.

He cursed, grabbed his hood, and pulled it back up, automatically hitting the diagnostic to make sure there were no leaks in the environmental suit. Then he ran for the airlocks.

He hadn't heard her move, but she was cunning and she was swift. She would have known to be quiet. He hadn't heard the doors, but she had only a few moments, and she wouldn't know the override codes.

The airlock would force her to stay inside for at least thirty seconds.

He ran for the doors, noting as he did that the galley door was now open. Damn, damn, damn. He had been preoccupied by that hand sticking out of the cockpit door, just as she had known he would be, and she had used that to her advantage.

The first airlock door was closed, and the rotating lock indicated that it was twenty-nine seconds into the cycle. Then he heard the inner door clang open—a sound he would have heard no matter where he was— and through the small window, he saw a suited body climb into the first airlock.

The door closed, and the second cycle started. Flint opened the inner door and stepped into the airlock. He could see her inside the other one, struggling with the panel.

Now she was at a disadvantage. She could no longer control the ship from the pilot's chair, resetting or opening controls at her whim. She might know the code she programmed but not the overrides.

He let the inner door close behind him, typed his code into the old panel, and overrode all commands, setting them to his code only. He jammed her door closed, making certain it would not open without three separate passwords from him.

Then he used the intercom, hoping she had her suit set for external sounds.

"You're trapped in there," he said. "I wouldn't try shooting your way out. Anything you do in that small space will probably ricochet and kill you."

For a moment, he didn't think she'd heard. Then he saw her move across the window and touch the intercom.

"What have you done with Paloma?" she asked.

42

The volunteers were wandering through the crowd in this section of the shut-off dome, getting them to line up for the various decon units. DeRicci forced Landres to get into line. He hadn't wanted to. He wanted to wait until she queued up before he did.

Van der Ketting had lined up long ago, and she didn't mind. She had actually given him permission. He had spent most of his time staring at the crews assembling the decon units rather than helping with the last-minute investigation.

DeRicci had done a few more interviews, gathered the rest of the surveillance equipment, and sent several different packets of information down her link. She'd isolated the dressing area so that no one would go into it accidentally, and she'd marked several other areas for HazMat to visit first.

She was grateful for the work. Otherwise she would be watching the crews assemble the decon units too, and wishing they would hurry.

They got the second one together fairly quickly, and then a third, and a fourth. They were working on a fifth. The units were fairly close together, so that there had to be only one line. When the other units arrived, they would probably be spaced out along the wall.

DeRicci got reports from various areas that the decon units already assembled seemed to be working.

So far, the people who had gone through had a later stage of the virus, but they were still mobile.

When they got out of the decon unit, the virus had left their system—at least so far as the diagnostic wands and blood tests could tell. But everyone who had been exposed would remain isolated for the rest of the night, to make sure this virus didn't hide in a person's system and then return.

The medical teams didn't think it would, but De-Ricci didn't trust them. This virus had been sneaky so far, and she expected it to continue to be sneaky.

Just like the person who had created it.

Landres had disappeared between the plastic walls as the line moved forward. DeRicci stood near the bungalow and stared Outside. Vehicles were parked near the finish line, and a few volunteers still remained at the tables, apparently cleaning up.

Those people probably hadn't been affected. They'd been wearing environmental suits all day, for hours before Jane Zweig even showed up at the race site.

They had agreed to wait Outside until the medical tent was cleared. Then they would go through that decon unit and join everyone else.

DeRicci wondered what it was like out there—not much to do, just wait, and hope that they didn't get ill like everyone else. They would be the last processed through the medical tent, which probably meant they'd go past bodies.

At the moment, she had no idea how many people had died. No one was releasing the numbers, and even though she could page the medical personnel and ask, she didn't. They were busy enough, keeping people comfortable.

She had a hunch a number of the medical team would die as well. They were on the front lines, and they weren't leaving until their patients did.

She wasn't leaving either. So far everything had

been orderly—surprisingly so—but she was afraid the order might not last.

If the crews couldn't get the remaining decon units running, then there wouldn't be enough time to help everyone who'd been exposed to this virus. These runners and volunteers weren't dumb. They'd figure it all out, that some of them might have to wait too long to be cured.

And if that happened, DeRicci fully expected some kind of riot.

She would do everything she could to prevent it.

43

Paloma? It was a trick. It had to be.

Tey must have read the registry on the *Dove* as Flint had approached this damaged ship. Then Tey would have discovered that the *Dove* was registered to someone named Paloma, and she would have decided to use the name to throw him off.

He didn't want to think about the fact that Frieda Tey might actually know Paloma. It raised more questions than he wanted right now, and it would distract him.

He saw a movement through the small window. Tey was floating toward the outer doors. Something glinted in her hand.

A knife. Of course. How else had she slit the pilot's throat? Frieda Tey was going to try to open the doors the old-fashioned way, with a knife blade and a lot of physical strength.

He didn't want to leave the area, but he had to. He had to make certain she had no real escape route.

Flint left the second airlock, headed through the inner doors, and hurried toward the cockpit. He stepped over the body of the first space cop and hurried to the pilot's chair. Paloma would hate what he had to do, but he had no choice. He reached for the exterior laser controls, the ones that prevented another ship from boarding. He had never done this before, not in this manner. He had used the external lasers on half a dozen ships, but he aimed them at the grapplers as they came toward the ship, not once they were attached.

He had no idea what severing the connection between the two ships would do to the space yacht. And he couldn't worry about that—not now.

His fingers slid across the blood-covered controls. He almost hit the wrong button. Fortunately, his environmental suit's gloves gave him some leverage, and he managed at the last minute to get a good grip on the correct part of the panel.

He hit the instructions for the lasers, then changed the viewscreen so that he could watch them work. The screen showed the edge of the hull. The lasers poked out of it, pointing toward the tunnel he had attached to the traffic ship.

With clear, bright red beams of light, the lasers severed the tunnel between the yacht and the ship. The yacht spun away, out of control.

The ship rocked. Flint grabbed the arms of the chair to keep his balance. He hadn't thought to strap in. Then the attitude controls kicked in and he couldn't feel the bucking anymore.

Flint hurried back toward the airlock doors. He wondered if Tey had gotten the main door open. If she had, she would be sucked into space the moment the tunnel separated from the ship. He peered through the windows, but couldn't see anything.

The exterior door seemed to be closed. He reached for the intercom when a scraping sound made him turn. Frieda Tey, so small she looked almost childlike, came at him from the passenger compartment, knife raised.

He managed to dodge, but not completely. The blade punctured his environmental suit and slashed down the leg, narrowly missing his thigh.

Flint grabbed Tey's wrist and pulled her around,

yanking her arm up her back so hard that he heard her shoulder dislocate. She screeched in pain. Then he pushed her toward the chairs, reaching for handcuffs—that he suddenly realized weren't there.

At that moment, she butted her head backward, her skull hitting his with such force that he lost part of his grip. She kicked upward, hitting him in the balls. His breath left his lungs, pain shooting through him, and somehow he found himself on his knees.

He was having trouble catching his breath. He was seeing red—pink, actually—and then he realized what was going on. He heard the faint whir of a fan, and knew that the air was leaving this part of the compartment.

She had looked at this ship's specs while she was alone in it. She knew that one of the many failsafes on board was isolated environmental controls, and she had this one set up—probably before he or anyone else got on board.

He looked up. She had vanished. The cockpit door was closed—she had taken advantage of his momentary weakness to go in there, and to regain control of the ship.

He put his hood up, but the suit informed him that it couldn't seal. The slash. She had planned this too. When he had turned on the lasers, she had reversed directions, using her knife to open the inner airlock door and come inside the ship.

She had taken those few seconds while he separated the *Dove* from this ship to set up a secondary plan.

He cursed mentally, and made himself concentrate on his own problem. She had no idea who he was, so she didn't know what kind of training he'd had.

He ripped one of the belts off the passenger chair and tied it around his leg, sealing the suit as best he could. Then he overrode the environmental suit's controls, the ones that blocked it from starting its protocol when the suit had a puncture. He put the hood back up and took a deep breath.

This wouldn't hold him very long, but it would give him the extra few minutes that he needed.

He went to the side panel that he had first used, punched in his code, and used the emergency code that had been valid when he was a traffic cop.

The system beeped at him. It had rejected the emergency code, and it shouldn't have, not since it took his other old codes.

Tey had changed it. She hadn't known about the individual codes, but she had known about the emergency override.

Somehow, while she was waiting, she had managed to find the code and delete it.

He pressed his hood close to the panel so that he could see what he was doing. He would have to hack his way in, and hope that the system didn't catch on to what he was doing. He also had to hope that Tey didn't catch on either. If she did, she would stop him.

No matter who stopped him, the result would be the same. A power surge, isolated to this panel, would go right into his fingers, which would burn through his suit, short-circuit it, and maybe injure or kill him as well.

Did Tey know that? Probably. Just like she had known about the individual environments and everything else. Those traffic cops hadn't had a chance. They hadn't known who they were up against.

Flint just hoped that he was stalling long enough for the reinforcements to arrive—and he hoped there were a lot of them. He had a hunch she'd take out at least two more space cops before someone brought her down.

His fingers found the right combination, and he suddenly had control of this section. He turned the air back on, then jury-rigged a block so that she couldn't access this part of the ship from the cockpit. That wouldn't last long—and there were warning bells inside the cockpit that notified her of what he was doing—but he didn't care.

He had gotten his extra few minutes. Again.

He hurried to the cockpit door. There was an override beside it, one that should respond to the same codes that had gotten him into the ship in the first place.

He had his laser pistol out, just like he had before. He now knew better than to assume that she was in the cockpit just because it was logical for her to be there. She might have something brilliant and completely unpredictable in mind.

That was what she had done all along.

When he reached the controls, he kept the pistol in his right hand trained on the door. He opened the panel, built into the plastic wall in such a way that the only way anyone would find it was if they knew it was there.

He started to type in his code when the cockpit door opened.

Frieda Tey stood before him, her environmental suit helmet off. He grabbed his laser pistol with both hands, making certain it was trained on her.

She had a pistol on him as well, probably the one that had killed the space cop near the door. Her eyes twinkled as she looked at Flint and he realized that, in any other circumstance, he would find her amazingly attractive. He found her attractive now, with her pixie-like intelligent face, her honey-colored hair, and a smile playing at her lips.

"Stalemate." Her voice was throaty and warm, its accent indeterminate. "The question is, can you shoot me faster than I can shoot you?"

That wasn't the question. The question was, Which one of them cared whether they got shot while killing the other? He figured he knew the answer to that, but he didn't enlighten her. In fact, he didn't say anything at all.

"You amaze me," she said. "I was beginning to give up hope. I figured Armstrong was my last shot."

She caught him, finally. Maybe if he kept her talking, he could get the pistol from her.

She had the pistol firmly in her hand. The other arm hung limp. But she was standing slightly sideways, so it would be difficult for him to get a good shot at her torso. Besides, the pink environmental suit she wore looked expensive. It probably had some reinforcements built in—the kind his suit didn't have.

"Your last shot at what?" he asked.

"Finding a person who didn't quit, no matter what was thrown at him. A lot of people have perseverance, but not combined with a working intelligence, one that allows them to solve any problem that comes their way, no matter what the threat to their life is."

She had the use of only one arm; she wouldn't be able to defend herself well. If he could get her to the brig, then the space cops could deal with her when they arrived.

"I think there are a lot of people like that," Flint said.

"Oh, no," she said, and her eyes twinkled even more. "I've been searching for them, hoping they'd reveal themselves to me. And you're the first one that I've found."

He tried not to look at her hand. The eyes gave away movement before anything else did. Maybe a warning shot would startle her, force her to shoot, and if he jumped forward, hit her wounded shoulder, then that might throw her off balance—

"You've redeemed it all," she said, and her words caught him again. He was actually listening. So she had charisma too. No wonder she'd been hard to pin down. No one would believe that such a charming person would be so thoroughly evil.

"Redeemed what?" He hit the last button on the code, just so that the door was in his control, not hers.

"The experiments. I was beginning to think I'd made a mistake, but now I know I haven't. You've made it all worthwhile. You've proven to me that I'm right. Given the proper circumstance, human beings will do great things."

His breath caught. He finally understood what she was saying, what she actually meant. He was not going to be the justification for all those deaths, not even for a minute.

"You think fighting you is a great thing?" he asked.

"It's chess," she said. "And you're the first person who has ever made it this far. So I have to congratulate you, Mr.—?"

"Flint," he said. "Miles Flint."

And then he shot her.

44

DeRicci stood inside the decon unit, her eyes closed. She leaned against the wall, the prickly heat of the various beams coating her entire body.

Someone had taken her uniform and her environmental suit. They promised her some kind of garment on the other side, but she had no idea what kind, and she really didn't care.

The unit was small and cramped. It was also too hot, and smelled of sweat and rotten apples. The light show in these things always made her nauseous. Combined with the bad food she'd eaten, the beginnings of a fever (no one had to confirm that—she recognized the feeling), and the emotional ride she'd been on, it was everything she could do to keep the contents of her stomach down.

So she shielded her eyes, and pretended she was somewhere else, somewhere better. What she really needed was a vacation, but she'd never get that—at least not to someplace interesting.

When they had gotten the last decon unit up and running, Chaiken demanded that she get in line. DeRicci had resisted, but Chaiken told him he had instructions from Gumiela. Apparently Gumiela had contacted him when she couldn't reach DeRicci.

DeRicci's links had come back up only half an hour

ago, sometime after the sixth decon unit started running.

The problem was, shortly after the seventh decon unit started to work, the press found out about the entire mess. Even worse, they'd found out that De-Ricci had been the detective involved. If she had thought her links were a mess before, they were unusable now—bells, whistles, red lights, scrolling text. She hadn't just sent the messages back. She had sent them back with the same kind of annoying alerts they had come with.

It wouldn't have quite the same effect, she knew, but it made her feel better.

Something had to.

The last death count was forty-one. She'd made the mistake of asking about a few people and getting real answers. Most of the medical staff was either too ill to go through the decon units or dead, including the man who had been in charge, Mikhail Tokagawa.

DeRicci felt bad about that, even though she'd never met any of these people. But the one who made her feel worse was the Tracker, Oliviari.

Apparently someone found her in the office shortly after DeRicci had signed off with her. Even though Oliviari had looked ill, DeRicci hadn't realized she was that ill. Somehow DeRicci had thought Oliviari would survive.

Maybe it was the woman's determination. Or maybe it was the aura of strength she'd had while she spoke.

DeRicci now understood what that strength was. It was sheer willpower. Oliviari had managed to stay alive long enough to give out all the information she could to save all of the lives that she could.

Oliviari had shown precisely the kind of courage that Tey had been looking for, the very thing Oliviari had been describing to DeRicci in the minutes before she died.

How many others had died like Oliviari, doing everything they could to make certain that everyone else would live? Had the heroes of Tey's first dome died first like the heroes had here? They'd get posthumous recognition, those people who had stayed behind to make sure the ill got care, but that was all they'd get. They wouldn't be able to live their lives, see their families again, run another stupid race, all because some crazy woman wanted to prove a point.

Even van der Ketting, as much as DeRicci complained about him, rose above his own natural tendencies. He worked as hard as his limited imagination had allowed him to.

She wasn't going to recommend a demotion for him. She would work with him. She couldn't give him any more imagination, but she could help him by letting him see hers.

The decontamination process made her itch. Her skin prickled, but at least the alternating sweats and chills had stopped.

So close. A few hours away from dying. And she was one of the lucky ones. She felt good about that—and she didn't want to. It was almost as if she were gloating for being alive.

She owed a lot to these people she was leaving behind in these tents. There was no way she would be able to give Tey the punishment she deserved.

But DeRicci would do everything in her power to make certain Tey was punished. DeRicci wasn't going to rest until that woman was caught.

45

The shot hit Tey squarely in the face, and she stumbled backward, but not before her own pistol went off, hitting Flint in the arm. Pain whistled through him, and he spun, slamming against the wall.

He struggled to regain control of his body, but he couldn't—not yet. He glanced at his arm, and saw that it was still there. The suit prevented some of the damage, just like it was supposed to. Hers would have prevented more. That was why he had no choice but to shoot her where he had.

Even if he hadn't killed her, he had probably blinded her, and he would be able to drag her to the brig.

She didn't come into the corridor after him. And when he could move again, the pain so severe that the entire right side of his body throbbed, he peered into the cockpit.

Frieda Tey lay on her back, arms above her head, just like the space cop she had killed earlier that day. Her face was a mass of burns, her hair covered with blood.

No one could live through that. Not even a woman who believed herself superhuman.

He turned away and slid down the wall, closing his eyes, trying to ignore the odd feeling of regret that filled him. She had been smart and attractive and charming, and despite everything, he'd liked the challenge she'd presented.

That moment when he pulled the trigger, he'd actually felt proud of himself. He'd found the one hole she'd missed.

She had cared about her own survival—and that gave him checkmate. A player had to have something to protect in order to have something to lose.

Flint had had nothing to lose—and she didn't know that because she hadn't known him.

She hadn't known that he didn't care if he survived.

46

It felt like DeRicci had been in isolation for a year, but she'd been in the building the city had set aside for only a night. The clothing she had been given was too big, but comfortable. She hadn't taken a cot, preferring to sit against the wall and doze.

If she slept too deeply, she saw too many faces, faces she wasn't sure had survived. The health officials had taken her hand-held away from her, along with her clothing, so she didn't have the case to preoccupy her, and she was apparently being kept in a different part of the building from Landres and van der Ketting.

She did see Coburn, however, and he looked like death himself. His eyes were bloodshot, his nose was red, and his cheeks were chapped.

The man had been crying.

He sat down next to her and hadn't said anything for a very long time. When he did speak, it had been so softly that she wasn't sure for a moment if she'd heard him.

"Is it true?" he asked. "Jane did all this?"

"Yeah," DeRicci had said.

"Jane? My business partner Jane?"

His former lover Jane. The woman he had described as being a little cold, impossible to get to on a deep level, a woman, DeRicci was beginning to believe, he had really loved.

"Yeah," DeRicci said.

Coburn had shaken his head, and stayed silent for the better part of an hour. DeRicci had almost forgotten he was there when he spoke again.

"When you start to set up a case against her," he had said, "you contact me. There were accidents, so many accidents, at Extreme Enterprises. I always thought it was a combination of her greed and inexperience. But now I'm beginning to think she did them deliberately."

DeRicci knew that they had been deliberate even without checking into them. But she didn't say anything. She didn't dare. Even though she believed Coburn innocent of all of this, she would still have to investigate him.

She would have to investigate everyone who came into contact with Jane Zweig, and determine whether they were guilty or not. If DeRicci did the investigation right, she would be able to clear their names. The last thing she wanted was for Frieda Tey to blame someone else for her crimes.

During one of her dozes, Coburn had moved away from her. Maybe he couldn't stand to remain there, or maybe she had answered enough of his questions.

All she knew was that when one of the health team tapped her on the shoulder and told her she was free to go, she didn't see Coburn anywhere around.

It took DeRicci until she reached the front door of the building to realize that "free to go" meant that she was no longer infected with the virus. She had survived it—when so many others hadn't.

She was so busy trying to deal with her mixture of elation and guilt that she didn't even notice Andrea Gumiela waiting on the building steps. There were no reporters around, and no volunteers either. The street was eerily empty, probably blocked off by uniforms and barricades.

"Noelle," Gumiela said.

DeRicci looked at her, and wondered what the woman wanted now. Probably to chastise her for all the deaths, for not seeing this sooner, for not understanding the crisis from the moment she got there.

"What?"

"I'm going to take you back to the precinct."

DeRicci sighed. She didn't have the energy to protest. Besides, her aircar was behind the wall, near the place where the bleachers had once been.

"Okay," DeRicci said.

They walked down the stairs together.

"I wanted to warn you before we got there that you're going to be getting quite a reception," Gumiela said.

DeRicci cringed. Here it came.

"The virus got contained. The case you mentioned out here was isolated and a different version of the virus. No one else got it. By closing down the marathon as fast as you did, you prevented a large-scale disaster. The entire city thinks you're a hero."

Gumiela had stopped on the sidewalk. She was looking at DeRicci, and there was no contempt on her face. She was being completely sincere.

"I'm no hero," DeRicci said. "The heroes all died."

Gumiela didn't say anything for a moment, but she didn't move either. Finally, she put a hand on DeRicci's shoulder. DeRicci suspected Gumiela was trying to comfort her.

It felt odd. Gumiela wasn't the comforting type.

"You're going to get a promotion, extra benefits, your long-overdue vacation. And you're probably going to get a lot more attention than you're used to." Gumiela's hand tightened on her shoulder, and then let go. "I know you're exhausted, but you did a good job. The team at the unit will help you through this. We're damn proud of you, Noelle."

DeRicci frowned. She had stepped into an alternate

universe. She was sure of it. Somewhere, everything had shifted, and she wasn't sure where.

"I didn't do anything," she said.

Gumiela gave her a gentle smile. "Yes, you did, Noelle. You did more than you'll ever know."

47

Three days later, Flint sat in his office, reconstructing old files. He had managed to avoid the media circus with help, in part, from the police department. They didn't want anyone to know that a civilian, acting on his own, had killed Frieda Tey. And he didn't want his name bandied about in the press. His actions on that ship had made him seem more like a Tracker than a Retrieval Artist.

They'd done the DNA testing and confirmed that indeed the woman who died had been Frieda Tey. But they were still grappling with how to present her death to the media. The police were afraid that she would become a martyr to people who held the same beliefs, and were also afraid that people who hated Frieda Tey would feel that death was too easy for her, that she deserved a greater punishment.

DeRicci had said as much to Flint, had implied, actually, that perhaps he had done the wrong thing in killing Tey. He had told DeRicci that he hadn't had any other choice, and he knew, deep down, that he was telling the truth.

He'd been thinking about it ever since he'd come back to Armstrong. If he had let Tey live, she might have found another way off that ship. She might have killed him, attacked the space cops, and taken their vessel.

Then she might have tried the same drifting-in-space technique she'd used to snare him to snare some other ship. That official police logo on the side of the traffic ship would make law-abiding pilots feel secure in approaching the ship to see what the trouble was.

The police had run the ship's logs. Tey had apparently known she was being followed. It had taken only a few shots to destroy the first ship and disable the second. Then she came aboard the ship, surprising the crew, and killing them.

Apparently she had set a remote-controlled self-destruct for the Extreme Enterprises yacht. Once she had secured the traffic ship, she had blown her own ship up, baiting the trap.

Flint, of course, had fallen right into it.

He had fallen into a lot of traps lately, and he finally understood Paloma's warning about the slow periods on his job. It led to bad decision making.

Wagner had hired Flint in good faith—Flint had actually been able to check that. Wagner had liked Rabinowitz and had worried about his death.

But Ignatius Wagner really was the lesser brother in Wagner, Stuart, and Xendor. He hadn't known anything that his older brother had known. From the files that Flint had gathered, Justinian had more than an inkling that Frieda Tey was on the Moon. He might even have known who she was.

It was clear that Tey's father had known who she was, and that was why he had revised his will. The question was why Tey hadn't taken the money when he died. Maybe she hadn't wanted her name cleared. Or maybe she thought the Armstrong "experiment" would clear it for her.

Whatever the reason, it had died with her.

So had a lot of other things, and Flint was content to let them. Only one thing nagged at him: a single word uttered in the middle of his fight with Tey.

Paloma.

He had justified it during the fight, thinking Tey had looked up the registration on the *Dove*, but she hadn't. There was no record of it on the traffic ship.

She had recognized the *Dove*—or at least the yacht's name—and she had been surprised when the person who had confronted her had been Flint and not Paloma.

He'd asked Paloma about it when he sent her the credits to pay her for the loss of her ship. She hadn't wanted to meet face-to-face.

She had denied ever knowing Frieda Tey or Jane Zweig. Paloma had said that she had no idea why the woman had spoken her name.

But Flint had a guess, and it had taken him days of reconstructing Paloma's files to find out that he was right.

Paloma had been working for Wagner, Stuart, and Xendor when Frieda Tey's father devised his first will. Apparently, old man Wagner had sent Paloma in search of Frieda Tey, and Paloma had found her.

But Paloma hadn't told WSX that. She hadn't told anyone. She had believed Tey, and Tey's account of that first experiment as an accident gone bad. Paloma had actually believed Tey to be a scapegoat, and, good Retrieval Artist that she was, she had let Tey continue in her new life.

Her life on Armstrong.

Experimenting with the lives of extreme athletes— and finally, with the entire city itself.

The knowledge disturbed Flint more than he could admit. He found himself pacing the office, trying to figure out what it all meant.

All he knew was that what looked to be the right thing at the moment might not be the right thing in hindsight.

And he wasn't sure how that made him feel.

But he did know he was not going to go to Paloma for advice anymore. He finally understood his own job. He was going to do it his way from now on.

And he would live with the consequences.

About the Author

Kristine Kathryn Rusch is an award-winning writer in several genres. Winner of the 2001 Hugo Award for the novelette "Millennium Babies," she has also won the *Ellery Queen* Readers' Choice Award for best mystery short story. She is also a winner of the *Asimov's* Readers Choice Award, the *Locus* Award, the World Fantasy Award, and the John W. Campbell Award.

She has published more than fifty novels in almost a dozen languages, and she has hit bestseller lists in the *Wall Street Journal, USA Today,* and *Publishers Weekly.* Her science fiction and mystery short stories have been in many year's-best collections.

The Retrieval Artist novels are based on the Hugo-nominated novella "The Retrieval Artist," which was first published in *Analog.*